Holy Knight

Pens and Needles

Green, Boyd, Green

ISBN: 0-578-03723-8
ISBN-13: 9780578037233

To order additional copies, please contact us.
Bookwelder Publishing
1-512-541-1747
www.bookwelder.com
www.holyknightbook.com

ACKNOWLEDGMENTS

As most stories go, this one would not have come to fruition without the help of a few friends. We had several beta readers along the way, and thanks to them, the book was finished.

Our good friend Jim provided input early on and the inspiration to keep going. Brad, Stephanie, and Jenny (perfectionist little sister) kept us on track and held our feet to the fire when we drifted off. And special thanks to our cover artist, Natalie.

Finally, there is you. We hope you have half as much fun reading the story as we did writing it, for that was our sole mission for the better part of a year.

PROLOGUE

April 5, 1995 A.D.

Bells rang out to a cloudless Boston sky as the full moon illuminated the two towers of St. Peter's Chapel. All was quiet on the campus of Brighton Latin College.

Thousands of miles away, another church bell rang its fifth and final time, the dawn lighting Vatican City in a golden blaze. A lone cardinal exited St. Peter's Basilica onto the piazza—the massive oval half in shadow from the early morning sun. Constructed to hold thousands when the Pope addressed the Vatican from his balcony, the magnificent plaza presently hosted just one guest. Just shy of a full run, he moved in a straight line toward the towering spike of the obelisk mounted dead center in the array of cobblestones. His footsteps slowed as he found his exit. Once outside the piazza, he turned left, catching his breath as he reached his destination. He trotted up the front steps and entered a very old, solid stone building, and proceeded directly up the narrow stairwell to the third floor; the sounds of a woman moaning grew louder as he climbed. There, he met a man wearing a dark suit, a bit wrinkled and disheveled—the look of someone who had been up all night.

"Everything is fine," he said to the cardinal.

He peered around the door jamb to witness the final push. She was surrounded by two women dressed as nurses and another man in a suit. The room was stark, with only a bed and side table hosting a large, flowered, ceramic pitcher of water and a matching wash basin. The push was accompanied with a brutal howl that echoed off the stone and tile. The next sound was that of a baby crying, followed by cheerful whispers from the small group.

After a minute, the doctor in the suit left the mother, baby, and nurses, and joined the two men.

"He looks perfect."

"Excellent!" replied the cardinal.

"Perhaps a miracle, indeed," the wrinkled suit man said with a strong British accent. "Or should I say, another miracle?"

The three joined the group to see the baby swathed in a blanket, cradled in his mother's arms. She looked to the men and smiled. They acknowledged her without words, all smiling back.

The silent celebration was interrupted when a tall man appeared in the doorway. He was dressed in a black suit with a pressed white shirt, a black overcoat folded over one arm, holding a black fedora. The cardinal excused himself and joined the visitor in the stairwell.

"It is done!" the Cardinal whispered. "When she is able, take them to my guest house to be with the others. When they are finished," he said nodding toward the others and lowering his voice, "bring me all of the files—everything. Then, Orsini, make this all go away. Make it go away forever!"

Orsini nodded: "It shall be done, your Eminence."

1

Fourteen Years Later

Come Labor Day, Boston is the U-Haul capital of the world. More than 60 colleges draw over a quarter of a million students into town toting duffels of clean laundry, mini refrigerators, music systems, computers, bicycles, and of course, Frisbees. On this given weekend, the side streets of Back Bay and Cambridge are clogged with overloaded vehicles and double parked rent–a–trucks, eliminating any chance of passage.

In the 2009 version of this annual show, a silver Mercedes sedan made its way up Commonwealth Avenue, offering witness to the phenomenon. And like so many other cars on that weekend, it did not have Massachusetts license plates. While most bore tags from Connecticut, New York, and New Jersey, this plate was from the opposite direction: Nova Scotia.

As it navigated the stretch of Boston's Back Bay predominantly occupied by Boston University, a green and white trolley emerged from underground. Traveling alongside the silver Benz in the center of the divided road, it looked like it had been stalking the car from below. The circled letter T on the side of the train car stopped directly under a sign with the same logo. A small crowd proceeded to board, while another moved away from the platform as the Benz pulled away. The next two miles previewed the chaotic, upbeat spectacle of moving day. On each block, the dividing side streets of the pre-war, cement and brick, four-story apartment buildings provided a slide show of different scenes, all with the same chaotic, yet festive, moving day theme. A couch bobbed along the sidewalk with its carriers out of view. Boxes tumbled out of a small moving truck scattering clothes on the street. A Frisbee flew aimlessly as a local radio station blared rock and roll. Two blocks further, the same radio station came back, resuming the song as people hugged, reunited.

The trolley caught up and passed the Benz. Then it crossed over its path and rode up the side of Commonwealth Avenue for a stretch. The Benz took the lead at the next light, all in a private game of cat and mouse between car and train.

They parted ways in Brighton when the Mercedes cut right over to Washington Street, then continued west, approaching Brighton's Oak Square. The college's presence was first felt by the large football stadium surrounded by other athletic facilities. Across the street, the buildings changed from commercial stores and food shops to campus facilities displaying the school's three-letter logo on the door or window. The center of Oak Square was marked by a well manicured brick and cobblestone rotary, surrounded by the college's lower campus buildings, each with symmetrical banners displaying a crest of arms with a sword and "Sentinels" written across the shield.

The car traveled around the rotary, passing one street and then a stone archway marking the entrance to a long, steep stairway up to the main campus. The sloping terrain was populated with red brick academic and administrative buildings. The Mercedes passed the main campus, crested the hill and turned right through a wrought iron gate.

The Oak Hill Campus sat atop the hill which made up most of Boston Latin's property. Just above the main campus, a group of three-story, red brick dormitories formed the perimeter of a square with all entrances pointing in at an old, stone house which served as a student center. The dorms were trimmed in white and showed their age with ivy climbing the brick and stone, with mature trees and shrubs making the area look like a historic landmark or re-creation of a colonial town square. The Benz parked on the grass next to the first dormitory, Fernwood Hall.

Under a tree 50 yards away, David was lying in the grass, taking it all in. He arrived earlier, flying in on the red eye from Anchorage. His duffel was still unpacked and pushed up against the window of the dorm room, which was all of five paces deep and having a parallel arrangement of closets, beds, bureaus, and desks linked wall to wall.

"Is there a knight here!?" howled a distant voice from behind.

David stood up, picked up his flannel shirt and walked to Fernwood's row of first floor dorm windows, one which was wide open, letting in one of the last summer days New England had left to offer. He wore green cargo pants, a black tee shirt and light hiking boots. He looked fit enough to have just graduated from boot camp, the byproduct of living his last five years off the grid in Alaska. And though his hair was a little too long for the military, his un-tanned skin all around its edges confirmed a recent, and significant haircut.

He stuck his head in the window.

"Hey, Brian!"

It had been three years since David Knight had seen his cousin.

"I'll come around," he offered, as he slid his flannel back on, leaving it un-tucked and unbuttoned.

As he reached the side entrance, Brian's father rounded the corner with his arms full of luggage.

"Hi, Uncle John!" David exclaimed, gesturing to shake hands as he held the door open.

John nodded, as he had no available hand. Brian held the inner door open.

"Right this way, Dad. First room on the right."

David poked his head around the corner to see his aunt wrestling a large duffel bag of clothes out of the trunk of the Mercedes.

"Let me get that, Aunt Ruth!" David offered.

"Why thank you, David! We thought you were coming in tomorrow. Shoot! We would have made plans to stay the night and have dinner together. How are you?" Aunt Ruth said all in one breath, as she grabbed a grocery bag, then placed a kiss on David's cheek.

David followed her into the dorm. The group filled up the tiny room as they stood exchanging greetings.

"That's David's side," Brian informed his mother just as she set a bag of groceries on a bed.

"Oh, I haven't picked. Whatever side you want."

"I was just going by the tape," answered Brian, referring to the masking tape on the overhead door jamb outside the room.

A small strip on the left side had "Knight" handwritten on it in magic marker, the one on the right, "Anderson." They all sat on the beds, as if on two sofas facing each other.

"What do you think of our chances of getting a hotel room?" Aunt Ruth asked her husband.

"On Labor Day in Boston? Zip!"

Not happy with the answer, she changed the subject, turning to David. "So, how are your parents doing? I have not talked to your mom in, well, too long."

"They're fine. Dad is his usual self. I think they couldn't wait to get rid of me."

"Oh, come now."

"No, really. He bought an old schooner, and they're taking off as we speak."

"Where to?"

"Here!"

"You're joking!?"

"No, 'fraid not. They're doing Christmas in the Galapagos Islands, and then they'll pick me up in Boston at the end of the school year."

"And then what?" she laughed.

"Then, we all head up to Nova Scotia—to see you!"

"My brother never did have all of his screws tight, you know," giggled Ruth, "and that mother of yours is a saint. She will go—well, I guess she *is going* to the end of the earth for that man. So, what about the homestead?"

"Shut it down for a year. The neighbors are working the gardens in exchange for keeping an eye on the place. So how is the import/export business treating you, Uncle John?"

"As long as there are bagels, the world will need lox! No complaints," he said. "We loaded up Brian with samples, although I bet you get your fill of salmon up there in no man's land."

They conversed for the better part of an hour, mostly about Alaska.

"We better shove off if we want to make it to Augusta tonight," Brian's father announced.

David stood up straight and tall.

"I do wish we could have stayed and spent more time together, David. Would you come home with Brian and join us for the Christmas break?" Ruth pleaded.

"Sounds like a plan, Aunt Ruth."

"And *please*, let some of your charm and manners rub off on your cousin."

Brian rolled his eyes behind his mother's back.

The two silently unpacked their duffels, much in the way they would hang out together, years ago in Vermont. Before any conversation began, Brian's father reappeared in the doorway.

"Bloody thing won't start. Well, it starts, then, stalls out when I give it some gas. I'm gonna need a phone book."

"May I take a look?" asked David.

"You think you can work on a German car? This isn't a snowmobile, ya know," Brian said.

"Do you have any tools?" David asked, as they moved quickly to the car.

"There is a small toolbox in the trunk, I think."

David grabbed the tools and disappeared under the Benz. After a minute of silence, Ruth chimed in, "He thinks he can get three hundred thousand miles out if this thing. I say it's time to trade it in."

"I'm more than halfway there," said Brian's father.

At that point, David sprang to his feet with a small wrench in his hand.

"You'll make it, Uncle John. Just keep the fuel filter clear."

"Uhhh, fixed?"

"Yep."

"How'd ya know?"

"Had the same problem on our seaplane."

"I'd fly with you any time, David!" Ruth charmed out the car window.

As the Mercedes drove out through the gate of Oak Hill Campus and turned left, the two walked back to the dorm. Brian picked up a small stone and flung it at a trash can.

"Oh, great!" he cracked. "At least *David* wouldn't let a lady carry your laundry. *David* has manners. *David* flies his own plane. *David* rescued us when we broke down. Jeez, I think I'm gonna puke…"

David smiled, then gave Brian a friendly shove with his elbow.

2

The silver Mercedes emerged from the Allston toll booth and entered from the eastbound ramp onto the Massachusetts Turnpike. As he got the Benz up to speed and merged with traffic, John noticed a shiny black Buick ahead in the fast lane moving with the other turnpike traffic. He saw his opportunity and went heavy on the gas, darting to the furthest right lane as Ruth sat in silence. She was taking in the sights, half paying attention and feeling melancholy about Brian's leaving home.

As John passed the slower center lane cars, the Buick signaled and moved in ahead of them from the fast lane, landing door to door with John and blocking him in behind a slower car. Annoyed, he hit the brakes and fell back, then moved two lanes left and gunned it around everyone. John glared over as he flew by the Buick, only to find tinted out windows, making for a faceless opponent. Ruth looked at John with her eyebrows tight, a look he had seen many times that meant disapproval. Now in his mirror, the Buick signaled right and disappeared up an exit ramp, and Ruth resumed her unfocused gaze out the window.

The Buick crossed the Charles River and cut through Cambridge, finally parking on the street in front of a small professional building in Somerville. The parking lot was empty, as one would expect on Labor Day weekend. A tall man in a black overcoat and fedora got out of the car and entered the building. Moving swiftly and silently, he arrived at a first floor door and took out a small tool from a red leather portfolio. He picked the lock in an instant.

Within minutes he emerged, carefully closing the door behind him and retracing his steps back to the car.

The Buick came to its next stop on a nearby corner of a residential street. The man walked up the side street and turned into the driveway of a green, single-story home with no cars in the driveway and no sign of anyone being home. He walked past the house and around the detached garage in the rear, moving to the furthest corner of the property, where a chest-high chain link fence stopped his progress. He reached into his overcoat pocket and pulled out a small black object the shape of a pack of cigarettes, with a wire antenna dangling from it. Gloved, he flipped a switch on the side, lighting a small green LED. He tossed the device over the fence and into the neighbor's yard, where it landed in a bush next to the basement door. He spun and quickly walked back around the garage, as the large, red-shingled home's alarm went off behind him. He slowed his pace as he hit the sidewalk and listened to doors opening and people yelling to each other over the security system's screech.

At its third stop, the Buick entered a small industrial complex and disappeared behind a long building housing multiple businesses.

"Hello, Appledore Security. Bob here," a round-faced man in blue work pants and shirt answered. "Again? Yes, I see it," he acknowledged, looking at his computer screen. "That's three times in ten minutes. You say it's in the *off* position? That's weird. There must be a problem in the controller. We'll be right over. Oh, no problem. You're welcome," he said, hanging up the phone.

Bob got up from his desk and yanked a yellow and blue jacket off of a rack of several more and left the office.

The security company occupied a bay in the long, metal multi-tenant building, each tenant's slice consisting of an office to the front and a warehouse and garage, with a large roll-up door, to the rear. The technician got in the yellow and blue van and pressed the remote door opener clipped to the visor. He started the van and rolled forward, timing his exit with the door opening as he had done many times, but stopped short when he saw the car blocking his exit.

The black Buick was parked with its rear to the door, its trunk wide open.

"What the...?" he muttered.

There was no sign of anyone. Bob got out of the van and slowly approached the car. The driver's side door was also open and the car was running, but there was no one inside. He stepped closer to the car and looked into the trunk.

He barely felt the cold steel press against the base of his skull, barely heard the pop of the silencer. As he fell, the man in the black coat flung an oversized trash bag over Bob's head and pulled it down past his shoulders, then let him collapse into the trunk. He flipped his legs up and pulled another bag over his feet before rolling him all the way in, only the torso now exposed. After slamming the trunk shut, he walked quickly into the office and found the rack of yellow and blue work jackets.

The Appledore Security van came to a stop in front of the big red house with a number "6" on its yellow front door. A man in his 30s answered.

"Thank you so much for coming out here on such short notice and on a holiday," he said. "Everything is closed. You shouldn't even be working."

A woman of about 70 greeted him with the same gratitude.

"It is no problem," the technician responded, revealing a slight European accent. "Has the alarm sounded again?"

"No, just the three times," the elderly woman answered. "And a good thing too, my husband isn't feeling well and is trying to sleep."

"Is the control box in the basement?"

"Yes," the man responded. "This way."

They went down the stairs to the unfinished cellar, finding the control panel for the alarm system mounted on the wall next to the fuse box.

"I should be no more than five minutes," the technician advised, as he pulled a screwdriver out of his tool belt and opened the control panel.

"Take your time; we'll be up in the kitchen."

The man closed the door at the top of the basement stairs; the technician opened the back door and retrieved the electronic device from the shrub.

"All set. It was a short in the wiring," the technician reported as he entered the kitchen and closed the basement door behind him.

"That's great news," the elderly woman said.

Another woman, the wife of the middle-aged man, was making dinner.

"I need to make sure all of the alarm sensors are in a closed position. Otherwise, it will start going off after I reboot the system back at the office," the technician said, holding out a schematic with a blueprint of the house. "It won't take but a minute."

"By all means," the elder woman said.

"Thank you, be right back."

As he left the kitchen, the homeowners were grateful the alarm dilemma was resolved, and on a holiday no less. So grateful, in fact, that they did not even notice that the technician's jacket was too small, the sleeves an inch too short. Nor did they notice the $400 Italian leather shoes under the black dress slacks, or the white surgical gloves.

3

Crash! David jumped to his feet and raced to the open window. Outside, four students were standing around laughing. A fifth student was lying on the ground about 10 feet from the window next to a metal trash can, his skateboard upside down, near his head. David had slept for only an hour when the door to his room slowly opened.

"Hey, you're up," Brian said softly.

"What time is it?"

"Six. Wanna grab some dinner?"

"Why not? Sounds like the natives are still restless."

"Then we can check the place out for a bit."

As they walked out of the dorm, they witnessed another attempt to jump the trash can with a skateboard. "Thud!" Then more howls. They trotted down the stairs between two cornering dorms flanking the stairwell. A strong smell of marijuana permeated the air.

"Good stuff." Brian said, raising his eyebrows.

"You smoke?"

"Not if I want to make the team."

The stairs were the only direct way out of the Oak Hill Campus, acting like a giant funnel, condensing the foot traffic of the 500+, 18- and 19-year-olds residing in the brick dormitories. At the bottom of the stairs, the funnel's output fed the giant mouth of McGuiness Hall, a multilevel, beige, contemporary building that looked out of place with the rest of the campus architecture. They entered the top floor through a wall of glass doors, which handled the intake at peak traffic.

Built into Oak Hill's sloping terrain, McGuiness was the perfect Rube Goldberg processor of humans. The large dining hall sat behind the wide lobby, providing the hopper that swallowed the masses of hungry underclassmen. Under the hall resided a snack bar and deli, faculty restaurant, post office, ATM, bookstore, and administrative offices. Two stories down and to the rear, McGuiness dumped its processed contents onto the main campus and into academia.

The dining hall echoed with lively conversation. Tall ceilings and dozens of tables on the hard floor created a loud, booming environment, especially when near capacity. After falling in line and sliding their trays along the aluminum piped racks of the chow line, the two devoured a non-offensive dinner of ham, roasted potatoes and green beans.

Without words, they bounced down the flights of stairs and out onto the main campus, just as the human processor was designed. The academic buildings were laid out in a grid-like pattern on the hill's sharp slope toward Oak Square. In the center stood St. Peter's Chapel, with its two square towers jutting up to the sky.

The church-like library sat low on the slope, sitting almost directly above Oak Square. The intimidating staircase sat to the right of it, taking the foot traffic on a steep climb through the bushes and trees to the rotary below.

"My dad told me about this. He called it 170-something steps," David said, as the two stood at the top.

"If we go down, we'll have to climb back up," Brian replied.

"He said that when he went here, some students drove a jeep down them for fun."

"The drinking age was eighteen back then, wasn't it?" asked Brian.

"'Nuf said."

"I have hockey practice down there tomorrow, so I can wait to see it, if that's OK with you."

"Sure, my brain is still a few hours out of whack."

They started walking, but after a few paces Brian stopped.

"Hey," Brian said, as he pulled out his cell phone. "While I'm thinking about it, gimme your cell number. Mine is…"

"Uh, I don't have a phone," David interrupted.

"What?"

"Really…"

"Listen up, Daniel Boone. Down here in the civilized world we have cell phones. That's how people communicate with each other. We talk, we text, and we can even send pictures to each other."

"What if I don't like people?"

"Very funny."

They both smiled and walked in silence back to Fernwood Hall. It was good to be back together.

They were the best of friends, spending many summers together in the hills of Vermont at Brian's family's farm. They could go for hours on end without talking, just milling about the farm, whether it was skipping stones on the pond, horse manure fights, or just watching the clouds go by while lying in the tall grass of the fields of the 75-acre spread. And there was always something to do with all of the chores, which somehow didn't seem like work when you were in a beautiful place, hanging with your best buddy.

John Anderson had worked as a buyer for a grocery chain. When the owner of a seafood brokerage from Nova Scotia of-fered to sell the business to him, the decision was very tough, as the move would rip the families apart, Aunt Ruth and David's mothers being as tight as the two boys. The deal was just too good to pass up.

After the move, David's family followed a similar path, albeit a more extreme one.

The Knights owned a Victorian right in the middle of Chester, which came with the conveniences of village living; it was the perfect setting to raise a child and be close to the Ander-sons. The beautiful New England village had all of the charm Vermont had to offer, and reaped the economic benefits of lo-cal skiing and summer tourism—many of the weekend warriors from Connecticut and New York would stop to shop on the way to and from the slopes. Chester's streets were lined with beauti-ful homes, many of which had been turned into boutiques and antique stores.

It was when the Andersons moved away that the Knights quickly realized it was their farm that drew them to Vermont. They now had no outlet to open space and the busy little center of town quickly drove David's father mad, according to his mother. The state road the house sat on saw a lot of traffic, including 18-wheelers pounding into town, down-shifting and up-shifting as they rounded the corner, the antique windows rattling from the percussion of the engine brakes. In the summer, the addition of straight pipes on motorcycles made gardening in the small side yard unbearable.

One spring Sunday, a New York City lawyer stopped in town on his way back from a last chance to ski at nearby Okimo Mountain. "I have been admiring your house for a couple of years now," he said to David's father, who was painting the front steps. "I am thinking about opening a B&B up here."

David's father calculated that the small fortune they made was enough to live off of—that is, if their next place cost less than $100,000, and they had a little bit of income. It happened so fast, David could hardly recall the series of events—the parents taking just one trip; almost everything else had been done over the Internet. Suddenly, the Knights were on their way to Alaska to homestead!

Tuesday morning brought a buzz of activity to Oak Hill Campus. Scrambling down the stairs and crossing the street into McGuiness, everyone hurried as if they were about to miss a train. Inside, the doors to the dining hall were constantly swinging, and the stairs echoed a consistent rumble of people tromping in a downward flow. David felt as though he were inside a giant pinball machine. At mid-level, he bailed out into the crowded post office, and searched for his mailbox. The box contained some welcome information from the school and a couple of flyers from local pizzerias. But what David found most interesting was not in his hands.

Heather was reading her junk mail when he noticed her. She came close to his six-foot-two stature, with Converse high tops peeking out from her faded blue jeans.

Whoa, not even heels! thought David, as he stuffed his eyes back into his head and tried to focus on the blurred print of the pizzeria brochure. He glanced back. Her short black hair was a little messed, leaving David to wonder how long it took to get that look. He could get it any morning, instantly. He looked down at his mail and smirked at the thought. When he looked back, she was staring at him, the dumb grin still on his face. He locked onto the most brilliant, ice blue eyes he had ever seen, causing him to stare right back at her. After the awkward moment, they both grinned and moved back into the flow of humanity, losing sight of each other in an instant.

At two o'clock, he emerged from Dexter Hall and found himself underneath the two towers of St. Peter's Chapel, done for the day. He wandered past the library and stopped at the top of the stairs.

Why not? David thought. He had all afternoon to get back up.

He lost count around 140, descending rapidly, trying not to think about the return climb.

David exited the stairway through the stone arch, took a left on Faneuil Street and walked, passing multi-family homes that the school had purchased over time, converting them to housing for upperclassmen. On the opposite side of the street, next to the football stadium was the hockey arena and sports complex, all sharing a parking lot. More athletic fields followed the structures. The Sentinels were out on the artificial turf, looking very impressive with what looked like a hundred players suited up. He continued on, now observing a lacrosse team practice; he recognized a couple of players from the dorm.

Must be sophomores, he thought.

They looked more like a club team than the high profile Sentinels out on the turf.

In high school, David played no sports. Not only was he six-foot-two, but the football coach could see the physical strength the demands of homesteading had yielded in his shoulders, arms and legs. For four years, David turned down endless efforts to recruit him, as the property provided all of the physical challenges one could desire.

In spring, there was prepping and planting the large gardens that would provide most of the Knights' food supply. Summer added some sort of construction project to farming, whether of stone or timber. Junior year brought a new stone smoke house, each stone dug and moved manually from its origin, stacked, then cemented into their final positions with hand mixed cement.

Recreation consisted mainly of fishing. The back of the property bordered a three-mile-long lake, which was well stocked with trout. David alternated between the canoe and the outboard-powered aluminum skiff, depending on which fishing hole he wanted to visit. The seaplane his father bought two years prior was also kept there, until he traded it for the schooner. Just a few miles in the other direction was the ocean, where David's father kept a fishing boat and a sea kayak, the latter of which was pretty much left for David to play around with. The boat had an enclosed wheelhouse and could get well out into the bay to do some serious fishing.

David enjoyed the ocean the most, as it presented the ultimate quality time with his father. On the water, it was quiet as they drifted or trolled, and the scenery was spectacular. The surrounding landscape of the islands, mountains and glaciers was a magnificent background for the seals, birds and whales. These times were most unforgettable, not to mention the hauling in of a salmon or halibut. Sometimes, David's mother accompanied them when the weather was nice, photographing the scenery and wildlife for their Internet business of prints, post cards and calendars of Alaska's beauty.

At home, they heated and cooked with wood, so there was always a need for cutting, chopping, or splitting. Trees downed by last winter's storms were cut into moveable pieces during the spring and summer months. Splitting and stacking was a constant pastime, along with the canning, smoking, and prepping of food for the long winter.

After passing the athletic facilities, David came upon a small train station, marking the end of the line for the trolley that ran up to Brighton. On his side of the street, the homes ended and strips of single-level stores began. David found a convenience store and emerged with a cold bottle of water. He looked to the blue sky and thought about home as the sun heated his face. *At least there is one thing that's not different here,* he thought.

4

He was not sure how long she had been standing there, or how she got so close without his noticing, but as he lowered the bottle she came into focus standing less than five feet away. Not only was she tall, but she filled out her frame perfectly.

"Hi," said Heather.

"Hi, uh, can I get you a water?" David said, after almost choking on a large gulp.

"Sure," she smiled.

"Oh, I'm sorry. I'm David," he said, blinking to break being once again locked on to her brilliant blue eyes. He felt as though she were looking right through him.

"Hello, David. I'm Heather."

"What do you think so far?"

"About what?"

"About this place. You're a freshman right? Or, I'm sorry, is that fresh-person"?" he stumbled.

"It's OK. I think freshman works fine."

"Excuse me, I'll be right back."

David disappeared into the Store 24 and reemerged seconds later with an ice cold bottle.

"Thanks."

Heather opened the wet bottle and took a sip.

"I like the green trolleys," David said, watching one leave the station.

"It's called the T. This is the Green Line."

"Huh. How easy is that?"

"I have Anthropology tomorrow over at St. Mathew's Parish," she commented. "I thought I would check it out today, so I wouldn't get lost. It's supposed to rain and the walk over here will be enough."

"Three o'clock?" asked David looking at his schedule.

"Yeah," smiled Heather to her new classmate.

"Mind if I tag along?"

"That'd be nice."

"So, where is this St. Mathew's?" he asked. "I see it on my schedule, with *remote campus* in parentheses."

Heather smiled, then led the way down Faneuil Street; the wind blew warm as the sun popped in and out of friendly clouds. Side by side, they looked as though they'd been together for some time. She wore jeans, a flannel shirt and a down vest. He, a fleece jacket, jeans, and light hiking boots. As they walked, they looked into the storefronts that lined the street, but David's eyes were focused on the glass of the windows, and the reflection of Heather as she passed by each one.

God, she's beautiful! I don't stand a chance with her.

After a few quiet moments, Heather attempted some conversation.

"I hear the church sold the place to the school as part of the lawsuits, ya' know, to raise money for the settlements."

"Yeah, I remember reading about it. They sold off a ton of real estate to pay for that mess."

They turned right on Turner Street passing several homes, half of them college owned, evident by little signs designating their purpose. St. Mathew's followed after the Foreign Studies house, and consisted of a church, a small private elementary school, a large stone rectory, and a carriage house, which was located directly across the street.

A group of students, some wearing Brighton Latin College tee shirts, were playing ultimate Frisbee on the ball field in front of the former elementary school, which now served as administrative offices.

As they approached, the rectory seemed oversized in comparison to the rest of the property. It stood three stories tall and was made of stone with iron-framed windows and an intricate slate roof with round towers at the corners. The detail made it look like a small castle and made David think, but not be so lame as to say, *They sure don't make 'em like they used to.*

"They sure don't build 'em like this, anymore," Heather announced, as she marched ahead toward the entrance. David raised his eyebrows and smirked as he followed.

The receptionist looked as old as the building. She wore her silver blue hair up in a bun, which went very well with her octagonal frameless glasses. She pouted a little as she looked over her glasses to read Heather's course schedule.

"Ah, yes, Anthropology. They stuck you on the third floor, 312. Straight to the back. The stairs will be on your right. All the way up to the top. Room numbers are on the doors."

Room 312 was a small, dingy classroom. The walls were pea green, rising up to meet an ornate, tin ceiling. Hanging from the ceiling were fluorescent light fixtures that looked like the insides of old-fashioned, metal ice cube trays. On the wall above the antique chalkboard, there was a horizontal cylinder housing a projection screen of similar vintage.

"Guess there isn't a big demand for Anthropology," David sighed.

Heather and David continued down the dimly lit hallway toward a set of swinging wooden doors with bright, rippled glass windows. They approached in silence, their steps muted by their rubber soled shoes.

David slowly pushed the door open to reveal a small library with a very old world feel to it. Thick, curved moldings bordered the ceiling, while the walls housed built-in bookcases of dark wood and iron framed windows with stone sills. Over two tables hung the same, ice cube tray-light fixtures.

As he continued to open the door, the right side of the room came into view revealing plush accommodations of leather wingback reading chairs, a rocker and a small couch, all arranged around a beautiful stone fireplace—and all occupied. Four priests were a bit startled to see the door swing open, and jumped to their feet when they saw Heather.

"Well, hello!" welcomed an elderly priest of at least 80, holding his tea service by the plate.

"I'm sorry. Um, we're sorry!" David exclaimed. "We didn't know this was private."

"Private indeed," said the elder, "but I'm afraid we are the intruders on *your* property. You see, it is now yours, or the college's that is, after the acquisition."

Heather maintained her grip on the door, holding it open so as not to complete their entrance.

"We have been, for the most part, reassigned to the carriage house across the street," the priest continued, motioning in the direction with his head.

"Could have been worse. They could have tossed us in the street!" another chuckled.

"Do come in, come in!" said the man to his right, of probably 70 years, while the others finished their laughs under their breaths.

"We beg you not to tell on us," he grinned. "We've been having tea here for so many years that we are compelled to sneak in, somewhat regularly I must confess, and continue our little tradition. Father Dan, in fact," he said, pointing to the first speaker, "outdates many of the books you will find here."

"You are so kind," Father Dan said, displaying a long smile.

"And most of us were here when this furniture was brought in as new. Please, come and sit with us for a bit."

Two of the priests grabbed chairs from the study tables and arranged them into the circle and quickly sat on them, forcing the two students to sit together on the small leather couch. Once they had taken their seats, the youngest of the group, a man of about 50, got up and disappeared through a wooden door, also with a rippled glass pane. He reemerged moments later with tea service for two on a serving tray.

"So tell us, how was your first day?" Father Dan asked.

"Is it that obvious?" replied Heather.

The man with the tray bent over and handed Heather a steaming cup on a saucer. As she accepted the cup she noticed he was taller than David, and also how small the tea service looked in his large, rugged hands. His dark hair and complexion convinced her that he was Greek or Italian.

"Thank you," Heather said. "Just milk, thanks."

"An easy wager when we see students scouting locations prior to the actual class time," Father Dan continued. "So, what do you think so far?"

The elders made Heather and David feel very much at ease. Like good hosts, they engaged them in conversation about school, majors, and where they were from. After about 20 minutes and a second cup of tea, the guests, attempting to be as polite as their hosts, offered their gratitude.

"Thank you so much for your hospitality, but we must get going," said Heather.

"Another big day tomorrow," David added.

"It was entirely our pleasure."

"Most enjoyable," said another.

David made the rounds shaking hands, trying to remember all of their names. As he shook hands with the man who served the tea, he stumbled on his name.

"Father…?"

"Scordo. Anthony, not Father," he said with a slight Italian accent.

"Oh, I thought…"

"I spent many years working here, so they let me maintain an office, well at least for the moment," he smiled, nodding to the single glass pane door. "I expect to be evicted any day now. I guess I wear black to blend in," he chuckled. "If I wore red pants, I would look like—"

"A lost golfer from Chestnut Hill!" finished the priest to his right with a laugh.

"Remember," Father Dan smiled, "if you keep this place to yourselves, it will be just yours, and ours," he said, putting his index finger to his lips and nodding.

5

They walked back down Faneuil Street and took an early right up Perthshire Road, which looped to the right and climbed Oak Hill at a lesser angle of attack than the brutal stairs, bringing them to the rear entrance of the main campus. As they continued on toward McGuiness, the lacrosse players approached from behind, returning from their practice session on lower campus. They merged around Heather and David as they set out across an open, grassy area. About halfway across the small field, a voice called from behind.

"Hey, Heather! It's Eric, from Psych class."

Eric jogged a few steps to get even.

"Hey, I was wondering if you would like to grab a bite to eat, maybe Friday or Saturday," Eric asked, as if David was not there.

"Oh, thanks, but I'm visiting my aunt this weekend."

"Then, maybe some other time, huh?"

"Maybe," Heather replied with an uncomfortable tone to her voice.

"Cool."

Eric jogged a few paces to join the players, never looking back.

"That was weird," said Heather.

"Nice fellah," David said, sarcastically. "Lives in my dorm. I guess he didn't recognize me..."

They slowed their pace a bit, allowing all of the lacrosse players to get far enough ahead so they would not have to climb the stairs inside McGuiness Hall with them. The two then did their usual routines of checking their mail then continued up. As they reached the dining hall, David asked, "Do you want to head in?"

Technically, this would be a date, right? David asked himself.

Actually, Heather had no other option, if she was hungry. So, maybe not…And there would be several hundred other students dining in the large hall.

Heather went through the door that David held open without answering. He figured it would come down to where they or she sat to eat dinner. Once they navigated the aluminum slide line, he followed her to the condiment station. He made certain to let her lead, stepping back to grab a purposely forgotten fork. Heather moved toward the table on her left occupied by some of her dorm mates.

"Hey, Heather."

"Hi."

"Hi, Heather."

"Hey, Jane."

David was not quite sure if she knew he was following her.

This is going to be awkward.

Heather did not sit, but kept moving until she put three tables between her and her dorm mates, then parked her tray on an empty table and turned around.

"This OK?"

Date!

"Uh, sure…" David calmly replied, as he sat down across from her.

"You went for the meatloaf, that's brave," commented Heather, as she started in on a large Caesar salad.

"Is that what this is?" smiled David. "I've never had gray meatloaf."

"So what *do* you think so far?" Heather asked, remembering the polite response back at the rectory.

"OK, I guess. I don't really know what to expect."

"How about you?"

"Pretty good, but I've only had two classes so far."

"Mmmm, same here."

They ate for a bit in silence.

"So you're from Alaska? *That* is sooo cool."

"I guess it's my parents that are cool. We moved there five years ago from Vermont."

"So, is it like the pictures and videos we see down here?"

"Oh, yeah. We lived *in town* in Vermont, and they wanted peace and quiet. We got that and more!"

"So, you're out in the wilderness?"

"As in, two hundred acres, off the grid!" he replied. "How about you? Are you right in the city in Chicago?"

"As in high rise overlooking the bay!"

"Wow."

"It's a little weird, but my parents love to travel, so they are into all the conveniences of the high rise lifestyle. They work in town so we only need one little car for getaways.

"Brothers and sisters?" asked David.

"Nope, you?"

"No. That's weird."

"What?"

"You're an only child, I'm an only child, and my cousin's an only child..."

"Who?"

"Oh, he's my roommate. You'll like him—uh, I mean if you're ever in the dorm, I will introduce you."

Ugh, that came out all wrong.

"You didn't finish your meatloaf," Heather commented as she organized her tray for departure.

"You were right; never attempt to eat anything gray."

"I think I'm going to get my act together for tomorrow, spend a little girl time with the gang, and get to sleep as early as possible. What about you?"

"Sounds about right for me too. Uh, I mean, except for the girl time."

Heather stood up, slung her day pack over her shoulder and picked up her food tray.

"Besides, they will want to know who the cute guy was that I had dinner with tonight," Heather smirked as she started to walk away.

"Oh?"

Nice response! What a dope! Now what?"

He followed her past the table of dorm mates, noticing a few looks.

Don't screw up!

But everything was working against him. Everything in his path was trying to trip him. Each chair leg was positioned perfectly in front of him. Someone stood up, suddenly shooting their chair out in front of him.

Get to the trash bin without falling down!

He made it. Then he clobbered the corner of the trash can opening with his tray, sending the plate and silverware flying in. He quickly caught the plate as it ricocheted off the side of the opening, but the silverware was a goner.

My bad, he thought as he dumped the tray onto the conveyer and walked after Heather, looking totally spastic.

They exited the dining hall without further incident, climbed upstream on the steps and headed toward the dorm. Heather was in Regina Hall, which was directly to the left of Fernwood, their respective end doors about 30 feet apart. As they approached the split in the worn foot path, Heather created some distance between the two.

"See ya at three," said Heather.

"Good night, Heather," David softly replied.

He walked into Fernwood in a daze.

What was that? It was good, no? Did I do OK?

6

Anthony Scordo emerged from his office and traversed the little library. In the opposite corner stood the fax machine; he loaded a small stack of papers face down. He entered the number, starting with "011" for international, then country code "379," Vatican City. As he started to enter the rest of the numbers, he heard the library doors swing open behind him.

"Good evening!" Professor Harrington announced.

In one motion, he pressed stop, pulled the papers from the feeder and spun around, holding the papers behind his back as he greeted the intruder.

"May I help you?" Scordo inquired with his Italian accent.

"Oh, no, just saying 'hi.' I am the new anthropology professor, John Harrington. Just came in to make sure everything was set for tomorrow, big day you know."

"Yes, I see," muttered Scordo.

Professor Harrington held out his hand to Scordo, who shifted the papers to the other hand behind his back, and brought out his right, accompanied with a short bow.

"Anthony Scordo," he said in a low monotone. "Pleasure."

"Why yes, same here," Professor Harrington replied, offering a slight bow in return.

Scordo did not offer any conversation, so the professor made for a polite exit.

"Best be off. Gotta get the handouts ready for tomorrow."

Scordo nodded, then turned and walked back to his office. His fax would wait until the professor had left the building.

Scordo opened the lower door of the cabinet that held the silver tea service and produced a bottle of scotch. After he poured, he slid the papers into a red portfolio on his desk and downed his drink. He retrieved a small duffel bag from under his desk and unzipped it. Inside was a yellow and blue jacket and surgical gloves. He reached into the red leather case and retrieved two small electronic devices, placed them in the duffel, and zipped it back up. After locking the door to the library, Scordo went out the opposite office door, locked it, and trotted down the front stairwell, continuing all the way to the basement. He moved swiftly through a maintenance area then down a dimly lit hallway. The rumble of the archaic furnace grew louder as he approached. He reached the furnace room and grabbed the firebox door handle. The room lit up yellow from the blaze of the furnace. Scordo's expressionless face glowed as he tossed the bag in.

Returning to his office, he refilled his drink, placed it on his desk, and moved to the library door. He looked down the hall to the back stairs—the lights to room 312 were out. He sat at his desk and pulled some papers out of the portfolio. Sipping his drink, he organized the small stack, separated the first two pages, returned the rest to a folder, and went back into the library.

He returned to his desk and finished his drink while looking at the papers one more time. On the first page he wrote: "Faxed, Sept. 3, 2 pgs" and circled the note. He added them to the folder and placed it in the red portfolio.

7

A week of classes had barely passed and David was already behind. Perhaps it would have been better if those first few days were cold and rainy. That might have focused his attention toward academics rather than the beautiful campus and the daily search for Heather. He had not seen that much of her since their first "date." No sign of her on the weekend. He wondered about Eric from down the hall; hopefully, Heather did go to her aunt's house.

David's last five years in Alaska were very exciting. His education included building his own house, then outfitting it with wind and solar power; growing and catching his own food; operating boats and planes, not to mention the wilderness experiences he enjoyed alone and with his family.

Plus, he maintained an "A" average in school on the "important stuff." There was one thing David did not excel at in those five years: girls.

There were girls in Alaska, and David was extremely good looking. The problem was more of logistics. The high school was a regional one, so students came from up to 30 miles away to attend. Also, during the school year, it was pretty much dark when school let out, so there was not much to do except make your way home in the snow.

David did date a girl during his junior year, though dating takes on a different meaning with Alaska's terrain and weather. It was almost impossible to get together. She lived 20 miles away, and the homestead commanded most of David's attention. He did manage to get her to stay with his family for a week during the summer. She helped put the finishing touches on the smoke house project, with plenty of time remaining for them to enjoy each other's company. She just didn't seem into the homesteading lifestyle, and David remembered her comments about being bored while they worked. When the school year started and the daylight faded, so did their relationship. They were still good friends; they just could not overcome Alaska's challenges to keep it going.

In the second week, things were settling in to a bit of a routine. Anthropology class was David's favorite, as it provided an opportunity to see Heather. The only problem was that the students walked back to the main campus as a group, pretty much eliminating any chance to talk privately, only allowing for the "So, howzitgoing?" exchange.

On both class days the next week, David waited for the group to dwindle on its way back, looking for the opportunity to talk to her. Unfortunately, the group did not dwindle enough. One of the students was a Regina Hall resident who was rather talkative. As a matter of fact, Donna could not shut up.

On Wednesday's return trip, the students moved up the final flight of stairs, into the Oak Hill Campus. One peeled off to his right.

"See ya later!"

"Bye, Steve!"

A moment later, another dropped off, leaving just three of them. The remaining steps were brutal. Donna streak-talked in her native Long Island tongue, replete with a nasal twang. She was rambling about her boyfriend back home. Heather was politely nodding and threw in an occasional "Really?" or "No kidding?" Donna was one of those people who looked straight ahead as she walked and talked—loudly.

David bailed out where the worn path split and headed toward Fernwood.

"Take care," David bid them.

There was a goodbye thrown in to the middle of a sentence, but it barely interrupted Donna's streak.

"Yeah, bye-bye, and so I says to him, listen I wanna know right now what she said, and no B.S., ya got that?"

The last thing David heard as he headed inside the dorm was Heather:

"Really?"

Friday's return trip saw a smaller group making its way up the hill. Steve hung a right.

"See ya!"

"Later, Steve."

David had the full stretch of campus to wedge himself into, and Donna out of, the conversation.

Donna was blasting into Heather's right ear. David was a pace behind Donna, staring at her enormous hoop earring, bobbing along in sync with her bleached blond ponytail as she blathered. Today's rant was about a recent date.

"I hope you don't expect me to eat any of this crap, I says to him. I mean how dare he? This guy is *supposed* to be taking me out on a date and he pulls into a friggin' Denny's! What's up with that? I mean, I'm not a snob or anything, but come on, a friggin' Denny's? At least Roger took me to a steak house, even though it was one of those chains, you know, like an Outback or something. Or maybe it was that Bugaboo place, I can't remember, well it doesn't matter, cuz I really love steak, how 'bout you? I mean I really love steak and those chains are great for steak. There, I said it, I like food chains. See, I'm not a snob it's just that..."

David concluded she had gills behind her ears, because she never inhaled. It just kept coming out like the continuous howl of an old-fashioned police siren. It was hopeless. He remembered reading *Harry Potter* and thought about the different spells. He held his right arm down at his side, then extended his index finger and pointed it at her. He stabbed the air with it.

Jaw-us, lock-us! he said to himself.

Nothing. He poked harder as the babbling continued.

Tongue-us, bite down-us!

No luck.

Ankle-us, sprain-us?

She walked and talked on.

David bid them good evening at the same point. Heather sneaked him a look, smiling with raised eyebrows, with a kind of "Help me!" look on her face.

I'm afraid there is nothing I can do, David shrugged.

Other than commuting to class on Friday, no Heather all weekend. Not even a distant sighting. Saturday brought quiet to Brighton Latin's Campus, enabling David to hit the books all day. He was very productive and thought if he could do the same on Sunday, he would be on top of everything. As evening came on, the place was like a ghost town.

David didn't want to push it, but it would have been nice to see Heather. He thought about love at first sight, *Nah, couldn't be,* he thought. But then he thought about how many times a day he pictured the first time he saw her in the post office. Man, she was pretty. And those eyes! Those incredible, hypnotic eyes!

What was just as amazing as her looks was that she was for real, not like a lot of the girls he met in the first few days. She showed no interest in making the scene or dressing the part. In some ways maybe she was like him, perhaps a bit of an outcast or loner. Maybe not...

What do I know about this stuff, anyway?

He did not run into her at dinner, which, on this day, took him twice as long to eat. Nor did he find her on the commute to and from McGuiness, which he walked in a painfully slow pace, just in case she was in the area.

Brian popped into the room around seven; David was on his bed reading.

"Got anything going tonight?"

"No."

"Why don't you come with me? A couple of the varsity players are having a party."

"OK, I'm in! I'm gonna' grab a shower first, OK?"

"No hurry."

With the drinking age now 21, the parties David and Brian heard their parents talk about were a thing of the past. Most attempts at a party would occur in upperclassmen housing down around Oak Square, and even those were kept low-key as the penalties for having under age students present were severe. The big parties happened off school property.

As they descended the 170-something steps, it was noticeably livelier in Oak Square. The street traffic was heavy as people moved about. The sports complex had people in sweats coming and going, catching an evening workout or tennis match. As they moved up Faneuil Street, Brian led the way up the driveway of a converted duplex where the hockey players were hosting the party.

In the back yard, there were some beach chairs and tables set up, but no people. On the patio, one of the hockey players attended to a gas grill.

"Hey Brian, wanna dog?"

"Sure!" he responded, grabbing the squeeze mustard off a table.

The player loaded another into a bun and gestured to David. "Thanks."

Brian spied a couple of JV players sitting on a couch in the lower apartment. He entered through the open door and sat down. David followed, eating his dog.

"Mis-ter An-der-son!" The two called out in unison.

"Hey, wassup Hosers?"

"Ready for a beer? I tink Sully's tappin' da keg."

"Sure," said Brian.

"OK," said David.

"Cups are in da kitchen. Keg's in da sink."

"George, Paul, this is my cousin, David."

The cousins enjoyed a couple of beers, listening to the JV players talk about northern Minnesota with their genuine accents. International Falls, Minnesota is about as good as it gets for being in the middle of nowhere, yet, somehow a school scout knew where to look. And what a find these guys were. It looked like they were going to be moved up to varsity before the season even started.

Although David was a bit of a wallflower, things lit up when they asked where he was from.

"Now dat's gotta be coder den what we're used ta up in Minn-a-soder, ay' Georgie?"

It was getting on 11:00.

"Thanks for the brewski. I think I'm gonna head up," David said.

"Really? The party is 'bout ta start!" laughed George.

David did notice there was a small crowd growing in the yard, and another group was stationed in the kitchen, minding the keg. It didn't matter; he was done and was looking forward to a solid night of sleep on the now quiet upper campus.

8

The small emblem next to the door read: "Cardinal Vincent." A nun of about 40 years entered.

"The bank records show Mr. Scordo has paid the school," she said with a thick Italian accent, placing a folder on his desk. "It seems a waste to pay for a full year's tuition. Perhaps Mr. Scordo can get reimbursed after the move is complete."

"It's insignificant, Sister Sarah," a man in a suit responded in an American voice. "We are on the doorstep of something so great that money cannot gauge its value."

Vincent closed the folder of paperwork having lost interest and beamed at Sarah. He moved around the desk smiling widely and placed his hands on her shoulders.

"We will now see the fruits of our efforts. Bringing them together—bringing them home—this is what we have worked so long and sacrificed so much for."

Sister Sarah offered a smile of agreement in return, but it did not contain the glee of the cardinal's. She excused herself, minutes later leaving the building and navigating the narrow, cobblestone side streets of Vatican City.

The afternoon sun hung low, casting long shadows across the small cemetery as she entered through the rusted, iron gate. In the furthest corner she knelt between two identical grave markers bearing the same name: Lombardo. The simple crosses and graves were clean and neat, in an otherwise much neglected cemetery. As she prayed, she produced a bouquet of flowers from her overcoat and divided tem into two small bunches, placing one on each grave.

After praying for several minutes, she exited the cemetery as a swift breeze rattled the rusty gate. She walked to a busy area of an open air market and found a taxi.

The sky was clearer outside of the city, the window cracked wide as the taxi weaved its way through the hills pulling in crisp air. Turning through an unmarked gate it made its way down a gravel driveway bordered with neatly manicured lawns, stopping in front of a white clapboard building with a large front porch. The sign next to the front door read, "Amadora House."

The nun breezed up the porch stairs and entered, greeted by a nurse sitting at the reception window. Without much dialogue, she handed Sister Sarah a visitor's badge. Unescorted, she walk to the end of a long hallway and entered a room filled with sunlight and a single occupant.

"Sarah!" the woman in pajamas exclaimed, rising out of her chair and placing a strong hug on her.

"Rose," Sarah hugged back.

They sat in two armchairs that faced the large window looking out over the private, park-like grounds of Amadora House. Birds darted about, stopping at the feeder hanging just a few feet away.

"How are you feeling?" Sarah asked.

"Fine," she said as she leaned a little closer. "I spit out the meds when I can," she whispered.

Sarah giggled. A man in a white uniform pushing a bucket with a mop stopped in the doorway. He said nothing, just looked at them, then left.

"Guardian angel?" Sarah asked with a grin.

"More like guard," Rose replied. "They're always watching."

"You would think, after three years, they would understand you have no intention of betraying them."

"Never should have spoken my mind," Rose said slightly shaking her head.

"We keep it bottled up all the time. It eats away at us like acid," Sarah consoled. "How could they blame you for caring about them? How could they blame you for feeling..." she stopped and sighed.

They watched the birds for a moment and soaked up the sun. Sarah broke the silence.

"Can we go someplace and talk?"

"How about a walk?" Rose said, standing up.

As they passed the empty front desk, Rose stopped and buttoned her overcoat, waiting for the footsteps to come around the corner.

"We're going to get some fresh air," Rose said to the returning nurse.

"Sure," the nurse replied.

The man in the white uniform was outside, tending to a garden hose. They walked, arm in arm, until they were out of earshot.

"They are bringing them home," Sarah started in. "They are considering the project a success and are moving to the next phase."

Rose shook her head. "No, this can't happen, Sarah. It must not happen!"

"I know, I know."

"Once they have them, any chance they had will be gone forever," Rose argued. "We have sacrificed so much, we cannot let it end like this."

"We have sacrificed so much," Sarah repeated in a low monotone. "That's what Vincent said."

Rose lowered her head as she walked. "'Sacrificed so *many!*' is what he meant," Rose said shaking her head.

"When the boys are brought together, we will die. You know that, don't you?"

Rose hushed her. "That kind of talk put me in here," she cautioned.

"I know," Sarah whispered. "Can we stop them?"

"We must."

"I am not sure I can."

"Sarah, they watch my every move. I cannot contact the boys. You—you must do it. You must get to them before they come. They deserve our help. Regardless of what happens to us, they deserve a chance to live a normal life."

"I know," Sarah nodded.

9

Wednesday brought them together again. When the class let out, the group formed a little commuting club bound for the main campus, except for Donna who remained behind, talking to the professor. David quietly took the stairs two at a time until he was at her side.

"Hey."

"How's it goin'?" asked Heather.

"Good. Uh, is it unusually quiet in here today, or is it just me?" David asked.

Heather smiled, knowing who he was referring to.

"Be nice," she cautioned.

"Always," David said.

He took a deep breath, "So how are you doing?"

David could hear Donna's voice as she entered the stairwell above. He only had moments before she would catch up to the pack.

"Oh, not so good," said Heather. "I have a paper due tomorrow and I haven't even started it. I am sooo screwed."

"Ouch! I have a test tomorrow and I'm not in much better shape," he lied, having studied for it all day Sunday. He could hear Donna's feet stomping down the stairs, just one flight above him.

"Hey guys! Wait up for me!" squeaked that loveable voice.

"I have an idea," whispered David. "Do you have your report stuff with you?"

"Yeah?"

"Why don't we grab a couple of veggie wraps at the Store 24 and go back to our senior friends' private library?" David asked, remembering her choice for dinner at McGuiness. "It'll save you over an hour getting dinner. No interruptions, I bet you can get it done there."

"How late do you think it's open till?" she asked.

"No clue."

Heather paused for a moment, then smiled. "Well, let's find out!"

"Hey guys, wait till you hear what the professor told me!" Donna cackled as she caught up to the pack.

Date!

Even if she didn't think they were dates, he didn't care; they counted for him. As the group exited St. Mathew's rectory, Heather glanced over to David and smiled. They crossed Faneuil Street and Heather stopped in front of the strip of stores to let David catch up. Donna stopped too, while the rest moved onward.

"Whattaya doin, stopping for somethin'?" asked Donna.

"Uh, David and I have plans," said Heather.

Donna's voice dropped an octave.

"Oh, well, I'll see ya up at the dorm."

Donna bounced along, quickly catching up to the shrunken pod.

"What would you like to drink?" asked David.

"I could use some of that Smart Water right about now."

David and Heather went in and stocked up on mineral water, veggie wraps, and a bag of kettle chips.

"These are sooo decadent," she said. "I promise to go for a run right after I hand in that paper."

David grabbed a couple of energy drinks and put them on the counter.

"Just in case," he said.

As the cashier rang it up, Heather reached into her day pack.

"I got it," said David.

"You sure?"

"Next time."

Hey! That was pretty smooth.

They found the little library just like the first time they saw it, albeit, empty.

"This is all right," said David softly.

"Works for me," whispered Heather.

They set up their laptops and dumped study materials out of their day packs and got to work. David started reviewing what he already knew, while Heather started typing.

"I suppose we shouldn't eat in here," said Heather.

"When you're hungry, we can take a break and go outside. But, we can start up here with those chips," David reasoned.

"Better crack me a Red Bull," said Heather. "I know I'm going to need it."

David pulled out some napkins for drink coasters and placed them on the beautiful old oak table.

"No evidence," he whispered.

About 6:30, Heather was hungry. David grabbed the bag with the rest of the food as she powered down and unplugged her laptop.

"What are you doing?" asked David.

"I'm not going to just leave it out in the open."

"I think we can trust those men we met here the other day. Besides, we are just going to the back steps."

"You think it's all right?"

"I think maybe you got a little too much of that city thing going on," he smiled.

They left the little library, trotted down the stairwell and out the rear exit, making sure the door wasn't locked from the outside, and sat on the steps. It was a crisp New England evening.

"So, I haven't seen you around on the weekends," David said between bites of his wrap.

"I've been going to my aunt's house in Belmont. My uncle had surgery and I've been helping out with laundry, cooking, general company, you know, stuff like that. I guess they could use some help all the time. Sometimes it takes someone getting sick to get you to do anything at all."

"Do they have anyone else?"

"A daughter in Sturbridge, about an hour from here. She comes during the week. It's tough though, with kids and all that.

"You are a good niece, Heather Connor!" David said firmly.

They returned to find everything in order. But, as they sat down, David noticed something was different. The large windows were now darkened, leaving the ceiling lights' neon glow colored the room, reflecting off the glass panes—except for one.

"Hey," he whispered. Heather looked up. David nodded toward the leather chairs and the fireplace. The rippled glass door to the adjoining room glowed from within.

"It's the Tea Man!" Heather whispered.

David chuckled under his breath then went back to work. After a few minutes, they heard a drawer open and close, a chair move, then steps. The light clicked off as they heard a door click shut, then the sound of a key in a lock.

"I guess the big shots get to use the front stairs," Heather whispered.

They spent three hours studying in the little library and chatting about Alaska and Chicago. After all, this was a date. Having his economics material down cold, he asked her several times if there was anything he could do to help on the paper, but she said "no."

One thing they had in common was a love of the water. David liked to fish and she loved sailing on Lake Michigan. In high school, she sailed in a racing club of day sailors. She even crewed on some larger boats. The biggest race, Chicago to Mackinaw, traveled the span of Lake Michigan.

"I got really sick in a storm," she confessed. "But I would go again in a heartbeat."

It was a little after 10:30 when they heard someone walking down the hall, outside the library's double doors.

"Looks like we're busted," David said.

An older man in dark blue pants and a tan shirt appeared in the doorway. He was a small man and looked even smaller the way he was hunched over as he walked.

"Hello. I'm the caretaker," he announced proudly, as he checked the thermostat on the wall. "It's good to see some students finally using this beautiful library."

"Hi," said Heather.

"No one usually comes up here," he continued, "especially at night."

"We were just leaving," she said.

"No rush, no rush. I quit at eleven, I just like to start locking up a little early," the caretaker said, bouncing a large hoop full of keys on his leg.

"We were on our way out anyway," said David, "but, thank you kindly."

Heather and David packed up and left, saying goodnight to the old man.

On the walk back, David asked, "How far did you get?"

"You won't believe it, but I'm almost done. I'm sure I can finish it up right after breakfast. Thank you so much for taking me there."

"I like it there. It's kind of like we're not at this place, you know—school," David sighed.

When they arrived at the dorms, David walked Heather to the side door of Regina Hall. As they walked the last 10 paces to the split in the path, Heather put her arm around David's waist and gave a light squeeze.

"Thanks again for tonight."

She released the squeeze and took the path toward her doorway, glancing back, smiling.

Should I have kissed her? he thought. *Oh, I suck at this.*

David was just inside Fernwood when he heard a high pitched shrill from Regina's open stairwell window.

"HEA-THER…EEEEE! OH MY GOD! He is sooo freak-king hot! Who is he?!"

"Shhhh! He lives right down there," Heather's voice cautioned.

He heard them all giggling as they faded out of earshot.

David grinned and rounded the corner.

WHAM!

A solid blow sent him into the wall. It was Eric's shoulder. He had his buddies in tow, heading out in a hurry.

"Uh, sorry," Eric muttered, obviously not meaning it. David stood up straight, but they kept hustling along out the door, never looking back.

He knew the type all too well. He had been taunted in high school, after refusing to play football. The worst was at his locker one day, just as school let out.

It was three on one, but he had no choice. When he saw the first one make a move, he charged him and crashed him onto the lockers, knocking the wind out of him. The second had jumped on his back; he quickly spun him off, then grabbed him by the hair with both hands and flung him into the third, knocking the two of them over. David took a couple of punches in the process and was standing over them when the teachers arrived.

"So, how did this happen?" the nurse asked when checking out the ribs of David's first assailant.

"I think he's nuts. He just went crazy on me!" the fullback responded in the presence of his coach.

"That would be, on you and two of your football buddies?"

The embarrassed fullback stared at the floor.

"You should know better than to mess with a guy that wrestles grizzlies," cautioned the nurse.

The fullback looked up with his jaw slacked.

"That's right, stitched him up myself."

The story was true. But, what the nurse didn't say was that it was a baby bear of about eighty pounds wanting to play with David. After tackling him, the two rolled around in the leaves for a bit, the bear licking his face and David laughing as he got free from its playful, but sharp grip. He had barely noticed the gash on the back of his neck when suddenly, the 400-pound mother showed up. David could have named his college, had someone been there to clock his 1000-meter dash.

"Where you been?" asked Brian from a full recline on his bed, watching the Bruins highlights on the 11 o'clock news as David closed the door.

"Oh, studying over at the rectory. It's quiet there."

"With that tall babe with the short black hair?"

"Yeah, how did you know?"

"I saw you staring at her on the way home the other night with that Donna chick hanging all over her. You had no chance, man!" Brian laughed.

"So, are you two an item?"

"God, I hope so!" David blurted out. "I mean, I think we're getting there."

"She is somethin' else, Davy!"

"Yeah, really something." David said, mostly to himself.

He sat his pack on his desk, kicked off his shoes, and flopped onto his bed.

"Hey, Brian, what do you know about the lacrosse payers down the hall?"

"Major league dicks! Especially that total asshole Eric! Hey, ya know, he has the hots for your friend—what's her name?"

"Heather."

"I watched him hit on her in the mail room today. She looked all embarrassed. Was telling her he was from Cherry Hill and had another place *down at the shore.*" He finished while jutting his lower teeth forward and giving a bad impersonation of someone sophisticated.

"Where's that?"

"I dunno, North Dickville! Who cares? He's an asshole!"

"Yeah, he did it right in front of me one day when I was walking with her." David smiled.

"See, what'd I tell ya?"

If there was one thing David could count on, Brian would tell it like it is. No beating around the bush, and, for the most part, no grace. At times it was refreshing, as Brian kept life real, only focusing on the big things. He was actually a very kind and caring person, off the ice, that is. And when it came to family and friends, Brian would go to the ends of the earth for them— they just better be prepared to laugh along the way.

10

Over the next few days, the leaves started changing to gold, red, and orange—the days having difficulty recovering from autumn's increasingly colder nights.

It was around dinner time on Thursday when David entered Fernwood and saw his door ajar. As he pushed it, the voices on the other side stopped their conversation. He found Heather standing next to Brian; she wore a fleece jacket and was holding a small paper bag. Her loaded day pack hung heavy on her shoulder.

"Hi."

"Hi."

"Have you two been introduced?" David said, stunned by her unexpected presence.

"We just met. I'm heading up to my aunt's a day early. My uncle has to go to the hospital tomorrow for tests, so I'm going to go along and keep them company. I just wanted to say have a nice weekend."

"Thanks, you too," he said smiling a little.

She came to me! I must be doing something right.

David then noticed that Heather was a little taller than Brian, who he knew was five-eleven. They were both wearing sneakers, so he calculated her height right at six feet.

"So, Brian was telling me about how you two used to live in the same town."

"Yeah, then his dad wanted to get rich, so they bailed to Nova Scotia."

"So, how did you two end up here together?" she asked.

Brian jumped in, "It was all *my* doing! We made a pact to go to college together. He never thought I'd pick Brighton Latin. Davy here had to do a late application and snuck in under the wire—and here we are! So, like, I'm kinda responsible for you meeting him. So...if you have a twin sister who's looking for something to do..."

"No twin, sorry," Heather blushed, "but, I will keep my eye out for you."

"Thanks!"

"Oh, my roommate made these cookies. I'm afraid they're pretty bad. I tried one on the way over."

She offered David and Brian the little paper bag; each drew out a cookie. David took a small bite, just in case.

"I'm afraid you're right," he said, swallowing hard on the little chunk.

"Whoa!" Brian gagged and spit out the cookie into the wastebasket. "You ain't shittin'. They're awful!"

Heather and David looked at Brian, then each other.

"Pinkies out, Brian—we have company!" David joked, as Brian spit out the last bits.

"I gotta run. My aunt's waiting."

"I'll walk you out."

"Nice meeting you, Brian."

"Same here, Heather. Have a good weekend."

David walked Heather toward her aunt's car.

"Take good notes in class tomorrow. Will I see you Monday?"

"Sure," he smiled. "I'll come find you around dinner."

"Great," Heather said, looking him in the eyes and growing a very large smile. Then she turned around and ran toward the car.

I think she just asked ME for a date!

This was huge. David had wondered if it was all him. He was completely nuts about her, but did not know how she felt. Everything was so new at college—maybe she just needed a friend to study with. Maybe she had a boyfriend back home. He just wasn't sure, till now.

On Saturday, Brian left for an overnight scrimmage in Syracuse, so there would be no beers with the boys in Oak Square. With everything seemingly at a standstill for the moment, David indulged in one of the great luxuries of independent campus life —a three-hour impromptu nap!

When he awoke, he threw on his fleece and headed down for an early dinner. With no reason to dawdle, his commute time to McGuiness was much faster than last weekend. He pigged out on all-you-can-eat Buffalo wings and downed a couple of sodas, not even noticing who was around him.

On the return trip to Fernwood Hall, he joined the guys who lived in the room across from him. As they passed the student center, they could hear a live band plugging in their amps and doing sound checks.

"Anyone know what that's about?" asked David.

"It's an Amateur Band Night thing," said Billy.

"You goin', Eskimo Joe?" asked Billy's roommate, Steve.

"No. I have a killer test on Monday that I haven't even started on."

David liked Billy and Steve. He often played backgammon with them in their room, as they had re-rigged it with bunk beds and added a couple of nice, wingback reading chairs like the little library had—creating a great place to chill. On the main campus, Billy and Steve could usually be found on the lawn behind McGuiness, tossing a Frisbee with whoever would stop to play. They were definitely the *Fun Guys*.

Steve spun around and walked backwards directly in front of David.

"OK, Mr. Bookworm, I challenge you to backgammon. My place, ten minutes!"

"Wager?" David inquired.

Steve reached into his pocket, pulled out a crisp dollar bill and stretched it out in front of David's face with both hands.

"Thems are shum high stakes!" Billy quivered.

"I'm in," David said accepting the challenge.

Billy then whistled the opening line to *The Good, the Bad, and the Ugly.*

"Whah—Whah—Whuh." David finished the tune, staring down Steve, still in reverse.

David returned to his room after going down two in a row and paying Steve two dollars. He thought it might be best if he left for the evening, as the lacrosse guys were in the dorm, tossing the ball in the hallway and drinking beer. While he wasn't afraid of them, it would be nice to have Brian nearby, as they always seemed to travel in a pack. Other than tangling with Eric, there was nothing else to look forward to, except maybe running into Donna, since the Fun Guys were heading up to Band Night.

St. Mathew's! he thought. *I could go there and study in peace and quiet. Maybe some of the elders were there having tea and enjoying a nice warm fire in that beautiful stone fireplace.*

He packed up and headed out into the crisp evening air toward the rectory. The sky was clear and brilliant with stars.

Nothing like at home. But then, what could be?

He was disappointed to find an empty library and no roaring fire. He plunked his pack down on one of the wingbacks and sat in the other. He put his feet up on a small ottoman and reviewed his notebook for a while.

There goes five years of callus build up, he thought, noticing the flaking skin on is finger tips.

His hands were like leather from the constant handling of wood and stones at the homestead. Maybe his dad was right. This was no place for him. Maybe he should be at some hippie, granola school in the hills of Vermont or learning about oceanography on a ship somewhere. He loved Vermont and Alaska, and, like his father, hated the "in town" noise of their previous house.

And now, here I am in Boston?

He thought about Heather, how she was from Chicago and how maybe this whole scene may be good for her.

Maybe I'm just a misfit, he conceded.

The book grew heavy in his hands as he thought about those electric blue eyes, their image lulling him to sleep.

11

David jumped up, startled by a wind gust pelting rain on a window. Looking about, the lights were off and the only thing he could see was a reddish glow shining dimly through the rippled glass of the double doors of the library. He now realized where he was.

How long did I sleep?

He cautiously felt his way past the familiar bookcases, then crossed over the study tables, until he reached the double doors to the hall. He softly padded down the door for the latch set.

Locked!

He lined up one eye to peek through the gap where the two doors met. He focused on the glowing light—an "Exit" sign mounted at the end of the short, unlit hallway.

The caretaker! It must be after 11. Or maybe not. He liked to lock up the library early.

David pounded on the doors and yelled. The two doors made a huge echoing racket, flexing where they were connected by the lock, but refusing to break free from each other. He stopped, pressed his ear against the gap, and waited a minute. Nothing. He banged and yelled again, this time for a full 10-second burst. He listened again. Nothing.

The caretaker must have gone home, he concluded.

He felt around for a light switch on both sides of the door; he could not see them mounted on the wall just outside in the hallway.

It was obvious no one was coming. Carefully, he made his way back through the room to the leather chairs, using the tiny bit of red light the exit sign offered to avoid the study tables. Anxious as he navigated, his movements were muffled by the rain pounding the roof and windows.

That must be it! The caretaker couldn't see me. The chairs blocked his view! he thought, holding on to the back of the wingback chair.

Now, how to get out of here?

There was only one other door to the library—the Tea Man's office. He felt his way to the door, twisted the knob, and to his surprise and relief, it opened. Stepping inside, he could see another glowing red light through another door across the dark office. Grateful, David backed up a few paces, scooped up his pack, felt for the notebook on the other chair and shoved it in. Making his way toward the red glow, he closed the door to the library behind him, then, turned and with a great crash, David felt his feet knocked out from under him! His shoulder collided with something solid. Things were falling on top of him—heavy, painful things. Scrambling on the floor backwards and trying to stand up, he felt a cool, hard object under his hand. Through the darkness, he made out the brass shaft of a fallen floor lamp.

On his knees, he gasped. After a moment, he took a deep breath, righted the lamp and turned it on. The office was cluttered with an overturned reading chair and a brown bookcase—its contents littering the floor. Scanning the rest of the room, he saw in his path a shin-height leather ottoman. David stood up quickly, embarrassed and glad no one had witnessed him tripping. The rain continued to pound the roof, drowning out any other noises that may have come from inside the building.

Stepping carefully through the mess, he unlocked and opened the second door, confirming the other Exit sign atop another flight of stairs. David rubbed his shoulder. His shin ached, too. He went back into the office and looked at the mess.

"Oh, great," he said, noticing his unzipped backpack had dumped its contents, including his small lap top.

David sat on the floor next to the mess and attempted to power up the laptop. It responded.

Whew! That would not have been good.

He put the laptop in the pack and then gathered some papers and quizzes into their manila folders along with a notepad and zipped his pack shut.

He did his best to put the rest of the puzzle back together. The lamp had a dented shade, which David straightened out to an almost undetectable dimple. He arranged the chair, its feet settling into the marks on the rug, and placed the bookcase— shoulder injury no doubt—right side up, leaving a mess of books and papers on the floor. The larger books must have come from the lower shelf, as they were underneath it. The smaller ones, maybe went on the top shelf? And finally, a red leather portfolio, with its contents of paperwork and folders had slid onto the wood floor toward the far door. He carefully slid the scattered papers back into their respective folders as best he could and placed them in the red portfolio. Now it was a guess as to where it resided in the brown bookcase. When he was done, it looked good to him, although he had no idea know how it looked before he plowed it over. David took one more look around the room to ensure everything was picked up, then, turned off the floor lamp. Closing the office door behind him, he realized he had no way to lock it.

I guess they're gonna know someone came through here no matter what, he thought.

David decided that it would be best if he stopped in and told them what happened. He would go back on Monday and find one of the elders. Since nothing was stolen or broken, save the dented lamp shade, they could hardly be angry. In fact, he was certain they would be relieved. It would be disconcerting, David thought, to feel like your personal things had been violated by an intruder. Admitting his blunder would eliminate any speculation and concern as to what happened.

As he left the rectory, there was no sign of anyone. The hard rain soaked David as he tucked his pack under his fleece to protect his laptop and books as best he could, then ducked into the Store 24 to purchase a coffee and a box of trash bags, covering his pack with one as he left the store.

Back home, you never leave without rain gear.

"Not too bright," he muttered to himself, noticing the rain letting up a bit. He walked up Faneuil Street, then, cut up Perthshire—his pack covered, and his hot coffee cup warming his hands as he sipped.

A band was still thumping away over at the student center when he finally arrived home. He put the pack on the floor and peeled off the soaked fleece. He looked at his alarm clock.

"Ugh," David grunted out loud.

He emptied the day pack on the floor. The laptop was pretty dry, which was good, and everything else was at worst, damp. He spread the notebooks and folders out on the floor to dry, then grabbed a towel. Gladly, the Fun Guys were still out, David dodging a certain ribbing. He stripped out of his soaked clothes and took a long, hot shower.

Leaving his wet clothes hanging in the shower area, David grabbed his wallet and key, and returned to his room in just a towel. After throwing on a pair of sweats, he killed the light and pulled the covers over his head.

12

Sister Sarah's hand shook as she wrote on a plain sheet of paper.

They must not come, she thought. *They should be allowed to grow up, like any boys. 'Too much has been invested,' indeed. I have too much invested. Rose has too much invested.*

She continued to write and finished the letter, then sealed it in an envelope, only writing "Sarah" in the space for the return address. She stopped short before exiting the building, looked about, then dialed a long number she had committed to memory.

"Hello, Glen here," the earpiece responded.

Sister Sarah hung up the phone.

13

The second best luxury of independent campus living: sleeping in! David opened one eye: 11:15 a.m.

That was great! I think I'll grab brunch.

David exited the dorm in his sweats. As he walked up the path, he saw Eric and his entourage going back into Fernwood.

At least I don't have to watch out rounding corners.

"You headin' down?" Billy called from behind.

"Yup," replied David, half spinning around with his hands stuffed in his pockets.

Steve was in his pajamas, with a plaid bathrobe and slippers, Billy in street clothes.

"Nice," David said to Steve, admiring his garb.

"Hey, I bet *you're* wearing what you slept in."

"OK, you got me there."

"It's just that, I am a slave to fashion," Steve said flipping his blond bangs to the side.

"You haven't even combed your hair," Billy commented. "Your tall babe must be out of town."

"How does everyone know about her?"

Steve stepped back and slapped the back of David's head.

"How about 'cuz she's freakin' gorgeous, you moron!"

"I know, I know!" said David, half reeling from the friendly blow.

"So what's the verdict?" asked Billy, as they as they trotted down the stairs.

"Oh, I could easily flunk out over her."

"Atta boy!" said Steve, with a last playful swat to the back of the head.

"You up for a rematch later?" David challenged Steve as they walked back to the dorm.

"Oh yeah, big boy. I'm ready for ya," Steve laughed.

David found Brian in their room unpacking his duffel.

"How was the scrimmage?"

"I got like, no ice time. I don't think I'll make the cut."

"Come on, they can't do that. You're Canadian. Well, sort of..."

"Is the dining hall still open? I'm starving."

"They were still serving when I left. Oh, sorry for leaving the mess. I got caught in the rain last night."

"No sweat," said Brian, as he pulled off his socks.

In one motion he made a free throw with his socks in the general direction of his closet, missing badly, and pulled his flip flops out from under the bed. Standing, he put one on. Then, as he reversed the move for the other beach sandal, his bare foot stuck to a manila folder, and launched it—sending its contents flying. David tried to catch the empty folder before it hit the ground, but missed. He swatted at the papers as they floated to the ground like leaves off a tree.

"Oops, my bad!" said Brian.

"It's just economics junk. No biggie," David said as he picked up the papers.

His jaw dropped as he looked closer at the page in his hand.

"Oh, no. I grabbed the wrong folder!" David cried.

"Heather's?" Brian guessed, as he zipped up his wind-breaker.

"No, over at the rectory. It's a long story."

"Tell me later. I gotta fly if I'm gonna make brunch!"

Brian swung open the door and just as he stepped out, a Frisbee whacked the exit door right in front of him. He caught it as it bounced off, and spun around.

"Go deep, Steve!" Brian yelled as he gave the disk a good fling, then exited into the stairwell, leaving the door to the room wide open.

David quickly shut it, and gathered the papers up. Then, he examined everything else laid out to dry. It was all his.

The top page was staring at him. It was a print out of a letter with a handwritten note circled at the top of the page, "Faxed Sept. 3, 2 pgs." The letter was addressed to Card. Vincent. No address, just the name.

He read:

> *"Your Eminence,*
> *I require funds in the amount of $23,000 transferred to the U.S. account for payment of Luc's private school tuition. This will cover his final year at the Day School.*

David sat up straight on the bed. "Hmmm, the Tea Man has a kid," he whispered. He looked around to make sure the door was closed and the shades were drawn. He felt like a snoop, but kept reading.

> *...Luc is doing well in school. Glen continues to do an excellent job acting as father and keeps me appraised of Luc's development, which, to date, is perfect.*
> *I need the wire transfer to be completed by the 13th, as tuition is due on the 15th of the month.*
> *I will forward the final medical exam shortly.*
> *All is well,*
> *Scordo*

OK, not his kid. Glen's kid? David thought.

He found an invoice from a private school that had been faxed to Anthony Scordo: Beacon Hill Day School, Luc Jennings, 214 Beacon Street, Boston, $23,000 due, 8th grade. The invoice was addressed to Glen Jennings of the same address.

David sat back and breathed deeply. He felt uncomfortable reading documents which were someone else's private property. Yet something seemed odd to David. It was the wording of the letter. Why would someone "act" as father?

Maybe the Tea Man is the real father?

Then there was the request for money to the "U.S. account." David popped open his laptop and Googled: "Abbreviation, Card." The first hit was some sort of Catholic encyclopedia. "Card.: Abbreviation for cardinal, or cardinals."

Wow! Scordo knows some heavy hitters, David thought. *And this guy is paying for his kid's school.*

He propped himself up on the bed with his pillow and continued to read.

He found medical reports for annual physicals on Luc, the most recent occurring in August. Scanning the reports, they were consistent. Luc was in excellent health. A Dr. Devito was the name on all of the reports. The exams were done at the Jennings' home, including a blood test.

He found another request for a wire transfer from Vincent. The amount was $5,000 for a large gift. It read:

> *...Our friend does not know about Dr. Devito, nor does he know the child's identity. He asks no questions and does the blood tests as asked. He has been a valuable asset and this gift will ensure his loyalty. As before, he returned all samples, no questions, and I ensured their destruction.*

That's weird!

He read it again.

Why would he destroy the blood? Shouldn't it say 'disposal'? Also, the secrecy. Who is this kid? Does he have some sort of disease that they are hiding from the family?

David got up and grabbed a couple of sheets of paper off of the printer and a pencil. First, he listed the facts:

Luc J.—8th grade
Glen J.—"Acting" as Dad
Lives in Boston
Beacon Day School
Private school—8th grade
Paid for by Mr. S.
Mr. S. gets money from Card. V
Mr. S. sends reports to Card. V
V not in USA?
Doctor Devito
Private physical
Secret blood tests
Secret lab guy

Nothing jumping off the page, he thought. *But there is definitely a puzzle here, and the medical stuff is right in the middle of it. And the father must be bogus, as the others are making decisions about and funding the kid's education. Hmm…*David pondered the list.

He made a diagram with *Luc* at the center and the other data orbiting around the name. It made no sense. On another sheet he put *Scordo* in the middle. All of the U.S. comments went on the left, all of the international comments on the right.

That makes sense, sort of. I guess I'm no Sherlock Holmes.

Brian entered the dorm room on his cell.

"Unbelievable! Hang on, I'll ask. Wanna go to the Patriots game tonight?"

"What? Sure."

"He's in! One hour. Right! We'll be here!"

Brian jumped on his bed and started a running in place celebration dance.

"Woo-hoo! Were goin' to the Pats game!"

"Hey!" David attempted to calm him down. "So how do we have tickets?"

"Sully's bein' looked at by the pros! They were at the Syracuse game and slid him four tix to the Pats home opener! Pro bono! Gratis! For no! As in Free-beez, Cu-zin!"

"And he called you?"

"I'm not asking any questions! And B-T-W, what you have to realize cousin, is that I am a great guy! And make sure your girlfriend knows that, so she can set me up."

"Did we hear the sweet sound of *Pats tickets?*" Billy asked, his head appearing around the open door.

"Sorry, guys," consoled Brian, "I only scored two."

Billy looked at his roommate.

"OK, Steve-a-reeno, Rock-Paper-Scissors for the extra tick!" Billy challenged.

"Two out of three!" agreed Steve.

"Wait, guys!" Brian said as they cocked their fists. "David's going."

"What? Whoa, no way!" said Steve. "It seems Davy here, has a big killer test to study for, re-mem-ber? He couldn't possibly have the time, I mean—if he couldn't go check out a little music across the street, then, there is nooo way he's going all the way to Foxboro!"

"Right!" agreed Billy.

"Ready?" announced Steve.

Billy re-cocked his arm.

"Damn!" Billy yelled on the first throw.

"Oh yeah!" he screamed on the second round.

They both pumped three times and let go the final throw. Billy was silent. Steve flung his hands into the air waiving two thumbs up. He spun out of the room and started to chant, "Yeah baby. Right here! That's what I'm talking about!"

Billy followed, his head down in defeat.

Sully picked them up in a little blue Honda. David squeezed into the back seat, as Sully's roommate slid the passenger seat forward a bit so he could wrestle himself in.

"Thanks, Rick."

David was clearly the largest of the group, but the other three were close with solid athletic builds, filling the car completely with shoulders and legs.

"Game's at six; we got plenty of time," said Sully.

"Grill and a cooler in the trunk," announced Rick.

"Can we stop and stock up?" asked Brian.

"That's the plan," said Rick.

"That was nice of those scouts to give you the tickets; they must be looking hard at you," David commented.

"*They* didn't give them to me," replied Sully. "That's illegal."

"But, I thought—"

"You thought wrong, that's all," informed Rick. "The tickets were given to Sully by the bus driver. He said he couldn't make it to the game. I saw it myself."

David squinted, trying to sort it out, then his eyes opened wide.

They sat in silence, sporting identical grins.

The little blue Honda pulled into the supermarket and its occupants muscled their way out. David exited the store with a bag of charcoal, a big bottle of Pepsi, and a full grocery bag with a bag of chips sticking out of the top.

"Let's roll," a voice shouted from behind.

Sully had a case of beer under one arm and a bag of ice dangling from his free hand. He handed Brian the beer then smashed the bag if ice on the ground and poured it into the cooler. He tossed in the beer, hot dogs and soda, slammed the lid, then the trunk, and they were off.

As they drove west on the Massachusetts Turnpike, David could not stop thinking about his little chart and what it possibly could have meant. Maybe he was reading too much into it. Scordo's secret child? More likely the cardinal's! Or, perhaps a family with a sick child being helped by these kind people was a perfectly plausible theory. Nah, there were too many little things, like all the secrecy and the *acting as dad* comment. The mental image of the chart kept his mind spinning.

The Tea Man is the man in the middle, he thought. *He must be in charge of everything in the US. He obviously reports to Cardinal Vincent who is overseas, funding everything.*

There, clear as mud.

The kid must be a secret; the cardinal or some priest probably had an affair with a young girl and they are hiding the offspring over here.

That would make perfect sense! Abortion was obviously out of the question. The private doctor and blood tests could be to hide any evidence that might warrant some type of paternity suit.

"You're awfully quiet, David," sounded a voice from the front seat.

"Yeah," said Brian. "Maybe I should-a brought Steve instead. But he can't help it Rick. His mind is completely preoccupied these days."

"Oh, what's her name?"

"Heather," David said, smiling.

They all chuckled.

"In Regina?" asked Rick.

"Yeah."

"I've seen her. Oh man, he's a goner!" Rick laughed.

David stared out the window, smiling in agreement; he was a goner. As the scenery flew by he thought about the papers and the puzzle; he had solved it, at least in theory. The illegitimate child plot was sound. The only question was, Should he return the file knowing they'd know he looked through it?

He could sleep on that one.

14

Breakfast was missed without regret. They awoke after nine, showered and got their act together. Brian had a class he had to dash to make; David had until eleven.

"I'll never schedule a morning class on Monday again," Brian declared as he threw on his jacket.

"Or any day, for that matter," added David.

"Later, cuz," Brian said, disappearing out the door.

David decided to get down to St. Mathew's and tell them what happened and return their paperwork. He slid his laptop into the padded sleeve of the backpack. He gathered up his notebooks along with the folder, making sure he removed his little sketches of clues. As he opened the pack to insert the small pile, something from the bottom of the pack glistened. When he moved his head, the reflection flashed back at him. He laid the paperwork down and reached in.

It was the size of a postcard, shiny and black. He pulled it all the way out, the flexible vellum material still damp.

He rubbed it dry it on his flannel shirt, held it up, and examined it. It was too dark to be a negative of a photograph, but it was not solid. He turned on the desk lamp and held it against the white shade. There was a pattern of tiny squares, perhaps a hundred or more, visible in the vellum. He looked closer, spotting images too small to make out. He put the velum into his chest pocket of his fleece, zipped it up, and packed the daypack.

David hit the stairs and trotted into McGuiness. He dropped a level and went into the Oak Tree, a cash deli and grill which catered to students not on the meal plan. David bought a muffin, coffee, and orange juice, and sat alone. He pulled out the film and held it up toward an outside window.

Too small to make out, he thought.

When his first class was over, he had two hours to kill before his exam. He was going to use this time to run down to the rectory to straighten everything out; but instead, he went to the library. He walked up to the information desk and presented the vellum.

"Ah, microfiche," said the librarian. "Haven't seen that stuff in years. I'm afraid we don't have a reader here. Try the basement of Dexter. There is a study hall there; I think that's where they retired it."

Dexter Hall, one of the oldest academic buildings on the campus was similar to the library at St. Mathew's, with work-tables, bookshelves and comfortable old chairs, plus the ice cube tray light fixtures. But there was no fireplace, and the windows looked out into concrete wells that let light into the lower level. Also, unlike the rectory, there were students.

The microfiche reader was in the back left corner of the room, past the tables hosting a few students working on their laptops. It was a large machine, standing upright at about five feet tall. A large screen was mounted on top, with the reading mechanism at desk height. David pulled up a chair and sat in front of the viewer, then bent over and spied the plug on the floor.

"As I thought…" he whispered to himself.

He plugged it in and turned it on. The screen barely glowed. The machine was a bit of a contraption, with a fixed scope mounted under the viewer, angled toward the work table. The reading mechanism looked like a metal tray; he swung the top piece of it upward and dropped the microfiche in. It was a perfect fit. When David moved the little black handle mounted on the front of the tray the viewer flashed by hundreds of images.

Whoops! David thought, jerking it back and getting the same effect in reverse.

He focused by turning a large black plastic knob on the side of the viewer, but he could not make the images clear. *Was it in another language? Hebrew?*

Dohhh! It's in backwards!

He reloaded the vellum. The document was familiar. It was another medical report on Luc, this one being from five years prior. Now using both hands, one steadying the other from jerking the joystick, he slowly moved it to his right.

Ooops, wrong way,

The next several documents alternated between the familiar physicals, and what appeared to be lab reports on the blood samples. He studied the second one.

The lab report looked normal, being a standard form with check boxes. The comments stated, "No abnormalities—excellent health." The report was not signed. In fact, nowhere on it was any reference to who filled it out or conducted the analysis. No hospital, lab, doctor, or technician's name was to be found.

Our friend with the $5000 gift.

He continued scanning, sliding the tray all the way back and starting on the second row of images. "Genetic Workup and Marker Analysis" was a multi-page document of small print, with check boxes. He scanned forward. The form repeated several times. David rewound to the first. "Luc Jennings, Aug 5, 2006, Age 11. The address, phone number, and next of kin boxes were all blank.

Again, looks like our secret lab tech's work.

He read the document, which listed a myriad of diseases, all checked "No." The second and third page continued with more diseases, then mental illnesses, and finally behavioral patters, such as "Prone to Violence," "Suicide," and "Sexual Deviance." Again, all checked "No." David read the comments on the last page.

> *...DNA direct match to sample, with no changes to markers...*
> *Physical development on track...No abnormal characteristics or evidence of non-human attributes.*
> *Continue treatment and review in 3 years.*

The next one was from August 3, 2003, age 8. With the exception of the date and age, the documents were identical. The reports were all the same, staggered several years apart; all for Luc Jennings, all with the same, consistent check marks. Finally, a three-page doctor's report of a physical exam done at six months of age, but rather than Luc Jennings it was for, *"Child, DOB: April 25."*

He didn't have a name when he was born! Or found...or kidnapped!

David's mind ran wild.

As he continued reading, he found what looked like a copy of the previous page, but there was something different; the handwriting was the same, but a line was crossed out, then rewritten. This was not on the other page.

The bells of the chapel started their melody signaling the time.

Crap! Two o'clock!

David pulled the microfiche out and stuffed it back in his fleece, grabbed his pack, and ran.

He missed the start of his accounting test, but it hardly mattered, because he could only think of what he had just seen. His mind raced over the data, trying to sort it all out: DNA profiling, markers, samples, matches, treatment, abnormal behavior, extra reports. He finally tried to focus on the test; he would go back to Dexter right after he finished.

When the professor called for time, David was not even close to being finished. And, he had no recollection of any of the questions he did answer, so it didn't look like today was going to boost his grade point average.

Back in research mode, David slid the little tray and found the report. With the exception of the scribble, it all looked the same, until he reached the very top of the first page: "Child, DOB: May 2." And there was only one page.

What the? Who the hell is this?"

He combed the partial document. Other than the scribble, only the name block was different. David sat and stared.

By now, he was supposed to have returned the file and cleared up the mystery of the mess he made in the Tea Man's office, but this was too weird. He jumped ahead to a series of letters and reports. He thought he saw an invoice from the school, but we went by it too fast to be sure. He retraced his path on the microfiche viewer and started to read the documents; he found a letter to Cardinal Vincent describing the favorable results of the DNA test. As the others, this was from Scordo.

He sat back, trying to digest it all at once. An unnamed child, "DOB: April 25" is apparently Luc and we have a second child, "DOB: May 2." Both had physicals by the same doctor at six months of age. Then Luc—at least Luc—was periodically genetically tested. He tried to make sense of it.

David discovered the print button on the front of the viewer. He aligned a page in the viewer and pressed it, and nothing happened, not even a click. He looked around on the viewer and underneath the desk and found the printer cable. It had a couple of adapters in it with the final connector being a USB. Any printer for the microfiche reader had been pirated long ago for another use.

David packed up and shut down the viewer. He ran up the hill from Dexter and took the stairs two at a time into Oak Hill Campus, kicking back into a full run across the grounds.

He reemerged from Fernwood a few minutes later with a gym bag containing his printer and a stack of paper.

He hooked everything up and reloaded the microfiche, finding the first Genetic Workup report. He pressed the red button on the front to the viewer. Nothing happened at first. As David stuck his head underneath the contraption to check the wiring and connections, it made a noise, paused, then, started up. The image on the viewer faded to black and the machine started humming. The printer lit up and, after what seemed like an eternity, the paper was finally sucked through and emerged printed. He printed the next page, then many more, each taking as long as the first.

The chapel bells rang eight times.

Heather! Oh, no!

He double-checked his vest pocket for the microfiche as he jetted up the stairs of Regina Hall with the gym bag in hand. He knocked on Heather's door. No answer.

15

He awoke in disbelief—he had blown her off.

David slid out of the room without waking his cousin. Once in McGuiness, he filled his tray with breakfast matter and positioned himself facing the door. His breakfast grew cold as he kept getting sucked into the printouts while trying to monitor the traffic. After 90 minutes and many coffee refills, David had to get to his class. No sign of her, and only a few pages reviewed.

He worked his way through his classes, then parked himself in a corner of the Oak Tree Deli for more reconnaissance and reading. No sign of Heather. Around five, he headed up to the room. As he passed Regina Hall, he could see her lights were out.

Where could she be?

He remembered their tea party with the priests was on a Tuesday, so she should have been done by now. Brian was getting ready to leave when David arrived in the room.

"Wanna grab dinner?" asked Brian.

"No, thanks, I just had a couple of slices at the Tree. Are you going to hockey practice?"

"Yeah, right from dinner, why?"

"Good, because I have this project I need to spread out all over the place."

"I'll bet you do!" Brian laughed.

"Gimme a break," grunted David.

After Brian left, David started to sort the papers. He flattened out a blanket, covering Brian's bed, then did the same with his. On Brian's bed, he laid out the medical and genetic makeup reports. He scattered the rest of the documents on his bed then started reading through them, line by line to see if there was something, some clue of information, or some inconsistency.

As Brian hit the top of the 170-something steps, Heather was summitting the climb with three girlfriends, including Donna.

"Hey," Heather puffed.

"Hey, Heather, how you doin'?" replied Brian.

"Out of shape, I guess."

"Nah, these stairs will do it to anyone."

"Hi, Brian."

"Hey, Donna."

Heather's friends walked ahead a few paces and slowed, to let her finish her conversation with Brian.

"Havin' a little study session with David?" Brian winked.

"Huh?"

"He's up there now, probably cleaning the room," Brian laughed. "See 'ya later—and don't forget me on the-you-know-what!"

Brian repelled down the stairs two at a time, vanishing into the dark.

"They're still serving. I'm goin in," announced Donna as they entered the lobby.

"You comin', Heather?"

"No, I'm going to head up."

She stopped and stared at Fernwood Hall. The room furthest to the left had the shades drawn, displaying moving shadows. She stood there frozen, not able to make out if he was alone.

Of course he's not!

Otherwise, why would Brian have made that comment? Her eyes welled up a bit as she completed the scenario in her mind. First, a no show on Monday. Now this. Being away on the weekends, it was bound to happen. She allowed open season on David. He was far too good looking and nice *not* to have it happen.

He's gone! she thought.

"Hey, Heather!" a voice called from behind.

Heather got herself together in one quick sniffle and turned around.

"Oh, hi, Eric."

"What are you doin' out and about?"

"Oh, just walking."

"Can I buy ya' a beer?"

Heather looked at him, confused.

"Got a cooler in the room," he smiled.

"Sure, why not?" she said.

Eric guided Heather into the main entrance of Fernwood, and took a right.

"Heather!" David said out loud, looking at the alarm clock on his bureau.

She should be home, the perfect opportunity to explain yesterday's absence. He headed out the side entrance and glanced left, observing the main door swinging closed, but not seeing Heather and Eric on the other side, heading in.

"Haven't seen her since this morning," her roommate Cindy said. "She said she was going to do some stuff later with Donna."

He chatted with her for a minute, hoping Heather would show up while he was there, then plodded his way back at about the same pace when he went to the dining hall the first weekend after meeting her.

Heather entered Eric's room where two of his lacrosse buddies were drinking beer. The beds were stacked into bunks across from a couple of canvas backed director's chairs and a foot locker serving as a coffee table in the middle. Lacrosse gear filled the corners behind the occupied chairs.

"Hi," she said.

"Hi," two lacrosse players said in unison.

"Heather!" Eric said with both hands out, presenting her.

"Bob," said one.

"Jimmy," the other replied.

Neither of the two got up, forcing Heather to sit on the lower bunk, bumping her head as she sat down. Bob reached into the cooler between the chairs and pulled out two Rolling Rocks, handing one to Heather and one to Eric, who walked by and grabbed it on his way to his desk.

"Thanks," said Heather.

"Sure," Bob said.

Eric had his iPod hooked up to a boom box and was fiddling with his play list. Heather took a long, hard swig of her beer.

"The Boss will rock forever!" said Eric as he turned up the volume on a live version of *Born to Run*, then plopped himself down on the bunk next to Heather.

The two across from her played the air drums to the opening beat. The song blasted along and then, all of a sudden, the two players got up.

"Gotta get going!" Bob said, as he lifted the lid to the cooler and grabbed another Rolling Rock.

Jimmy dove in before the cooler lid shut and snagged one too.

Heather thought about what was happening and quickly jumped up, wedging herself between the guys and the door.

"Where you goin'?" asked Eric.

She held up her hand and lunged with her long legs, placing her unfinished beer on the footlocker.

"Listen, you guys, stay and relax. I'm the one that has to get going," she explained, as she stood up straight. "Thanks Eric, but there's some stuff I gotta do."

No one said anything as she backed out of the room and closed the door. As it clicked closed, she bowed her head forward, resting it for a second on the door.

"Stupid, stupid, stupid," she mouthed.

David stood with his key in the lock, watching Heather with her forehead on Eric's door. He blinked hard.

I blew it!

Heather took three or four paces in David's direction before she looked up.

"Oh, shit!" she blurted to herself as she locked eyes with David.

She hung an immediate left and walked quickly out the main entrance.

David was in a panic.

What do I do? I blew it. Let her go? Or should I go after her? What would I say? Oh, I suck sooo bad at this.

Tears streamed down Heather's cheeks as she ran to the side door of Regina. Barely holding back a full cry, she just needed to make it to the privacy of her room where she could dive face first into her pillow and howl. As she entered, she was suddenly jerked to a stop by a strong grip on her right arm. She spun around and stood face-to-face with David.

"I just wanted to say I'm sorry about yesterday. I screwed up, completely."

Heather looked at him and sniffled once.

"And today?"

"Been lookin' for you everywhere, all day. I just didn't know you were—I just want you to know that I am sorry," he said, letting go of her arm.

"I wasn't...I mean, I'm not. It was just a stupid beer," she whimpered, wiping her tears and looking away.

David looked down, not knowing what to say next. A long, silent moment passed.

"David?" she sniffled one last time.

"Yeah?" he said softly.

"Will you go on a date with me tonight?"

"Where to?"

"Right here..."

Heather flung both arms around his neck and kissed him so hard his head jerked back, sending him off balance into the door jamb. Some seconds later, he returned the favor. The kiss seemed to last a very long time—a very, wonderful, luxurious, long time. When they finally separated, they stood forehead to forehead, staring in each others eyes.

"I owed myself that," Heather whispered.

"I hope you stay in debt," he whispered back.

They hugged for a minute in silence.

"I need to show you something," David whispered.

He took her by the hand and led her to his room. When he closed the door, he pointed to the beds.

"This is how I screwed up."

Heather stood amidst the mess of papers.

"OK—what is it?"

David spent the next ten minutes telling her the story of Saturday night at the rectory, the tripping over the ottoman, the discovery of the microfiche, and torturing himself with his little diagrams of an internationally-funded, covert operation.

"It all added up to a cover-up and funding of an illegitimate child," David said. "Till I dug into the microfiche. Look, he has a brother, and see, over here there's two physicals with different dates of birth on them. They're even drugging them! Look at the reports!"

It was a lot for Heather to digest, especially since her mind was still back on the doorway kiss. She tried to participate, sitting down as David flipped through the papers.

"So you don't think the kids are the products of an affair?" she asked, attempting to sound interested.

"Maybe, but more than that, they're some kind of lab rats to these people. Some kind of genetic experiment, maybe."

Heather played along. She examined the documents and compared them to David's diagram.

"Something doesn't work," Heather said, scrunching her eyebrows as she compared two pieces of paper. "*Brothers,* just doesn't make sense."

"It's in a memo from a medical report," David said as he started sifting through the papers. "Here, in a letter from Scordo about the DNA tests:

> *Luc's test results are excellent. And I see from the report on the brother that he is developing perfectly, as well."*

"But how could they be brothers if one was born in April and the other in May?" she asked, flashing the two medical reports.

"Ugh! You're right. This makes less sense the more I look at it. Maybe I'm way off track, trying to make something out of nothing!"

Suddenly, a large "BANG!" outside the room stopped their conversation. It was the exit door being flung open into the wall.

"If I had known you were a Cowboys fan, I would have brought you instead of Davy," they heard Brian yelling down the hall to Steve. "It would have been sweet rubbin' your nose in it all the way home. FOUR–TEE–TWO to NUTH-IN, BABY!!"

David and Heather gathered up the papers when they heard the key in the lock.

"Whoops! Sorry. Hey! You *are* studying. How about that!?"

"I'll walk you over," David said picking up the last of the piles.

Once in the stairwell, David looked around, then gently guided her to the wall.

"I'll say good night here," he whispered.

They both giggled as he put his arms around her and kissed her.

"Good night," he whispered. Heather looked him in the eyes. "As in good, David Knight," she smiled and kissed him back.

"Mmmmm."

They hugged, Heather putting her mouth close to David's ear.

"Half brothers," she whispered.

David jerked back.

"They could have had the same father, as in: improper relationship*s*," she finished.

"Breakfast?" David smiled.

"Eight thirty?"

"OK."

16

They talked more at breakfast. Maybe it was an overly active priest with a couple of indiscretions. The genetic analysis and medical monitoring may just be secret to keep it that way, just in case there is a claim.

"So, maybe this guy, or priest, is pretty high up the ladder. Or maybe it's the cardinal. I mean, to want to put that kind of effort into a cover-up..." speculated David.

"Did you bring the files?" Heather perked up.

"Yeah."

"Maybe we can make more sense of it later. How about after Anthropology?"

"You don't have to do this."

Walking down Faneuil Street, they were joined by classmates making the commute. As they stepped onto the front walk of St Mathew's, a tire squealed, followed by the sound of a car accelerating. They turned to see a big black Buick with tinted windows speeding by. The Buick squealed to a stopped in front to the stone carriage house. They recognized Scordo as he got out and hurried across the street into the rectory. He wore a full length, black wool coat and a black hat.

"The Tea Man," Heather whispered.

"That's Mr. Scordo, to you," David whispered back. He disappeared through a side entrance to the rectory.

"I can only imagine why he's in a hurry," David said with a slight grin.

"I'm gonna check something out; I'll catch up," David said to Heather, just as she started her descent in the stairwell with the other students.

He made his way to the little library and cracked the door. The window pane glowed as David witnessed a small racket from inside. A drawer opened, then, closed hard, a chair slid and banged into something.

Well I guess he knows.

David caught up to his classmates as they trekked up Turner Street. Donna was on her game.

"So, then he says to me your paper is late. And I says, but I put it under your office door on the day it was due. And he says it was due on a Friday and he didn't see it until Monday. I mean come on! If you're gonna have a stick up your butt about it, then maybe you need a time stamper thingy mounted to the bottom of your freakin' door! I mean, what's the big deal?"

David slid up next to Donna who was wearing out Heather's right ear.

"So, David, how you doin?" Heather saw an opportunity to rest her ear and took a couple of large steps to get even further ahead.

"Good, Donna. How do you like this class?"

"Oh, it's all right I guess."

Before Donna started the next sentence, David whispered quickly in her ear:

"I am dying to ask Heather on a date tonight, but I don't know where to take her—can you help me?"

"I like the fact that there isn't much homework, so I guess it's good," Donna finished, then jerked her head to the right.

"No sweat. Watch this," she whispered.

Donna caught up to Heather on her left side and waited for the others to finish talking about what was for dinner at McGuiness.

"Ya know Heather, I went to this cute little café down on Cambridge Street. Its like, two stops on the T. It's really cozy, you should try it some time. Ya know, with—"

David was now at Donna's side and she said it loud enough as if she were talking to the two of them.

"Hey, I'm sorry," she interrupted herself, "I don't mean to get in the middle of anything, maybe you two should talk."

She darted out from between them and joined the others, sporting a proud look on her face. Heather looked at David with raised her eyebrows, impressed.

"He was in there all right, and it sounded like he was tossing the room," David whispered.

"So are you asking me out to the café?" she asked, ignoring his reconnaissance report.

"Huh? Oh, yeah, sure. It sounds kind of nice."

Heather swung over to the others and grabbed Donna's sleeve.

"He's taking me there tonight—right now! Thanks for bringing it up!"

The two dropped out at the T stop.

"Very smooth," Heather said to David.

"Not too bad, yourself."

"You could have just told her to butt out."

"She's not a bad person. You don't do that to good people."

"You're a good person, David Knight," Heather said, placing a kiss on his forehead.

On a bench at the T station, they were silent for a long moment.

"Do you think they're all in on it?" asked Heather.

"I'm not sure, I think he was alone in there...but he came back in a hurry, so someone must have called him about the office. Maybe the caretaker?"

After another long moment of silence, David continued.

"I guess its time to make a decision. I mean, *I* need to make a decision. I've gotta either come clean right now and return the files or keep digging and wait for them to come."

"Why would they come?"

"Because, while I ended up with some of their files, one of my Eco quizzes is missing, so it's just a question of time before they wanna know how my test got in their messed up files."

Heather's eyes were wide open.

"When did you realize that?"

"Last night, right before we, uh, got together."

"Well, maybe we should hide out for a bit tonight?"

"The café?" David said with a bit of a smile.

"Where did you say that microfiche reader was?" she asked.

David looked at Heather.

"You really don't need to."

"Let's get this done," Heather interrupted. "I want to go to the café with David Knight—not some guy off in another place contemplating his conspiracy diagram. See, it's all about me, not you," she laughed.

She leaned over and gave him a soft kiss on the cheek.

"Veggie wrap?" David asked as he got up from the bench.

"Don't forget the chips and Red Bull," Heather smiled. "No wait! It's my turn," she said as she jumped up.

"Not yet. Enjoy the moonrise. I'll be right back."

It was a gigantic, orange, harvest moon, rising over the residential neighborhoods of Brighton. When he returned, it had shrunk quite a bit and was much whiter in color.

"It was even more beautiful a moment ago," she said as they started their walk up Faneuil Street. "I bet the night sky is beautiful up in Alaska," Heather said, as she gave David her arm.

He took it and smiled.

"I'd sound like I'm braggin' if I told you how magnificent everything was up there."

They cut right on Perthshire Road and started to climb Oak Hill.

"Brag a little," she encouraged him.

David took a few silent steps before he started.

"Well, try going kayaking and havin' a whale the size of a school bus do a full breach twenty yards away."

"Whuh?" Heather said, jerking her head.

"At first you wonder if it was just by luck that it didn't land on you, then, you see the wave comin'," he laughed a little. "You ride it, and by some miracle, you don't get tossed. Then, from behind you, this big shadow covers up everything and you think— oh, crap—it's at it again. This time, the wave wipes you out. And as soon as you get the boat upright, a huge tail slams down right in front of you, and BAM! You're hangin' upside down in ice cold water."

Heather looked at him in amazement, shaking her head.

"What did you do?"

"What could I do?" he paused, then smiled. "Ever been kissed by a whale?" he asked with a big smile.

"No way!" she laughed.

"Came right up close. I was just hanging there," David said, then stopped for a second as the laughter overtook his ability to talk. "I mean, it could have eaten me right there, like snack food, but it just howled and blew bubbles on me," he laughed, then sighed, tightening his arm up on hers. "I think it liked me…"

"Over there, in the corner," David said softly, pointing.

They slid a couple of chairs over and spun the reader to hide the screen from the room's view. He turned it on and popped in the fiche.

"So how far did you get?" asked Heather.

David navigated the scope to what he thought was the last page he printed.

"I think here," he said, looking at one of the medical reports.

"So we have two kids, maybe half brothers, and some people who are messing with their DNA. OK, what's next?" Heather summarized.

David nudged the joystick over and the screen jerked a little. The next page was a letter.

It appears Bryce has some behavioral issues this year in and outside of school. While his medical profiles don't show any negative traits, he has had a couple of brushes with the law. Though minor, they do raise questions regarding his future development and may jeopardize his acceptance into a private high school. We may want to consider some form of medical intervention.

Please advise,

Henry

"We have a name," said Heather.

"And it looks like Bryce is not such a good little teenager," added David.

"And again, the quick answer is medication,"

"Hold on," he whispered.

David pulled out a notebook and wrote down the X and Y coordinates on the grid table on the edge of the monitor, noting: *Henry letter, Bryce is bad.*

"Wanna drive? Maybe your touch will find something good."

Heather grabbed the joystick and the screen flew across the pages.

"Whoah!" she cried.

"Let's see what you found…It appears to be in another language. Spanish? No, Italian. Of course! Right in front of me the whole time! Devito, Scordo…Italian. Scordo even speaks with the accent. So the boss man Cardinal Vincent is definitely in Rome!"

"Don't all the cardinals live in Rome?" she inquired.

"Beats me," David replied. "I may have grown up in God's country, but we didn't get into the formalities."

Heather grabbed the joystick.

"Ready?" she asked

"Here, let me show you," he said.

David put his hand on Heather's and slowly nudged the joystick, scanning over four or five documents.

"Got the hang of it?" he asked.

"Not yet," she said, placing her other hand over David's.

She started to work the joystick under David's soft grip without any assistance.

"All of these are part of some large Italian report or document."

"Get back to the top."

She inched the joystick up.

"More letters from Henry."

"Let's look at that one," David said, releasing his grip. "A letter and an invoice."

"Just like Luc, they are paying for the kid's private school." Heather pointed to the screen. "Look, it's the Early Years School. He was in the second grade here."

"Four grand for second grade?" David balked. "And look here; it says Bryce Boddington House on the top of the invoice."

Heather continued while David wrote down the coordinates.

"Bryce Boddington. Sounds sort of stuffy, no?" David commented.

"Seems were getting further back in time," whispered Heather.

The screen moved quickly over the documents, but slow enough to scan the content. Then she stopped.

"Check this out! They were both born in Vatican City," she said.

They examined a photocopy containing two birth certificates, both with the same date of birth. One was for Luc Jennings and the other for Bryce Jones.

"Why does it say they were born on the same day?" David mumbled. "And it's May 14. That's a new one."

"And we know that Jennings isn't the dad," Heather jumped in. "And check this out—it's Bryce Jones—not Boddington."

"Jones?" David raised his eyebrows. Heather found a handwritten letter.

Orsini,

Both certificates are attached. Assign them and relocate as discussed. Glen is ready to leave for Boston today. As a final request, please deliver Bryce to Boddington House. An immediate departure is best.

"It's a place!" whispered David. "Look, no apostrophe after Boddington. And look back here."

He grabbed the joystick and navigated back to the invoice.

"Bryce, see, a comma—as in Bryce *at the* Boddington House..."

David popped the screen back to the letter.

...Scordo is in place to oversee all tactical issues in raising the boys, from finances to medical monitoring. He sees it best to stay in Boston and I agree. I can trust him explicitly. Your loyalty and service will not be forgotten.

Godspeed,
Vincent

"Well, that kind of puts it all in place. Two unknown kids born a few weeks apart with forged identities," Heather said matter of factly.

David stared at the screen.

"Forged to place them under people's care...14 years ago, and they still keep it a secret?" David questioned. "Ugh, you hungry?"

"A little."

David took the microfiche out of the viewer and zipped it in his fleece. They grabbed their packs and went out into the crisp evening air, deciding to eat on a far bench.

"Want to split one? I'm not that hungry," he said.

They ate, mostly in silence, with the harvest moon hanging in the evening sky.

"Well, now you know," said Heather softly. "I suppose you could report it to the authorities. Say they are mistreating them and drugging them."

"Are they? For all we know they could have a rare disease like leukemia or something. Maybe this is all a good thing for these kids, like a covert rescue. Or maybe they are just illegitimate kids and their parents are doing their best to bring them up. All we know for sure is that *I* am in possession of stolen property," David stated, standing up.

"We can dig a little more tonight," Heather said, as she stood up, offering him some chips. "Or, David, maybe you would feel better if you knew they were OK?"

"How can we find out?"

"One of them is right down the street."

"You mean?" David raised his eyebrows.

"Let's go tomorrow. I want your head clear for our date to the café," she said, smiling and wrapping her free arm around him.

He put an arm around her and with the other, grabbed some chips.

"OK, I'm up for that.'"

Back at the microfiche reader, they learned little more, just details supporting their theory. As they walked back to upper campus, they planned for Thursday.

"I have a quiz at 10:00, which I need to cram for," she said. "If we meet at the T at noon, we should have plenty of time."

"Look Heather, you really don't need to do any of this. I may be nuts and making this conspiracy theory up in my mind. I mean, sometimes I think that. I'm sorry I dumped these crazy ideas on you."

"It's not crazy, David. Something is clearly going on here. Maybe the kids are sick and just being cared for by good people. Let's find out."

She rubbed his back as they approached the dorm. They found their private spot at the bottom of the stairs and made out for a long minute.

17

David printed out the directions from Mapquest for both the Beacon Hill Day School and 214 Beacon Street, folded them into the back pocket of his jeans. It was chilly and breezy when he met Heather. She wore her usual faded jeans and black Converse high-tops, with a flannel shirt and a dark green down vest.

God, she looks great, he thought.

"Last time I didn't bring a raincoat and paid the price," he said to Heather as they got on the trolley, a jacket bunched in his hand.

"No rain in the forecast," she ensured him.

"I guess back home it rains so much, I always bring it."

Others piled into the train, most heading in to the Red Sox playoff game. The trolley became a festive environment of young baseball fans pumped up for the event. Heather and David took it all in as the trolley made its way into Back Bay. It was, in fact, a beautiful fall day, and the colors of the trees flashed in the bright sun and cool breeze.

The trolley submerged, then stopped. The fans all exited, whooping it up as they jumped onto the platform and headed for Fenway.

After a couple more underground stops, they exited and climbed back into bright day on Beacon Street. The last block of Beacon Street has the Commons, a park facing the gold-domed State House on its north side. A few doors up from the corner of the park sat the exclusive location of the brick brownstone townhouse bearing the number "214." David motioned to it as they stood on the corner of Beacon Street and a busy cross street.

"Check it out. The school is four blocks that way," he said, now motioning the other way.

They walked for a block, then turned right, exiting the busy street lined with a Starbucks, a Store 24, and commercial shops.

In just a few short steps, everything changed. They now stood in the heart of Beacon Hill. Located behind the State House, narrow, winding streets created a maze of neighborhoods that were on a hill. Everything was made of red bricks. The buildings were all narrow townhouses. The gas lanterns and cobblestone streets completed the look of a setting 200 years prior. This is the place where the senators, diplomats, and "old money" lived.

"Wow!" said Heather. "It's beautiful back here."

They found the Day School, which was converted from two adjoining brownstones.

"So, he's in there," Heather said.

"Looks like we have about an hour before school lets out," David said, looking at his watch. "How about a coffee back at that Starbucks?"

"Sounds good."

"Can this count?" David asked as they walked on the cobblestones.

"What do you mean?"

"As a date. I haven't really taken you out on a date and although this is just a few minutes in a coffee shop, I would like to be on record as taking you on a date. I would consider this a start, from which I promise to improve."

"I really liked our second date in the little library," Heather said, smiling and giving him a squeeze.

They sat in Starbucks, sipping hot coffee.

"This is a little crazy, don't you think?" asked David.

"If you dropped the whole thing that would be crazy, or at least it would drive you crazy—crazy wondering what was really going on."

"I guess."

"You're not nuts. I least *I* don't think you are," she smiled. "When we see the kid and he's fine, you can return the files, case closed. But at least you will know you didn't leave someone out there. I can see you care, that's why it's driving you—"

"We better get up there, before they dismiss them," David finished.

They walked back up the hill and passed the school.

"Up there," David said pointing to the next corner. "We can get a good view of them and stay behind the flow of traffic."

A few parents gathered near the front door where moments later, a stream of little people poured out. Parents met up with the youngest children, while some of the older ones walked with lunch boxes in hand and colorful rucksacks on their backs. A group of eighth graders emerged last.

"Let's go," David whispered.

A couple of the kids were going the opposite way, passing them as they descended the hill. They followed the crowd and watched it thin, a girl taking a left down a side street, then a boy entering a doorway of a brownstone to the right. The group continued to shrink as it progressed toward Beacon Street. Heather and David kept a good distance, letting them go momentarily out of sight as they took the turn.

As they approached the corner, a man in a black trench coat and a black, felt fedora crossed in front of them, following the boys to Beacon Street.

"Wait!" announced David, holding out his arm to stop her progress. Heather saw him.

"Is it the…?"

"No, never seen him before."

They followed, the foot traffic popping the boys in and out of view. They saw them split up, just as they reached Beacon Street. The man in black crossed the busy side street through a break in the traffic, and started down the far side of the street. Heather and David stayed on their side for the last block watching a young teenager with a red jacket and a blue daypack over his shoulder cross the street, then wait for the light to cross Beacon, where #214 stood, three doors further down. As the man in black got closer to the child, the light changed and the red jacket moved with the small crowd across Beacon Street. He did not cross, but walked on, staying across the street from the boy and #214, watching from a safe distance.

"Let's hang back and make sure it's the right kid," David said, as they stepped off the curb.

Suddenly, a black Buick with blacked out windows whipped by, traveling up Beacon. It screeched to a stop, double-parking next to the man in black. He walked between the parked cars and approached the opening passenger window.

"Do you see that!?" Heather asked, as they stepped up on the curb, the Buick stopping just up ahead.

The man cut his conversation and lifted his head from the Buick's window, looking around, first at the child, who was approaching the brownstone. He then scanned the busy sidewalks, turning their way.

"Down! Go, go, go!" David barked.

They darted into the entrance to the T and descended the stairs two at a time. Once on the platform, they found a packed train.

"That one!" David yelled; the two squeezed through the closing doors with nothing to spare.

For a few seconds neither of them could breathe. The trolley had barely accelerated, when it slowed to a stop. They got out and went to the end of the platform where no one was standing.

"Do you think they saw us?" panted Heather.

"I don't know." David said hunched over with his hands on his knees, attempting to catch his breath.

"That was them right?

"It sure looked like the Tea Man's car."

"Well, that makes two of them," she said in an exhale.

"At least."

"What next?"

"I didn't have a plan for this."

"Should we go up?"

"In a minute."

It had been nearly an hour since the brush with the black Buick, but David's heart was still pounding. They were only a few blocks from the scene, finding refuge in a small coffee shop. They sat in the back, facing the front windows, monitoring the foot traffic as it passed the café's windows.

"Did you see the kid go in?" asked David.

"No, everything happened so fast. Do you think the Dark Men grabbed him?"

"The what?"

"Those men."

"You said *Dark Men*."

"I did? Yeah, I did. What else would you call them? They're kinda creepy and dressed in black."

"We should finish this," David said.

"You mean go back there?"

"Yeah."

"Do you think it's safe?"

"Not sure. Let's walk back there. If we see any of your *Dark Men*, we'll bolt, I promise."

"All right," Heather agreed. "If they are there, that car is probably parked somewhere."

They exited the coffee shop and walked down the street looking in every direction for men in black and black cars. As they approached the brownstone from across the street, the massive wooden front door opened and the boy in the red jacket trotted down the steps. A man emerged and closed the door. He was about 40 years old, wearing a Red Sox jacket and carrying a baseball glove. They noticed the boy also had a glove; they crossed the street and entered the park.

Heather and David walked slowly down Beacon Street, passed the brownstone and entered the Commons.

"Must be Glen Jennings," Heather said, as they spied him playing catch with Luc in the middle of the park. "Let's get closer."

"Maybe we shouldn't," David said, admiring her courage.

"Come on, we'll just walk by them on the sidewalk."

Heather took David by the hand and they strolled along on the sidewalk looking like the perfect couple.

"I kinda like this part," he said softly. "Any sign of those Dark Men?"

"No," she said glancing around, then putting her arm around him.

As they approached, the father overthrew the ball, which bounced onto the sidewalk and then picked up speed, veering off the path in front of them and rolling down the gentle slope to the pond.

"I got it," David said to Heather, letting go of her and jogging after the ball.

It barely made it to the pond, coming to a stop in the tall grass that edged half of it. He lifted the wet ball and tossed it back to Heather. Luc and his father were on the sidewalk walking toward them.

"Here you go, young man," Heather said, placing the ball in his glove.

"Thank you," Luc said, bashfully looking up at the gorgeous, six-foot-tall woman.

"Thanks," added the father.

David caught up to them and received the same thanks, albeit without the bashful look.

"Are you guys married?" Luc asked.

"No," replied Heather, grinning.

David blushed a little.

"We just met this fall. We're students," she added.

"Brighton Latin," David interjected.

"My dad went there too!" Luc exclaimed.

"That was along time ago," Glen said.

"We're freshmen, so it's all very new," she said.

"What are you studying?" Glen asked Heather.

"Anthropology. I would like to study or work abroad, but that's about the extent of my career planning so far."

"You are right on track. Keep it loose. I ended up working overseas and it was a great experience." Glen said.

"I was born in Italy!" Luc chimed in.

"Did you like it?" she asked.

"I don't remember. I was little, but we're going there in a couple weeks, when I make my confirmation."

"That's exciting!" responded Heather.

"Well, I wish you a very happy trip," David said to Luc. "Keep working on that side arm, and I'll come watch you at pitch at Fenway in a few years."

All exchanged friendly waves and moved on. Their exit was perfect. David put his arm around Heather and kissed her on the cheek.

"Just in case they're watching us," he whispered.

"I'm sure they are," she said, kissing him back.

They found an almost empty trolley and sat in the back.

"He looks fine," David sighed.

"Happy too," added Heather.

"Now what?" David mumbled.

They rode in silence for a few minutes, then David perked up.

"Let's print out what's on the film and put it in a safe place, just in case. Then I'll toss the papers and film on the table in the library, or maybe under his door. Then, maybe this thing will just fade away, and I can focus on being less of a dud to you."

"One last study hall date?" Heather asked smiling.

"Then the café, I promise."

18

"I have not been able to get hold of Luc; he doesn't answer the house phone," Sister Sarah said.

"You must keep trying," Rose answered. "Kids probably have cell phones…"

The man in the white uniform appeared in front of Rose's door pushing a mop. They changed the subject and talked about the Vatican and the upcoming Christmas celebration until the man could be heard moving his bucket down the hall—his reconnaissance completed.

"I sent a letter to Luc, I asked him to call me. I wrote about his coming for his confirmation and that I need some information. If his parents open the letter, they will hopefully let him respond."

"Good. Now what about Bryce?" Rose asked

Nothing. I left him a couple of messages at the orphanage. I have heard nothing. He's a bit of a hellion from what I hear."

"Keep trying. We only have a couple of weeks before they come," Rose said.

19

David arrived at Dexter with his small gym bag. Heather was already there and had a paper bag at her feet.

"What do you have there?" David asked.

"The usual—my turn."

He unloaded the printer and hooked it up.

"Crap."

"What?" she asked.

"I only have a few sheets of paper."

"Uh-oh."

"Hey, the Store 24 on the way to St. Mathew's has an office supplies aisle. I know they have printer paper. Why don't you start in and I'll run."

David unzipped his fleece and handed Heather the microfiche.

Three of them blocked David's descent down the stairs. Jimmy and Bob stood behind Eric's respective shoulders.

"Gentlemen?" David greeted them.

"I've had about enough of you!" Eric replied.

"What!?" David said with raised eyebrows.

David did not need this right know. The lacrosse players held their ground on the stairs.

"Listen," David reasoned. "I really don't have time—"

"You're gonna make time!" Eric demanded.

"Here we go," David thought.

He ran the scenario through his mind in one second. There were three of them, but he was positioned above them. He lined two of them up. The important thing would be to take two of them down and land on top of them—make sure to land on top of them as they go down the stairs backwards. Whoever is on the bottom will probably break their back or skull on the concrete. Then go for the third one.

Stay on top!

He stared the three down, shifting his eyes from one to the other, then resting on Eric's tee shirt. The graphic was two crossed lacrosse sticks with the words underneath "Chix Luv our Stix." He slowly mouthed the words, with Eric watching intently.

"So how's that workin' for ya?" David asked motioning to the shirt with a nudge of his chin.

Poised to launch, he watched the three lacrosse players turn, look down, and walk off, taking a foot path to the library. David was anticipating rage from at least Eric with the comment. Maybe they realized he was going to land on them like a ton of bricks? Out of the corner of his eye he saw movement. He jerked his head to find Brian and three hockey players standing right behind him.

"Hey cousin, havin' a little trouble with the pretty boys?"

"Nothin' I can't handle."

"Suuure," Brain smiled.

"Hey," David greeted the other players.

"If you weren't so damn intimidating, we could have had a little fun here," one of them replied.

"Yeah, yeah, yeah." David said under his breath, as he fist bumped the two players.

"Goin' to practice?"

"Yep, my last one. I'm gonna get the axe tonight."

They trotted together down the stairs, then the four split right, across the street toward the rink. It only took David a minute to get in and out of the store and head back toward Dexter.

They were in front of the stone arch entrance to the stairs, heading right at him. As he got within 20 feet, Eric broke out into a run—no words this time. David dropped the bag with the paper and went on autopilot. He got as low as he could just at the right moment. Eric dove on top of him, but David had ducked him, grabbing a fistful of shirt and his waist, lifting and heaving him, like a farmer tossing a bail of hay. Eric executed a half flip, his back meeting squarely with the windshield of a moving baby-blue Hyundai. As it skidded to a stop, Eric was launched forward and bounced along the ground until he came to a groaning stop, leaving a dense web of safety glass and a buckled hood.

David never stopped moving. Now in the middle of the street, he ducked the second one's swing then shoved him out of the way and received the third, tackling him and driving him back, the way a linebacker seeks extra yards when sacking a quarterback. He carried him across the street as far as his momentum would take him, then lifted him and slammed him down with his shoulder planted firmly into his chest. The alarm on the parked, new BMW 330i went berserk as the hood imploded under the weight of the two flying bodies. David hesitated for a moment, felt no movement from underneath him, then sprang to his feet, spinning around to receive the last one, who looked at him, then turned and ran toward the sport complex. The remaining two lay on their backs moaning in agony. The occupants of the Hyundai, two female students, were out of the car, assessing the mess. Opposite traffic stopped, as Eric was lying in their path. David grabbed the bag and bolted up the stairs into the darkness.

By the time he got to the top of the stairs, the car alarm had stopped and his heart was pounding in his chest and head. He walked slowly to the front door of Dexter, attempting to catch his breath.

"Fun stairs?" Heather said.

"Oh, yeah! Great workout."

"You OK? You look a little rattled."

"Oh, I just saw Brian. He's sure he's getting cut tonight."

"Bummer," she sympathized.

"Major. He really loves hockey."

They could hear a siren off in the distance—a couple of distinct tones, getting closer. One stopped, then the other.

"What do you think that is?"

David was still puffing.

"Maybe they caught the guy who set off that car alarm."

He looked at Heather. She had something else on her mind.

"What's up?" he asked.

"You're not going to believe me," she said. "Unless your see it for yourself."

"Isn't that my line?"

She spun around to the microfiche machine and inserted the vellum.

"I went all the way back, past the report in Italian. Here, a birthing report. And before that, the medical reports on the impregnation of two young nuns, Sarah and Rose."

"You mean the mothers of these kids are nuns?" David whispered a little louder than intended, still out of breath. He panned the room, making sure no students looked up after his comment.

"More like hosts."

"I don't get it."

"They weren't an accident; they were planned. The whole operation was to create these kids."

David squinted in confusion. Heather looked around the room, then leaned closer to David.

"With DNA!"

He stared at her for a long moment.

"You mean, cloning?" he whispered.

"It's right here in the impregnation report."

"Holy shit!" he said, studying the report on the viewer. "Print it!"

"I already did."

"This is bizarre!" he said, trying to keep his voice down. "Who is the father?" he asked.

"Huh?"

"If the nuns were the hosts then whose DNA fathered them?"

"It's not fathering, it's recreating—cloning the person."

"OK, then who are these kids supposed to be?" he shrugged.

"Take a guess."

Heather slid the viewer over a couple of pages. At the bottom of the report, the comments contained a note from a Dr. Leonard.

"Read right here," she said pointing at the screen.

The same procedure was followed for all samples. Successful impregnation of Sister Sarah on the first attempt with the DNA recovered from the ossuary of James. All attempts with the sample from the Shroud failed. However, the sample from the Sudarium was successful and we are excited about the quality and the immediate results. Sister Rose is the host and the procedure went without issue.

"What the hell are they talking about?" David said. "Shroud...Not *the* Shroud!?" he looked at Heather.

"It looks like they had a DNA sample and were trying to..." she took a breath, "I can't believe I'm saying this—clone Jesus! As bizarre as that sounds, it looks like it failed. But, they were successful with the brother, James."

"Who?"

"Jesus had a brother," she whispered, looking around. "His name was James."

"Sorry, I'm not that..."

"They found what are believed to be his bones in an ossuary back in 70s. That's where the DNA came from."

"An ossuary?"

"The bones! An ossuary is where they place the remains, like a little mausoleum."

"What's a Sudarium?"

"I don't know, but that sample worked. That's our second kid," Heather said, biting her upper lip and staring at the report.

She started printing. David's breathing was back to normal; the encounter seemed to have occurred days ago.

"Check this one out!" Heather said. "It's another handwritten letter to that Mr. Orsini—right after the birthing report."

...When they are old enough to relocate, the children will be raised privately and separately, until they make their confirmation. At that point, they will be old enough to make our final evaluation on the success of the project and decide on the future. We must remain ready at all times to terminate this project in its entirety, should medical conditions warrant it or security issues pose any threat to us or those who might be impacted. As

before, you have the authority and trusted responsibility to manage a complete shutdown.

We of course do not foresee any such issues and look forward to the point where we can welcome the beginning of a new world order. These are exciting times, my friend, and you know how much I appreciate your loyalty and dedication. Please advise me of anything you require to be successful.

Vincent

"His confirmation's in two weeks," David said.

They printed stacks of documents, then shut down the machine and packed up the printer.

"I think they're in danger," Heather said as they hurried across the grass toward McGuiness.

"You're starting to sound like me," David chuckled in disbelief.

"Luc is going to Italy to make his confirmation," Heather reasoned. "That's when they will make their final evaluation on the project. What if it's not a positive report? What do they do with him then? And what about Bryce Jones?"

"It also says they would shut the whole thing down if there was a security breach, maybe like the one I caused. My falling over a friggin' footstool may have put these kids in jeopardy."

"They also said, *'like before'*. Maybe some bad shit went down with that Orsini guy," Heather sighed.

"Orsini must have been the go-to guy," David acknowledged. "And now it's our friend the Tea Man. Remember in the letter where he was put in place—after Orsini delivered Bryce to Boddington House?"

In his room, David sat down on the bed, while Heather plopped into the chair at his desk. From the paper bag he handed her half a veggie-wrap and a bottle of water, leafing through the pages, while he bit at his sandwich.

"May I?" she asked, taking his laptop out of the pack.

"'Course."

The screen clicked brighter as she plugged it into the wall, then she started searching on Google.

"Guess where Bryce Jones lives?" she asked in a cocky manner.

"Boddington House."

"OK, smart guy, where is Boddington House?" she smirked back and took a bite.

"England."

"Wuh?! How did you know that?"

"Well, because the request for payment from his private school here states 4000 *pounds sterling*. What do you have?"

"A British newspaper article from about a year ago. It looks like there was a small fire in the kitchen of the Bodding-ton House. It says, '*Henry Jones, the proprietor of the 100-year-old orphanage, reported the kitchen fire during a Friday night dinner service for its 15 young male residents. Damage was estimated at 5000 pounds and no one was injured.*'"

"You gotta love Google. Can you get an address on that place?"

"So, the kid was documented as Henry's child, not an or-phan. What was that other source of DNA called?"

"Hang on a sec," David said, putting down his sandwich and sorting through the file folder.

"Here it is—*Sudarium*...that's S-U-D-A-R..."

"It's HIM!!!" she cried, her mouth dropping wide open as she stared at the screen.

"What?" he said, jumping up.

She read, "The Sudariam of Oviedo was a smaller face cloth used to wipe the blood off the face of Jesus after he was crucified."

David moved to the desk, standing over her shoulder as she continued.

"It was kept separately form the other artifacts, but has been genetically proven to match the Shroud of Turin, which wrapped Christ's entire body."

"Oh, my God," David mumbled in a bewildered voice, staring at the screen.

"Son of," corrected Heather without looking up.

The two stared at the webpage with images of the Shroud of Turin, a crucifix and an image of the face cloth. As she read it again, Heather slid her food to the side, causing the water bottle to fall off the desk. As it hit the floor, neither flinched—they remained frozen, hypnotized by the computer screen. Finally, David reached down and retrieved the now almost empty bottle and tossed a towel on the spill, while Heather continued to gaze at the screen. He raised the impregnation report and stared at it.

"This is too freakin weird," he said shaking the paper.

After a long pause, David looked up, "Then who is who?"

"Not sure," answered Heather, finally freeing herself from the laptop's trance.

David took all of the papers, including the originals from the Tea Man's office, stacked them up, and divided the pile in half.

"Here. Any clue as to who these kids are, or belong to— anything you can find. We've got one Jesus kid and one, brother of Jesus kid..."

He handed a stack to Heather, who hopped onto Brian's bed and assumed a semi-reclined position, beginning her search. David did the same on his bed.

"This is about as bizarre as it gets," he mumbled to himself.

"Makes me want to wake up and laugh about a weird, bad dream," she replied.

They continued going through the papers.

"One thing I do know," David quietly said. "They never found my test."

"How can you be sure?"

"Because we still exist. Think about it. You clone Christ and I find out about it? What would you do?"

After a long moment of silence, Heather perked up.

"We? Who besides you thinks we are actually dating?"

Before David could look up she was next to him, placing her arms around him.

"This is getting a little freaky," she said, burying her face into his neck.

The two leaned back onto the wall of the tiny dorm room, holding onto each other.

After a few minutes, Heather got up and took the kettle chips out of the bag.

"Oh well, live for today!" she said pulling out a small handful.

She resumed reading, the two of them close.

"Anything?" David asked as he completed the stack.

"No, you?"

"No, not even on the birthing report from May. We have that DNA guy Leonard, another doctor named Diorio—must be the birthing doctor—and two more sisters.

"More nuns?" interrupted Heather.

"The report refers to the sisters Florence and Fiona acting as midwives for the birth, but no mention of the mother's name."

"Which kid?"

"Uh, the May second child, so Bryce?" David said inconclusively.

"What about the other kid, Luc?"

"It's the only birthing report in the file."

"There should be two, no?"

"Maybe we missed it."

"We need to warn Luc," Heather said after finishing the remains of her water. "But the story is just too weird, especially for a kid. Maybe we just tell him he has a brother, and that the people in the Vatican, including his father know all about it. It's a secret they keep from him because they—I don't know," Heather leaned into David, shrugging her shoulders.

"No, that's good!" David encouraged. "They keep it from him because both of their births were a secret. There, lay out the truth—almost. He can't comprehend the cloning thing—hell, I can't, but if he connects the dots with the private doctor and tests, it might make sense to him. If he knows his dad knows, then he can at least skate with his head up."

"What about his trip to the Vatican?" she asked.

"If he goes, he could be gone forever. Let's take this one step at a time. There may be some bad stuff going on from my busting up that office, and he needs to be careful."

"I want to go tomorrow. He needs to know."

"*We* will go tomorrow, but it's a good idea if you do the talking; he thinks you're cute."

"Get out!"

"Hey, I was thirteen once, I saw the way he looked at you."

"Really, how?"

"The same way I look at you now, when you're not watching," David confessed, stuffing the files into a brown expandable folder, then, leaning back on his pillows and letting her curl up in his arms.

They kicked off their shoes and were quiet, with eyes wide open, until, one at a time, they dozed off.

20

A mile away, a red leather portfolio sat on a hardwood floor, getting files jammed in it. Anthony Scordo leaned back and put his feet up on the little ottoman, the very one that had tripped David Knight. He could not believe that after two days, he had no answers as to who had broken in, and why only a partial set of his documents were missing. He took a large gulp of his scotch and stared at the ceiling. He pulled the file out of the briefcase again, though he had done it so many times there was no need. There were documents and a single postcard-size piece of vellum. He flipped through the file looking for more. The documents and the other microfiche slide were gone.

Must report this to Vincent.

Scordo poured another scotch and returned to the chair, starring back at the ceiling. He took a sip and breathed deeply. It was the middle of the night in Italy, so he had a few hours before he would call.

Half my life, and now this...

He remembered waking up 25 years earlier on a table in the Allston/Brighton YMCA locker room. His head was pounding and his vision went in and out of focus.

"It looks like you will have to keep your day job," Father Vincent smiled, placing a wet towel on his forehead as the room finally came into focus.

A trainer was at his side, removing his boxing gloves. It was to be his first—and last—amateur fight.

"Looks like he has a bit of a glass jaw," the trainer commented. "He was clobbering the other guy pretty good, then suddenly, he came down like a redwood."

The priest came to the YMCA often, working with the after school programs, helping keep kids off the street. Like many of the neighborhood's kids, Father Vincent knew him from Sunday mass, where he towered over his mother as they stood singing hymns.

When he was younger, they lived in Boston's North End. He first learned Italian, as his mother was an immigrant and her English was not good enough to properly teach him; she would leave that for the schools. He never met his father, but his mother did her best to raise him alone, taking him to church on Sunday and getting him involved in the YMCA after school, since she often worked two jobs.

When she landed a better paying job, they moved to Allston, the city that connects Boston University to Brighton Latin College and Boston College, next door in Newton.

With not much to do, other than the Y and with little money, Anthony cruised the streets with his friends, looking for unlocked cars and unattended valuables. If they saw a back door to a store left open, they would duck in and grab whatever they could, selling what they couldn't use.

When he graduated, there was no place to go, except into the military, but he thought it would be best to stay and help his mother pay the bills, even though he had no skills to land a good job. He soon found out he was good at stealing cars—at least until the fourth one.

At 22 years old, he held part-time jobs, working as a bouncer at a local bar and filling in at the corner liquor store. Cars, however, presented the opportunity to make some serious cash. One of the local kids knew somebody who would pay $500 for a good clean car. The car would be driven away and—as it was understood—chopped and sold as parts.

Scordo never told his mother, nor flashed any money around. He would sometimes buy her a gift or offer to pay a bill, telling her he had a good night at the club, the bartender sharing his tips with him. His mother was too busy herself to notice if he was actually working or not, but she knew the neighborhood and didn't like the youths he hung out with, though there was not much she could do about it except caution him.

He wasn't sure what went wrong, only that on his fourth car, he made it just a few blocks before a police cruiser cut him off and he was staring at a service revolver. Scordo, of course, insisted he was joy riding and did not give up any of his associates in the little crime ring.

His mother was devastated. She knew he wasn't alone and that this was probably not his first time, recalling some of the sudden increases in available cash in the household.

Father Vincent appeared at the courthouse just before his arraignment. He approached Scordo, who sat with a public defender in the courtroom's outer hallway. He was nervous and looked out of place in his borrowed, wrinkled suit; Father Vincent sat down beside him.

"I would like to speak with Anthony privately," he requested of his lawyer, as he sat down next to Scordo.

The attorney nodded, got up, and walked away.

"Tell me, Anthony, is it the thrill of stealing cars or the money that makes you do it?"

"I only did it to get the money to help my mother," Scordo answered. "Now she is ashamed of me and I will never be nothing more than a felon to her," he added.

"Anthony," Father Vincent whispered, "I can help you. But I will only do it if I have your word that you will trust me and do as I say. I can get you out of here and provide you with a job that will take care of you and your mother. But you must commit to me that that this is what you want—not that you just want to get out of jail and back onto the street."

The words still rang in his head. There was no question Scordo had made the right decision. After that day, his mother lived a modest, yet comfortable life, only needing a part time job until she retired. After, that, Scordo paid for everything, until she passed some years later.

Father Vincent worked with the judge to grant Scordo probation, provided he maintain a full-time job. Vincent also provided the job as driver for St. Mathew's rectory in Brighton, where Father Vincent lived.

The cars were large Buick sedans, keeping with the Catholic austere practice of no Cadillacs or Lincolns. For the most part he drove Vincent places and ran errands for him, but the service expanded to more members of the rectory and, at times, the neighboring college for airport runs and driving visitors to and from hotels.

For a few years, he worked alone. When Father Vincent was elevated to Bishop, he instructed Scordo to find another driver. Scordo brought in a trusted friend.

He was never quite sure where the money to pay him came from. The first year, he was paid with personal checks from Father Vincent, saying the Church reimbursed him. Then, the Fontana Limousine service started appearing on the checks—the bank account that he would soon administer.

Vincent's assignment to Palermo, Sicily, for a humanitarian mission did not affect the driving service, as Scordo had taken on a management role, with two drivers being deployed at the rectory's and college's will. He would now only drive when overloaded, or when an important task was requested.

It was after he became cardinal that Vincent came home and told Scordo of the project. How long it was in the works he did not know, but the significance of it, and the trust he had in Scordo to include him was immeasurable. He assured the cardinal he would serve with his life on such a project. Secrecy was most important, as Cardinal Vincent assured him that no one at St. Mathew's, in fact, no one in the United States knew about the project.

"The church would be devastated if there was outside knowledge of this," Vincent told him, "Only a few of us will ever know—and we must do whatever it takes to keep it that way."

Scordo was on board. Glen Jennings was the first step. Using Cardinal Vincent's letterhead and St. Mathew's connections to the school, there were many applicants for the position to work in the Vatican. Glen was just what they were looking for: young, energetic, religious, and engaged. Vincent came home to interview him and Glen and his fiancé soon graduated with plane tickets to Europe in hand.

When the experiments were successful, Scordo purchased the brownstone and readied it, as Boddington House was simultaneously acquired and Father Henry put in place. Only Glen was brought in on the plan. Anne was advised that the child was an orphan, and that the church wished to groom him for the clergy, requiring his return when of age. She was honored to be presented the opportunity to serve the Vatican in such a way. They would have Scordo for anything he needed, once back in Boston.

Scordo was also well aware of Orsini. He was Vincent's right hand man in Italy and very instrumental in the project. He was pleased when Orsini vanished after placing Bryce in Boddington House. In his mind, this restored him to Cardinal Vincent's most trusted disciple.

In subsequent visits to Boddington House, Father Henry filled in some of the blanks on the project's history—as disturbing as they were when they involved Orsini. But his work was done and he was gone; it was all necessary, at least in Scordo's mind. The last 12 years were exciting, watching the boys grow into young men, looking over them like a godfather on behalf of the man who made everything possible: Vincent.

A tear streamed down his cheek as he sat in the leather reading chair pondering the disappointment he was about to bring. He could not go on after such a failure. Everything was lost. Then, he noticed the corner of a piece of paper sticking out from under the far side of his desk. He sat and stared; it was only a single piece of paper and there were many more missing, plus the microfiche. He sipped his scotch, paused, then slowly got up and walked over to the desk. He bent over and blindly reached under, feeling for the paper. He stood up straight and stared at David's economics quiz.

21

Heather awoke in David's arms at 7:30. She looked over and saw Brian asleep in his bed, explaining the blanket now over them. From her slight movement, David awoke. He looked over at Brian, then at Heather. It was nice and warm under the blanket as they cuddled, enjoying each other's body heat. As they looked at each other, Heather's nose scrunched up.

"What is that?" she winced.

"Oh man, that stinks!" David whispered.

They slowly sat up and looked around. Brian didn't move. Behind the door laid Brian's hockey bag, with a big number 12 on the side.

"That is foul!" David said, waking up Brian.

"Uh, oh, sorry," he said rolling over.

As the two got up, Brian mumbled as he attempted to pick up his head: "I came in pretty late. Yeah, that's what a hockey bag smells like."

"Thanks for the blanket," said Heather as Brian's head hit the pillow.

"I got cut with three others last night, so the boys helped us drown our sorrows."

"Sorry, cousin," David consoled.

"No worries. If I really wanted to play hockey, I would have gone to another school. These guys are on top in division three, so the odds were against me, but hey, it was fun."

Brian sat up, rubbing his eyes and scratching his head as he let out a yawn.

"Can we do something about the smell?" asked David.

"Yeah, sure," he said yawning again. "I gotta wash my jersey and socks and return them today. I'll throw the bag in my locker at the rink; they let me have it for the year."

Half asleep, Brian dragged the bag down the hall to the showers and returned with the shirt and socks.

"Will your stuff be OK there?"

"Who's gonna stick their head in that thing?" Brian grunted.

Brian sat on his desk chair and bent over, looking at the floor. He let out one last, enormous yawn.

"I think I'll grab breakfast while these wash."

Then he stood up, wearing the gray sweats he slept in, and put on his flip flops.

"Be back in an hour."

Brian stumbled out the door clutching his little load of laundry.

"What time do you want to head into town?" David asked, reality setting back in.

"Oh, we have to wait till the end of school, right?"

"Sure, but let's get out of here, anyway," David said.

"Maybe you didn't leave the test behind. Maybe they won't come. They haven't yet."

"I went through everything again last night. I don't have it."

"What will happen if they come?"

"I guess that all depends on who they is. I can't imagine the police being involved, but what do I know? And this Scordo guy is not a priest or a member of the school staff, but he could very well be working with either, or both—or neither—Ugh!"

Heather became invigorated.

"OK, let's assume that they're coming. What do we do? I mean, are we ready to deal with these guys and can we help the kids? First, we know that there at least two of them, in the US, that is. And they probably know what we have. So let's start by keeping them from getting it back."

David took out the microfiche and looked at Heather.

"Any ideas?" he asked.

She was up and pacing.

"Somewhere safe, locked up, but not in your room. Or mine, since the rumor is that we are dating," she smiled.

"How about locked up in that smelly gym bag down at the rink?"

Heather lit up.

"Nice!"

David grabbed an envelope from his desk and went down the hall, finding the bag in the empty shower room. He slipped the microfiche under the bottom reinforcement panel then zipped it back up. As he left the bathroom, Steve passed him, toting a towel and shaving kit.

"Mor-nin'!" Steve announced, clad in his pajamas.

"Hey," replied David.

As he walked down the hall he heard Steve's voice echoing in the shower room.

"Geez! Oh man! What died in here!?"

David smiled as he walked into the room.

"Everything OK?" asked Heather.

"As long as they don't call in a hazmat crew on that bag, it'll be safe."

"So, what about the files? Let's take the birth certificate and the birthing report to show the kid. The rest we can hide somewhere. How about my locker at the sports complex?" Heather rattled off.

"Really? You have a locker at the gym?"

"I was supposed to work out or swim every day, but some guy I met has completely dominated all of my free time."

Cindy answered David's knock.

"Hi, David," she said with a smirk.

She opened the door wide to reveal Heather stuffing gloves into her pockets. Her hair was still wet from her shower.

"Ready?" she asked.

"Sure," smiled David.

"Heading into town for a day of fun?"

"Something like that," Heather replied.

As they descended the stairs to Oak Square, the chapel bells tolled nine times.

"What's in the pack?" asked Heather.

"My laptop, the files, and a raincoat."

"It's not going to rain."

David zipped up his grey fleece as a cool breeze kicked up.

"So who do you think we are going to see today, Christ, or his little brother?" asked Heather.

"How bizarre does that sound?" he replied. "It is amazing to think that one of these kids is *the one*."

"And the other is not that far off."

They exited the stairs through the stone arch and crossed the street. Once in the parking lot, without words, she took the files and walked into the sports complex.

At 2:30, Heather took her position inside the Starbucks coffee shop, directly across from the side street where Luc would appear. David was outside, pretending to window shop at the boutique next door. He would keep an eye out for any Dark Men, then knock on the window as Luc exited the side street. If there were Dark Men, he would abort the meeting.

Heather watched the side street from her tall, round table. She saw Luc appear, wearing the same red jacket and heard two clunks of a knuckle on the window as David walked by.

She exited the shop and Luc immediately saw her.

"Hey!" Luc yelled.

"Hi!" she yelled back. David went the other way down the side street and continued his patrol. Luc ran up to the intersection, crossed with the light and then backtracked to the coffee shop.

"What are you doing here?"

"Shopping. I just saw David, now where did he go?"

She looked about, then said, "I left my coffee inside. Come on, I'll buy you a soda."

David showed up right as they sat down with Luc's soda.

"I saw you from across the way. So, how are you doing kid?" he asked.

"Great!"

He sucked up some soda through a straw, while looking at Heather. Heather looked at David. There was no time to waste.

"Do you need to get going? We don't want your mom worried about you?" Heather inquired.

"She's in California. Her aunt died and she flew out yesterday for a couple of weeks. My dad won't get home for a couple hours. I have a key," he said, taking another sip.

"Luc—"

"How do you know my name? I don't know yours."

"It's Heather. And I know your name because of my anthropology studies," she quickly explained. "I was researching the church and I found some records that were apparently misfiled. The file had your name and address on it. Luc, I have to apologize to you, we actually came down yesterday to see if you were a real person. But, before we could knock on your door, you were heading into the park to play catch."

"That's weird. Why would the college have my name?"

"We think we know. Your dad worked for the church right?"

"When he lived in Italy," Luc answered.

"They helped him out; it's not the school that had the records, but someone who worked for the church and the school, like your dad. We got them by mistake. Anyway, it's good to see that you are a real person and that you are OK."

"Why wouldn't I be OK?"

"Well, the few records we had showed you were under the care of a doctor, so we thought…"

"I don't like this; I'm going to go now."

"Here."

Heather handed him the photocopy of the birth certificates.

"Hey, that's me!"

"You can go if you want," Heather offered. "I don't want you to be uncomfortable or scared. It's the truth. We just got this stuff by mistake."

"Who is Bryce Jones?"

"He is your brother, we assume."

"What!? I don't have brother. My parents would have told me."

"More like half brothers. We think he's living in England," David said, finally joining in.

"Hey, it says we were born on the same day!"

"Actually, the doctor's report shows you are three weeks older than Bryce," Heather explained. "We think it's kind of a big secret with the people your father worked for, so he probably can't talk about it.

Sorry, I know this is weird, but we thought you should know about it. That's all. We're not creepy people, we just wanted you to know," she pleaded.

"The doctor keeps an eye on you, right?" David asked with a positive tone. "And you feel good and strong, right?"

Luc just stared at them, confused, but a little more comfortable as they pleaded their case.

"We thought you might be sick, from the little we read. But you are fine. That's all we wanted to know," Heather said.

"Listen," David interrupted, "we should let you get home. We just want you to know that it looks like you might have a half brother out there somewhere named Bryce Jones and to be on the lookout for him—especially if you're around the church or your dad's work. Who knows, you may run into him over in Italy."

"Do you have a cell phone?" asked Heather.

Luc hesitated, then pulled it out of his jacket pocket and handed it to her.

"I'm putting my number in here under "H," for Heather. You don't ever have to call me, but if you ever want to ask any questions or just talk, you can, OK?"

Luc barely nodded.

"Luc," David said quietly, "have you seen the men with the dark clothes and the big black cars?"

"Yeah, they come around and talk to my dad sometimes."

"That's where this came from," David said pointing to the birth certificate. "If he's really is out there, we'll let him know about you. Maybe he's not. This could all just be a big mistake."

"Can I keep it?" he asked holding on to it.

"It's best if you didn't have this. And, we need it for our research," David said, gently taking the paper from his hand.

"This is really weird." Luc said.

"We know. We're sorry if we upset you," said Heather. "We're still figuring it out ourselves."

They all left the coffee shop and went to the corner.

"We'll watch you get home from here, OK?"

"Sure," Luc replied without concern.

David leaned over and placed a brand new baseball with a Red Sox logo in his hand.

"You hang in their kid."

"Wow! Oh, I mean, I can't!"

"Tell them you found it in the tall grass by the pond, looked everywhere for the rightful owner. Now get along, it was nice knowing ya," David said, in an attempt to convince the boy they were not going to stalk him.

"Good luck in Italy!" Heather said smiling.

He half smiled, and followed the small crowd across Beacon Street, gripping the baseball tightly in his hand. Heather watched him until he was inside #214, while David did a slow spin, observing his surroundings.

"All clear," he whispered to Heather, as they stepped to their right and descended to the subway to find a green trolley loading. They hopped in and found an empty area away from the other passengers.

"How do you think we did?" asked David.

She was on the verge of tears.

"Well for starters, we may have just lied to Jesus. And the best case scenario is we just told a stranger he has a mysterious brother living in Europe and it's all a big secret his father is in on. Years of therapy to follow on that one."

"I think it went well," David said with a positive tone. "I mean, we did what we could, without the kid's head exploding from too much information. Now he knows something weird is going on and if something does happen, he will know where it came from. I think you did great, Heather and I didn't hear any lies."

After a pause, David continued, "Although, he probably thinks we're a couple of psychos."

Ten minutes later, when the trolley emerged from underground, things did not look right. At an intersection David saw the sign "Entering Brookline."

"Crap! We're on the wrong train!" he said to Heather.

They quickly figured out that they were on the Brookline run, which ran west, parallel to their route, but several miles away from where they wanted to be.

"Well, it's not a total disaster," he said looking at the map on the wall of the trolley.

"I could use the walk," said Heather.

22

The train stopped at the intersection of Route 9 and Hammond Street. They walked silently down Hammond Street and rounded neighboring Boston College's campus. They crossed Commonwealth Avenue, then headed down toward Oak Square, when David suddenly stopped.

"I have an idea," he said.

Heather stared.

"I deliver a copy of everything to Scordo. I tell him I know. It puts the ball in his court. He knows it's a copy, so what can he do?"

"I don't know," said Heather, "maybe we should wait a bit."

Their minds ran every scenario as they silently completed their journey and entered through the stone archway, climbing the stairs, arm in arm.

They walked into Fernwood and rounded the corner to find an open door and crowded room. Brian, Steve and Billy, were standing in the middle of the mess. The mattresses were on their sides and the contents of the two bureaus, mostly clothes, were dumped on the bed frames and floor.

"What the?" David said.

"Security tossed the place," said Brian. "I came home and they were going through everything. I asked for a warrant and they said this was their property and they didn't need one."

"What did they look like?"

"A rent-a-cop with a big guy in a dark suit."

"Black trench coat and a fedora, six-three or four?

"Yeah, how'd ya know?"

"Not a priest?"

"Right! Just wearing all black you know, like regular clothes; just looking through stuff—never talked."

"Did they say what they wanted?"

"No, but the security cop kept asking about you."

Billy jumped in, "Hey, I told him I was calling the real cops—this was an invasion of private property—this is leased space. Then they took off—as in 'illegal search' baby, yeah!" said Billy, boasting his pre-law savvy, then toning it down. "So, what the hell did you do, man?"

"At first, I thought it was about your run-in with the lacrosse dudes," Brian interrupted. "B-T-W, Sully saw the whole thing; he wants you to know number three didn't get away. But they didn't mention that."

Heather's eyes opened wide, staring at David.

"Did they take anything?" David continued, feeling her eyes on him, but not looking back.

"One of your folders," Brian answered as he reloaded his clothes into the drawers. "The guy in the suit was looking at some diagrams you drew. That's when Billy said he was calling the cops and getting a lawyer—invasion of privacy and all that. They left, but I think they already had a pretty good look through everything."

"Shit, when did this happen?"

"Just now! They left maybe ten minutes ago."

Heather pulled out her cell phone and dialed.

"Hey, it's me. Don't say anything. Is security there? I'll call you back. David, they're in my room."

He looked at Heather.

"Right now!"

"We have to get out of here!" David said to Brian.

From the desk drawer spilt on the floor, he grabbed a Leatherman Multi-tool and a flashlight and stuffed them into his pack.

"Brian, I need an extra jacket for Heather," he demanded as he jammed in a pair of sweat pants and an extra tee shirt.

"More violations of our civil rights! What can we do, bro?" Steve asked.

"They're on the second floor of Regina tossing another room. Got a camera?"

"Were on it!"

Billy and Steve disappeared out the door.

Brian reached into his closet and presented a hooded BLC sweatshirt.

"Maybe something a little less obvious?"

He tossed the sweatshirt into the closet top shelf and pulled a denim jacket off a hanger.

"And that ball cap," David said. "And your pack."

"Geeze."

"You can use mine. It's in my room, Heather offered as she stuffed the jacket into the surrendered pack.

"It's not pink is it?"

"Teal."

"Oh, just great."

"Thanks, we'll call you," said David.

Heather slung the pack over her shoulder and pulled out her cell.

"Number?" she asked Brian.

As they exited the side door, they saw Steve and Billy through the stairwell windows, running up to the second floor of Regina.

"Black Buick, six o'clock!" Heather yelled. The car was parked on the side street, behind the dorms.

"Anyone inside?" David asked, keeping his head down.

"Windows are blacked out, but its running," she said, noticing the steam from the exhaust. "I think so!"

As they walked, they noticed the security cameras hanging off the buildings, suddenly confronting them by their existence.

"Just walk and don't look around," David said.

"Where are we going?"

"Don't know—someplace to think—keep moving."

"What did they take from your room?"

"My conspiracy theory diagrams. I left them out of the file after you figured out the whole cloning thing."

"So *they* know..."

"That *we* know..."

"Oh, shit!"

They descended the stairs with a flow of students heading in for dinner. Heather spotted a campus security car sitting off to the right on Washington Street.

"Two o'clock!"

"Keep walking. McGuiness, Go! GO! " he blurted.

They slipped into McGuiness, then, darted down the stairs as everyone else flowed into the dining hall. The post office presented a momentary refuge, but there were several students moving about, so they calmly checked their mailboxes and read junk mail in silence until they cleared out. As the last person disappeared around the corner, they simultaneously dumped all of their mail into the trash bin.

"What now!?" Heather asked.

"Let's check out in there," he said, motioning to the door to the administrative offices. It was unlocked; they went in. The hallway was long and empty, lined with closed doors with rippled glass panels, much like the ones of the rectory.

"Everyone's probably gone," she said.

They hurried to the end of the hall, where David stopped short.

"Wait!'" he said as he looked around the corner to his right, spying another long empty hallway with closed doors on one side and windows on the other.

He slowly eased across to the wall of windows.

"Come check this out!"

Heather bobbed her head over to try to get a quick peek at the street below. She bobbed again. Popping in and out of view was another black Buick with blacked-out windows. It was parked so the driver could see all of the foot traffic coming and going onto the main campus. Exhaust steam confirmed it was occupied.

"We're trapped!" Heather cried.

"Maybe that security car was just waiting for traffic. Let's try back that way."

They exited the offices and jogged up the stairs past the dining hall, stopping before the large bank of glass doors.

"Looks clear," Heather said.

There was no sign of security. At that point, a small white shuttle bus appeared from the left, turning off Washington Street and entering the campus. It stopped curbside, in front of McGuiness.

"Let's go!" said David. The two hustled onto the bus, as the last student got off. The other students boarding blocked their view of the black Buick slowly turning in from Washington Street and the security officer on foot, descending the stairs, constantly looking about.

The bus pulled away and descended the hill to Faneuil Street. The first stop was the T station near St. Mathew's. They stayed on board, wanting more distance.

"Do you know where we're going?" David asked, maintaining a constant lookout.

"No."

They sat in silence as the bus rolled along.

23

They disembarked in front of a small apartment building in a residential neighborhood with no signs of campus security or any Buicks.

"This way," Heather said, crossing the street. "It gets busy down here about a half a mile; there are stores and we can catch the T there."

"How do you know this?"

"I drive around here; my aunt doesn't live too far."

"You have a car?"

Within a few minutes they were crossing the busy intersection in Newton that straddles the Massachusetts Turnpike, creating an oversized, quasi rotary, with cars entering and exiting the highway from below, local traffic navigating in an oversized circle, above, and right in the middle of it all, the T, with tracks crisscrossing the traffic lanes. They crossed the gauntlet of quickly maneuvering vehicles, and ducked into a coffee shop. David went to the counter, while Heather found a table in the rear, where they could watch the front door and street. David sat down with two coffees.

"I should call Cindy. She's probably freaking out about this."

"Blame me," David offered.

"Hey, it's me. I'm OK; did they take anything? No, I didn't do anything, really!" She looked at David cringing, "No, they searched David's room, too. I think they thought he or Brian was involved in drugs. He's going to talk to them on Monday. It's gotta be a big mistake." After listening a moment she chuckled, "I gotta go. I'll be home later."

She smiled at David as she pocketed the phone.

"They didn't take anything. And then Steve and Billy showed up with their camera, claiming to be with the campus newspaper and asked for a statement on the illegal searches of student housing. The Tea Man snatched the camera and left."

David smiled.

"I love those guys. It's probably best they gave up the camera—they don't need any trouble. I hope they don't think Brian was part of this, he has enough going on with getting cut from the team and all."

They both sipped their coffees, then, Heather looked David straight in the eye.

"So are you gonna tell me about Sully and the lacrosse players?" she asked.

David looked down at his coffee.

"Eric and his buddies jumped me last night."

"Oh, my God!" she gasped.

"I got away. I ran all the whole way up those stairs," he said proudly.

"And..."

"That's it. Well, I think Eric may have got a little hurt.

"A little?"

"I shoved him onto a car, *then* I ran."

"That hurt him?"

"Well, the car wasn't exactly parked."

Heather's eyes popped open.

"So, that was the car alarm?"

"Well, no, that was Eric's roommate."

Heather stared and waited.

"He kind of fell onto the hood of a parked car and set off the alarm."

"Oh, fell. And Sully and number three?"

"The third guy ran, I guess right into Sully. I just got out of there."

"It my fault," said Heather. "I never should have talked to that jerk."

"He *is* a jerk, but forget about it," David said looking into his cup, not knowing how she was taking hearing about him fighting.

It was self defense. She does realize that doesn't she?

After a long moment, Heather got up and bought another round of coffees.

She seems OK with it.

"I guess we can't stay here forever," said David, starting in on his second cup.

"How about we go to my aunt's? We can crash there."

"How far?"

"We could take the T, but I'll need a map to figure out which one."

"I'm up for a hike."

"Probably take a while."

"The longer, the better."

It was after eight o'clock when they ordered.

"Do you have any Indian restaurants back home?"

"Near us?" he chuckled, "There is nothing near us!"

They ate for a minute in silence.

"You know what sucks?"

"No?" Heather cautiously replied.

"The fact that I am here with you in this cool little restaurant and I should be holding your hand and telling you how friggin' crazy I am about you. But, instead we're running from some goons with a bad science project."

Heather blushed. David looked down at his food.

"Well, I am…"

Heather teared up, lifted slightly out of her chair and placed a long kiss on David's forehead.

They walked the last mile with an arm around each other.

"David?"

"Yeah?"

"Maybe your idea would work. You know, drop a copy of everything on the Tea Man's desk and say 'Here's a copy for you, now back off.'"

"I don't know, it sounded good at the time."

"What else can we do?" she asked.

"Well, we certainly have enough to go to the authorities, or at least the media."

"Wow! It would really hit the fan if the media believed everything," Heather pondered, "Could you imagine? It would bring the church and the school to its knees."

"Even though they probably don't have a clue about any of it," he laughed. "I think there's more on that fiche, not that we need more—the letters spell it out."

"So, David, which way do you want to go?"

"Do we have to decide this moment? What do you think… You're part of this whether you want to be or not, so you get a vote."

"Ugh, you vote first."

"No way!" David laughed.

"OK, why don't we make a couple of copies, then deliver a set to the Tea Man. We can use the media and authorities as plan B. Who knows, maybe he'll thank us and offer an explanation."

"OK, but I wouldn't count on any thank-yous," David laughed.

"What's your vote?"

"I think to make this go away, at this point, they would have to think they got everything back," David said. "That means getting the original files and fiche back. I think if we deliver copies of the print outs it will just raise the stakes."

"OK, then *we* keep the copies and deliver the film and the originals."

"I guess it's the best we can do," David conceded, smiling a little.

They arrived at her aunt's house at 10:00. Her Uncle Joe, still recovering from surgery, had gone to bed, but Aunt Shirley was awake and excited from Heather's call that they were en route.

"Hi, I'm Shirley."

"Nice to meet you. David," he responded, accompanied by a gentle handshake.

Heather kissed her aunt on the cheek and went inside.

The home was typical of two retirees. The front porch of the 1930s gray and white Dutch Colonial was replete with rocking chairs that were actually used and not for decoration. Inside, the white mantle over the living room fireplace was jammed with framed family photographs. The oval coffee table held only a small box of four drink coasters. The fireplace had white birch logs in it that were for decoration, not heat. The room was so meticulous that David wondered where the den was—they obviously didn't "live" in the living room.

"Please sit!" Shirley insisted. "What can I get you? Coffee, soda, beer?"

"Beer!" said Heather.

"Sure," Shirley said, then looked at David. "I know the drinking age is 21, but when my daughter was growing up, it was 18, so this house is grandfathered in at 18, provided, of course, that you're not going to be driving anywhere."

Shirley emerged moments later with a serving tray with two Heinekens and a pair of pilsner glasses.

Talking to someone removed from the whole thing almost took their minds off their drama.

"How is Mr. Hughes doing?" asked David.

"Much better, thanks. He still needs his rest but he's getting there."

When they finished their beers, Shirley got up.

"Another, David?"

"Oh, no thanks Mrs. Hughes."

"Call me Shirley. Heather?"

"All set. In fact I think I'm gonna crash, it's been a long day."

"OK, kids. Heather, I made up Cheryl's old room for you. David is in the guest room; I figured he didn't need to sleep with bunnies and dolls..."

"Thank you, Shirley," David said.

Heather led David up to his room, stopping to kiss goodnight in the hallway.

24

"Pancakes!"

The smell was intoxicating. He changed out of his sweats and into his street clothes and ran into Heather who was coming out of the bathroom wearing a blue terrycloth robe.

"Hey," he said.

"Hi. How did you sleep?" Heather asked as she rubbed a towel on her wet head.

"Okay," he nodded.

"There's a toothbrush and razor in there for you. Towels are in the closet."

"Thanks."

He went in and got cleaned up. When he emerged from the bathroom, they crossed paths in the hall again. This time she was fully dressed and her hair almost dry.

"Find everything?"

"Yes, much better," he sighed, clean shaven.

"Let's see." Heather put her hand on his cheek and followed it in for a nice long kiss.

Shirley was flipping pancakes while Joe was making a second pot of coffee. The round kitchen table was set with a glass of orange juice at each place setting.

"How did you sleep, David?" Shirley asked.

"Great, thanks."

"Hello, David," Mr. Hughes said, spinning around from the coffee pot.

"Hello, Mr. Hughes," David said as he thrust his hand out. "It's a pleasure to meet you."

"Likewise here."

"It's on the table!" Shirley said, and slid a stack of pancakes onto a platter centered on the round wooden table, which separated kitchen and the den.

"Wow! Real food! I haven't seen this in over a month," David gushed, downing his juice.

"Heather's been coming out every week to help out, so we try to give her some home cooking. Although, there's nothing wrong with a good pizza pie now and then."

"Do you follow the Sentinels, David?" Joe asked.

"Uncle Joe's a big sports fan," Heather said.

"Only one game so far."

"Really? It's right there at your fingertips! I like the local college stuff and the Pats and Sox, of course. But the college sports are much easier to catch. I even head into town to see crew on the Charles River, if the weather is good."

David was working on his third pancake as Joe was talking about the BU hockey team's chances at a national championship.

"...really tough to get tickets with them doing so well. Hey, did you hear? Tough break on the lacrosse team."

David gagged on his pancake.

"Uh, sorry?"

Heather snuck a look at David as he cleared his throat with a gulp of coffee.

"Looks like their season is over before it even started. It's right here in today's paper," Joe said, as he reached behind David and picked up the sports section of the Saturday *Boston Globe* off of the end table next to the recliner.

He started to unfold it and stopped.

"Right here…it says 'Brighton Latin Lacrosse players hospitalized after incident in Oak Square.'"

David could feel Heather's eyes on him again.

"Sophomore and Assistant Captain Eric Styles, sophomore defensemen Jimmy Kowalski, and junior and Co-Captain Bob Sawyer, were all taken to Newton-Wellesley Hospital by ambulance with multiple injuries, including bone fractures, a concussion, and a broken jaw. The incident appeared to be motor vehicle related, as two damaged vehicles were seen being towed away from the scene. Sawyer was treated and released for a broken jaw, but the other two were admitted."

Sully! David thought.

"Here's the weird part," Joe continued. "Brighton Latin College had no comment on the matter other than their thoughts and prayers for a speedy recovery of those injured. However, an anonymous eyewitness told reporters that the two more seriously injured players were actually thrown onto the cars by an unidentified individual, not struck by them. The police have not released any information at this time."

He folded the paper and tossed it onto the recliner.

"Smells like a brawl to me. Maybe the Sentinels can find that guy and make him a defensive back."

"Is the Camry drivable?" Heather said changing the subject.

"Sure," Joe answered, "It was just a dead battery. Charged right back up."

"David and I have an anthropology project to do. We were thinking of heading to the library."

"You could walk, it's only a few blocks," said Shirley.

"We have to jet into campus first and pick up some papers."

"Is she blocked in?" Shirley yelled to Joe, as he headed into the garage.

"I'll move it!" he yelled back.

After breakfast, they headed out in Heather's little red Toyota Camry. Shirley and Joe gave Heather the car when they weren't offered anything in trade when purchasing their new car. It was 14 years old, had 120,000 miles on the odometer, but was maintained by a mechanic and Uncle Joe. It was perfect for Heather. When she came out to see Brighton Latin in the spring, she bought a one-way ticket, then bought the car for one dollar and drove it home. When she drove back in the fall, carrying all of her stuff, she simply went to Belmont for the first weekend and left if there, because underclassmen couldn't get campus parking permits.

"My body work project is coming along, Heather. I hope you don't mind driving it around with the big patch on it," he said looking at the rear right side.

"It's fine, Uncle Joe. You don't need to fix all that stuff. Its perfect for me the way it is."

As they backed out of the driveway, David thanked them for the accommodations and complimented Aunt Shirley on the wonderful breakfast.

"They are so nice to me. They gave me the car and now they garage it and fix it while I'm at school."

"Your uncle looks like the type of guy who needs to keep busy with a project."

They immediately recalibrated their conversation to the business at hand.

"Same plan as yesterday?" Heather asked.

"Unless you came up with a better one this morning."

She pulled over in front of the Belmont Public Library.

"I'll run in," he said.

David reappeared in about a minute and hopped in, smiling.

"They have a microfiche viewer—with a printer!"

"Let's go!"

Heather smiled as she drove off, handing David her cell phone.

"How do you work this thing?"

"Press and hold the five."

He did and the screen lit up: "calling Brian."

"Hey," David said into the phone.

"You two OK?" Brian asked.

"Yeah, we're fine."

"Where are you?"

"Around, just staying away from the dorms. Anyone looking for us?"

"I saw that same weasel rent-a-cop hanging out under a tree this morning. So, what the hell is going on with you two?"

"It's a long story."

"Unlimited nights and weekends, go ahead."

"You're not going to believe it."

"Still waiting…"

"They think I stole some documents from the rectory. I guess I did. But it was a mistake. Anyway, that's what they were looking for."

"And why did you steal them?"

"I didn't! I picked them up by mistake. I didn't even know I had them, till your smelly foot launched them all over the room!"

"Don't drag *me* into your life of crime, cousin. So what's in the documents?"

"You wouldn't believe it."

"Again with that? I think you're forgetting who you're talking to."

"OK, sorry. They uh..." David paused, then, took a deep breath. "The guys who tossed the room are from St. Mathew's. We found out that they cloned Jesus Christ. He's living in Beacon Hill."

Heather gawked at David.

Dead silence.

"We met him. He's fourteen."

Dead silence.

"Pretty good sidearm...you there?"

"No friggin' way!"

"See."

"No, uh, I believe you but...what the...?"

"Pretty weird, huh cuz?"

"How do you know this?"

"The documents are the medical reports and more."

"Wow! Who are these guys?"

"Not completely sure. Definitely that big guy in the dark suit. Not sure who else. He has an office over at the rectory. Hey, go over there and check out the black Buicks—that's where they hang. We counted two so far, plus that security guard. There are also some people in the Vatican. That's where this whole thing started."

"The Vatican and a Jesus clone!? That is some freaky shit, cousin!"

"Yeah that's what it looks like. Look, I need to ditch some laundry and I don't want to come to the room. Can you give me the combo to your locker at the rink?"

"Sure, its number 131, combo 1-0-5. Are you two all right?"

"Not really."

"Can't imagine you would be. What's the plan?"

"Uh, we are figuring that out right now."

"Let me know what I can do."

"I will, cousin. I'm sure we'll need you."

"I can bring in the crew if you need reinforcements. You're the man! Hey, you *gotta* read the paper!"

"I saw it."

"Eric's got a broken arm and shoulder. And Kowalski's got five broken ribs—FIVE! They're done for the season!"

David looked at Heather to make sure she didn't hear the voice yelling in his ear. She didn't flinch; she just drove.

"And Sawyer's gonna be drinkin' Budweiser through a straw for six weeks!" Brian continued as he laughed.

"Yeah, thanks to Sully," David said cautiously.

"Hey, you're getting credit for all of it. You've been crowned *Royal Ass Kicker of the Dick Squad.* You 'da man, cuz!"

"David pressed the phone hard against his ear to keep Brian's voice from escaping into the car.

"Hey, and cheer up Heather and tell her that all the chicks are really digging my teal daypack. Thanks for that!"

"OK, she'll like hearing that," David smiled.

"Stay low man, and call me."

David wrote the combination on his hand and set the phone down in the center console.

"So you just told him that there's a clone of Jesus running around Boston and he believed you?"

"Yes, sort of. We're a little tighter than most. I would believe him if he said aliens were trying to abduct him. It just works that way."

"It must be special to have someone in your life like that."

"He's my hero."

"And you're his Royal Ass Kicker?"

25

Saturday lower campus activity consisted mainly of people going in and out of the sports complex, as the Sentinels were away that weekend. They parked several rows away from the entrance.

"I'll come with you," he said reaching for the door handle.

"We're more noticeable together. I'll go, you wait here."

Heather put on the black ball cap and went inside.

It was too quick. She reappeared suddenly and moved briskly to the car, empty-handed. Heather hopped into the driver's seat and slammed the door.

"Did someone see you?" asked David.

"They're gone!" she said. "The files are gone!"

"Shit."

Heather started trembling and crying.

"The lock was missing and the files were gone. I...I thought I was in the wrong locker, but my gym stuff was sitting there on the bottom!"

"It's OK," David said putting his arm around her.

"What do we do now?" she cried.

"It's all right. It's all right." he assured her. "Let's go get the microfiche."

They sat for a minute until Heather got it back together.

"You ready?" he asked.

She took a deep breath and nodded, then got out of the car and headed for the rink. The locker room was accessed by swipe cards, but there was enough traffic that they caught a closing door before it could catch. Once inside, they could hear a couple of guys around the corner in the shower room. They followed the numbers down and turned the corner at locker 120. They both stood and stared. Locker 131 was cracked open. David slowly opened the door. The crow bar mark was clearly visible, the latch destroyed. The only thing inside the locker was a hockey stick with a number 12 written in black marker.

"Let's go!" David said.

They darted to the parking lot, tears streaking her face as they ran.

"What now?" she cried.

"First, let's get a couple of miles away from here."

"Then what?"

"I'm not a good planner. Let's just get out of here," he said just short of a full run.

Heather tossed the keys to David and they jumped into the car. He took a deep, measured breath.

"Easy…" David said to himself, pulling out of the lot, while Heather panted, trying to keep back more tears.

The Camry made its way down Faneuil Street, following the bus's path from the day before.

"They have the printouts from the film," Heather said, now calming down. "They know that we know everything. And they have it all back. All we have left are copies of the birth certificates and the birthing report," she said, her voice still trembling. "Maybe it's enough to go to the police and say these guys are after us."

"After us for what? No one will be able to get their hands on those documents again."

"Where to?"

"I don't know. How about that library? Maybe something will click there. Can we crash at your aunt and uncle's again?"

"We're expected for dinner," she smiled as she sniffled.

The Belmont Public Library looked like a safe place to kill a few hours. It was busy, but not so crowded that they couldn't find a table off to the side where they could talk quietly. David pulled out his laptop and connected to the library's wireless network. Heather pulled out a notebook and started to write.

"What are you writing?"

"Everything I can remember about what we saw. I'm trying to list the documents. What are you doing?"

"Trying to find out who those Dark Men are."

As she wrote, David Googled for information about the St. Mathew's rectory and the purchase by Brighton Latin College.

"Aha," David whispered.

Heather put down her notebook and slid her chair close to David.

"Where are you?"

"I'm in some sort of news post link on the Brighton Latin website. It says here that the transition of the rectory is done from a legal standpoint and blah, blah, blah—then, right here: the building known as the carriage house shall be sublet to provide quarters and offices for members of the archdiocese who work closely with the college, as well as the Fontana Limousine Service, a small limousine company that offers car service to the church and school that has operated its business out the carriage house for many years. Mr. Scordo of the company has signed a ten-year lease with the college, from which the income alone will cover the overhead and maintenance of the facility."

"So these guys write out a big check and camp out at the rectory," Heather said.

"Basically. Let's look them up,"

He Googled Fontana Limousine Service, Boston. Nothing. He modified the search replacing "Boston" with "Massachusetts." He got one hit—the article he had just read. Then he removed the state. A Tony Fontana Limo service in Hollywood. Nothing else.

He switched over to Yahoo's yellow pages. No results.

"These guys don't even have a phone number," David said.

"I wonder how business is," smirked Heather.

"We can assume the limo company is the front for the U.S. operation."

"Or maybe part of the operation?" Heather offered.

"I don't think so. In all of the documents and letters, Scordo is the man. He is in control and there is no mention of the church or the school, nor are there any records of anyone in the U.S., other than Glen Jennings, who even knows about this."

"There's that lab technician," offered Heather.

"Right, but he knows nothing, per the letter from Scordo to Vincent in Italy. So the good news, if there can be any good news, is we're dealing with just a couple of people, maybe just Scordo."

"Can we find anything on him?"

The Google search for Anthony Scordo gave over 600,000 results.

"This could take a while…"

Heather slid back and kept writing, while David tried combinations of searches on Scordo, Massachusetts, and limousines.

After 20 minutes, David gave up.

"This guy just doesn't exist," he sighed, looking over at Heather. "So how is that going?"

"I'm writing a cover letter explaining our theory and how it all happened, to go with the list, in case we vanish."

She said it. Their lives being in danger was just too bizarre to talk about. He had half joked earlier about them not having his economics quiz, but the things that had happened since then made the statement too plausible to say. If it was all true, then the stakes just might be that high.

"We just need to be careful for a few days, that's all," David reassured her. "This will all work itself out, now that they have their stuff back."

David continued to surf.

"What about the doctor?" he wondered.

Heather perked up.

"If we can get him to agree," David continued, "then we would have someone to confirm our theory. He probably has some sort of records or evidence."

"Don't you think we should just let it lie?" Heather asked. "Like you said, they have their stuff back."

"If he knows that we know," David said, stumbling on the expression, "then he would know if the kid is really in any danger. He would want to help, no? Here he is, Dr. Devito, in Somerville," David said, jotting down the address.

"Wanna go for a ride?" he asked.

"We have plenty of time before dinner," Heather confirmed.

They found themselves in Somerville in minutes.

"Left at the next block," David instructed.

Heather parked the car on a residential side street.

"What will you say to him—if he is home?" Heather asked.

"Not sure, but I think just mentioning Luc's name ought to do it."

They walked up the side street and approached a large, red-shingled home bearing a gold "6" mounted on the yellow front door. A man in his 30s was on the front lawn raking out a flower bed.

"Dr. Devito?" David asked.

"Yes!" he said, as he spun around greeting his guest.

David walked onto the lawn so he could speak more quietly.

"I am sorry to bother you on the weekend. But, I need to talk to you about one of your patients."

"I can listen, but, as I'm sure you know, I cannot talk about my patients."

"Not even about Luc Jennings?"

The doctor looked puzzled.

"I have no patient by that name."

"Two-fourteen, Beacon Street. I have copies of your medical reports from the in-home exams. I think you know what I'm talking about," David said firmly.

"No, I am afraid I don't," the doctor stated. "Unless...when did the examination occur?"

"The last one was in August," David answered, softening his tone a bit.

"Then you are probably looking for my father, Dr. Nicholas Devito. I am Dr. Robert Devito."

"Oh, I am sorry," David said, embarrassed by his aggressive approach. "Can you tell me how to find him?"

"You are at the right house, but my father passed away on Labor Day."

"I'm so sorry," Heather offered. "We didn't mean to bother you."

"It's all right. You know, I am taking on most of his patients, but I haven't seen any records for a Luc Jennings, and I've gone through everything."

"Thank you again, sorry to bother you," David said.

The doctor went back to his raking as the two returned to the car and headed for dinner.

Shirley and Joe had invited their only child, Cheryl, and her children from Sturbridge.

"My cousin is divorced and has three boys—all terrors. Sorry to subject you to this," Heather apologized.

"Compared to what I have subjected you to, this is nothing," he smiled.

While stopped at a light, David leaned over to the driver's seat and put his hand gently on her cheek. Instead of talking, he slid his hand around the back of her neck and drew her lips to his. The light changed. After a short honk from the car behind, the Camry moved forward.

26

Bacon! Two in a row!
He could hear conversation down in the kitchen. It was nearly 10:00 according to little alarm clock on the night stand when Heather poked her head in the door.

"Sorry, I overslept," David whispered.

"It's OK. Ready for breakfast?"

"Sure, just let me brush my teeth."

Heather disappeared down the stairs. David scrambled, throwing on his clothes and shoes, then doing a quick pass with the toothbrush. His hair was a mess, but he was still damn cute, thought Heather, as he sat down at the breakfast table, apologizing for sleeping in.

"Don't be silly," said Aunt Shirley, "We know you're comfortable here when you get a good night's sleep."

David and Heather thanked their hosts for the weekend lodging as they got into the Camry and backed out of the driveway. A few moments later, they were parked next to the library.

"Well, we have all day to come up with a plan," said Heather.

"Longer, if you think about it. At the moment, I guess I'm homeless!" David said, laughing.

Although only one night had passed, it seemed to put some distance on the whole thing. There was not much more they could do, other than go to the authorities and plead their case.

"You surf, I'll write," he said, sliding over the laptop.

He took the pad and reviewed her notes first, then started to make comments.

She started in on Google.

"Keyword?" asked David

"Dr. Devito, obituary. Well, he wasn't lying," confirmed Heather. "Says he died of natural causes, respiratory failure; passed away Labor Day weekend, while he was taking an afternoon nap. Not a bad way to go, I guess."

She typed in more keywords.

"Poking around in Italy and the Vatican, thirteen years ago," she said before he asked.

Fifteen minutes passed, then Heather gasped, staring at the screen.

"Oh no!"

"What have you got?" he said, putting down the notebook.

"Newspaper article. It looks like the birthing doctor, Diorio, died on May 9th, right after the births."

"How did he die?"

"Car crash off a cliff."

"What are you reading?" he asked.

"A Rome newspaper converted to English on their website."

"How many Diorios do you think are in Rome?

"Doctor Diorios? Obstetricians? It's gotta be him," she said.

David went back to his notes. After another minute Heather shuddered.

"David! Oh my God! It's the sisters!"

David got close.

"The nuns?"

"No, they were actually siblings."

"Were?"

"It says, 'in a follow up on yesterday's reported tragedy, the deaths of two sisters Fiona and Florence Lombardo were determined to be from carbon monoxide poison emitted from a faulty gas heater. The odorless poison filled the apartment, killing them while they slept.'"

Heather pounded the keyboard as her breathing quickened. She jumped to the May 8th edition.

"Here it is. Oh, no. It says, 'nursing sisters who were known and loved by many in the town were found dead in their Rome apartment yesterday morning, after not showing up for an appointment.'"

"That would be the seventh," said David.

"'Fiona Lombardo, 36, and Florence Lombardo, 38, of Rose Terrace Lane, were found around 11:00 a.m., according to police. Cause of death is under investigation, but it is suspected to be accidental, as the sisters were found in their beds with no sign of any trouble. The two nurses had delivered many of the babies in the village, often without charge to those who could not afford it. 'They will be dearly missed,' said a neighbor.'"

"Dr. Leonard. Search for it."

Heather's hands shook as she typed in the name. She clicked "Go."

The headline appeared: *May 14, 1995—Genetic scientist falls to his death hiking in the Alps.*

Heather was bewildered.

"They're all dead! All of them!" she cried.

"As before, the authority to manage a complete shut down," mumbled David. "Orsini!"

David grabbed Heather's arm.

"We need to get to the cops! These guys aren't gonna let us walk away with what we know. Even if we don't have enough, we can get help. Heather, we need to get help."

Heather's phone vibrated on the table, slowly spinning as it buzzed.

"It's my aunt."

She pulled herself together and flipped it open.

"Hey, Aunt Shirley."

"Hi, Heather. I'm afraid I have bad news."

"What do you mean?"

"David's grandmother died."

"Wuh? How did you find out?"

"The man from the college was just here. He said David's roommate told him he was out here for the weekend."

Heather covered the phone.

"They're here!" she cried jumping up, her eyes wild.

David jumped up and packed the laptop and notebook.

"Aunt Shirley, where is he?"

"He just left. I told him he could find you at the library. Are you still there?"

"We just left."

They started for the door, then Heather motioned to the window. The black Buick had just come into view traveling down Main Street.

David motioned toward the rear exit sign. They walked looking back to the windows.

"Oh, too bad. Maybe you should go back. Please tell David we are sorry to hear the bad news."

"I'll tell him," Heather said, as they watched the car come to a stop directly in front of the library.

"By the way Heather, he is cute with a capital 'C'! Are you two an item?!"

"I gotta go, I'll call ya later."

She snapped the phone closed as she reached the back door. David poked his head outside.

"Clear, let's go!"

It was a short dash to the Camry. Heather adjusted the interior mirror as she inserted the key in the ignition as he rounded the corner.

"Down!" Heather yelled.

They both slumped down in their seats. Heather grabbed the little knob that controls the side mirror and lowered it until he came back into view.

"It's the guy from Luc's house!" she said. "He's going in the back door. Let's go!"

"Easy," cautioned David.

Heather looked at David and took a deep breath, then started the car and slowly pulled out, taking the first right. David looked over his shoulder to make sure the Dark Man stayed inside the library.

After another block, Heather turned again and accelerated.

"He told my aunt your grandmother died and Brian told him where you were," she said, gripping the wheel.

"Brian doesn't know where we are. And all my grandparents died years ago."

"How did they know to check my aunt's house? How did they even know I have an aunt?"

"On your enrollment paperwork, who is to be contacted in an emergency?"

"Oh, shit!"

27

The bedside table's alarm clock read 11:30. With his mother away, Luc's Sunday morning was absent of the inviting smell of a hot breakfast. Still in pajamas, he went downstairs finding a note on the kitchen table that said his dad had gone out for a jog and he would be back to make him lunch. He foraged through the refrigerator, but nothing looked good. He settled on a package of blueberry Pop-Tarts, which he found in the pantry.

It was boring without his Mom around. Not that his dad wasn't fun, but it was just too quiet in the house. He heard something sliding across the hardwood floor in the living room and poked his head out to see their new kitten batting his iPod across the floor like a puck. The cat and gadget came to an abrupt stop at the Oriental carpet, the cat catching his prey. The kitten scurried behind the couch as Luc grabbed the iPod away from it.

"Now where'd you go with my earphones?" Luc called out.

On his hands and knees, he crawled behind the end table to see the kitten behind the couch wrestling with the white wire of his ear buds.

"Come here, you!" he yelled.

The cat rolled over, tangling itself in the cord. Luc crawled behind the antique couch, untangling his pet from the head phones. Freed, it darted under the sofa and sat down just out of arm's reach.

The front door rattled. Luc heard his father coming in, talking to someone. As they walked down the hall, he could hear the voice of another man and his shoes tapping on the hard

Floors—not a jogger. They came into the living room talking in hushed voices.

"He's up in his room. Anne flew out yesterday to California for her aunt's funeral."

Scordo slid closed the massive pocket doors that led to the main hallway and the staircase.

"It is serious enough that we have to move quickly. They have the details of our activities," he said in a clipped Italian accent.

"How could this happen?"

Luc remained still, parked on his elbows and knees.

"It was a break-in at my office. We always knew something like this could happen. You knew the risks all along."

"It just seems that after so much time, we should think about this. Anthony, we, uh, Anne and I were talking—"

"You told her about this? You said you never would."

No, I did not tell her about the project, just that we are now faced with Luc's return to the Vatican for a higher education. She accepts that this was the agreement all along but we decided…"

"We must shut it down now," Scordo interrupted. This could expose everything. It would take down so many, so many who had no knowledge."

"The church?" Glen speculated.

"The church would be blamed. We cannot, must not, allow that to happen."

"Just who stole the information?"

"Two students. We know they have gone though the files. We know they know about this house and who lives here."

"Wait, male and female, both tall?"

Scordo pulled back, raising his eyebrows.

"Yes, David Knight and Heather Connor."

Luc's eyes opened wide, *They're for real!*

"They didn't introduce themselves, but I met them in the park," offered Glen.

"What did they say?"

"Nothing, really. Just that they were freshmen. Oh, and she studies anthropology.

"Nothing else?" Scordo prodded.

"No. It was very brief."

"Did you or the boy say anything?"

"Lets, see, I said went to Brighton Latin too. Oh, and Luc said he was born in Italy and that we were going there in a couple of weeks. That's everything."

"That was enough to confirm that you are the people in the files," Scordo's voice grew louder.

"What do we do now?" Glen asked.

"I will fly the boy out tonight at midnight."

Luc's jaw slacked. His heart rate was soaring and his breathing became difficult. He made every attempt to be perfectly still and not breathe loudly, but he was certain they could hear his heart pounding, as the pulses throbbed in his head.

"Luc and I were going to Provincetown for the Columbus Day festival."

"That's good. Don't cancel. Are you taking the ferry?"

"Yes."

"Be back by seven-thirty. I will meet you at the dock. This will give you some time with him—time to explain. Tell him you must go the West Coast to be with your wife. There is an old friend from the Vatican visiting who can take him to Italy a little ahead of schedule for his confirmation. You will be a few days at most."

Scordo looked down at the side of the couch. Something had his attention. He looked closer, then dropped to one knee. Luc stared at the knee from two feet away, under the antique sofa's tall, French Provencal legs. His heart was in his throat as he saw a hand touch the floor as the man lowered himself. His shadow grew larger as he came closer. Just as Scordo dipped his head to look under the sofa, from out of nowhere, the kitten attacked, pouncing on his hand. His gold and emerald ring was in the grasp of the microscopic lion. Scordo picked up the kitten and stood up. Luc could not breathe; the kitten clutched the ring.

"OK," Glen sighed, "We will follow in a week."

"No," Scordo said, as he slowly stroked the kitten's back; the little ball of fur purred loudly. "That cannot happen. You can no longer be connected to us."

He gently put the kitten down and watched it run back to its lair under the sofa.

"We will relocate the child to another safe place," he said standing back up. "Your work is done here, Glen. We will take over from here."

Luc could not believe what he just heard. He was being taken away from his family, and his father was in on it!

"But, we were planning, rather, Anne and I are planning to relocate—to be with him in Italy." Glen's voice reeked of distress as Scordo scoffed, half laughing.

"What? Don't be ridiculous. That was never an option. We will take care of him. It will all make sense to him once we are in the Vatican."

"What about Anne? She thinks we can stay together, as a family."

"You have all weekend to figure that out. As I said, we must move quickly. It's for the best, for the child's best interest too. You know that. Those two students are out there somewhere and they will come again."

"What if we stop them?"

"When we find them, we will deal with them. If you see them or hear from them, you call me."

Luc was trembling. Tears streamed down his face as he held his mouth wide open trying to pull in air silently when the kitten pounced again. The earphones clenched in Luc's fists were the new target. Six inches from his face, he watched a battle to the death with the dangling ear-buds.

"I must go and prepare. Seven-thirty will give us enough time to stop here for his things," said Scordo, as he slid open the pocket doors.

"I'll walk you to your car," Glen said, his head down.

He heard the door close and waited a couple of seconds to make sure his dad had walked out, then scrambled out from behind the sofa and ran as fast as he could up the stairs to his room. The kitten kept pace with him to the bottom of the stairs, then gave up the chase and sat looking up the curved wooden staircase.

When Glen returned, Luc was upstairs. He slid the pocket doors closed and walked quickly to his office. He paused as the computer booted, holding is head in his hands.

"Vincent will make it all right," he muttered.

Once fired up, Glen opened up his Yahoo account and skipped the 13 messages in his inbox, clicking "new" and started typing. He didn't have much time, yet there was so much to say.

28

"I think we're clear," said David.

Heather continued to maneuver through the side streets of Belmont while David scouted for the Buick.

"Do you think…" she swallowed hard and continued, "they killed Dr. Devito?"

David stared out the window, "Let's get to a police station."

Her cell phone rang and she handed it to David.

"Caller ID says 'Jennings.' It's Luc! You better answer," David said handing her the phone.

"Hello?"

She listened for a long moment.

"Wait, wait, slow down. OK, who is going to take you away?" she said, as the car swerved, almost taking out a "for sale" sign.

Heather brought the car to a stop.

"Where are you?"

"In my bedroom," Luc said in a panic.

"Did they say why?"

"You stole some files, so they have to shut everything down. That means they take me away to the Vatican."

"We didn't Luc, but what about your dad?"

"He doesn't like it, but they said his job was over. I don't think he's my dad!"

"He's your dad, Luc. He loves you."

"The man is going to take me!" he cried.

"Who?"

"I didn't see him. He sounded Italian. I think its one of the guys in the dark suits."

"When is this going to happen?"

"Tonight. Midnight. My dad's taking me to Provincetown today and when we get back, I go right to the airport. I'm never coming back!" Luc whimpered.

"Luc, listen to me. We will help you,"

"My dad is coming!"

"Luc, text me when you can!" Heather blurted, "We're coming. We'll be there!"

The line went dead. Heather hung her head.

"We'll be there? Is there a plan I should know about?" David asked.

"The Tea Man is shutting the project down. They fly him out at midnight!"

"Shit! Where are we going?"

"Cape Cod."

"Are you all right, son?" Glen asked, seeing that Luc was upset.

"I feel really sick. Stomach ache. I think I am going to throw up."

"Now, now, let's see,"

Glen placed his hand on Luc's forehead.

"No fever. You're fine. Let's get you up and have a glass of ginger ale and some rye toast. Fixes everything…"

Luc got dressed, put his cell in his pocket, and went downstairs with his father. Glen popped two slices of rye bread in the toaster oven and poured a glass of ginger ale.

"Son," Glen said with his back to Luc, "we're going to the festival in P-town today, remember?"

"I don't feel that great," Luc said, then realizing that the ferry trip to Provincetown may be better than sitting around waiting to be abducted. "But I think the toast will help."

"Attaboy."

He turned and looked at him. Luc could see the distress in his eyes.

"I'll get us some jackets; it will be chilly on the ferry."

Glen returned with Luc's favorite jacket with a Red Sox logo on the sleeve.

"We'll be twins," Glen said as he put his red jacket on, "unless, you don't want to be."

"It's OK, Dad," he said, finishing his toast.

"Well, I don't know how you kids think. You're getting older and sometimes this stuff matters."

Luc smiled a little. They walked to the front door of the brownstone.

"I better go to the bathroom," he said as his father opened the front door.

"Good idea," Glen agreed.

He ran up the stairs, closed the door and pulled out his cell. He typed in: "goin to ferry" and sent the text message to Heather. Within 20 seconds his phone vibrated.

"meet u in p town," he read.

He flushed the toilet and ran down the stairs.

As they exited #214 Beacon, Glen noticed the box next to the door was jammed with junk mail. He pulled the stack out and placed it on the table just inside, not noticing the yellow envelope with *Sarah* written in the corner.

"Maybe we should call the police?" David said, as Heather entered the on ramp of the interstate.

She was focused, gripping the wheel firmly with both hands, as she responded.

"They could have us tied up for days questioning and validating our story. This is happening now! If we're gonna help, then we need to do this. We can go to the authorities after we save this kid."

Heather suddenly realized her authoritative tone.

"I mean, don't you think?" she asked as she turned the radio down.

David looked at her and smiled.

"I couldn't have said it better," he said, reaching over and placing his hand on her knee.

He had dragged her into this and felt terrible about it. Had he kept the puzzle to himself, she would not be on the run with him; maybe this nightmare would not have occurred.

"It will be better now than later," he added a few moments later. "We'll only have Mr. Jennings to deal with."

They drove for a while, then, Heather looked at David.

"Once we get Luc, how do we get off the Cape?" she asked him, looking over.

"They can't report it, so I guess we have to decide where to take him."

"Uh, David?" Heather said, as she navigated through high volume traffic.

"Yeah?"

"You've never been to the Cape, have you?" she asked, clicking the radio off.

"No, why?"

"OK, here's the deal. There are only two bridges to get on and off of Cape Cod."

"OK…"

"Provincetown is all the way at the end of the Cape, two hours from the bridges. Mr. Tea Man and his buddies can be at the bridges in under an hour. So, if Luc's father doesn't like the idea of us kidnapping his child…"

"We'll have a welcoming committee when we return to the mainland," David finished.

"Black Buick at each bridge," she nodded.

David tapped his knee as he thought.

"Maybe we wait. Hide out for a day or so, then go. They can't sit there forever."

"Maybe tomorrow afternoon?" Heather suggested. "Traffic will be crazy with everyone coming home after the long weekend. Maybe we can blend in."

29

He did not acknowledge Sister Sarah's stare, grabbing his coat and exiting the stone building in a rush.

Once in the church, Vincent slowed down. He moved to the candle station, knelt and prayed, his head hanging low. Activity in the church was light—every sound echoed off the hard surfaces that made up the building's ornate interior. Shoe heels clicked loudly as someone walked quickly. Someone coughed. One of the large entrance doors creaked, then a muffled thud confirmed it was closed again, the shoes now outside. Someone sniffled. More footsteps, only softer and slower. Another sniffle. The footsteps grew quieter until they were gone. The church was silent. Another sniffle. Without raising his head, Cardinal Vincent reached into his coat and produced a handkerchief and raised it to his face.

30

Luc and his dad walked along the beach.

"I've never seen a Frisbee go that far," Luc said, holding the disk under his arm.

"I think I had a little help from the wind," Glen reasoned.

The sun was low and the temperature was starting to drop.

"I'm getting cold. Can I have my jacket?" asked Luc.

Glen pulled both coats out of his daypack. After they put them on, Luc looked at his dad as they walked along the high tide mark of the beach. For a moment, he had forgotten about the Italian man and the plans to take him away. He loved his dad and this was how it was supposed to be.

"Maybe we do look a little dorky as twins," he said, smiling up at Glen.

The ring tone on Luc's phone was the opening of the James Bond theme song. As it grew louder, he pulled the singing and buzzing phone out of his pocket.

"we r here—where u ?"

"Who is that?" Luc's father asked.

"It's Billy, he wants to go to the park. I'll let him know I'm with you."

"Good," Glen said.

"beach," he texted.

The sun was setting over the water. They sat in the Camry in a crowded parking lot just outside of the downtown area of Provincetown, the streets closed for the festival.

"He's at the beach," Heather said pocketing her phone.

"How do we find them?"

"We don't. The whole Cape is a continuous beach. Let's give him fifteen minutes and I'll try him again."

Time was short. Luc knew they had to catch the ferry soon, as his father was looking more and more depressed. As they walked into town, Glen put his arm around Luc's shoulders.

"We need to catch the six o'clock ferry, so if there's anything you want to do," he offered.

"I'm OK just walking around. Can I get a tee shirt?"

"Sure."

The Bond theme started up again. Luc opened the phone.

"where-u?"

"Billy again?"

"Yep."

"in town"

The song started back up before he could put the phone back in his pocket.

"go to army-navy store"

As Luc and his father wandered about, they saw a lot of Provincetown's festive nature, in full swing for the holiday.

Sitting at the outermost part of Cape Cod, Provincetown's landscape mimics a scorpion's tail. The ocean side has one long, continuous beach, while the tip hooks in and creates the bayside, protecting the large commercial fishing fleet, and the beautiful village.

Over the years, the charming, predominantly Portuguese fishing town evolved into an upscale, yet quaint summer haven. At the height of the season, the downtown area is packed with tourists visiting boutiques, art galleries, bookstores and food vendors.

Finally, he saw the Army Navy Store. Luc did his best to attempt to act cheerful.

"Let's go in there!"

"Sure, son."

The store would be difficult to navigate with no one in it. The Army Navy Store was packed with shoppers, moving around cramped clothing racks and bins. The store sold everything: new and used clothes, army surplus gear, toys, souvenirs, etc...The walls in the front of the store were lined with bins containing sea shells, starfish, candles, small toys and trinkets; in the back were the marine supplies. Lobster pots and buoys, war memorabilia, and an old-fashioned hard hat diver's suit hung from the ceiling. Every step required Luc and Glen to focus on the traffic as they navigated the deep, narrow store.

From across the street in an art studio, David and Heather were watching.

"He's in," said David.

The two crossed the street and went down the alley on the side of the store.

"OK, here we go. Is the car ready?" she asked.

"Keys are in it," he quickly replied. "Don't wait for me. Just go if I'm not there. We can meet in half an hour along the highway, one mile down."

The plan would take less than ten seconds. *Heather sweeps the kid out the back door, then David blocks the door, stopping the dad.* He rehearsed his line in his head one more time: *Look, Luc doesn't want to go away with your friend. We'll call you in a few days. This is his request. He's in safe hands.*

"Ready," David whispered as he confirmed the rear door of the store was open.

Heather flipped open her phone and entered: "meet...back of store."

She pressed send.

The Bond theme started up and Luc quickly flipped his phone open.

"Who's that?" his father asked.

"Oh, no one. Just another friend looking for something to do."

He closed it and put it in his pocket.

Heather slipped in through the rear door wearing the black ball cap and Brian's denim jacket with the collar turned up. She saw them, about halfway back in the middle of the store looking at tee shirts.

At the back of the store, atop a cabinet, stood a polished suit of armor.

"Check that out!" Luc said, finding a reason to move to the rear.

He walked over to it, glancing about, then up to the suit of armor.

"It looks like it would fit me!" he said.

"People were much smaller back then, son."

As his father admired the armor, Luc spotted Heather off to the side, positioned about 15 feet from the door. She nodded toward the door as Luc saw a display counter with hundreds of knives.

"Can I get one dad?"

"Well, not a big one."

He selected a folding pocket knife with a serrated blade and a blue metal housing. The vendor behind the case handed the bag to Luc; he took the knife out and put it in his pocket while catching a glimpse of David, outside the partially open rear door. Heather was in position behind a rack of used, bright orange military raincoats.

"Ready to go?" Luc's dad asked.

"OK."

As they weaved their way up the makeshift aisles, they approached the orange raincoats. Luc saw Heather's back was to them. She gave a quick glance over her shoulder and made eye contact. He inched closer to the coat rack and swallowed hard. Heather took one step back, looked down, hiding her eyes under the visor, and started a slow, clockwise spin. As she turned, she extended her left hand outward, while her right hand was on the orange raincoat rack to blindly calibrate her position.

Here we go, she thought.

Three-quarters of the way through her spin her face hit black wool, colliding with the middle of the back of a black coat. Scordo stood between them! She ducked to the floor pretending to pick up some dropped clothes between the racks.

Shit! she thought, peeking out from under her cap.

Scordo glanced back, half ignoring the brush in the hectic store. She kept her head down, Scordo blocking the view of Luc and his dad.

Slow down!

Heather's heart raced.

"Hello, Glen. You must be Luc," Scordo said.

Luc instantly recognized the accent form that morning. Scordo gestured as to put his arm around them and pointed to the front door. Heather slowly stood up and headed around the circular coat rack for the back door.

"I thought we were meeting in Boston?" Glen asked.

"Of course, of course." the Italian accent thickened. "But it was such a fine day and rather than wait around, I though it might be nice to join you. Have you explained your predicament to Luc?

"No, not yet."

"Oh, I am so sorry, I should leave you two for a bit," he said guiding them out the exit and to the right, back toward the ferry.

Heather's chest pounded as she fled the Army Navy store.

"What the hell was that!?" asked David.

"I don't know! He came out of nowhere!" Heather gasped.

"He was supposed to be in Boston!"

"How many were there?"

"Just Scordo," David said.

"I crashed right into him. God, that was so close!"

"Maybe the kid had it wrong?"

"Maybe."

Luc looked up at his dad, trying to appear curious, rather than frightened.

"It's your mother's uncle. Here, sit down."

The two sat on a park bench along the pier while Scordo stood a polite distance away, able to hear but not so close as to be part of the conversation.

Here it comes, Luc thought.

"After the funeral he had a stroke. He's not going to make it. I need to go out there and help mom see this through. I was telling Mr. Scordo about the problem and he had a good idea. Luc, you may not remember him, but he works with the people that I worked for when you were born. He's a very good friend. In fact, we're going to be staying with him when we go over for your confirmation. He has offered to help us out and thinks it would be great to have you go to Italy a little early and he can show you around. You don't want to be around us with all that gloom."

Luc just stared as his father's voice cracked repeatedly while streaming the lie. The Dark Man stepped forward.

"There are a couple of people who would love to see you again and show you around Italy for a few days while your parents deal with this family crisis."

Stunned and speechless, Luc played along.

"When do we go?"

"That's the problem son, Mr. Scordo flies out tonight. He was going to meet us later and tell me if he could get you on the flight."

"All set," advised Scordo.

"That's it—I'm going?"

"I know it's short notice, but I just got the call from mom this morning. Your uncle had a stroke at the funeral—such a big mess, I need your help here. I am flying out first thing tomorrow."

"What about school?"

"Don't worry, it's a family emergency. I'll get all of your assignments sent over."

Luc gave up on the questions, as he knew there would be some sort of answer to make it all work. This was a done deal in his father's eyes as well.

How could he do this? And where did Heather and David go?

31

David and Heather bounced off of people in the mobbed streets as the parade began. They could hear the music of the procession getting closer and searched the adjoining stores and the side streets that housed more shops. The parade was closing in.

"Now what?"

"Back to the pier!" David said.

They hurried, avoiding colliding with people. Evening had fallen on Provincetown and the streets were lit up in light and brilliant colors for the celebration. The crowd was squeezed as the parade arrived.

"What time is it?" David asked.

Heather looked at her cell phone.

"Almost six."

As she said it, the bells in the tower started to ring.

"The ferry. Let's go..."

They darted through a store and out the back, finding an alley where they could run to the pier.

Halfway down, the ferry was tied up behind a line of commercial fishing boats docked single file along the massive wharf. They bee-lined it for the boat.

"Look!" Heather pointed. In the distance, they could see three people boarding the ferry, the tall man unmistakable.

As they raced toward the ferry, the gangway was pulled off the boat onto the pier. The loud rumble of the engines confirmed the departure.

The twin hulled, high-speed ferry, was capable of cutting quickly through the water with a large load of people, making Boston a 90-minute, summertime commute. The large bridge deck connecting the hulls created a tunnel-like space large enough to drive cars through. Sitting over the tunnel was the passenger compartment, and, on top of that, the navigation bridge on the top deck. Outfitted with enormous engines powering water-jet drives, enormous roster tails of water shot out of the back of each hull when at speed.

On board the catamaran, Luc and his guardians were virtually alone. The festival was in full swing and most who would leave by ferry would catch the next one, so they could enjoy the parade and fireworks. They moved forward on the left side to the outside walkway.

"We're too late!" cried Heather as they ran.

"I gotta plan!"

David spied the kayak rental shack at the end of the pier, opposite the fishing boats.

The ropes were tossed to the pier and the ferry gave its engines a quick rev. Free from the dock it drifted sideways, clearing the fishing boats.

At the tip of the pier, David blew by the owner of the kayak shop, who was closing up.

"I just need ten minutes, I left something on my boat...I'm late!" he blurted.

"Sure, no problem."

He tossed his wallet to the shop owner and grabbed a kayak and paddle. He flung the kayak into the water next to the dock and ran along side of it as it slid forward. With one hand on the dock and the other in the air with the paddle, he jumped in, the move not perfect, as the boat wobbled, almost dumping David.

Luc was in a panic. The opportunity to escape was gone and this stranger was now in control. Suddenly, he did a U-turn and headed back toward the door to the inside passenger compartment. His dad blocked his way.

"Where are you going, son?"

"I'm not going! I know I'm not coming back! I know! I heard what he said at the house! I heard everything!"

"Luc, please listen to me. There are things you don't understand."

The ferry was now moving forward, the sound of its engines and jet pumps increasing in volume as it pushed by the fishing fleet. Scordo stepped in.

"Just settle down, young man!" he yelled over the engine noise. "We have a long way to go tonight."

"I won't go with you!"

Glen looked at Scordo.

"Look, this isn't working. We're going to have to…"

Scordo's long black coat opened, presenting a black 9-millimeter Beretta, with a silencer mounted to its barrel tip.

"Enough!" Scordo declared, as he blocked the entrance to the passenger compartment.

Luc's father jumped in.

"This has all gotten way out of control!" he yelled, stepping toward Scordo.

The pistol popped twice.

Glen grabbed his stomach and looked at Scordo in disbelief, a blackish red stain spreading on his shirt; blood oozing between his fingers.

Luc watched his father drop to his knees as the ferry passed the last fishing boat.

"Dad! Noooo!"

His cries were drowned out as the engines and jet pumps roared to a full boil. Luc's cell phone vibrated in his jacket pocket as his father fell forward clutching Scordo around the legs. In this bizarre, surreal moment, Luc stood confused. He did not know why or how, but in a flash his instincts were controlling him— instincts he did not know he had.

Survive! Run!

He turned and ran toward the bow while his cell phone continued to buzz and ring, the engines blocking any chance to hear it. Scordo released Glen to the deck, looked around to confirm no witnesses, and went after Luc.

Heather ran down the pier, catching flashes of the ferry in between the fishing boats' masts, nets, and pilot houses. She hit speed dial on her phone as she made out the gun and the scuffle, gasping when Luc's father dropped to his knees and lurched onto Scordo. She saw Luc rounding the corner at the front of the passenger compartment as the big catamaran picked up speed. Nearing the end of the pier, Heather came to an abrupt stop at the sight of David accelerating from behind a moored sailboat in a kayak on a collision course with the ferry. She glanced back to Scordo who rounded the corner and stopped.

"Answer it, come on Luc, answer it!" she pleaded into the phone.

David paddled furiously away from the rental dock. He reached the closest moored boat, a sailboat, just out of the channel. As he emerged from behind it, the ferry had cleared the dock and the bows were lifting in response to throttles opening up.

He accelerated, shooting out into the channel, clearing the first hull with 10 feet to spare. As the cat straddled him, he looked up and saw Luc with his cell phone to his ear.

Scordo rounded the corner and stopped 10 feet from Luc. Their eyes locked as Scordo raised the gun; Luc had the phone to his ear.

"JUMP! JUMP NOW!" Heather screamed into the phone.

Luc closed his eyes, dropped the phone, and rolled over the pipe handrail, like a high jumper clearing the bar.

"Pop-clink, Pop-clink!"

As he went over, Luc did not see the sparks of the two rounds hitting the handrail directly in front of his chest. He dropped into the dark abyss.

Luc inhaled seawater as he thrashed about, trying to get to the surface. For a moment, he couldn't tell which way was up in the pitch black water. He breathed in more water. After the second intake of ocean, he stopped fighting and started to go limp. He hung motionless for a split second, then felt himself being dragged.

David had him by the collar of his jacket, pulling him against the kayak as the ferry ran them over. Luc's head surfaced, greeted by the engine's deafening howl echoing off the metal hulls and bridge deck above. He vomited seawater, then took in air. The accelerating cat trampled them and spit them back into the evening, bouncing in the churning white foam wake accompanied by the fire hose-like spray of the portside jet pump's growing rooster tail. As they cleared the cat's mayhem, David's eyes, stinging with salt, could see people on the back of the ferry pointing at him. In a reflex, he raised his paddle over his head.

"Woo-hoo!" he yelled, realizing Luc was on the far side of the kayak and hopefully out of view.

If he was successful, he could imagine the people on the back of the ferry.

What an idiot!

That jerk is gonna kill himself joyriding like that!

He should be arrested for that stunt!

To that last imaginary comment, kept David moving. He paddled behind a fishing boat while Luc clung to the kayak, still gagging. Heather's head appeared from above.

"Can you climb?" asked David.

"I think so," Luc gasped.

"I'll help you," Heather called down.

Luc grabbed the wooden ladder affixed to the concrete pier and pulled himself up as Heather reached down to grab a hold of him.

David paddled back out and quickly made his way back to the rental shack. As he climbed the gangway, the owner appeared, noticing that David's shirt was soaked.

"Oops?" the owner said.

"Oh, I rolled it getting back in," David laughingly replied as he rested the kayak on the rail.

"What do I owe you?"

"No charge," said the shop owner, tossing David his wallet.

He jogged the length of the pier and parking area and was consumed by the colorful mob. He popped out on the other side of Main Street and kicked into a full run. As he headed for the parking lot, the Camry whipped around the corner and stopped next to him. He jumped in the front passenger seat and Heather navigated through the twisty side streets to the highway. David's breath became a little longer and more controlled. Heather cranked the heat on full, as David could finally talk.

"How'd we do?"

"Not so good."

"What do you mean? We got him! That was so damn close!"

"He shot Luc's father."

"Scordo?"

David looked in the back seat; Luc was doubled over and crying. He shook his head.

"No, this can't be happening!"

"David," she said softly, then leaned over and whispered in his ear, "he shot at Luc, too."

"Turn around!"

"Where are we going?"

"The police! We have that guy on the ferry for the next hour and we have Luc, so we can stop this right now!"

The red Camry slowed and moved into the breakdown lane, waited for the next car to pass, and hung a U-turn.

32

Inside the station, the lobby had a glass window with a round hole in it, behind which sat an empty desk. After a moment, a man appeared in the window and spoke through the hole.

"How can I help you?"

"We were just involved in a shooting," David said succinctly.

"Stay right there!" the voice behind the glass ordered.

A moment later, the plain clothes policeman emerged through a side door.

"Come with me."

He held the door for the three and guided them into a small conference room.

"Get some blankets!" he yelled to someone in the office.

Luc had on David's fleece but was still soaked head to toe. David was half soaked, his chamois cloth shirt taking the blast of the ferry's rooster tail. He asked them to sit and said he would be right back.

"Here you go," a uniformed officer said, plying them with blankets. "How about some hot chocolate and a couple of coffees?"

Luc did not answer.

"Sure, thank you," Heather replied.

A minute later the plain clothes officer returned.

"Sorry, it's a little crazy tonight with the festival. I'm Detective Brown. First tell me your names."

David replied, looking at the others, "Heather Connor, Luc Jennings," then nodding, "David Knight."

"Tell me what happened."

Luc came to life.

"The man on the ferry shot my father!"

"What man?"

"Mr. Scordo."

The uniformed police officer returned with the coffees and hot chocolate.

"Thanks, Ron," The detective said, and looking to a shivering Luc, offered, "Why don't you take a sip of that first then we can talk some more."

They all sipped their drinks while the detective started jotting some notes. Heather looked at David. It seemed best, at least at this point, to let him continue to do the talking.

"OK, Luc, where did this happen?" the detective continued.

"On the ferry."

"The one that just left?"

"Yes!"

"And you were on it?"

"Yes."

"How do you know this man's name?"

"He knew my father, through work, I think."

"Did you actually see this man shoot your father?"

"Yes, right in front of me. My father fell."

Luc's eyes teared up.

"And how did you go overboard?"

"I jumped. He pointed the gun at me and I jumped."

"And you got him out of the water?" The detective asked, shifting his eyes to David, who had a blanket around his shoulders.

"Yes. The ferry was pulling out when it all happened."

"Luc, do you know why the man shot your father and would want to shoot you?"

Heather and David perked up. How would he explain all of that?

"No."

They looked at each other then back to Luc.

"They argued about something this morning, then he showed up here."

"Could you hear what it was about?"

"No, I was upstairs in my room."

The detective turned to Heather and David.

"How do you know this boy?"

Heather went first, "We actually just met him a week ago, in Boston, in the park."

"And did you just happen to run in to him down here?"

David chimed in, "No, we knew he was coming and thought it would be a good idea to come. I'm new to the area."

"Where are you from?"

"Alaska."

"Really? Why are you in Massachusetts?"

"I'm a student—we're students," he explained, gesturing to Heather.

"Do you know this Scordo guy?"

"Yes, we do."

The detective sat up straight.

"He has an office at the school."

"What school?"

"Brighton Latin College."

"Go on."

"I guess that's how Luc's father met him. He—Anthony Scordo—works there in some capacity, I believe."

"We have a class in the building where his office is and we met him there in the library," Heather added.

The detective stood up.

"I need to contact the port authority and the state police. The ferry will dock in Boston soon and we don't want this Mr. Scordo to leave. Then we can get formal statements from all of you."

When Detective Brown left the conference room, Heather whispered, "You told him we know Scordo?"

"Remember Martha Stewart?"

"What?"

"She went to jail for lying to the cops, not for what she did. So far, I haven't lied."

Luc looked up.

"You don't have to worry. You're a kid," David smiled.

"I need to use the bathroom," Heather said.

As Heather approached the empty receptionist's desk, she could hear Detective Brown in the lobby talking. He laughed a little as the conversation came into range. Just before they came into her view through the glass window, she stopped and listened.

"No, I am fine. He makes these stories up. See, no bullet holes. I'm afraid he's a bit of a runaway."

Heather could see the reflection of the men in the glass of a framed poster for drunk driving awareness mounted on the wall of the lobby. She could make out a long black coat and a tall man with dark hair—the man from Beacon Street!

"I had the ferry turn around and bring me back after he jumped. I could see the young man plucked him out of the water. I owe him for helping my son. He could have drowned."

Heather burst into the conference room.

"We have to get out of here!"

David got up and shed the blanket.

"Scordo's man is with the detective. He's saying he's Luc's dad and that Luc's a runaway and made the whole shooting thing up."

David poked his head out of the door and looked both ways.

"Let's go!" David saw an exit sign the opposite way down the hall. "This way," he whispered.

At the end of the hall, the door was cracked open slightly and the policeman named Ron was standing outside with another policeman, smoking cigarettes.

"Everything OK?"

"Yes, thanks. Just a little lost getting out of here," David said, "Oh, there we are," seeing the street to his left.

Luc looked up at the policeman.

"Thank you for the hot chocolate."

Heather followed in single file behind Luc.

"Thanks, we'll bring the blanket back in the morning."

They rounded the building and broke into a full run, darting through the municipal parking lot and over to the supermarket. David looked back as they got in the car. No one had come out of the police station. He put the car in gear and paused, taking a deep breath, then slowly drove out to Route 6, and headed west on the two lane highway that connects Cape Cod from end to end.

"We need to get off this road!" David said after a minute of driving.

"There's ocean on both sides of us," answered Heather. "It's the only way out of here."

"How long before they have an Amber Alert out on us?" David asked.

"Do you think they want that?" Heather responded.

"Who would have thought he would march into police headquarters claiming to be the kid's dad?" David said, shaking his head.

They drove down Route 6 monitoring the rear view mirror as much as the view ahead. After a few minutes, the two heard sobbing and turned to see Luc shivering and crying, clenching the police blanket.

What the hell are we doing? David thought. *This kid's life has just been shattered, cuz of me...*

"No one knows about this car," Heather announced.

David barely heard her, his mind replaying the scene in Scordo's office of his falling over the ottoman.

"I didn't put it down on the enrollment form."

David glanced to her, "But if they know your name and that you're from Chicago, it will show up in the computer."

"No, it won't."

"Why do you say that?"

"Cuz, I kinda forgot to register it."

David looked at her with raised eyebrows.

"Heather, well done! So whose plates are we driving around with?"

"My friend's. She junked her Corolla and let me borrow them, so these plates are still legit. I just forgot to take care of it with all of the packing and getting ready to move."

"You are forgiven," David said smiling.

"It would be better coming from him," she said, gesturing to the back seat.

33

The National Seashore Park was closed for the season, but the gate was slightly ajar. David dragged the gate far enough for the Camry to get through, then closed it all the way. They parked near two other cars in the small parking lot.

David popped the trunk and got out. Heather turned to Luc.

"Hang in there kid. We're gonna get you some dry clothes."

She got out and went to the back of the car to find David taking out some of his clothes. Heather was trembling; he hugged her.

"We need to take care of him," he said after a long moment.

Heather continued the long, tight hug.

"I have some extra sweats I grabbed at my aunt's house; they will fit him better. You wear yours."

She released David, then pulled out a large wool sweater and pulled it over her head.

"My aunt knitted this for me."

"They do treat you well," he smiled.

They got Luc into dry clothes and David then changed in to his sweats.

"Let's walk a bit," Heather said to Luc, as she put the blanket around him.

As they crossed the grassy dune that obscured the beach, they discovered small bonfires on the beach, about two hundred yards apart. They walked between them toward the water, and when the sand became smooth and wet, they turned, as the people at the fire started picking up their things and calling it a night. Heather took quick steps in their direction, as one of them started to kick sand on the fire.

"Excuse me. We can put that out for you," Heather offered.

"Enjoy," the man said and walked off into the dark toward the parking lot.

The fire was going strong and there were four or five good size pieces of firewood piled nearby. Heather signaled to the boys.

"This is good," David said to Luc as they walked to the fire.

"I'll go get the wet clothes," said Heather.

As Heather disappeared into night, David and Luc sat close to each other, positioning themselves to avoid the fire's smoke.

"Thanks for coming for me," Luc said quietly.

"I'm really sorry about what happened to your dad."

"I'm not so sure he even was my dad."

"He raised you and loved you. That's more than a lot of people get. He's your dad."

Luc rubbed tears away with the back of his fist.

"Can you tell me what happened?" David asked softly.

"I guess, I freaked," he sniffled. "I thought you guys were gone after the store. Then they lied about me going away and I just couldn't do it. My dad got in the middle of us and he shot him. It's all my fault!" he said sobbing.

"Luc, it's not your fault. That man didn't come down here to help you. I don't think either of you were going to make it back to Boston."

David put his arm around Luc to warm him up.

"Why?" Luc asked as he sniffled.

"Luc, this is all my fault. I am so sorry."

"He said you stole some documents. That's why they had to shut it down. Shut what down? I don't understand. They said it was the plan all along—for me to go back," Luc said, confused.

"I tripped and fell."

"Huh?"

"Into a bookshelf in Scordo's office, I knocked over a brief-case and mixed his papers with mine. I didn't steal them. I wish it never happened."

"Those men, the Dark Men in the long coats, they have killed other people, Luc. You must understand that this was not your fault. They are killers and we are all just stuck in the mid-dle of it. You did nothing wrong."

David held him a little tighter, squeezing his shoulder. Luc was confused, cold, and in shock. Heather returned with the wet clothes and some dead tree branches. She stuck the branches into the sand and hung the clothes on them to dry. She placed Luc's sneakers on a log close to the fire and tossed in a couple of sticks before sitting in the sand across from them.

"This blanket's kinda wet," Luc said.

Heather stuck out her hand, smiling, as he unwrapped himself from it and handed it to her. She jammed another stick into the sand and draped the blanket on it. Luc began to shiver. David took off his denim jacket and wrapped it around Luc. They both shuffled closer to the fire.

"Your core temperature must be way down after being in that cold water," said David. "If this doesn't warm you up soon, we'll have to get you to a hospital."

Heather brought out Brian's pack. She rummaged through it, then tossed each a granola bar.

"I grabbed these at my aunt's."

"You should eat," David said to Luc, who just held the bar in his hand and stared at the fire. Heather shared their one bottle of water with them.

They sat, mostly in silence, until all the logs were burnt and the fire could no longer keep them warm. Luc had responded well to the small blaze and was no longer blue-lipped or shivering. The other visitors were long gone when they finally covered the fire with sand, picked their dry clothes off the branches, and headed for the car. David let the engine warm up. Luc got in back, avoiding the wet spot and wrapped the blanket around him. As the car came up to temperature, David cranked the heat up and got out. Heather zipped up her fleece and joined David, leaning on the hood of the car; she wrapped an arm around him.

"Do you think Scordo saw us?" asked Heather.

"The other one must have been around when the whole thing went down. He showed up at the police station too quickly to have been called in."

"I can't believe they would try to kill Luc if he is, you know, the one. And after so many years of work."

"In the letters they mention it, it's like some sort of pact they made, shut it down and protect the church at all costs. Let's get out of here first thing in the morning."

Back in the warm Camry, he shut the motor off.

"Try to get some sleep," David said to Luc, "then, we'll get out of here."

"OK. It's really hot in here," Luc said softly from under the blanket.

"That's good," he encouraged.

34

The sound of the police officer's flashlight knocking on the glass startled the three of them. David jumped up, almost hitting his head on the ceiling of the car. He noticed the little digital clock on the dash said 5:45 and powered down the window. The policeman surveyed the interior of the car, then, looked at David.

"I could bust you for sleeping here, but I guess I would want my kid sleeping it off rather than driving out of that festival. You better take off before the ranger comes. You're on federal land."

Without waiting for a response, the policeman returned to his running cruiser and left.

"Quite reasonable," David said as he started up the Camry. "Everyone OK?"

"Yep," said Heather.

"Yes," said a quiet voice from the back seat.

No Amber Alert had been issued, and they noticed no police or black Buicks on their journey back along Route 6 to the bridges accessing the mainland. Luc remained quiet in the back seat, still in shock. As they approached the bridge, Heather had the road atlas open.

"Take this exit."

"Not over the bridge?"

"No, this one is the way to Boston. We'll take the other one."

"Where does that take us?"

"In a big loop around Boston up toward Maine, it looks like."

"Where are we going?" asked Luc.

"Where do you want to go?"

"Home."

"Sorry, kid."

"I know."

Had they taken the bridge, they would have driven right by the black Buick that was parked at the other end. They made their way along the canal and took the ramp up onto the second big bridge that traversed the Cap Cod Canal. As they peaked, they could see for miles up and down the canal, including the ships working their way through it.

"Get ready!" David announced. "If there's going to be a police check point or a Buick, it will be here."

As they came down the other side, they were directly behind a white Wonder Bread delivery truck.

"Oh, shit. Black Buick!" Heather yelled.

She could see it a couple hundred yards ahead, but the van blocked David's view.

"Where?"

"On the right coming up! Luc get down!"

David floored it and swerved into the left lane, cutting off another car. It honked at him. He raised his hand to gesture "sorry" as he pulled along side, using the bread van as a shield. They passed the black Buick completely shadowed. He sped up, staying cloaked as they entered Route 495.

"Do you think it was them?" asked David.

"Yeah, it had blacked out windows!" Heather said, staring in the right side rear view mirror.

"Do you think they saw us?"

"I don't think so. Nice driving."

They drove for the next 10 minutes with their eyes fixed on the mirrors.

"I think we're clear," Heather finally said.

"Where to?"

Heather looked back at him; they had no plan. All they knew is that they were northbound on a highway in Massachusetts, with no idea where they were going or what to do next. They drove on, away from Cape Cod.

"We need gas," David announced. "We'll stop at a station with a store. What do we have and what do we need? Medicine, food, drinks, batteries—anything you can think of. Only one person goes in the store. They'll have security cameras. Luc, when we pull in, I need you to get under that blanket. Heather you go in—wear the ball cap," he said, handing her a pen. "Let's make a list. I need a pack of triple A batteries."

Heather wrote it down.

"How about drinks? We should do water and Gatorade," David continued.

"Red Bull?" Heather asked with half a smile.

"OK, sure. And a roll of paper towels, toilet paper, soap or hand cleaner."

"Are we going camping?" she asked.

"You never know. Luc?"

"Yeah?"

"What's your favorite food?"

"Lobster!"

"OK, what's your favorite snack food?"

"Oh," Luc responded, disappointed. "Do hot dogs count?"

"We can get some for lunch, if they have them. Think about stuff that's packaged, for tomorrow."

"I like beef jerky and Pringles."

"There you go!"

Heather wrote down the items. "And you?" she turned to David.

"Whatever you're getting. Only with meat! I'm starving."

Heather went through Brian's pack, taking inventory.

"I think I'm good," she said. "I need a cell phone charger, but I doubt they have them here."

She unzipped the front pocket and pulled out some papers and read for a minute.

"David, check this out!"

"Whatta-ya-got?"

"It's a packing slip for UPS. It's for one duffel bag, contents: hockey gear. Value: one thousand dollars."

David looked puzzled.

"Shipped to Nova Scotia—on Friday!"

"The fiche!" David yelled, swerving then snapping the Camry back on track.

"What's going on?" Luc said from the back seat.

Heather glanced his way.

"Good stuff, Luc. Really good stuff!!" she said, smiling.

They exited the highway after a blue sign promoting facilities of fuel, food, and lodging. The first station had a large convenience store and rows of gas pumps. Luc tucked himself under the blanket.

"What side?" David asked Heather.

"Left."

He pulled up on the right side of the pump. David checked all the fluid levels of the car. They were good, thanks to Uncle Joe. He topped the tank off, squeezing the handle until it would take no more. Heather emerged with her hands full of plastic bags and a six-pack of blue Gatorades, which she stuffed on the back seat floor while Luc remained hidden under the blanket.

They pulled out fully provisioned, with Heather behind the wheel. David reached behind the driver's seat and pulled up one of the bags.

"How about a hot dog for breakfast, Luc?" David asked, as Luc emerged from under the blanket.

"Sure."

Luc smiled a little. He handed him a foil package, then reached for a Gatorade and a sandwich.

"This one's turkey," David said digging for the other sandwich.

"Both turkey."

David scrunched his eyebrows.

"You eat meat?"

"Small doses."

He split the sandwich with Heather.

As they shared their food and drink, David asked, "Anything left on that cell phone?"

"A bit," replied Heather, handing it to David.

He pressed "5."

"Hello," Brian answered.

"Hey."

"How are you guys doing!?"

"Hanging in there…"

"What's the plan?"

"Some stuff happened. We are kind of on the run."

"What stuff?"

"Not now, cuz. We are in deep shit. Listen, exactly when did you ship your hockey bag home?"

"You found my slip, huh? Friday, on the way back to the rink. Another guy who got cut was sending his stuff home, so I thought I might as well get it out of the way, why?"

"Because I stashed what those guys are looking for in the bottom of your bag. It proves everything I told you."

"Someone told me my locker got busted into, but I had nothing in there, maybe a stick."

"Yeah, we thought they got it back. Listen, I need you to meet us."

"Where? You're *not* comin' around here, are you?"

"No, we need cash, so, can I meet you at your bank at ten o'clock."

"*My* bank?"

"Yeah, my bank is in Alaska only, so I need to wire some money to you."

"What about an ATM?"

"I can only withdraw three hundred a day."

"How much do you need?"

"A lot. We need to get to that bag."

"OK. Davy, do you know Newton Corner?"

"Yeah."

"Ten, Bank of Amer—"

The phone died with a parting beep.

"Battery's gone," David said, closing the phone.

"Where to?"

"Newton."

35

They exited the Massachusetts Turnpike into the rotary of Newton Corner at 40 miles per hour.

"Jesus!" yelled David as a car cut them off. Another followed, pushing her further right. Heather accelerated and cut left, sending David's face into the door window with a grunt as she sliced between the two cars exiting the rotary and got back into her lane. She stopped alongside a green T bus. She timed it perfectly, nailing the gas as the light blinked green and crossed in front of the bus before it could accelerate. David grabbed the dash and winced as she completed the move and came to a hard stop directly in front of the bank. Heather clicked on the turn signal—a first—and put the car in reverse, slowly and perfectly easing it into the space, six inches from the curb.

"Twenty minutes early. How about coffee?" Heather said removing the key from the ignition as David looked on in horror.

"You two go in, I'll catch up in a minute," he said, slightly out of breath, releasing his death grip on the dash.

Heather placed two coffees and a chocolate drink on the table as David came into the coffee shop.

"Where did you go?"

"I tapped in at the ATM machine."

David handed Heather five twenties and gave Luc the same. The two stuffed the cash into their pockets.

"This wire transfer might take awhile, so you'll need to occupy yourselves without hanging around in public. There's a Radio Shack a few stores down. Get a couple of cell phone chargers—one for the car, one for the wall—and another battery if they have one."

"Where are we going?" asked Luc.

"Canada," Heather said softly.

"Why Canada?"

"Some of the files from Scordo's office ended up there. If we can get them and go to the police with you, it will stop all this."

"Can't we go to the police right now?"

"No, that man said he's your father and he may try to grab you and run," Heather answered.

"We're not going to let anything happen to you," added David.

"Why is all this happening? What's in the files?"

"Luc," whispered David, "It's a long, complicated story, and we have a very long drive ahead of us. I'll explain it all as soon as we get going, all right?"

Luc looked down his straw into his drink, "OK…" he said without looking up.

"David, can I use your laptop? Heather asked. "They have Wi-Fi here and I want to send my aunt an e-mail."

David pulled the computer out of his pack and slid it across the table.

"We gave our names, so the police may contact them looking for you," David advised.

"Exactly," Heather said as she started typing, her fingers moving very quickly as the keyboard rattled.

"Wow! Are you some kind of programmer?" David asked.

"Texting and Facebook," Heather replied without looking up from the screen. "Don't tell me you've never texted."

"I e-mail Brian. Does that count?"

Heather fired away at the laptop, while Luc and David watched.

"What are you saying to her?" David asked.

"I am telling her we met a kid who has a strange uncle. He needed to get to Florida, back to his parents to be safe. So, if the police question them, they will just tell the truth."

"That's good," David nodded. "Maybe send another to your roommate saying I am taking you to Florida for a romantic getaway."

Heather smiled as she continued her assault on the keyboard.

When she was done, she slid the laptop over to David.

"Do you want to check yours?"

"People know better than to try to get a hold of me that way."

"Luc?" she said sliding it back across the table.

Not knowing what to do next, Luc took the laptop and, half paying attention logged into his Yahoo account while finishing his soda. In a flash, his eyes popped wide open, the straw sticking to his bottom lip as his jaw slacked, then dropping on the table.

"What is it?" Heather asked.

"An email—from Dad," Luc said staring at the screen. "He sent it yesterday."

Luc trembled. His mind flashed to night before on the ferry, where he watched his father die right in front of him. He teared up as he opened the message, his mind now racing through the conversation he heard from behind the couch. He refocused, and read it:

> Luc,
> By the time you read this, you will be in Italy with Mr. Scordo and Cardinal Vincent. I am not sure what they

may have told you, but I will tell you in my own words, because I want you to hear it from me.

I would have told you face to face on our trip to P-Town, but I didn't for several reasons. At least I don't think I will be telling you, as I want to enjoy the day with you, my son.

What is most important, Luc it that you go to the Vatican. This may sound strange to you, but you are very special. If I attempt to explain this today, there may be confusion and the trip could be in jeopardy.

Always know that we love you very much. When your mother and I received you when you were six-months old, you were the most beautiful thing we had ever seen. I am so sorry to tell you this way, in an email, but you probably already know by now. Not being your birth parents does not matter to us one bit.

Your life started in the Vatican and the church made our family possible. We all agreed that you were so special, that you would return to the Vatican when you grew up and continue your life with God and the church. You have a journey ahead of you that is more important than you could imagine. But rather than confuse you with this knowledge, we wanted you to grow up as kid, as our child, and not worry or wonder about it.

It is time for your journey to start and we are very proud of you. That plan has not changed. What has changed is that we love you so much, that we are making arrangements with Cardinal Vincent to relocate to the Vatican to be with you, to watch you become a man and still be a family."

Tears streamed down Luc's cheeks as he continued.

I will explain it all when we get there. We are excited about moving back. I know this is a surprise to you, but when you learn of the reasons, it will all make sense, as there is nothing more important than your life and the things we are about to experience together.
We will be there soon and we can talk—and answer all the questions you must have.

Love,
Dad

Luc was frozen. The only movement was tears dripping off his cheeks and onto his shirt. Heather reached for his hand.

"I'm so sorry, Luc," she said, barely getting out the words.

What have we done? she thought, feeling his grip tighten.

Luc slid the laptop to Heather and put his head down on the table, covering himself up with his arms.

"He should be here," David whispered as he got up, then moved to the window.

When he returned, Heather was reading the e-mail, crying in silence. Luc remained with his head in his arms as Heather stood up and put her head on David's shoulder, wrapping an arm around him.

"They were all moving to the Vatican," she whispered.

David hunched forward, an invisible blow to his stomach rendered him breathless.

I did this, he thought. *I took this kid's family away from him. I am the reason his dad was murdered!*

David collapsed into his chair as Heather wiped her tears.

"Is he here?" she asked with a quick sniffle.

"Not yet," David said in a haze, not able to focus his eyes on anything.

Heather placed a gentle hand on Luc's head as she walked around him, then moved to the window. She saw Brian getting out of a blue Honda and stretching with a large yawn.

"He's here," she whispered to David, sitting down beside him.

David looked at her. His face plainly stated he did not want to go on.

"David, you didn't do this," she whispered. "There has to be another reason. They could have all just left the country if they were worried about what we saw."

"They said they would shut it down."

"Leaving Boston would have done that, you have to believe that," she pleaded. "You saved him, not hurt him."

David slowly got up, and said, "I'll get started. Check in at the bank in a little while to see how long this will take."

"What about security cameras?" Heather asked.

David looked at her, confused. His mind then snapped back to reality.

"Duh. Right! Stay outside the bank. I'll come and find you," he said, then turned and went out the door.

"You OK?" Heather asked, placing her hand on his shoulder.

Luc picked his head up. The tears had stopped for the moment.

"Yeah, I'm thirsty," he said quietly.

"I'll get you a refill," she said, forcing a smile.

36

David met them in front of the bank.

"Hey!" Sully said. "How you doin', man?"

"OK, thanks for driving Brian over."

"No sweat. Hope you're not in trouble for me poppin' that guy. I just hit him once, I swear!"

"We better get started," said Brian.

"I'm gonna grab a bagel. I'll catch up with you guys in a few," said Sully.

As he went into the coffee shop, David and Brian entered the bank and wired $9000 from his bank in Alaska. After a few minutes, Sully reappeared.

"Howzitgoin'?" Sully inquired, sipping his coffee.

"Good, they said it will be done in less than thirty minutes," Brian answered.

"You would not believe this chick that was in the coffee shop!" Sully blurted. "I am in love, man. I mean, oh my God, totally hot! She has to be six feet tall!"

David and Brian just smiled, as a bank employee approached the small group.

"Mr. Anderson, your transfer is complete."

"Wow, that was quick!" said Brian.

Brian filled out a cash withdrawal slip and walked up to the teller. He returned and handed the brown envelope to David. They quickly exited the bank, and walked over to the parked cars. Sully turned around, then did a double take.

"Oh, man here she comes!" he signaled to them.

Heather was walking with Luc down the sidewalk dangling a Radio Shack bag from her right hand. She walked right at them, staring at the three of them. David looked at Heather and could hardly blame Sully. She was beautiful in her tight jeans, Converse sneakers, and that beautiful sweater her aunt knitted. She never wore makeup, and, as far as he was concerned, looked better than girls who spent hours painting their face. She walked right up to Sully, who opened his mouth to talk, just as she turned her head to David.

"How are you making out?" she asked.

"All done."

"Great!" she exclaimed.

"Oh, this is Sully," David said with a grin.

"Hi, I'm Heather. I've heard a lot about you," she said.

"Nothin' good, I'll bet!" Sully replied, deflated and sheepish.

"You'd win!" laughed Heather. "I'm joking. Oh, this is my nephew, Jimmy."

Luc nodded then faded back behind Heather.

"We better shove off," said David.

Heather and Luc got in the car. Sully and Brian walked to the Honda where David saw Brian say something to Sully, then pull out Heather's teal daypack.

"Not a word, promise!" David heard Sully say to Brian. "Good luck, Davy!" he yelled over the Honda getting in and speeding out into the chaotic traffic of Newton Corner.

Brian walked up to David.

"What? Does my pack not match my jacket?" Brian challenged.

"You *comin'*?" David quietly asked back.

"Who's gonna explain this to my parents? Besides, those bastards will probably blow up the dorm room and I don't need to be remembered as collateral damage in your crime spree."

"You're gonna miss some school."

"Whatever."

Heather was in the driver's seat when the two got in.

"We have a new passenger," said David.

Brian flopped into the back seat, his pack landing on Luc's leg.

"Eh, sorry. Hey! You're not Heather's nephew are you? You're the Jesus kid!" Brian announced.

Heather and David gasped.

"My name is Luc."

Brian raised his fist with his thumb and index finger extended like a gun and pointed it at him.

"Gotcha!" Brian said with a wink.

Luc looked at David from behind the driver's seat.

"Why did he call me that?"

David let out a sigh, "I can't imagine there ever will be a good time to talk about this."

He grabbed the lever on the side of the seat and reclined until he hit Brian's knees with the seatback. Brian realized his gaff and what was about to happen, allowing David to recline more so he could turn and talk directly to Luc. Heather drove as David started.

"Luc, what do you know about DNA?"

"We learned about it in school. Uh, it's the secret code that makes up a person or animal. It's your genes."

"Right. Well, back before you were born, these people your father knew in the Vatican got a hold of some DNA samples that were very old. They got them from artifacts. You know about the Shroud of Turin?"

"Yes, they taught me in CCD."

"Those kinds of artifacts. They got some DNA from Jesus and his brother James.

"Jesus had a brother? They never taught us that."

"Yeah, he did. They used the DNA samples in an experiment to make two babies—two baby boys."

Luc just stared at the back of Heather's seat. The silence hung as Heather drove as smoothly as she could down the turnpike. Luc thought about the birth certificate with the two names on it. Then the e-mail and the comments about his being special and doing God's work in the Vatican. He knew where this was going. His eyes opened wider.

"The experiments worked, but the people who did it swore to keep it a secret forever, no matter what. That's when your father and mother brought you to the US to raise you."

"Then who are my real parents!?"

That's kind of tricky. You were brought into this world by a young nun named Sarah, so she would be your birth mother."

"And, my dad…who is my father!?" he demanded.

"Luc, your parents are the people you know, who love you and raised you. That you have them makes you luckier than most people."

"Had," Luc said softly.

"I'm really sorry, Luc," David apologized.

Luc started to sob uncontrollably.

"Shit," David muttered.

After a minute of sniffling, Luc looked up.

"So, I have two mothers, my mom and Sister Sarah, right?" Luc said, almost sounding encouraged as he tried to make sense of the bizarre tale.

"That's one way to look at it."

"Then do I have two fathers?"

"Uh, no."

"Then my dad was my real dad."

"Well, no…"

"Then, who?"

"Scientifically speaking?"

"Yeah, huh? I guess."

"Joseph," David offered tentatively.

"Who? Oh! What? You mean Jesus and I are brothers?"

"More like perfect, identical twins," David said, thinking that it was about the most sense he had made yet. "But, just maybe, that is. We don't know whose DNA you have, Jesus' or his brother, James'."

"And that kid Bryce Jones, on the other birth certificate, is the other one?" Luc asked with interest.

"Yes. Bryce has one set of genes and you have the other, so you two are also brothers, by the way of your genes, your DNA." David added.

Brian maintained his silence, taking it all in for the first time, while Heather drove on.

"The files from Scordo's office explained what happened. After you and Bryce were born, they moved you both away, I guess to have a normal life with a family until you made your confirmation. Your going back to Italy was part of the plan."

"What was supposed to happen when I went there?"

"We're not sure. They would decide once you were there. Scordo was in charge of the secret and kept an eye on both of you while you grew up. But then I tripped over the files and they decided to, well…"

"Shut down the project," Luc finished, looking down at the floor. "That's what Scordo said to my father."

"That's what seems to be going on. They're afraid of what might happen if the secrets got out," David quietly replied.

"So, *I* am the project."

37

There were no police waiting for them at the New Hampshire border, leading David to think Heather's lapse in responsibility had paid off.

The Camry had traveled for some time without a word from its passengers, only the occasional sniffle from Luc. Brian had looked through the plastic bags and offered paper towels in lieu of a tissue. There was not much anyone could say to cheer him up or help him comprehend what he was told an hour earlier.

"Pit stop!" Heather announced, as she exited from the middle lane when she spotted the New Hampshire State Liquor Store and rest area.

"I'll take Luc in," said Brian.

"No, I will," said David. "Best to keep you disconnected from us on any security cameras."

Brian hopped out and jogged into the store.

"Can we call my mom?" Luc asked.

"Yes, when we get to Canada," David replied. "We all might be wanted for questioning and we need to get the evidence to protect us—especially you. Besides, Luc, we don't want her alarmed or running home into danger."

This was too much for Luc. The pain of what he had just experienced overwhelmed him; the thought of his family now gone was unbearable.

"I don't wanna to go to Canada. I want to go home!" Luc cried. "I don't want to be special! I just want to go home and see my mother! I want this to end—now!"

"I'm sorry Luc," Heather offered, "It's just not that simple. We believe you will be in danger if we stop now."

"I am only in danger because of you! Who are you people anyway? Why did you come?!"

David's heart sunk at the comment. It was true. Had this not happened, they would still be a family, on their way to the Vatican, probably to watch their adopted son grow up to be a cardinal, or pope. It could have all been that simple—until he decided to butt in.

"Luc," Heather pleaded, "that man Scordo, he has killed other people. The Dark Men are murderers. You cannot be safe if they have you."

The comment was for David as much as it was for Luc.

"I don't believe any of this, I just want to go back to my house and see my mom!"

He stopped, then whispered, "and my dad…"

He cried for a bit while David and Heather remained silent. David never felt worse. Heather had to keep it together, as she knew this was killing him.

After a long moment, Luc, wiped his eyes and blew his nose.

"I'm sorry. I know he's a bad man," he said. "I just wish I could go home."

"I will get you home, Luc," David softly said, the pain of what he heard still in his gut. "Just give me one day and we will call your mother and I will take you to her. I promise."

Brian returned with a big bag of Kettle Corn popcorn. He jumped in the back and ripped the bag open, spilling some, then offered the bag to Luc, who shook his head.

"You obviously never had Kettle Corn before," he said, gesturing with the bag. "Come on—it's salty and sweet. See, like it says on the bag."

Luc stuck his hand in and pulled out a few pieces. He chewed them, then smiled a little at Brian. Brian held the bag out and smiled back, popping his eyebrows twice, while Luc grabbed as much as his hand could hold.

Heather came back from the restroom and replaced David in the passenger seat. When David and Luc returned, David assumed the pilot's role. He started the car, but before he put it into *Drive*, he pulled out the brown envelope. There were nine, thousand dollar packets; he handed $2000 to each of them and stuffed the last three packets in his fleece vest pocket.

"In case we get split up. Brian, give everyone your address and home phone. That's where we need to end up."

They all stared at the money. Then, one by one, they zipped it away.

"This is some of your tuition money, isn't it?" Brian asked.

"Yeah, for next semester. Somehow I feel it's available..."

"I didn't think you wired this much," Brian said.

I would have done more, but when you pull ten grand, the IRS and Homeland Security get notified, and we gave our names to that cop in Provincetown.

"More?"

"Yeah, look! We have just one chance to do this right. Who knows what they will do next. And besides, with the shit that just went down on the Cape, *It's only money,* applies, no?" David said as he put the car in gear and got back on the highway. "Besides, I expect the unspent cash back..."

His last remark forced smiles as the red Camry finished its cut across the 20 miles of New Hampshire seacoast, and on to Maine and Canada.

Brian chuckled a little.

"What?" David said, looking at him in the rear view mirror.

"Nothin. I just was thinking how while you were out on that king crab boat last summer making all this money, you probably never would have guessed it could be more dangerous spending it!"

"Way true, cousin, way true," David replied with a hint of a laugh.

Interstate 95 split left as the road approached the small coastal city of Portsmouth, New Hampshire. In seconds they were climbing the big arched bridge that spans the Piscataqua River. The green bridge was tall enough to allow ships to pass underneath and provided a spectacular view to the right: the city, the river working its way to the sea, and on its east bank, the southernmost part of Maine.

"Toll! Anyone got any singles?" David requested a mile after the bridge. Heather pulled some cash from her pocket and handed it to David. The Camry chugged its way back up to speed as the highway shrunk back to three lanes, the long, gradual incline making it obvious the little car was carrying a full load. As they crested the hill, just behind a brown sign with tourist information about Moosehead Lake sat a filthy silver Buick, the windshield blacked out from where the wipers had cleaned it. Heather glanced to David who was also looking at it. The dirty car looked abandoned.

"Thank God it's not black," she quietly said.

David sighed and nodded in agreement.

The car lurched forward.

"Hey, it's the car from the rectory!" Brian announced, as the Buick started up the breakdown lane.

"I thought they were all black!" David yelled back, startled.

"Two black, one silver. I went over and checked them out like you said to. That one was in the back of the garage. Did you see? It was all covered with dust and pigeon shit!"

David stomped the gas pedal; the little Camry accelerated as best it could, moving to the fast lane around a tractor trailer truck.

"Are you sure it's them!?" David yelled back to Brian.

"Who do you think wrote '*WASH ME!*' on the fender?"

They put a hundred yards between them and the truck, then pulled back into the middle lane. In the right rear view mirror, the Buick was visible alongside the tractor trailer and coming fast.

"David!" Heather yelled.

"I see him!"

David floored it again, but the little motor barely accelerated. They hit 85 miles per hour when the silver Buick came up on their right side.

"DAVID!" cried Heather.

"It's not like they're gonna shoot—" Brian started to say, just as his window exploded into a million little nuggets of safety glass, falling on him and blowing around in back of the car.

"What the?"

David lost control of the car, slamming Brian into the door, his head bobbing out of the now missing window.

The car skidded over the rumble strip and onto the grass before David wrenched the wheel to the right, jerking the car back onto the pavement, screeching across all three lanes and flying off the other side of the highway.

At this point David gave up trying to get back on the road and concentrated on not flipping the car, which was now bouncing down the bumpy, grassy slope toward a small dirt road lined with a chicken wire fence. He steered the car directly between two metal fence posts and braced himself. The impact pulled the fence posts out of the ground and the fence was squashed under the tires. He aimed for the dirt road, but hit a huge bump sending them into the air.

The car slammed down onto the road, shedding the two right side hub caps, then, David quickly spun the wheel to the right, pulling the emergency brake. The car skidded until it was facing back down the road; David slapped down the emergency brake and hit the accelerator, leaving skid marks in the dirt as the Camry sped away in the direction from which it had come.

On the highway, the silver Buick had pulled over to the side of the road. A man in a black overcoat opened the door and stepped out, his gun still clutched in his right hand, and watched the red car drive off into the dense woods.

The tractor trailer truck pulled up behind the Buick and stopped. The Dark Man quickly stuffed the gun into his coat pocket as a beer-bellied man in a white tee shirt, jeans, and Chicago Cubs cap leapt from the cab and stared after the Camry, which had disappeared from sight.

"What was that all about?" the truck driver asked, stunned.

"Kids, I think their tire blew out," he replied.

"Wow, they got lucky. Could have hit something hard," the driver said shaking his head. He climbed back into the semi and drove away.

The Dark Man also got back into his car, but before pulling away, he leaned back and grabbed a map from a pocket behind the passenger's seat.

38

"Everyone OK?" asked Heather after a minute of silence.

There was a general muttering of assent from the back, which died out into another stunned silence.

"So, where to now?" David asked. "Brian, you know these roads better than anyone, right?"

"No, just the highways," he apologized.

"Is that safe?" asked Heather.

"Well, we could just take back roads and follow the highway," offered David.

"Sounds good to me," said Brian.

David stopped the car at the end of the dirt road, next to the Town Forest Service Road sign.

"Bang a Louie!" yelled Brian.

David looked back at him, slightly squinting. Brian rolled his eyes.

"Take a left," Brian explained.

They took a left onto a paved road and then another left onto a main road.

"Let's take another left," suggested Heather, "We need to find the highway."

After a short minute, they crossed the Town Forest Service Road and went underneath the highway. Instinctively, they all looked up at the overpass, watching for silver among the cars that flew by.

CRASH!

The Buick came out of nowhere, ramming the right side of the car, just behind Brian's door. The force of the impact crushed the rear quarter panel, sent the red plastic tail light lens flying, and flung the trunk open. Heather and Brian's head's were slammed into the side pillars of the car as it spun completely around. They all grunted as the two cars came to an abrupt stop in opposite directions, with both passenger sides touching. Brian's missing window was lined up with the Buick's front passenger window. He dove on Luc, forcing both himself and Luc down as the blacked out window disintegrated with the sound of a pop, revealing a pistol with a silencer pointing at them. A second shot shattered Luc's window on the other side as David slammed on the gas, disconnecting the two vehicles. The Camry came to life and pulled away, the trunk lid flapping off of the pushed in quarter panel as the car accelerated. The Buick spun its wheels in reverse, spinning around to make a two point U-turn.

"What are you doing?" yelled Heather as David turned left onto the Town Forest Service Road.

"How should I know!?" David shouted back over the sound of the car downshifting as he floored it.

"Here he comes!" exclaimed Luc.

David looked in the rear view mirror. The silver Buick, now missing a grill, was a hundred yards back and gaining.

"Can't this thing go any faster?" asked Brian, looking over his shoulder.

"I'm flooring it! Watch him Brian!" he yelled, with two hands firmly on the wheel, navigating the tight, winding dirt road. "What do you see!?"

"Thirty feet and closing!" Brian reported, watching the one-eyed, grill-less Buick through the cloud of dust the Camry threw up as it slid through the turns.

They sped down the dirt road, sand and dust flying out behind them, but the silver Buick kept closing the distance.

"What's that!?" asked Heather, peering out the front windshield and leaning forward to get a better look.

"I don't know," said David, squinting at the strange object that seemed to be in the road.

"A bridge!" David realized.

"He's on us!" Brian yelled.

He looked in the right mirror: *Objects in Mirror Are Closer Than They Appear.* As he read it, the mirror disappeared and was replaced with the Buick's front fender as the cars collided with a bang. David gripped the wheel harder, gaining a little on the swerving Buick.

The bridge was just one lane, spanning a river. The sides were lined with wood posts connected by steel cables, making guardrails. Heather glared at David as they both saw it was much too narrow to fit both cars.

The Camry was forced to the left side of the road as the Buick came up alongside of it. Heather ducked as the Buick's window drew up, but there was no need: The Dark Man had two hands on the wheel for maximum control, the cars bouncing off one another, neither able to force the other off the loose dirt road. As they reached the bridge, David unexpectedly jerked the car to the left at the same time the Buick moved to ram them off the road. The veering of the Camry left nothing to hit, causing the Buick to careen wildly left just as it met the bridge, snapping the first post and riding up the support cables and over the posts. The collision ripped off the oil pan, and, as the car slid along, the cable on metal contact shot sparks out the back like a skate sharpener.

David slammed on the brakes as the Camry spun 180 degrees down a sandy incline toward the river, then jolted to a stop on the gravel bank. They all looked up at the bridge as flames appeared from under the front of car and quickly spread across the underbelly, licking the sides. The Buick sat motionless as fire engulfed it. Suddenly, the wooden post under it snapped, dropping the car on its side, leaving it slung in the cables. After a moment of hesitation, the car, now ablaze, flipped over and smacked the water with its roof, causing a gigantic splash around the fire. In another moment, it was gone from sight. For three full seconds nothing happened until a deep, muted thud and a bright flash came from under the water. David and Heather jerked back in surprise. The gas tank had exploded. The water where the car had vanished bubbled and fizzed.

"We should get out of here," Brian calmly stated.

Wordlessly, David put the car in gear and pressed the accelerator. The car moved, then stopped as the engine revved, and the tires spun.

"We're stuck in the sand," Heather said, "Brian, come help me push!"

Heather found some sticks and put them around the front wheels and then she and Brian together pushed the car until it was out of the sand. They both jumped back in without the Camry stopping.

Brian said, "The highway's lookin' good to me."

Minutes later, the beat up Camry with its trunk lid bumping up and down, hubcaps missing, and two windows gone, climbed back up onto the northbound side of Interstate 95.

39

The Camry limped into Portland, Maine, its occupants still rattled and now cold from traveling the last hour on the highway without rear windows. David parked in the furthest spot from the street in a small municipal parking lot.

"Wipe it down!" David commanded.

Without words, everyone moved quickly, grabbing their belongings.

Brian and Luc stuffed all of the loose food and drink into the daypacks and grabbed the grocery bags of provisions. Heather unplugged her fully charged cell phone, stuffing the charger in her pack, and looked around. The back seat had popcorn and glass all over it.

"Nice," she said, observing the mess in her once immaculate car.

"Looks better than the outside," Brian retorted, then reached into his shirt collar and produced a nugget of safety glass and held it between two fingers. After briefly examining it, he flicked it into the front seat.

As David moved to get out, he unclipped his seat belt, held it out away from his body and let it go. It dropped onto his lap, rather then rewinding and stowing itself on the side of the seat. He turned and saw that the retract mechanism, located an inch from his head, was split in half. Looking closer, he spotted shiny metal, the back of a nine-millimeter slug lodged in the headliner between the plastic pieces. He said nothing and got out.

Brian grabbed a tee shirt out of the teal daypack and started wiping off every hard surface inside the car. He then walked around the outside of the car rubbing the body, taking extra time on the door handles, mirrors and window frames.

At the back of the car, Heather lifted the wobbly trunk lid and looked for valuables, then closed it, though it would not catch. Brian wiped down the trunk lid after her. David removed the Illinois license plates with his Leatherman tool.

They all regrouped behind the car, then David finally spoke.

"Ready?"

The rest nodded and they moved out, abandoning Heather's little red Camry.

They walked down the side streets of Portland, working their way toward the water. Brian ducked into a gift shop and reappeared with a brochure on the Fast Cat to Nova Scotia.

"Sixty bucks," Brian read. "Let's see, here's the schedule. One leaving at three, that's a half hour."

"Let's go," said David.

The four marched on, toward the harbor. Portland's downtown was busy, cluttered with bars, restaurants, and shops catering to tourists. As they descended the slope toward the ocean, the sidewalks filled with shoppers forced them to weave in and out of the foot traffic. Now at sea level, they traveled away from the shops and crowds, toward the ferry terminal a quarter-mile down. As they walked, David pulled out a license plate from his fleece, wiped it down with the end of his sleeve, and slipped it into a storm drain without breaking his stride. David looked about for witnesses, then deposited the second plate in the next drain.

"We better hurry," Brian announced when the parking lot came into view.

David stopped, signaling to the others to do the same. Looking around, he spotted what he was looking for: three security cameras, positioned at different angles on the tall light poles in the parking lot.

"Up there!" he motioned. "All right, we need to split up here," he ordered. "Heather and Luc, you guys stick together. Find a family and get in line for tickets behind them. Make it look like you're with them. Go now, we'll follow."

Heather put on the black cap and pulled up the collar on her denim jacket as she and Luc stepped out into view and entered the main gate, heading for the crowd at the ticket window 200 yards away.

"OK, we're just a couple of college kids visiting Nova Scotia for the weekend," David said. "Let's go!"

Traversing the parking lot, it was the first time they had been alone.

"How'd you know to send them with a family like that?" Brian asked.

"That's how I snuck into the county fair," David confessed.

"Wait until my mom hears about that one!" Brian threatened.

"Look, they killed his father on the P-town ferry last night," David interrupted.

Brian looked back with his eyes wide open.

"No friggin' way!"

"Shot him right in front of the kid. Then shot at the kid, but he dove into the bay."

"Awe, Je-sus!" Brian exclaimed.

"We've been running from them since. They have some kind of orders to shut this cloning operation down and that means no evidence whatsoever."

Brian was speechless. They parked themselves on a bench 50 feet from the crowded ticket window. From there, David and Brian looked on as Heather and Luc stood in line behind a boisterous family of six, bought their tickets, and followed the family onto the Cat, the ferry was enormous compared to the one feeding Provincetown. The two cousins stood up and casually walked over to the ticket line, talking animatedly, reliving the best parts of the most recent Pats game, while their eyes monitored the crowd and parking lot, looking for a dark overcoat or a black Buick, or the police. They bought two one-way tickets and walked up the gangway onto the deck of the Cat.

Inside, walking to the front of the boat, David and Brian passed Heather and Luc who were sitting in two of the airport-style chairs facing the rear. David caught Heather's eye and mentioned loudly to Brian that they should go to the bar and get something to drink.

"Two Cokes please," said Brian to the bartender, as he and David slid onto two of the padded, leather stools at the bar. They sipped their drinks and talked about the Patriots' chances against the Bengals, agreeing the spread would easily be covered. Heather and Luc slid into seats next to them and ordered.

"Hey," Heather murmured as the bartender went to the far end of the bar to serve more customers.

"How you guys holding up?" whispered David as he glanced at Luc who was staring down into the Doctor Pepper he held with both hands.

"He's still pretty shaken up," Heather replied in an undertone.

"Me too," Brian whispered back, talking more to himself than to them. "You guys didn't tell me they had guns and were shooting you one by one. That teal backpack didn't look so bad on me that I had to die to get mine back."

Heather ignored him. "All right, so we should probably split up for the ride. It's going to be five hours, give or take. I'll take Luc to the back where we can sit and watch the wake of the ferry. I came on with the bags of food and stuff, so I should keep them. You guys find something else to do. We can meet once we're off the boat."

"Oh, I know a great little coffee and sandwich shop near the docks," Brian chimed in. "Just take a right outta the parking lot and it's on the left. It's called Papa's."

"Okay, see you there," said Heather, slapping five dollars on the counter and dragging Luc, who was still clutching his full can of soda.

"Well, there *is* a casino on this boat," informed Brian.

"Let's kill a little time," David replied. They parked themselves at neighboring slot machines, each with a hundred dollars in tokens. The buzz of the casino allowed them to talk privately while they played.

"So how did this all happen?" asked Brian.

"Bet slowly, it's along story."

David brought him up to speed while Brian gambled away David's tuition money. Brian heard about the putting together of the puzzle with the microfiche, the two trips into Boston, and the mad dash to Provincetown where they watched Glen Jennings die.

David blindly put in coins and kept pulling the lever as he told the story.

"All because of my friggin' economics test!" David said, as he yanked the lever extra hard. "They never would have come and none of this would have happened."

"Don't be so sure," Brian said. "They could have done their worst without you knowing. You said they were going to Italy for his confirmation. No tellin' what would have happened once they were over there. They could have killed them all, including the mother."

"Maybe. It just looks like I put the whole thing in motion— the wrong way. All I know, is I have to fix it for this kid."

"You already have, cuz." Brian paused, "He's still alive because of you."

David nodded, unconvinced.

"And, it looks like I owe you fifty bucks," he said, counting the remains of his tokens.

David smiled at Brian. He had a knack for making people smile.

"No worries," David said looking down at his machine's coin tray, "looks like I'm up a hundred."

Heather sat with Luc, watching the twin rooster tails of the high speed catamaran, much in the way a campfire hypnotizes its guests.

"I want to go home," Luc said, pulling a blanket up around his chest and semi-reclining in the seat.

Heather put an arm around him.

"You will. David promised. I promise. We are almost there. When we get off the ferry you can do whatever you want. We need to get to the film; it will protect us all. But if you want to go to the police, call your mom, or just walk away, you can. You have been through a lot Luc. No one expects anything from you.

You can do what you want and we will support you—help you, if that's what you wish. It's your call. It's not fair what happened to you."

"Not fair that I am a clone?"

"Not fair that a boy should have his father taken from him, especially that way."

Luc stared out the windows at the ocean going by at a fast clip. He was not who he thought he was.

"What do I do, Heather? I mean, what am I supposed to do? I am supposed to be so special, but I don't feel it. Should I do something religious? I don't feel very religious right now."

Heather pulled him closer.

"Like I said, no one expects you to do anything or be anyone other than Luc Jennings. And when this is over and we get you to your mother, remember that. No one, no man in a dark coat with a gun, no crazy cardinal, no nosy college students, no one can make you become something you are not. So don't feel you have to. And don't be afraid that you have to. Luc, you are special in that you are Luc Jennings, a great fourteen year old boy, with a pretty good side arm."

"I'd like to be playing catch right now," he said.

"Me too," Heather replied, slightly tightening her grip.

Luc accepted the one-armed hug and stayed close to Heather, as the rooster tails continued their endless plumes of water, gradually lulling him to sleep.

40

Yarmouth sits at the south end of Nova Scotia and, though it has the closest proximity to the US and is the ferry port, it remains a small fishing town. Tourist dollars come from the people who start and end their Nova Scotia vacations here, putting their cars onto the ferry rather than driving the 10 hours via the mainland.

Only a small portion of the town had been built up; most looked straight out of a time capsule a hundred years prior. A cluster of fishing boats occupied the inner harbor, surrounded by weather beaten, clapboard houses, making up the small neighborhoods of fishing families.

It was almost 9:00 when Heather and Luc reached Papa's Diner, which was closed. A few doors down stood Mac's Pub. They found Brian and David at the bar, each with a 16-ounce draft beer.

"Eighteen is legal up here," said Brian.

"Good! I'll have one of those," said Heather, dropping the grocery bags on the floor.

"You want anything, Luc?"

He shook his head.

Brian apologized, "A big 'Duh!' on the coffee shop being closed. I spaced on what time we would arrive. After six, this is the only place in town open."

They finished their beers and Brian stood up.

"Ready?"

"Yep," David replied standing up and grabbing his pack.

Heather looked at Luc and waited for a response.

He looked her straight in the eyes.

"OK."

At 9:30 they were standing in front of Brian's parent's house.

"This oughta be good," Brian said.

"Brian?" Ruth exclaimed, stepping back in disbelief, then hugging him.

She looked over his shoulder to see the rest of the group.

"David!" she said as she squeezed Brian tight. "You too? What brings you all the way up here?"

Mr. Anderson appeared, having heard what was going on at the front door.

"Hey, kiddo!" he exclaimed.

Ruth released him, then hugged David.

John then received Brian with a hug and a pat on the back.

"Come in! Come in!" John said to the group.

They all move into the house, David starting the introductions as Aunt Ruth closed the front door.

"This is Heather Connor and Luc Jennings," he said, "and these are the Andersons, Ruth and John."

They exchanged handshakes as they spread out into the den.

"So why are you here?" Aunt Ruth asked again.

"We were in the neighborhood and thought we'd stop in," Brian laughed.

"Ha, ha," Ruth said sarcastically.

"It's a long story, Mom."

"Is there a short version?" she smiled.

They all stood in the Andersons' den in a circle, still with their coats on, everyone focusing on Brian.

"Eh, sure, Mom," he said. "Ya see there is this death squad from the Vatican chasing us. They won't stop till we're all dead, so we had to flee the country and hide here."

Ruth paused, then, looked very serious.

"Oh, very funny! David how do you put up with him in that little dorm room?"

They all looked at each other and chuckled, even Luc, as they knew they were about to blow Aunt Ruth's mind.

"Who would like something to drink? Please, have a seat," Aunt Ruth insisted, ignoring Brian's joke.

"Is my hockey bag here?"

"It arrived today," Brian's father said. "I'm really sorry son. I know you had big hopes to make the team."

"Thanks, Dad. It's not the end of the world."

"It needs a good washing, if you know what I mean," Aunt Ruth said as she went into the kitchen, "so I put it in the basement."

"More like gasoline and a match," Heather mumbled under her breath.

"You got that right!" Aunt Ruth laughed as she came out of the kitchen with some bottles of cold water.

"Be right back," Brian said walking to the cellar door.

"It's in the bottom," David said, then turned to Aunt Ruth before she could repeat the obvious. "Luc could use a shower. Well I guess we all could. Would that be alright?" David asked, thinking Luc did not need to hear this story again.

"Sure, no problem!"

Aunt Ruth put down a basket of potato chips and a dish of mixed nuts, and guided Luc upstairs.

David started in with his uncle. He decided the original, illegitimate child of someone high up in the clergy theory would be best believed, with the addition of Glen's murder.

"Oh my God!" cried Aunt Ruth as she came back in the middle of David explaining how they shot his father in cold blood. "You mean, he wasn't joking? How could that be!?"

"The boy is the illegitimate child of someone in the Vatican, who has a couple of mafia types trying to snuff out the whole story," John succinctly explained to Ruth.

"One of them is now claiming to be Luc's father," David continued, "and that he's a runaway and we're helping him. If we go to the police, they may get their hands on him, and we're certain they will kill him if they do. They've already tried a couple of times."

"To kill that boy?!" Aunt Ruth gasped. "And what about you?" she asked, her eyes darting back and forth between David and Heather.

"And us," added Heather.

"My word! We need to go to the police right away!" cried Aunt Ruth.

"Not so fast," said Mr. Anderson. "David is right. If the police think this guy is the kid's father, then as far as they're concerned, this is kidnapping with international border crossing. And, even if you do explain it, to your point, they will get their opportunity to grab the kid while they sort out the truth."

"Exactly," said David.

"What do we do? We must do something!" pleaded Aunt Ruth.

Brian appeared from the basement holding the microfiche.

"What's that?" asked Mr. Anderson.

"Evidence. A set of documents about who Luc is and what they have done over the years," said David, as he took it from Brian and zipped it into his chest pocket, patting it as it was back where it belonged. "I got it by mistake. My mistake is what started this whole mess. I need to fix it for him. I can't let this end with him unsafe."

Luc entered the room, bathed and with a fresh set of sweats on.

"They're a little big," he said.

"They're Brian's old high school sweats; you look like a new man, Luc," replied Aunt Ruth.

"Thank you," he replied.

"Heather, would you like to go next? Why don't you all take turns and I can do a big load of laundry."

"Is anyone hungry?" Mr. Anderson asked. "It's only ten, why don't I throw some steaks on the grill while we figure things out."

41

Heather opted for the shower, while David, Brian, and Luc followed Mr. Anderson out onto the large back patio. Aunt Ruth disappeared to get more clean clothes ready.

John dropped three large steaks onto the gas grill, twisted the knobs up full, then went to the edge of the patio and grabbed two handfuls of sticks from a pile and put them in an outdoor fireplace centered on the stone patio.

"We invited the neighbors over for a cookout tomorrow. We can always get more of these. I love steak. How 'bout you?" Mr. Anderson said, smiling at Luc.

Luc nodded and smiled a little. He stared off into the evening sky, which was clear and covered with stars.

"They will come here soon," he calmly said.

"You think so?" Mr. Anderson asked, as he splashed lighter fluid on the pile of wood and tossed a match, exploding the pile into a small, roaring fire.

"They found us before," Brian said.

David looked at his uncle, who was inspecting the steaks.

"They'll figure out who Brian is and why we headed north. Or maybe that's why they were waiting for us in Maine," David added. "It won't take them long. The car we ditched in Portland will confirm we're here."

As the fire grew, they sat on the benches that circled the fire pit, orienting themselves to the center.

"This is all very confusing and sounds dangerous!" exclaimed Aunt Ruth as she put a winter coat around Luc, who was still damp from his shower.

"I'm sorry about this big mess I caused," David apologized, "and by being here we are dragging you into it. We're going tomorrow—to get Luc to his mother. We will figure out the rest after that."

"Nonsense, we're here to help. This is now a family matter!" declared Mr. Anderson as he turned over the steaks. "We will take care of Luc and you kids."

As he poked at the meat, Aunt Ruth looked on.

"What are you serving with them, John?" she asked.

"More steaks!"

Aunt Ruth disappeared into the kitchen shaking her head at her husband's menu. Mr. Anderson moved closer to David, who sat closest to the grill, the crackling of the fire providing a little privacy.

"How many people make up 'they'?"

"Not sure. It looks like a few people in the US and maybe more in Italy. One was killed in Maine."

"What?!"

"Chasing us today—crashed."

"My God! You *have* been through the wringer!" exclaimed Uncle John.

Heather appeared with wet hair and a fresh set of clothes. Her black jeans and sweat shirt were a little baggy, obviously Brian's. She zipped up her down vest and sat the bench with Luc.

"Steaks are ready! Do you want to go in or eat out here?"

"This is good, thank you," said Heather, accepting her plate." Oh, that's too much! I can split it with Luc."

She put half of her steak on Luc's already loaded plate as it went by.

Aunt Ruth brought out a large bowl of salad with two types of dressing and a large plastic cup full of knives and forks.

"Here you go," she said, handing Heather a knife, fork and napkin, which she put down, helping herself to a large portion of salad.

"Are you sure you want to eat out here? It's kind of chilly," she asked.

"It's nice next to the fire," Heather replied.

After serving the rest, Mr. Anderson plated the remaining beef and shut off the grill, then joined the circle around the fire. As Aunt Ruth started the relay around the patio with the dressing bottles, Mr. Anderson sat and helped himself to a piece of steak.

"All right then, folks," Mr. Anderson addressed the group, chewing a piece of meat. "So we need to get this boy to his mother ASAP. Where is that?"

"California," David replied.

"OK, we can get a flight out of Halifax in the morning. Who's going?"

"I will take him," David answered, "but those guys are coming, maybe we should all go."

"Maybe not, cuz," Brian answered. "If we split up, they won't be able to get us. And we can drop your evidence off at the FBI, or somewhere safe—even the media."

Heather looked at Brian. The plan was sound—very sound. Brian looked back at her.

"What? Just because I have teal pack doesn't make me a dope. I told you—I'm a great guy!"

"That's good," David said. "But where will you go?"

"We have to save my brother!" Luc cried, standing up and looking at everyone over the flames. "If we go to the police, they will kill him!"

Luc's statement shocked everyone. Until now he had been a victim in a bizarre nightmare, one that had unraveled in just two days and dragged him from Boston to Canada. He stood as tall as he could.

"You knew you had to save me. It's the same with Bryce!"

Luc was almost angry with his claim; the unspoken part of the conversation was now in play.

"Who is Bryce?" asked Mr. Anderson, putting some larger sticks in the fire, which was doing its job in the 45 degree air.

"There were two kids, Uncle John."

"My brother's name is Bryce."

"Luc, I don't think he's had time to deal with Bryce," David said. "There's a letter we found on the film. Scordo was watching over both of you."

"*Is* the other kid in danger?" John whispered.

"I think as long as we have the film and are running he is," David replied quietly.

"Luc," Heather said, "is that what you want?"

Luc looked at her. She said on the ferry she would support any decision he made. He now realized his outburst was a decision—a decision he made unconsciously. He stared at the fire.

What do *I want? What do I want to do? How can I end this?*

As he stood like a statue in front of the fire, they could only imagine what was going through his mind. They had all been through a lot, but Luc's world had been shattered—and there would be no recovery. His life as he knew it was gone, and there was only confusion and death in the one he was now living. And he was just a kid.

"Yes, it is what I want," he calmly said without shifting his focus from the fire. "It is what you did for me."

A long moment passed; Luc remained motionless.

"What about your mom?" David asked. "We should get you in touch with her. She needs to know."

Luc continued looking into the fire—it was easier to speak to the flames than the people.

"My mother is in California," he said in a monotone. "She will only be in danger if she comes home."

He paused, thinking about how devastated she will be when she hears the news. He inhaled and continued.

"She doesn't know anything about the project. Those men know that, so she is safe if I stay away from her. They must be watching her, thinking that's where I will go. If I show up or contact her, they will kill her."

David could not believe what he was hearing. Luc was calm and calculating, reasoning his options in a plot to murder his own family!

Luc paused, then raised his head and looked around him.

"*Anyone* I am with will be killed," he said, putting them all on notice.

"If we can get to England," Brian started.

"You've done enough, Brian," interrupted Heather. "Really, you don't need any more of this. You should just go back."

"Back to what?"

"This has got to end," she muttered, lowering her head.

"We must go, Heather," Luc said. "Bryce probably doesn't even know what's happening," he added, looking at her squarely, "At least I had a chance, because of you…"

Mr. Anderson stood up.

"Your brother is in England you say?"

Luc nodded. Mr. Anderson excused himself and closed the slider behind him.

"I made a pot of decaf," announced Aunt Ruth.

"Sounds nice," said Heather.

"Yes, thanks," David added.

"Luc?"

"Three sugars please."

David collected the plates, silverware and leftover steak and followed Aunt Ruth to the kitchen.

Luc, Heather and Brian sat in silence around the fire. It was only a couple of minutes when Mr. Anderson returned.

"There is a freighter heading for Liverpool. I can get you on it."

Luc jumped up, "Really!?"

David and Aunt Ruth returned with the coffee service.

"My friend owns the ship. I give him a lot of business. He's just about ready to leave."

"Where are we going?" asked David.

"England," Heather replied.

"I was only gone for a minute," David mumbled. "How long to get there?"

"Ten to twelve days, depending on weather."

"That's too long. Once they realize we've gone, they can fly there."

"What if we delay them at this end?"

"No, Uncle John, we need to get out of here and not get you involved."

"Too late, nephew. Your showing up means we are involved—targets, in fact, if I understand what's going on here."

"I'm—"

"Don't apologize, I would be very angry if you *didn't* come to us. Now we know they're coming here, right?" he asked as he sat down.

"Pretty sure," said David

"Oh, yeah!" confirmed Brian.

"So we aren't going to stay put and let them get to us."

"You have a plan?" Heather asked Mr. Anderson.

"I think so. First, protect everyone. If they're coming, we must leave. That's a given. Second, delay them. This is a small town—I have connections. If we can tie these guys up for a few days with the Canadian police, and they come and find everyone long gone, we could burn just enough time for you to get across the pond and help this young man's brother."

"Dad, how are you gonna get them arrested?"

"They have guns, right?"

"With silencers," Brian added.

"I'll tell my friend at the police station that Brian got mixed up with the wrong people in Boston betting on sports. Someone is coming to collect."

"Oh, thanks, Dad!"

"Use me, Uncle John, Brian lives here."

"OK, good point. You are running to me to borrow money."

"Where will we go, John?" asked Aunt Ruth.

"How about the Virgin Islands for a couple of weeks?"

Aunt Ruth lit up.

"Can you just take time off from the company like that?"

"Well, last time I looked, I *owned* the company."

"When do we leave?" asked the four in unison.

"First light. I told him I'd have you there around three."

"You knew they'd go?" asked Aunt Ruth.

"Our kids would do anything for each other. Luc and his brother are now in good hands," ensured John.

"Brian was just along for the ride to get us home, so he should go with you," David said, thinking about the worst case scenario.

"I'm in, cousin. I'm not nosing in on Mom and Dad's second honeymoon and I got no other place to go. Can't go back to Boston, and I can't stay around here, 'cuz my mom just gave away all my clothes."

"I know what you're thinking, David. We couldn't bear to lose either of you. I think safety in numbers applies here. Get Luc's brother then get to the police or Scotland Yard, or whatever the hell they call it over there!

"That's the plan, Uncle John."

42

No one went to bed. Luc rested on the couch for a short time, but there was no significant sleep as departure time was approaching. David and Brian cycled through the shower.

"You will leave in the morning, right?" David asked Mr. Anderson.

"We'll take the shuttle out of Halifax and connect in Boston or New York. I'll call my friend right as you leave, he doesn't need to know you were ever here. Don't worry about us, we'll have a police escort out."

Just prior to leaving, David bumped into Mr. Anderson exiting his bedroom.

"Here," John said, holding out his hand and presenting a chrome-plated, semi-automatic pistol, with mother of pearl handle inlays. "We taught you how to shoot when you were kids."

"No thanks, Uncle John," David responded. "I don't need to give anyone another reason to shoot at me. You take it and keep Aunt Ruth safe."

"All right, then."

He stuffed the gun into the back of his pants belt and pulled his sweater over it.

As David came back down the hall, Aunt Ruth was presenting the rest of the travelers with a duffel bag of laundry.

"I also stocked up your supplies. I can't imagine the boat will have snacks," she said, handing them the two bags they brought now stuffed full, plus another. "It's a long trip; I hope this helps."

At three in the morning the group squeezed into the silver Mercedes for the quick ride to the dock. The four youths were in the back, with Heather sitting on David's lap, bent sideways to keep her from hitting the ceiling. They all exchanged hugs at the bottom of the gangway to the freighter.

"When you land, contact me through the company. My secretary will know where we are," Mr. Anderson said. "And I have Heather and Brian's cell numbers, though I doubt they'll work in England."

"Be careful!" Aunt Ruth said, giving Luc an extra hug and patting Heather on the shoulder. As they were about to enter the gangway, Brian spun around and gave his mother a hug, practically picking her up off the ground. She burst into tears.

"We'll be careful, don't worry. I love you mom."

He then gave his dad a hug too.

"Take care of mom. They could come any time," he whispered.

"Don't worry about us. Watch each other's back," he said, releasing Brian and slapping him firmly on the shoulder.

The captain greeted them at the top of the gangway and gave a nod and short wave to Mr. Anderson below.

"Mike Beaumont. Time to shove off," he announced to them.

They introduced themselves and were quickly guided below deck to the crew's cabins located at the stern of the ship. The little cabin had bunks on either side of it, and not much more.

"I'm short on crew for this run, so you'll earn your way," smiled Captain Beaumont.

"Glad to help wherever we can," David offered gratefully.

"Some of this is food," Heather said.

"All food stays locked up in the galley; you don't need any critters gnawing on your nose while you sleep."

He could have worded that better, she thought.

After stowing their bags below the bottom bunks, they found the galley and stowed the food in locked metal bins. They climbed back up, all the way to the bridge, where they stood outside on the wing bridge and watched the dawn light up Yarmouth.

The shorthanded crew ran about, handling the lines while Captain Beaumont backed the ship into the harbor. There was a little fog, or sea smoke, as the captain called it, on the calm water of the harbor, which the light of day would dissolve in the next few minutes what the ship did not run over. Brian stuck his head into the bridge, where the captain was alone working the controls.

"Need any help?"

"No, just stay put right there till we get going."

He was very busy timing the shift from reverse to forward so the ship would turn and be dead center in the channel, then darting to the wheel and adjusting the course, all while maintaining a 360 degree lookout for other vessels. He was a trim man of about six feet. Everything about him was neat. His shirt looked pressed, and he maintained a clean haircut. His looks would have you guess low at 50 years old.

From high astern on the wing bridge they watched the blue steel ship swing out into the harbor. As the momentum shifted from backward to forward, the flurry of activity ceased, and they were underway. Yarmouth grew smaller as the freighter worked its way through the harbor, the sun rising off the bow. A breeze kicked up that chilled Heather's ears. On the side of the hill that lined the harbor, the road to town was no longer visible except for the flickering blue lights of a motionless police car.

"Ya think?" Heather whispered to David.

43

At 150 feet, the Scotia Star was miniature in comparison to the freighters that went in and out of Halifax. The hull was blue to the water line, which sat a few feet above the water, as the boat was not loaded to capacity. Its age showed in many rust stains. On the nose of the bow, a gold emblem with three lines heading aft on each side mimicked a royal seal standing proudly amongst the peeling paint and rust blisters. She looked much like her larger siblings, sporting a high bow, replete with hawse pipes loaded with anchors, low freeboard amidships, then a white superstructure atop a rounded stern. Rising up two stories it had look of a little super tanker.

The guest crew stayed above deck as the scenery changed from harbor to bay, then to open ocean. The day had grown into a sunny and relatively calm one, the breeze tolerable as they were bundled up in down and fleece. On the bridge, inside, the captain maintained a hot pot of coffee in the day galley, which helped warm their hands and stomachs.

"Got any cream and sugar?" Brian asked as he filled the mug the captain handed him.

The captain did not answer but looked at him as if it was the most ridiculous request he'd ever heard.

"Black is good, too," Brian quickly adjusted.

The bridge deck was more wide than deep, with everything from floor to ceiling made or housed in honey stained wood. Two of the eight small square windows looking forward had thick, plexiglass circles mounted to them to spin rainwater off in severe storms and high winds, where a traditional windshield wiper would fail. The walls were crowded with gauges and electronics, including radar displays, radios, chart plotter/GPS displays and vintage throttle controls. In the middle of the cabin stood the ship's wheel mounted on a pedestal which housed another large, brass compass. Conflicting with its museum worthy appearance was a black rubber belt on a smaller, chrome disc half the wheel's size, which drove the ship when on auto pilot.

The four came in to warm up.

"We do six-hour shifts; each of you can take one. That will let me rest my crew," the captain said.

"No problem, glad to help," said Brian.

"This is Billy and Pedro," the captain said. Billy nodded, standing next to the self steering helm.

"Allo," said Pedro, who was fiddling with a GPS plotter mounted on the chart cabinet.

Billy was about the size of David, maybe 40 years old and spoke with a southern accent. Pedro was much smaller and struggled with his English.

"You should all get some rest, then we'll put you to work," Captain Beaumont advised, knowing they had been up all night.

It was time to sleep. David asked the captain to wake him first for anything they might need help with.

"We can't thank you enough for this," he added.

As they entered the saloon, they met the young blond man who tended the mooring lines when they departed.

"I'm Ian," he said softly in a Russian dialect.

"Hi! I'm Brian, and this is—"

Ian interrupted him by pressing his finger to his lips.

"Mickey is sleeping," he whispered, pointing to the ladder down to the crew's quarters.

They whispered the rest of their introductions and quietly climbed down the ladder. David entered the small cabin last and climbed into the top bunk, above Heather. They all slept hard for hours.

It was mid afternoon when David arrived on the bridge.

"How can I help you, Cap'n Beaumont?"

"Can you cook dinner for nine?"

"I'll do my best," he replied.

"Pedro will take you to the galley and show you where everything is. We keep it simple at sea: pasta, soups, maybe a chili."

David noticed a magnifying glass on the chart table.

"May I borrow that, Cap'n?"

"Go ahead."

David pulled the microfiche out of his fleece and held the glass up to it. It wasn't powerful enough to read the pages, but just blew them up enough so he could see the image of the documents and whether they were typed or handwritten.

"What do you have there?" the captain asked.

"No government secrets, promise," assured David with a quick smile. "Just medical records for the most part but," David sighed, "the glass isn't powerful enough to read them."

"There is a microscope on board, down in the medical closet."

"Maybe after dinner, thanks."

Pedro showed David around the galley.

"I recommend spaghetti," Pedro said with his healthy Spanish accent. "One, it is easy. Two, we have fresh bread to go with it."

"I'm sold!"

The meal went together very easily. The galley offered ample workspace, being designed to support a crew of 10 to 15 mates sharing bunks as their work shifts rotated. David worked on the stainless steel countertop along the outside wall. The two interior walls provided a large stove with oven and a wash station with a deep double sink on one wall, and a refrigerator/freezer next to three rows of metal food bins on the other.

He found canned sliced mushrooms for the sauce as well as some sausages in the freezer, which he prepared as a side dish in case anyone, Heather in particular, was not a big meat eater.

When dinner was served, everyone was up. Brian was up on the bridge with Billy and Ian, while Captain Beaumont, Pedro, and Mickey were in the saloon with Luc. Heather helped David bring dinner to the on watch crew, then joined the others in the saloon. Even though everyone was awake, conversation was still kept low out of habit.

Like the bridge, the saloon was for the most part wood. In daytime, the small portholes glowed like bright headlights, making the room bright. Now at night, the dark wood walls reflected the flickering flames of brass oil lamps, the largest of which hung over the dining table, providing a warm glow to the dining area, much in the way of a campfire illuminates just those who are around it.

The captain said, "Luc, you're on at eight, with Pedro and me. Are you up for it—or do you need more rest?"

"Sure, I'm ready," replied Luc.

"Mickey, you can go on at two, then KP for lunch."

Luc raised his eyebrows.

"Kitchen Patrol," the captain explained. "Old military expression." He turned to David. "You and Heather will have to flip for the graveyard shift. Billy is the mechanic, so he doubles up his shift during daylight hours."

"Can I have a look at that microscope?" David asked Captain Beaumont, once he was certain he was finished with the duty roster.

"The medical closet, next to the day head."

David returned with an older microscope, which had a light under the slide. David held up the cord.

"Is there any one ten on the boat?" he asked.

"Right behind your head. There's also one on the bridge if you're looking."

David turned around and saw the outlet with "110V" written in white marker on the wall next to it. The scope lit up and David placed it on the saloon table and pulled out the fiche. He carefully lifted the metal slide holders and inserted the fiche. He twisted the knob and the documents came into focus. Then he rotated the circular lens holder to increase the magnification.

"Perfect!" he said, as he was looking at one of the documents of the first row. But the slide holders prevented him from moving the microfiche to scan down.

"I think those unscrew," Cap'n Beaumont offered.

David fiddled with the scope for a minute and a nut dropped onto the table freeing one of the slide holders. He unfastened the other then gathered up the loose components. The Captain handed him a small glass in which David deposited the hardware. He spent a half an hour looking at documents, re-reading the important ones.

When Luc started his shift, Brian returned and sat with Heather and David.

"Not so bad. Just hanging out drinking coffee for the most part. Whatta-ya got there?"

"It reads the microfiche," David replied.

"Cool. Find anything?"

"Just started."

David took the microfiche out and zipped it away.

"I better catch some Z's since I'm taking the graveyard shift."

He unplugged the scope and placed it in a cubby which held a few books and a flashlight, then leaned over and placed his head on Heather's lap and hugged her. He could have slept right there.

Mickey knocked twice on the cabin door. David slid out of the top bunk, grabbed his jacket, and quietly exited the cabin where Heather and Brian slept on the two lower bunks. As he topped the ladder, Luc appeared.

"Hey, how did you make out?" asked David.

"It was fun," he whispered, though not sounding overly enthusiastic. "Cap'n Beaumont showed me how to use the radar and read a chart."

"Cool, maybe Mickey can show me."

"I gotta crash. Are they asleep?

"Yeah, I think so," answered David.

Luc nodded goodbye to David and quietly climbed down to the crew's quarters.

Up on the bridge deck, the captain was talking to Mickey and Pedro. The cabin lights were off except for a red glow from the gauges and a small lamp with a red light bulb on the chart table. As his eyes adjusted to the darkness, the outside world came into view. The dim red lights were just enough to work your way around the bridge, yet not affect the view outward. The moon was waning, about one-third full. Stars blinked and the ocean sparkled from the moonlight.

"At night, we stay inside unless we have to," Captain Beaumont said to David.

"OK."

"That's Aye, Cap'n!" he said with a laugh as he slapped David on the shoulder. "See you tomorrow," he said heading out the door.

Pedro opened a toolbox and went to work repairing a small pump. Mickey picked up the binoculars for a scan of the ocean, while the shiny disc steered the ship.

Pedro did not say much, but when he did his accent hinted at Mexico or Spain. Mickey looked like he was sixty years old. He was actually 50, the years of sun at sea had aged his skin to a tough, olive-toned hide. As he took another look with the binoculars, he started humming a tune, then softly sang the song.

"What is that?"

"A song my mother sang to me when I was a little boy, back home."

"Where's home?" David asked after listening to a few more lines, trying to guess the language.

"Italy."

"I thought I recognized that accent."

"Where is home for you?"

"Alaska for a while, nowhere now. Right here, I guess…"

44

David woke Heather with a kiss.

"Mmmmmm," she said.

"Time to go to work," he whispered.

"Damn," she whispered back.

As Heather closed the door, David rolled onto her bunk and immediately fell asleep.

When he awoke, he was alone in the cabin. It was almost 11:00 when he emerged with his shaving kit, the smell of good coffee wafting down from above. David climbed the ladder to find Brian sitting at the fixed dining table, drinking coffee and talking to his watch mate, Billy.

"Hey," Brian said, as David filled his mug.

"Hey."

"How's life at sea treating you?"

"So far, OK. You?" David replied.

"I'm good."

"Any cream or sugar around here?" David asked.

"If you have to have it, you'll find some in the galley," Billy replied.

"Seen Heather?" David asked, as he sipped the bitter black coffee.

"Yeah," Brian replied, widening his grin.

"What?"

"Seems the day shift goes out on deck; they have her up in the bow painting the anchor winch. That is, if she's not puking her guts," Brian laughed.

David immediately noticed the movement of the ship. Until now, they had been motoring in calm seas, so calm they barely knew they were on the water. But now there was a gentle, but definite movement to the room—up and down.

"Storm's comin'," Billy said, smiling a little.

David walked out of the saloon and onto the deck, standing directly under the port wing bridge. The bow of the boat was rising and falling as each 10-foot wave passed beneath it, then the motion flattened out into a gentle roll as the stern of the ship passed through what remained of the waves. He could see Heather all the way up in the bow, wearing a yellow oilskin coat, painting with one hand and hanging on to the windlass with the other. He wanted to go and help, but he didn't want her to think he thought she needed it. He recalled her story about being sick on Lake Michigan as he watched the spray shoot out from the left side of the bow. The captain was directly above David, standing on the wing bridge.

"Heather!" he yelled, startling David.

Heather turned and looked back. David could not see the captain motioning for her to come in.

"One minute—almost done!" she yelled back.

"OK!" David heard from above.

She looks like she is actually enjoying it, David thought.

"What's on the menu for tonight?" Captain Beaumont said, greeting David on the bridge. He must have made a good meal, he thought as he watched Heather climb down to the main deck, holding a can of paint in one hand, the other sliding down the handrail of the metal ladder as if she had done it a hundred times. She disappeared into the bow to stow her supplies.

"Not sure," David replied. "I'll take a quick inventory."

Captain Beaumont didn't talk much, his mind staying focused on the ship and the course. Being short on crew, he was constantly monitoring the ship's systems, plotting the course, and checking the weather.

David exited the bridge and climbed down the outside gangway, greeting Heather on the main deck. She had a small smudge of red paint on her cheek, but was otherwise intact. She looked beautiful in the black wool cap and yellow slicker. David thought she was the perfect model for it, whatever she wore.

"Having fun?" he smiled.

"Actually, yeah," she smiled back. "I thought I would be sick as the waves got bigger, but I'm OK. I guess big boats agree with me. How are you?"

"Looks like I'm the cook," he said, locked on to those eyes, which in the bright daylight glistened more than the sun on the ocean.

"That's even better than taking me on date. What are you making me for dinner?" she laughed as she leaned off of the ladder and kissed him, then started her ascent to the bridge to report in.

David went inside to the galley and rummaged around, reviewing his options. There were potatoes and onions. He found ground beef in the freezer, but wasn't sure how long it would take to defrost. When he saw the enormous, bulk-sized cans of chopped clams, his decision was made. The leftover bread would go nicely with clam chowder. He confirmed two quarts of un-opened non-dairy creamer as he moved the ground beef from the freezer to the refrigerator anticipating he would cook again the next day, as it seemed they had established a work routine for the journey.

Everyone had their shift; sleeping on the off-shifts kept them from any extended time together. The afternoons and dinner found them all awake together, but Brian's shift and David's KP duty occupied much of that time. In a way, it was a good thing. David did not have to plan the next step and Luc was busy with the captain who had taken him under his wing, distracting him in the evenings with seamanship lessons. The ship's schedule now commanded their lives. It was a welcome break for all of them, for when they hit land they would be back in high gear— and probably back in danger.

As they finished dinner, the seas were getting higher and the saloon's motion had increased, but not to a point of concern, as the bow and first hundred feet of the ship kept knocking down most of the waves.

"Storm will hit later tonight," the captain said. "Shouldn't be so bad as to knock you out of bed, but extra care needs to be taken when moving around. Always hang onto something. Watch for things bouncing around. And we don't need to be looking for anyone during any kind of weather, so make sure you report in and someone always knows where you are."

The temporary crew nodded, as these instructions were directed solely at them.

David broke out the scope and plugged it in. He read a document or two then hopped around randomly, gently nudging the fiche under the lens. Mickey looked on from the end of the fixed dining table.

"Mickey"

"Yeah, David?"

"Can you read Italian?"

"Of course."

David fumbled about in the storage cubby and produced an elastic band, which he wrapped around the slide plate and film. He adjusted the microfiche then slid the microscope across the table. Mickey put his eye up to the lens and focused the scope a little.

"It's from the Vatican," Mickey whispered.

"Yes. Can you tell us what it's about?"

"It's from ten years ago—an investigation—it says *by the Prefect of the Inquisition, Vatican City. An investigation on life form experiments conducted with secret artifacts of the Vatican.*"

Mickey looked up, "Oh my! Where did you get such a thing?" he asked in a pensive, thickly accented voice. The crew in the saloon perked up. Captain Beaumont focused too.

"Does this have anything to do with why you're hiding on my ship?"

"Everything, I'm afraid," David whispered. "There are people out there who want this back. Very badly..."

"And so you are running away with it?"

"They killed my dad!" cried Luc.

The captain and crew stared at Luc with frozen faces. No one in the saloon moved.

"They shot him, shot at me, too!" he added.

"I'm very sorry," said Captain Beaumont.

The captain turned to David.

"John Anderson is my friend. Is he in danger?"

"They left the country right after we got on board. They'll be all right," David assured him.

"It's about a twenty-five page report," Heather said. "Mickey, could you translate it for us, maybe a few pages at a time?"

"I don't think I should be reading such things."

"You're right," David said. "There are things in there you will not believe...will not comprehend," he said nodding toward the fiche.

There was a certain air about the situation, people slipping out of the country with ruthless men in pursuit, now safe in the belly of a freighter in the open ocean, discovering the micro-film's secrets as the oil lamp lit the wood-lined room as it gently rocked.

"OK, maybe a little more," said Mickey.

He put his eye to the scope and slid the film under the rubber band.

"Oops!" he said, looking up apologetically.

He slid it back to the left and found his spot. Everyone focused on Mickey, as if he were telling a ghost story. "It says:

Subjects of Investigation: Cardinal Joseph Vincent, Mr. Michael Orsini, and Dr. Henry Leonard, PHD (deceased).
Opening statement: This inquiry is to understand the activities of the subjects surrounding the violation of certain sacred arti-facts as well as the activities of their efforts to create human life with the genetic residue from them."

As he paused, the crew looked at each other, confirming they all heard Mickey clearly, Pedro making a quick sign of the cross about his upper body. They all stared at Mickey and nod-ded, encouraging him to continue.

First, the tragic death of Doctor Leonard does not allow his...

Huh, how do you say it," Mickey asked, "to be speaking in court?"

"Testimony?" offered Heather.

"Yes, thanks.

...testimony for this inquiry."

"Fell of a cliff," interjected David, "and no accident."

Mickey took a sip from his coffee mug and swallowed hard. He looked back into the lens.

Complete cooperation has been assured by the surviving subjects and they will answer all questions or make written statements upon our request. Mr. Orsini will speak on behalf of the subjects unless specific questions require Cardinal Vincent's comments.

Mickey looked up.

"This has a bad smell to it," he said.

"Yeah, this is a pretty dark group of people you are talking about," David acknowledged.

"No, I mean the film. It smells like—like old socks."

45

David's shift saw the storm come in. The wind gusted to 40 knots and the waves rose to 20 feet, the Scotia Star's bow crashing into each one, then blasting upward. Outside, David held onto the rail that surrounded the deck-level saloon and worked his way to the metal stairs to the bridge. White spray spewed higher than the bow, like an overactive geyser. Lights mounted under the wing bridge guided his way. He held on tightly as he climbed, not able to see much with the wind and rain in his face. Once inside the bridge, the rain pelted the windows relentlessly. The small spinning circular windows were idle, as there was no chance of visibility in the dark with the heavy rain.

"When you go below in this weather, the bridge needs to know you made it inside," Mickey lectured. "When you get in the saloon, you call back up on this, letting the bridge know you're in."

Mickey tapped at a pipe that came up through the floor next to the door and traveled up the wall about four feet, ending in a small funnel.

"Same when you come up. Someone has to know you are outside. You keep calling until someone calls back. If we get water on deck, we will use the hatch in the day galley."

Water on deck? That would mean the bow went under! I can miss that.

The bow stayed above water throughout his shift, but they rode each wave hanging on to something, as the huge waves grew too powerful to be conquered by the little ship; the swells lifted the middle and back of the freighter as it passed over them.

Dawn illuminated the show. The waves still pounded the bow, but the rain had let up a bit. This was a sizable storm, but had not produced any awe or concern from the crew, who for the most part, did nothing different in their daily and nightly routines.

At 8:00, a voice came through the metal tube: "Two comin' up!"

"Aye!" Mickey barked into the funnel.

The door flung open and the wind howled loudly as the next shift entered.

"Pedro will be up in a bit," Captain Beaumont said to Mickey, "He's making breakfast. Billy's checkin' the bilge pumps."

Heather hung her slicker on a brass hook then held onto it as the ship crested another wave.

"Breakfast, then sleep. Mmmm," David said, as he kissed Heather and warmed her up with half a hug, his free hand holding on to a grab rail mounted to the ceiling of the cabin. She released the hook and hung on to David, rubbing his back.

The captain immediately went to the control panel on the back wall and studied all of the gauges, then moved to the chart plotter to review their progress across the Atlantic.

"I am heading down. I'm hungry," Mickey said.

"I'll be down in a bit," said David, seeing the opportunity to be with Heather as no chores would be issued in the storm.

Heather and David looked out at the ocean and watched the sea repeatedly assault the bow, releasing explosions of white spray. The movement of the boat was significant, but steady.

"I'm in!" Mickey's voice shot out of the tube.

"Aye!" The captain returned into the funnel.

With just the three of them on the bridge, the captain took the opportunity for a private conversation.

"So they shot this kid's father over that film?" he asked.

"Yeah," replied David as Heather continued her hug. "Now they're trying to get rid of all the evidence, including us. Luc's father was working for them."

"Evidence of what…?"

"Experiments. Illegal genetic experiments."

"Who is they?" the captain continued.

"It's all in the film. Mickey is reading about them. Plus there are a couple of others."

"So, how did you get the evidence?"

"Entirely by accident. I literally tripped over it."

The captain had heard enough and settled into his shift.

"He has a brother," Heather added.

The captain looked up from the chart, raising his grey eyebrows.

"Luc does. He lives in England. We're not running away. We are going to help him, just in case."

"Comin' up!" Pedro's voice sounded through the tube.

"Aye!" the captain squawked back.

Pedro appeared in the doorway donning his slicker and a wool cap, holding a pot with a ladle in it. David could see the end of a loaf of bread sitting in the pot just below the rim. Without words, Pedro went into the day galley and clanged around, using only one hand to avoid launching himself about the room. He emerged and, one at a time, served the captain then Heather a large mug filled with scrambled eggs and a piece of bread.

"Coffee?" asked the captain, parking his food in the corner of the chart table.

"We just made a pot," answered David.

Captain Beaumont went into the day galley and poured a half cup of coffee from the metal pot secured on the small, two burner stove by rails, like you typically find on the stove on a sailboat, then returned to the chart table.

"I better get some sleep," David said.

He kissed Heather again and put on his slicker, being careful to hold onto the ceiling's grab rail, switching hands with each sleeve. Heather relocated her grip from him to a grab rail just below the windshield.

"There's more eggs and bread below," Pedro said, as David reached the door.

David descended, the force of the storm hitting him on his back. A wind gust nearly blew him off as he slipped on the wet metal steps. Tightening his grip, he did not let go of the stairs until he had a firm grip on the grab rail wrapping around the main deck saloon. After closing the door behind him, he took his slicker off in the same manner as he put it on and hung it in the wet locker by the door. He grabbed the rail on the ceiling and worked his way toward the galley to join Mickey.

"Oh, right!"

He spun around and shuffled his way back to the door, finding the tube that came down from through ceiling, ending at about five feet off the deck in another little funnel.

"I'm in," he said bending over, speaking directly into the funnel.

He turned his head to orient his ear to the funnel and listened for a few seconds.

"I love you," her voice whispered back through the tube.

David found Mickey wedged into the dining table so he could eat without holding on to something.

"In the pot in the fridge, still warm; bread's in the bin."

David served himself and joined Mickey at the table.

"Keep all food in the fridge or the bins," Mickey went on. "There are critters on the boat. No way to avoid it when you are moving freight in and out of those filthy ports."

David nodded and ate in silence, thinking about the three words he had just heard.

When David emerged from his bunk, the portholes that lit the saloon were noticeably brighter and the motion of the ship had definitely lessened. He poured a cup of coffee and looked in the refrigerator. The eggs were gone and the pot must have been cleaned and put away. He opened a food bin and spied the bags that Aunt Ruth had filled.

"Pop-Tarts!" he said out loud.

He opened a box of blueberry ones and took out a pack of two pastries, stuffing the box back in the bag and locking the bin. He zipped up his fleece and headed outside, taking a bite then stashing them in his pocket to keep a free hand while he held his coffee. The seas were still unsettled, but the sun was out for the moment, popping out from behind the storm's trailing clouds. White spray still shot up from the bow, but not with every wave, as most of the ferociousness was gone. As the brisk wind blew his hair back, his mind raced through the events that had brought him here to this very strange, surreal place: from Brian's phone call announcing his acceptance to Brighton Latin College, all the way through to the car chase in Maine. His life had been flipped upside down; now he stood on the deck of a freighter in the middle of the Atlantic, in hopes of reuniting two kids—not just kids, the clones of Christ and his brother!

How freakin' bizarre is this? I didn't see any reference to any of this in the course catalog!

Nonetheless, this was far from over and the importance of these next days clamped down hard on him. They were the only hope the world had to protect the existence of these two special beings. He breathed deep and remembered those three words.

David climbed the metal stairs as the wind blew the last drops out of his coffee mug, which dangled from one finger. He entered the bridge to find Heather and the captain working the chart plotter while Pedro scanned the horizon with the binoculars.

"Everything OK?" David asked.

"Excellent!" Captain Beaumont responded cheerfully. "Storm's behind us and we've got great weather for the next few days."

David was more interested in Heather than the forecast. And she had been waiting for him as well.

"Hey," she said, looking for a sign that her little comment was well received.

"Hi," David smiled, staring at her.

"What does dinner look like for today?" asked the captain.

"I think chili," he said without shifting his gaze from Heather's eyes.

"You know if you run out of ideas, we have a few tons of smoked salmon on ice in the hold," The captain chuckled.

Chili was served in mugs with a torn piece of bread from the now half-stale last loaf. Mickey and Heather ran three servings up to the bridge while David set up the microscope, resting it at his side while he ate his dinner. As they finished their meal, David turned to Mickey.

"Will you read more for us, Mickey?"

"Sure, just help me with the dishes," he smiled.

"Can do!"

David jumped up, leaving the microscope on the settee. He rolled up the sleeves of his flannel shirt and started scrubbing the empty chili pot.

"You can probably have a job here if you want. That was the best chili this boat has ever seen."

"Thanks."

A few minutes later they reappeared in the saloon. Everyone was waiting for Mickey to start. David set up the film with the rubber band, then slid Mickey the scope; everyone perked up as Mickey translated:

The files forwarded by Scotland Yard from Dr. Leonard's widow reveal that he was experimenting with DNA samples. These samples were from artifacts in the Vatican's control as well as from the Sudarium, which is controlled by the Archdiocese of Spain. These files also reveal that the samples were provided by Michael Orsini. Furthermore, there is reference to Cardinal Vincent with respect to his relationship to Mr. Orsini and his providing funding to Dr. Leonard to conduct the experiments with the DNA. Copies of these documents have been provided to the other subjects of this Inquisition and they have had sufficient time to review them. Is that true?

Orsini: Yes.

Mickey lifted his head from the scope to find everyone frozen, focused on him. Heather nodded and smiled. He took a breath and continued to read.

What is your relationship to Cardinal Vincent?
Orsini: I worked for him for many years.

Do you work for him now?
Orsini: No.

Did you work for him when Dr. Leonard conducted the DNA experiments?
Orsini: Yes.

In what capacity?
Orsini: I was his driver and assistant.

Did you assist on the DNA experiments?
Orsini: Yes.

What did you do?
Orsini: I obtained the samples and provided them to Dr. Leonard, as the documents state.

How did you access the Shroud of Turin?
Orsini: I bribed the guard.

We have a sworn statement by the guard which summarizes his testimony he recently gave here. This statement accuses you of bribing him, after which he provided you entrance to the vault where the Shroud of Turin is stored. You entered the vault and he witnessed you tampering with the shroud. Have you read his statement?
Orsini: Yes.

Do you have anything to say regarding the accuracy of the statements?
Orsini: Accurate. All true.

How did you access the Sudarium?
Orsini: The same way.

Who did you bribe?
Orsini: I offer no comment to that question.

"They are confessing to everything," David said as he held onto the ceiling rail of the saloon. Brian was about to go on watch as David briefed him on the previous night's reading.

"Seems strange. Does that mean that the Vatican is in on it?" Brian speculated. "If so, cousin, we could have a small army waiting for us at that orphanage."

"I know. It just doesn't make sense with all of the other stuff we found. Ya know, keeping it a secret and shutting the whole thing down, just cuz we found out."

"How much more does Mickey have left to translate?"

"Another night or two, I guess."

46

Sarah nodded to the man in to the uniform as she made her way down the hallway, her weekly visit right on schedule.

"I've heard nothing," Sarah said. "Something is going on. Vincent hasn't even asked me to purchase the plane tickets for either of them."

"Maybe Scordo did it. It's not that big of a purchase," Rose offered.

"Scordo has left the US. He is with Henry. And there is more. Vincent is acting strange. He won't even talk to me. He was so excited a couple of week ago. Now he is very stressed. Something is definitely wrong."

"Sarah, call Glen. If Scordo changed the plan, Glen will know."

"I don't trust any of them, Rose."

"Then get a message to Henry. There is still time. Henry is not a bad person, he will help Bryce!"

"Scordo is there, Rose. If he tells Vincent I talked with him, he will know what we are up to. Rose, he will kill us."

"Sarah, we must."

47

The next evening had everyone, save the on watch crew, present in the saloon waiting the next reading, oblivious to David's simple pot of macaroni and cheese—except Heather.

"Can we get a vegetable around here? How about a salad night?" she complained.

The crew ate, oblivious to her request. As long as it was hot and tasted good, whatever the cook served was fine. Besides, they were waiting on Mickey.

"No thanks," Heather responded David's gesture to pass the cream and sugar.

"You take cream, no?" inquired David.

"I got used to being up on the bridge. It's too far to the galley," she replied.

"Yeah, same here," David agreed.

They settled in with their black coffees, as David unzipped the microfiche. Mickey pulled out the scope while David, Heather, Luc, Pedro, and Captain Beaumont listened attentively as he walked them through the laboratory experiments where they extracted DNA from the three samples.

Leonard received 500,000 sterling for his work, but died just after receiving the money.

Who paid him?
Orsini: Cardinal Vincent.

Where did he get the money?
Orsini: I don't know.

Cardinal Vincent: It was my money. I funded everything.

Where is the rest of the documentation about the experiments?
Orsini: I destroyed it.

Was it your intention to destroy all of the evidence of this experiment?
Orsini: Of course, yes.

Why?
Orsini: There was no point in retaining evidence of something illegal, especially after it all failed."

"What!?" blurted Heather. "Read that again, Mickey."

"Wait!" David said, getting up from the settee and moving to the door. He put his mouth to the funnel.

"Brian, need you down here!"

"Aye!" the tube answered.

Brian appeared in seconds, having slid down the outside stairs by the handrails, his feet never touching the steps.

"Wassup?"

"You gotta hear this. Mickey, go ahead, read it again."

The room was on edge, silent, as Mickey put his eye to the scope.

Why did the experiments fail?
Orsini: The experiments were a total failure, as the embryos could not be successfully created. I do not know the scientific answer to the question. It just failed.

What did you do next?
Orsini: The project was immediately shut down after the realization that the reincarnation could not be accomplished. The

samples and records were then destroyed, as there was no point in retaining any evidence."

The four looked at each other. Mickey, Pedro, and the captain could see the nonverbal communication.

"What is it?" asked the captain.

"It's a freakin' lie, that's what!" yelled Brian.

"The experiment worked and they lied to cover it up!" added Heather.

"Y'all mean they actually cloned Jesus Christ?" Billy said in amazement.

Pedro started muttering a prayer in Spanish and rapidly made the sign of the cross about his upper body.

Mickey put his hands together and bowed his head, shaking it slightly, mouthing something in Italian.

"Yes," David responded, "It was successful all right, and so was the cloning of Jesus' brother. It's all there on that film."

Pedro made the sign of the cross again and continued his low volume, high speed chant in Spanish. Captain Beaumont's eyes flew open as he recalled the conversation on the bridge where Heather talked about Luc's brother. He looked at her then refocused on Luc. The excitement in the saloon settled down. Mickey's thick accent cut in, as he clenched his hands together on his forehead.

"David?" he whispered without looking up.

"Yeah, Mickey?"

"Are you saying that we are to believe, that, as we sit here, that Jesus Christ has been recreated and is somewhere out there walking among us?"

David looked at Mickey, who was now staring at him, then shifted to Pedro, who was riveted on David, eyes wide open in terror, awaiting the answer. David glanced over to Luc. Luc stared back at him, fearless. He didn't even blink. Luc nodded.

"No," David calmly answered.

Mickey and Pedro were puzzled, but both gasped in relief and looked at each other, smiling and shaking there heads at the thought of the possibility. They turned back to David smiling.

"He's not out *there*," David qualified.

David, Heather, Brian, and the captain, slowly turned their heads in unison to Luc. Luc smiled a little. Pedro took it all in, then rolled his eyes and fainted, collapsing to the floor of the saloon. Mickey started muttering in Italian with his head bowed, in prayer.

"It's OK, Pedro!!" Luc said. "Don't be afraid!"

Pedro came to on the floor and curled up on his knees praying in Spanish. Brian stepped in, "Hey! Let's not freak the kid out any more than you have to, geez!" he said, then looked at Luc, who sat up straight and then whispered, "I bet *he* could go for some of that Kettle Corn right about now."

Brian smiled back at Luc. Mickey and Pedro pulled themselves together, trying not to stare at Luc. The room was silent, until the captain spoke.

"It's time. Pedro?"

"Ready!" responded Luc.

Pedro was up on his knees, bewildered.

"Come on, Pedro," Luc encouraged. "You can teach me that prayer you were saying; I should probably learn some, ya know."

Pedro looked up as Luc extended his hand, smiling at him. He took it, smiling back. As the crew exited, David, Heather, and Brian slumped back in their seats.

"Do you believe this shit?" Brian blurted.

"Not in a million years," laughed Heather, gently banging her head against the wall.

David stared at the ceiling. "We gotta finish this. We have no choice—for these kids—maybe for the world, if you think about it. I mean, the secret goes only as far as this boat," David said, breathing deeply and continuing. "At least I have the two of you to ride it out with."

He stared at the ceiling and extended his open hand on the settee to Heather's side. She clasped it and looked up too, those three words bouncing through both of their minds.

48

It was noon when they arrived in port at Liverpool. As the boat docked, all hands were on deck. Heather worked the bowline under Ian's direction, while Brian worked the mid-ship springline. David was on the bridge with the captain, who was at the helm, and Billy stood at the ship's gauges. David stood ready to deploy any sudden redirection. On the stern deck stood Mickey, Pedro, and Luc, working the lines. As the ship slid sideways into the dock, Mickey and Pedro, feeling a bit overprotective, struggled to do all of the tasks.

"I can do this, you know!" Luc complained, as he grabbed the leader for the mooring line away from Pedro.

"Of course", Pedro said bowing his head down. "Of course you can."

"And stop doing that!" Luc cried out as he flung the leader with a monkey fist to a shore man on the dock.

"I am sorry!" replied Pedro, as he fed the thick mooring line to the ground crew. Mickey maintained the other end of the mooring line, ready to secure it at the proper length. As the ground crew secured their end, Mickey tied off the other end on the ship's massive cleat, the others forward doing the same, bringing the little ship to a halt.

Now relaxed, Pedro apologized again as he faked down the excess line.

"I am a very religious man and you, eh, you makes me nervous. But I am also glad. You are a good person. I can see it in your eyes."

"Thanks," Luc said softly. "If this works out, maybe I can give you a special blessing," he grinned, "once I figure out how to do that."

"You already have," Pedro smiled back. "It's time for you to help your brother."

David cooked one more meal for the captain and crew. At Heather's request, he worked with the canned goods and produced a three bean salad. He also cooked eggs, peppers, onions, and cheese in two skillets.

"I was going for quiche, but I don't know how they're made. I think I blew it," David said to Mickey. "Now I can't get them out of the pan," he added as he tried to free one with a spatula. He flipped the skillet on a big cutting board and the pie fell out, upside down, revealing slightly burnt eggs on the bottom. He repeated the process with the other one and got the same results.

"Oh, well," David sighed.

"Mmmm," Heather said, working on her salad as David emerged with the cutting board.

"Oh, and frittatas, perfect!" she exclaimed, admiring the meal.

"Uh, yeah, sure," David acknowledged, looking at Mickey, who gave a "why not?" shrug as he sat down.

"Brian, how did you do today?" David asked.

"Mmm-gub!" he said with a mouthful of eggs. "There is a car rental office a mile from here. Plenty of cars in the lot. Also, I got us prepaid cell phones, sixty minutes on each. Here, my man," Brian said, handing the phones to Luc. "Set up the speed dials so we don't have to remember any numbers. And here," he opened his pack by his feet and pulled out a couple of maps. "I found an Internet café and marked up a map," he said sliding one off the table and onto the settee, "Less than a day to Blackpool."

"So close, that's great!" beamed Heather.

"I also talked to my dad's office. They're staying another week."

"That's so romantic," Heather gushed.

"I don't need a visual on that. His secretary will get them a message that we are fine."

"Any word on out of town visitors?" asked David.

"Uh, didn't ask."

"I don't have a load for the ride back yet, so we may be here for a week or two," the captain informed his outgoing crew. "We can always use a hand getting back home if it works out for you," he added, smiling. "And your brother is welcome to sail with us any time," he said, giving Luc a quick rub on the head. "I'm sure he would make good crew."

"So we passed the test?" asked Heather.

"With flying colors. But, I'm afraid David will be assigned to KP forever—by popular vote!"

"Aye!" the permanent crew cheered in unison, clanging their forks off their mugs and plates.

Pedro and Mickey sat with Luc, still adjusting to their crewmate's newly discovered status.

"Your brother—the one from James." Pedro started in.

"We are not sure who is who," Luc explained. "We don't have all of the papers.

"See, what a rip-off!" cracked Brian. "You guys were losin' it and we may not even have the real deal here. He might *only* be the *brother* of Jesus Christ. How lame is that?" he laughed, getting up and going into the galley to refill his coffee mug.

Brian sat down with his cup and the pot, giggling to himself at his little jab. He passed the pot to Luc who filled his mug and slid the pot on to Heather. As the pot traveled, the room became quiet, the crew finishing up their food.

"Anyone for hot chocolate?" Billy announced as he disappeared into the galley.

"No, thanks," Heather replied.

The rest of the room did not acknowledge the offer.

"Luc?" Billy asked, returning a minute later with his mug steaming.

"Thanks, but coffee's workin' for me right now." Luc responded as he sipped.

The captain smiled at the comment. The others sipped their coffees.

"Luc," Pedro said in a soft tone, as if others were sleeping below. "If you need any help to get your brother safe, any at all, I will come, just say the word."

"Same here," said Mickey.

Several "ayes" were shouted about the room, the last being the captain's.

"Any of us, and all of us will go with you to help you and your brother. You can count on that," the captain stated as a point of fact.

"I know that," said Luc. "Thank you all."

David turned his back to the captain.

"Thank you for everything," he said. "Slipping in and out quickly will be our best approach, but we'll come get you if things get ugly."

"Is that the plan?" asked the captain.

"When we get Bryce," David answered, "we go immediately to Scotland Yard, or the U.S. Embassy, whatever is closer.

We'll be safe from them then; it's just a couple of hours of sneaking around. Then we immediately contact Luc's mother, Brian's parents, and Heather's parents."

"Do you have parents?" asked Captain Beaumont.

"Yeah, sure."

"Why not call them?"

"They're at sea, somewhere in the Pacific."

"Merchant Marine?"

"Fifty-foot schooner."

The captain smiled, raising his eyebrows.

"Who's on watch?" he said, spinning his head to address the whole saloon.

"I'll go," said Mickey.

"Want some company?" offered David.

Mickey smiled and the two headed up to the bridge for their last watch together.

49

With the ship in port, the purpose of the watch was security, so only one or two needed to be on at any given time. The two settled in. Mickey grabbed the flashlight.

"I will make the rounds," he said to David.

"I'll make coffee," David responded with a smile.

When Mickey returned, David had a pot of fresh coffee ready in the day galley. Mickey filled his mug and joined David on the bridge, the lights now off, except for the red ones used when underway. The now dark bridge deck offered a view across the river to the illuminated tower marking the entrance to the Kingsway Tunnel, which traversed the bay.

"I had no idea this trip would turn out this way," Mickey said. "As strange as it is, it is kind of exciting. Every other trip is so routine, like how you say, a rut."

"Well, we didn't mean to freak anyone out. I'm sorry about that," David offered.

"How can you be sorry, with such a crazy thing going on? If you think about it, this ship is delivering the most precious cargo in the world. You know what I mean?"

"Yeah, maybe," David sighed.

"Do you not believe David?"

"Whuh?"

"You said maybe."

"Oh, I meant because we're not sure if it's him or the brother."

"Precious nonetheless."

"You're right," David sighed.

David and Mickey sipped their coffees and studied the neighboring ships.

"So you do believe?" Mickey asked after a long moment.

"In the brother? I was never taught about him."

"Not just that," Mickey answered, "I didn't know about any brother either."

"Not sure sometimes."

Mickey flinched at the answer.

"I just wasn't raised that way. My parents didn't go to church. There aren't any churches for miles," he stopped, giving up on making excuses. "But hey, where I come from, things are so magnificent, so unbelievable, you can't help but be inspired. You know that there's something bigger than all of us, something spectacular."

Mickey looked at him, still in disbelief that David was not a devout Christian.

"And, yeah, I do believe in Jesus, Mickey. He was very special. I guess the question is, for me anyway, was he a man, you know a mortal. Maybe the message was that we are all special, and we all can be as special as he was. Wouldn't that be a breath of fresh air on this screwed up planet. I guess part of me thinks he was trying to tell everyone just that. He was just like us—all sons of God—and that he was no more special than the rest. So what would that make him—a very important 'man' or maybe the perfect messenger from God? Ya know, leaving the final decision for us to make."

David paused and looked down at the cabin floor.

"Sorry, Mickey. I don't disrespect your belief, really. I just struggle a bit with mine."

David knew his answer was completely inadequate. How could he not believe in something so powerful, or at least believe in something else as strongly. Mickey would probably respect that.

"So, you do not think the boys are special?" Mickey asked, breaking a long silence.

"Oh, they're special all right. But more important, they are just kids, and they have the right to be 'just kids.' These guys took that away. Well I did; I caused it, anyway. With their DNA, they are definitely special. Who knows what they could grow up to be?" David lowered his head. "I need to give them that chance."

David looked into his coffee and took a final sip, then got up and went to the day galley to refill his mug.

When he returned, Mickey was inspecting the ship's control panel, humming the tune David heard on his first watch of the voyage.

"Can you read a little more for me?" David asked. "There are some pages left and I need to know what they decided in the end. Apparently, these guys got away with it."

"Sure, David."

David slid down the outside stairs, tapping his feet on the steps as he supported himself with his hands. He grabbed the microscope from the cubby and returned to the bridge, finding the electrical outlet. He rigged the scope with the film, and handed it to Mickey one last time.

"Can you find the spot where the prefect makes a ruling, or final decision?"

"OK," Mickey said. He rested his cup on the chart table and put his eye to the lens.

He slid the microfiche around for a minute, reviewing the last of the documents of the Inquisition.

"Here is something from Vincent on the brother James…"

Mickey adjusted the screen and sat up as he focused his eye in the scope as David got closer.

> *Why did you consider the ossuary of James when, in fact, we do not acknowledge his existence?*
> *Vincent: I will explain. Dr. Leonard was hired to prove the ossuary's authenticity to the owner, after it was discovered. He believed the ossuary to be genuine, and he believed the DNA could be used for cloning. When we obtained the samples from the sacred artifacts, he compared them to samples he had retained, and they were a genetic match. This fact changes history for us.*

Mickey raised his head.

"Well," David sighed, "Now we know."

Mickey refocused and slid the film around and found the final page of the Inquisition report.

> *The Inquisition has reached its decision on the events and activities regarding the three subjects.*
>
> *First, Doctor Henry Leonard: His death prevents us from taking any action against him personally, and it is the Inquisition's position to seal the records regarding his activities.*
> *Next, Michael Orsini: Your role in this was clearly one of conscious disregard for the laws of the Vatican. We find you guilty of trespassing and vandalism to sacred artifacts of the Vatican. The Inquisition will offer, in exchange for a signed statement of sworn secrecy and a signed agreement to never again enter Vatican City, probation.*
> *Orsini: Agreed.*

"Got off easy, no?" David said. Mickey nodded in agreement and sipped his coffee. He read on.

Finally, Cardinal Vincent, the conspiracy that you led to perform the unthinkable is beyond the Inquisition's comprehension. The fact that all that remains of your activities are the doctor's files and this investigation presents a dilemma we have struggled with regarding your sentence and the good of the Vatican. It has been decided that you will be offered a life of probation for the following considerations: You will sign a statement of sworn secrecy, and also a statement admitting your guilt and the fact that all of your activities were conducted outside of, and without the knowledge of, any office of the church.
Vincent: Yes, of course.
And, you will resign your position of cardinal and agree to never seek any future role or activity with the church or its members, except for your right to personal worship and prayer, perhaps for your own forgiveness.
Vincent: I see, yes.

Mickey scanned another page.

"That's about it, David," he said.

"Thanks."

"Looks like they did not want anyone to know this happened." Mickey offered.

"Yeah," David agreed, "Keeping the proof of the brother a secret probably helped them make their decision. There would be a lot of explaining to do, plus the media would be all over it. It really would have caused a lot of trouble."

"What if the media heard the truth?" Mickey said with a growing smile.

"We thought about that," David replied. "But only as a last resort, for our safety."

Mickey laughed in agreement.

"But that wouldn't be good for the kids," he continued. "They'd probably be treated like freaks of nature."

"You are a good person, David. Look at all that you are doing for them," Mickey gently said.

David looked out at the illuminated tower to the tunnel.

"Undoing," he muttered to himself.

As Mickey refreshed both coffees, he asked, "Will you see this Ex-Cardinal Vincent when you get to the orphanage?"

"No, I doubt it. He is probably somewhere in the Vatican calling the shots. He has a couple of thugs working for him. I imagine they will be there or be called in when we get to Bryce.

"Orsini?"

"No, thank God! He's long gone, vanished as best we can tell. The Inquisition is the only record of him after he cleaned house. He must have come back to help the cardinal one last time. His replacement, Scordo, is the one we have to watch out for."

"What does that mean, *clean house*?"

"He killed the doctors and the midwives, we figure, maybe more. From what we read, he was authorized to kill everyone involved and destroy all the evidence of the experiments. He made it all *go away*."

"How you say, an *Ice Man*."

"We say *Hit Man*, but that works too," David sighed.

50

Brian paid cash for a week's rental, but had to use his credit card and passport for insurance and damage deposit purposes.

"They said come back in an hour or two and they would have one ready," Brian informed the group that was waiting on the corner.

Two hours later, Brian exited the rental office with the keys to a red Vauxhall Vectra, a 4-door sedan.

"First car in was a bit of an upgrade, I hope you don't mind, Davy," Brian said.

"Upgrade to what?" David cautiously asked.

"Somethin' big enough that we don't have to fold you in half and grease you up to get you in the door. Her either, for that matter."

Brian fiddled with the key fob. The doors clicked and the trunk popped open. They dumped their packs in the trunk and Heather pulled out the maps.

"Sweet ride!" she complimented, admiring the leather interior. "Shotgun!" she whispered to Luc, passing him on the right side of the car and hopping in the front seat.

Brian followed.

"What the?" she exclaimed looking down at the steering wheel.

She opened the door to see Brian standing there, dangling the keys in his hand.

"OK, if you want to drive that bad, here," he said.

"I don't," she said getting out with her maps.

Brian drove as Heather navigated through the streets of the industrial port city, finding their way out to the M6 highway, which took them north.

The M55 brought them west into Blackpool, which sits on the coast, looking out into the Irish Sea. As they turned north, the scenery changed dramatically. Ocean surf and beaches were on their left side, with amusement rides and arcades on the other. The coast line of Blackpool was consumed by three large amusement parks, with smaller venues of eateries and arcades filling the spaces between them. Opposite, a boardwalk seemed to stretch forever.

The parks were still open, but the crowds were light in the chilly fall air; the beaches empty, save a few joggers and dog walkers.

"I'm hungry!" Luc announced from the back seat.

"Plenty of grease along here," Heather responded as they passed a fried dough stand.

"Can we?" Luc pleaded.

Brian smiled and parked the car.

"What do you think?" David asked, scanning the many options.

"Idea!" Brian exclaimed. "Everyone fend for themselves. Meet back here in fifteen minutes.

"We're on their turf, remember?" David cautioned. "How about you and Luc go for your grease fix and Heather and I will find some real food. Meet back here in fifteen, and take a phone just in case."

Luc produced two phones.

"Your one, we're two," Luc said handing David a phone with his speed dial number written in magic marker on the back.

Heather and David were returning to the car with their food when they passed an arcade and spotted Luc through the window stationed at a video game.

"Let's roll," David said, sticking his head through the doorway.

"OK."

"Woo-hoo!" Brian yelled from over his shoulder, seated in a race car simulator.

"You, too!" David said, as Luc picked up his bag of food.

"No way! I am sooo settin' the high score on this thing!"

"Focus!" David yelled.

Brian slapped the steering wheel, spinning it as he got up.

As they drove off, Brian set his food up on the dash. Two paper baskets: one with fries, the other with batter fried fish. He held his can of soda between his legs as he carefully shifted through the gears, everything being backwards to him.

Whad'ya get?" he asked Heather as he munched on a fry.

Heather looked slightly embarrassed then produced a similar basket of fries from her paper bag, followed by fried fish. It would have been too easy to say something, so Brian just smiled.

"Well, when in Rome," Heather conceded, breaking off a chunk of fish and popping it into her mouth. They ate for a minute in silence, Heather reading the map while she munched.

"Boddington House is about a mile northeast of the last park," she said.

As they approached the third park, an enormous roller coaster loomed overhead.

"Wow!" Heather said, gawking through the windshield.

The neon sign mounted on it said "Kaleidoscope."

"That thing is huge!" Luc cried from the back seat. They then drove past the entrance, the name "Wonderland" spanning over the roadway into the park.

51

The orphanage was an old Victorian, painted off-white with grey-blue shutters and a red front door. They cruised by very slowly, observing well lit rooms, the yard, and driveway. Brian parked the Vauxhall a few blocks away. The small group walked back and stopped a short, but safe distance from the house.

"There it is," said Heather.

"OK, here we are. Now what?" asked Brian.

"I hadn't planned that far," said David.

"Well, let's think about who we are looking for," Brian said. "Young kids live here—a bunch of 'em. And, being an orphanage, they should all come around for dinner. If we keep a watch on the place till then, hopefully Bryce will make an appearance, if he's not already in there. We can approach them after dinner before anyone takes off. This will also give us time to see if any undesirables come and go, if you know what I mean."

David raised his eyebrows up, impressed at the solid plan.

"Wuh? You don't think I know what I'm doing?" Brian defended.

"It's not that…" David started.

"Good. You start the lookout, while I catch some Z's in the car." He interrupted, then turned and walked away.

Brian returned to find they had taken up a position behind a small retaining wall in a driveway diagonally across the street, at a house where no one was home.

"Wassup?" Brian inquired.

"You were right," Heather answered. "A few kids came in, but there hasn't been that much activity. They've got to be done with dinner by now. I saw a couple kids through the windows, but I don't think too many are home."

"Maybe there aren't many?" Luc surmised. "The whole reason for the orphanage was to raise Bryce, so why add any new kids after he arrived?"

Heather nodded in agreement.

"I'm going in," David said. "No sense in wasting any time. Here," he said, handing the microfiche to Heather, which she stored in an envelope and zipped it in her daypack.

"We'll call you if we see anything suspicious. Speed dial two or three for us," Brian said handing David the phone with a "1" on it.

David crept around the left side of the Victorian, hugging the bushes and watching the windows, and then disappeared from sight. Meanwhile, Luc, Brian, and Heather maintained surveillance from behind the retaining wall.

A few minutes passed without any sign of him through the house's windows. In fact, there was no sign of any movement in the house.

"Too quiet," Brian stated. "I'm gonna go around back and see if I can see him in there."

He followed David's route except that he disappeared into the bushes, not around the corner of the house. Seconds later he reappeared, with dirty hands and knees, running in a crouch out of the bushes and toward Heather.

"What's wrong?" she asked, seeing the panicked look in Brian's eyes.

"A black Jag," he whispered. "It's parked in the driveway in back!"

Without responding, Heather flipped open her cell phone and pressed one. It rang five times and cut to voicemail.

"He's not picking up!" She pressed redial and let it ring five more times. "Come on, come on!" she pleaded, but got voicemail again.

As she turned to Brian, he grabbed her, forcing her down.

"Luc, get down!" he whispered as he ducked behind the wall with Heather.

Luc crouched down, looking over Brian and Heather, and watched them come out of the side door of Boddington House, turning toward the rear of the house. From their vantage point, there was no mistaking Scordo as the first man out. The next two were supporting David under his arms, his feet dragging across the ground. His head bobbed, then he lifted it—confirming he was conscious—but also revealing a face covered in blood.

Like statues, they sat motionless as they watched the four disappear down the driveway. Moments later they heard several car doors close and the car start. They ducked the headlight's flash as the jag turned out and sped away into the night.

Tears streamed down Heather's face. Brian and Luc gasped and watched the car's red tail lights disappear. They were speechless. Brian teared up—he was losing his cousin. The trip across the Atlantic had put distance to the evil they had experienced just a short time ago; the thought they would all not make it through this was put out of their minds after surviving the confrontation in Maine. Brian's stomach knotted as he put his hands on his knees and breathed deeply, trying to keep it together.

Heather's phone buzzed. She put it to her ear and a chill went up her spine at the Italian accent.

"Listen very carefully. Bring the boy and the film to the amusement park called Wonderland. Be at the gate to the big roller coaster at ten o'clock. You know I have no issue with killing him, so do not be late."

The phone beeped. The screen read "Call Ended." Heather slumped down against the retaining wall with her head between her knees, trembling.

"What did he say?" asked Brian.

"Ten o'clock, at the gate to the big roller coaster at Wonderland. They want the film and Luc." Her breathing quickened as she tried to talk.

"I'll go!" volunteered Luc.

"The hell you will!" ordered Brian.

Heather wiped the tears from her face, but more followed.

"They aren't going to let him go, are they?" she sniffled, as she lifted her head.

"It's a set up, for sure," conceded Brian as he sat down next to her. "After all of this, they aren't gonna just let us walk away."

"Well let's set them up!" Luc piped in.

Heather stared at the sky as she cried, the reality taking its toll.

"Why the amusement park?" she asked. "Why would they want the exchange in such a public place?" she sniffled.

Brian raised his eyebrows.

"Maybe if someone gets shot there would be too many suspects," he speculated.

"Yeah, what do they call that, hiding in plain sight?" Heather added, sniffling and wiping her eyes.

"Like setting off a grenade to start a riot," Brian continued. "Then they take out the targets, grab the film, and walk out."

"And what about Luc?"

"His body can't be found, so they leave with him. Case closed, mission accomplished."

"You guys are really starting to creep me out," Luc said, crouching on the driveway.

Brian looked at Luc.

"Sorry, kid," Brian said, suddenly realizing his hypothetical was actually real.

After a long moment, Luc jumped up.

"Hey, what if *we* start the riot, like pull a fire alarm before they're ready to make their move!"

Heather refocused from the sky to Luc.

"I like that," Heather said with another sniffle. "Maybe we can cause a panic so *we* disappear in the crowd and meet after near an exit."

"And maybe they don't know I'm with you," Brian added. "Maybe we can surprise them a little. What time is it?" Brian asked as he stood up.

Heather looked at her cell phone.

"Nine-thirty."

"Better get moving," Luc said, offering a hand to Heather.

"God, I hope this works."

"Of course it will," Luc encouraged, "You saved me right?"

Luc paused, looking down, then pulled it back together. "And we kicked their big ass car a good one with your little Camry, right? This one will be easy."

Luc stared at Heather maintaining a confident look. To waver would be to fail—Heather had to believe.

The three tuned the plan as they drove to the amusement park, pulling in the north entrance.

"Park at the end near the road so we can get out if there is a traffic jam," Heather directed, still sniffling a bit.

"Smart," Brian replied as he brought the car to a stop.

"My dad used to take me to see the Bulls when MJ played— always sold out," she said, half paying attention, her mind stuck on the image of a bloody David being dragged away.

52

David climbed out of the back seat of the black Jaguar after Scordo, who had his coat over his shoulders like a cape, with free and armed hands underneath. The gash over his eye had stopped bleeding and his face had been cleaned up. Two other Dark Men followed, entering Wonderland Park through the east gate. It was a straight line to the tallest roller coaster. The closer they got, the more crowded it became. The last hundred yards opened up to a carnival-like scene with games offering stuffed animal prizes, cotton candy vendors, a small photo booth with flashes popping from behind its curtain, a clown selling balloons, and the entrance to the Kaleidoscope, one of the largest coasters in the world. Neon lights mounted to its complex structure created a brilliant, flashing backdrop to the busy square. The crowd swelled near the coaster's entrance.

"It's ten!" Scordo whipped around, looking for Heather and Luc. The second man gripped David's upper arm with one hand and kept the other stuffed in the pocket of his long black overcoat. The third nodded to the others and disappeared into the crowd.

David looked at Scordo, his ribs aching from the punches his cement block hands had delivered to his side. He was bigger than David and probably just as strong, even though much older. Then there was the gun. The gash over his eye stung and the back of his head throbbed from whatever had hit him from behind when he entered the orphanage.

As the crowd thinned, Heather appeared, standing less than 10 feet away; both of her hands clasping a manila envelope. She took a step forward. Scordo spoke.

"Where is he!?" he demanded.

"You get the film. I get David, *then* you get Luc."

"No chance!" he barked as he leaned forward as if he wanted to come out firing from beneath his coat. "You don't call the shots!"

"Then you don't get the film," she said with all the courage she could muster.

The train car from the Kaleidoscope flew by behind them, its passengers screaming as it rumbled the ground. The screams subsided as the train climbed the next hill, with a loud clacking sound of the track's safety ratchets. A woman walked between them, oblivious to their meeting, as the flow of foot traffic surged. For the moment, they all stood still, the two men flanking David and facing Heather who was motionless, maintaining a fix on Scordo.

His move.

Brian caught glimpses from 50 yards away, in position by a fire alarm mounted to a light pole next to the cotton candy vendor.

Two small children scampered between them, halting by a clown selling balloons. David's eyes darted about, looking for the third Dark Man, as the clown, in a striped jump suit and bright orange hair, gave balloons to the children. The children provided momentary cover; David thought, or at least hoped, they would not come out firing with kids that close. As the children left, the clown turned and his two-foot long shoe, flailing around like a scuba diver's fin, stepped on Scordo's foot.

"Watch it!" he barked, bringing out an arm and shoving the clown out of his way.

The balloon strings wrapped around Scordo's free arm, requiring his gun hand to untangle himself. David saw his chance. He turned and grabbed the other Dark Man by the coat pockets, clamping his hand inside, and drove him backwards until he tripped and fell.

"Go!" he yelled back to Heather, then darted into the crowd.

Her pause to assess the situation took less than a second. Scordo was wrestling himself free from the balloons and the other was flat on his back, scrambling to get up. She turned and ran into the crowd.

Must find David! she thought, cutting left. She bounced off several people, then saw an opening in the crowd where she could speed up to a full run.

As she took her first full stride she was suddenly jerked to a stop by a painful yank on her upper arm. The third Dark Man had her, spinning her around. He pulled her close, so they stood shoulder to shoulder, his hand jammed up under her armpit, cutting off the circulation and nearly lifting her off the ground. He jerked her even closer and put his mouth to her ear, his other hand remained stashed in his coat pocket.

"Scream, and I'll shoot you in the stomach," he said gritting his teeth and motioning from inside his coat pocket. "Now slide that envelope into my coat," he demanded with a smirk.

She reached across and slowly tucked the envelope into the inside pocket of his overcoat. He smiled a little more, then turned toward the vendors and dragged her along, keeping them shoulder to shoulder.

Scordo, now free from the balloons, shoved the clown to the ground.

"You fool!" he cried, then spun around and scanned the crowd.

Everyone was gone. The second man had recovered from David's shove and was battling foot traffic in the direction David had run. Scordo brushed himself off, adjusted his coat, and followed.

"Keep moving!" the third barked, as he dragged Heather by a stand where people were shooting water guns into balloons to explode them; the cotton candy was next, where he turned—this was his exit.

BAM!

From out of nowhere Brian cross-checked the Dark Man, sending him over the counter and into the water balloon game. Brian had Heather by the sleeve to ensure she separated from her captor as he flew. He was up on the balls of his feet, bouncing like a boxer, ready to go. For the moment, the Dark Man stayed down behind the counter.

"Let's go!" he said maintaining a fix on the counter.

They bolted back into the crowd toward the north gate.

David fought his way through the crowd, predicting which way Heather would be running. The second Dark Man was closing in.

Damn! David thought.

He had to lose him before he ran into Heather. He cut to the left, hopped a small fence, and pushed through some bushes. He heard the Dark Man grunt as he scaled the chain link fence, just a couple seconds back. David stood at the base to the first hill of the *Le Mans*, a double track, racing roller coaster. The car on the near track had just passed and was ratcheting up the steep slope of the vintage, wood-framed coaster. There was no time to think. David accelerated across to the second track, greeting its train of passengers.

He jumped, landing on the connector between the first and second car. The passengers in the front row of the second car were startled at David's sudden presence; the coaster started its climb.

"What the!?" a young man yelled.

"Sorry!" David apologized, his voice barely audible above the sounds of the two climbing cars.

David's feet rested on the mechanism that held the cars together, supporting him in a crouched position as he gripped the safety bar that crossed the passengers' laps. He offered an apologetic smile to his four new traveling companions.

After a long moment, the train car leveled off and David found his exit.

"Sorry about that," he reiterated to the passengers.

As he stood to jump he heard people from the rear of the car complaining.

"What the heck!?"

"Watch it!"

He turned to see the Dark Man working his way forward, scrambling over the passengers. He was a car back and coming. Suddenly, the entire coaster tilted to its left and started to accelerate, executing a smooth, sweeping left turn. The passengers were raising their hands in the air.

He jumped.

The coaster immediately dove, sucking its trailing cars—and the Dark Man—into the abyss between the white wooden-framed peaks.

David's body slammed into the four by four inch post supporting the wooden rail on the maintenance catwalk. He clutched it with both arms as the cars whooshed past, accelerating into the next valley; his feet and legs dangled a hundred feet above the park.

Everything ached. He wondered how many bones were broken, how many stitches he would need. He refocused.

Move!

He took a deep breath and started the climb down the outside of the white wooden structure, which cloaked him from the rest of the park. He moved between large triangles of wood, sliding down the angles and grabbing the next vertical beam, having nothing to grip for a second as he traversed each section. He dropped the last 10 feet into the bushes and collapsed to the ground; he lay there for a minute to catch his breath.

He stood, then collapsed back down to his knees. His foot throbbed. He felt it hit something as he landed, but now the pain told him it was more than a bruise.

The Dark Man exited the coaster as people pointed at him and complained to the attendant. He hopped the fence and took up a position in the bushes on a corner to monitor foot traffic in two directions.

Brian and Heather raced to the north exit and ducked between a row of hedges, diving out onto a small, private lawn.

They got to their knees and gasped for air. After a minute, Brian got himself to his feet and helped Heather up. She hugged him hard.

"God, that was close," she said, releasing him and bending back over to continue catching her breath.

"Where's Luc?" asked Brian. "He was supposed to be right here."

They surveyed the area; there was no sign of him.

"Did they get the film?" asked Brian.

"Yeah."

They moved to the darkest corner of the lawn and sat with their backs up against a fence, still breathing hard.

"Should we go look for them?" asked Heather.

"No, we should stay put. Those guys are probably still out there."

"But David doesn't know we are here. Where will he go?"

"He'll be OK. If we get caught, it will ruin everything. Where the hell did Luc go?" Brian whispered.

"I don't like this," Heather said after a few long breaths.

"One at a time," Brian consoled. "First, we're safe. We need to think about where Luc is. That's why we're here, dammit! That's what David would do. We need to find Luc."

They sat for a few minutes as their breathing returned to normal. Then, the bushes started to move. A single blue balloon floated above the hedge, tethered to the intruder. The bushes separated, and David limped out onto the lawn.

"David!" Heather cried as she jumped up and hugged him as hard as she could. The pain on his ribs was excruciating, but he held her tightly, releasing the balloon.

"How did you know?" she whispered.

David released the hug and sat down on the grass, taking the weight off his foot.

The bushes started to shake again. They all froze for a moment, then looked down to see a two-foot long clown shoe appear, then another.

"I found him on the way over. Sorry it took so long; I can't run in these things." Luc apologized, peeling off his bushy orange wig.

The three Dark Men reunited in front of Kaleidoscope.

"What happened to the girl?" Scordo grilled the third Dark Man.

"There was another one. He caught me off guard; she got away."

"David?" asked Scordo to the second.

He shook his head. Scordo glared at the third.

"The film!?"

The third Dark Man reached into his vest pocket and pulled out the manila envelope, smiling, and laughing a little while he shook it up in the air.

"Well, not a total loss, no?" he said.

Scordo sneered, grabbing the envelope and reached inside. He cracked a smile as his fingers felt the shiny vellum. As he pulled it out, his smile vanished. The film was much smaller than the microfiche. He pulled it all of the way out, revealing a strip of three instant photos. The first one was a close-up of Brian smiling, flipping the bird at the camera lens. The second was a little blurry, but it was obviously Brian's naked behind. And the third was a combination of the two, Brian bending all the way over and reaching through his legs to give the salute.

Scordo threw the photos at the ground in disgust and stormed off toward the exit as the others followed in a silent hurry, scanning the crowd a final time. Behind the instant photo booth, a single blue balloon floated into the sky.

"Where to?" asked David.

"We hadn't planned that far ahead," laughed Brian, as the four walked out the east exit, constantly scanning the crowd.

At the car, Heather inspected the gash over David's eye. She moved to touch the wound, but retracted her hand knowing she would not provide any comfort.

"I thought I lost you," she trembled.

"Me too," he said, hugging her.

As she squeezed, David grunted a little.

"Sorry, I think I busted a rib," David whispered as Heather eased her grip.

"Save it for later!" Brian cracked, starting up the car. Luc was already in the back seat, forcing David and Heather to split up. As David buckled himself in the front passenger seat, he felt something on his shoulder; he looked back; Heather was handing him a small manila envelope.

"You're best to take care of this," she smiled.

David smiled and zipped the microfiche back into his chest pocket.

"They must be really pissed right about now," Brian laughed, driving out the exit.

"Oh, yeah," David replied as leaned his head back and felt to see if his forehead was bleeding, "Nothin' funnier than pissed off people with guns."

53

A gust of rain pelted the Vauxhall's windshield, waking Brian. David was already up and signaled to Brian to get out. Brian eased the key out of the ignition so the door chimes wouldn't sound and slipped out without waking Luc or Heather. Tucked behind the public restrooms, the car was out of view from the street and the beach looked empty.

They took turns using the men's room and hiding from the rain under the eves of the building. David examined the cuts on his face in the mirror. It could have been much worse. He lifted his shirt to see a large purple bruise on his side. It hurt when he inhaled. His foot was throbbing and swollen tight in his hiking shoe. He reasoned it be best not to take it off.

Back outside, they stood resting on the wall of the building, watching the surf roll in.

"We should get a hotel and get cleaned up," David said.

"Where do you think they are right now?" asked Brian.

"Back at the orphanage would be my bet."

"So, what do we do?"

David shrugged, then poked his head out from under the eve and looked at the sky.

"It's letting up. How about some breakfast, then a shower?"

"And after that? Lemme guess…"

David smiled, "Then, how about we go back to that orphanage and see what they're up to."

Brian smiled back. "Hunting the hunter?"

"Something like that."

Brian looked down for a moment, his smile fading.

"Hey, if you ever want to know what feeling like shit is," he said looking up, "watch your cousin get dragged away all beat up by killers."

"Sorry, cuz. I should have sent you in. They never would have taken you."

"Huh?"

"They hit me on the head," David said with a grin.

With most beachfront establishments closed for the season, they had to drive a bit to find an open restaurant. It was small, with a "breakfast" sign in the window. They went in and, out of habit, sat at the table furthest to the back, Heather and David facing the front door and street.

The waitress placed a basket of biscuits on the table—Brian and Luc's hands instantly collided as they grabbed, nearly dumping it over.

"Gentlemen," David cautioned.

Luc sighed apologetically, while Brian dove back in for a packet of butter.

"We're going back," Brian announced to Luc and Heather as he took a bite of his biscuit.

"To the US?" Heather asked, as the waitress worked her way around the table, pouring cups of coffee.

She placed cream and sugar on the table, but no one moved for it. Brian waited for the waitress to leave before continuing.

"To Boddington House," he answered as he buttered his biscuit.

Heather looked to David.

"They're probably there. Maybe they have Bryce."

"That's what we're gonna find out," David said. "If they're not there, maybe we can lure Bryce out of the house, or sneak in disguised."

"Yeah, or we could just, ya know, go in and *ask for Bryce*," interrupted Brian.

David looked at him, surprised.

"Okayyy, we could try that."

The waitress returned and took their orders. As they waited for their food, they discussed the options.

"They'll probably be there, so we need to plan for that," David said.

"We should have a safe place to meet in case we get split up," Heather added.

"We need to find out which kid is Bryce, then maybe get someone to bring him a message—maybe written on the copy of his birth certificate," Luc offered.

"Das gub," Brian said with a mouthful of biscuit, pointing to Luc.

54

The Rhone River flowed at its slowest pace, waiting for winter's snow to recharge it. The second floor apartment's living room window provided a view from a single rocking chair to the river and the urban scenery of Basel, Switzerland. In the small kitchen, a tea kettle started to whistle as the phone rang.

"Allo," a man's deep voice said softly, as his free hand spun the knob on the stove, silencing the kettle.

"It's Vincent."

"It's been a long time," the thick Italian accent responded.

"Yes. It has. Of course best to keep it that way, until now. I have a situation that needs your attention."

"Where?"

"The orphanage. Scordo is there with his men, but they… Let's just say I need you there to make sure things get finished properly. He can fill you in when you arrive."

"I understand, your Eminence."

"Orsini?"

"Yes?"

"Now more than ever, do not fail me. Godspeed, my friend."

The phone clicked.

Orsini cradled the phone and finished his tea. He rinsed the cup and put it in the strainer next to the sink, then started moving swiftly. He opened a vintage suitcase and threw in some clothes then pulled out a black suit coat from the closet, laying it on the bed. He reached up to the ceiling panel of the closet and yanked on the trim; the panel fell out under the weight of a small gym bag. He dumped the black bag's contents on the bed: two passports, a 38-caliber revolver in a shoulder holster, a switchblade, and a box of ammunition. Orsini stayed in motion, loading the revolver, put on the holster over his pressed white shirt and slid the gun in. He dumped a handful of ammunition into the pocket of the suit coat and tossed the half full box into the suitcase. He spun around and opened the nightstand drawer and pulled out a derringer and tossed it in on top of his clothes. From under the stand, he yanked on the bottom, releasing a secret drawer full of money in multiple currencies. He dumped it on top of the derringer, taking two bundles of one hundred pound sterling notes and pocketing them. He latched the suitcase closed, the entire process taking just a couple of minutes.

Orsini put on the suit coat, then a black wool overcoat, in which he pocketed the switchblade and passports. He spun the thermostat down, grabbed the black fedora hanging on the back of the door, clicked the light off, and left.

He emerged from the apartment building and walked briskly along the river, crossing the first bridge and reaching a large cathedral on the other side.

The church was all but empty. Orsini removed his hat and walked down the main aisle to the front, dipped a knee while executing a quick sign of the cross with his hat in hand, and moved to his left. He lowered both knees on the pad at the candle station, and parked the suitcase. Dozens of flickering lights in little red globes illuminated his aged, chiseled face. He lit five candles and prayed. Motionless, the candle light danced about his face, scars and wrinkles flashing; Orsini sighed deeply as he prayed.

After a minute, he picked up the suitcase and walked quickly out of the cathedral, retracing his steps over the bridge, before flinging the bag into the back seat of a silver BMW 5 series sedan and speeding away.

Three hours later Orsini slowly pulled the BMW onto the train and parked. He reclined his seat all the way back as the trip though the Chunnel began. It was so many years ago that this all began, and so many years since he thought it had all ended.

He was a young street brawler in Palermo, Sicily, constantly in trouble with the law and those around him. By the time he was 20, he had accumulated a list of charges, including robbery and assault. It was only through sheer luck that there were no convictions.

When he was 25, he beat a man to death in a bar after an argument, the other man having spat in his face. After serving four years of a 10-year sentence, Orsini was released on good behavior. It would not be long before he was back in jail or dead.

Bishop Vincent was new to the city of Palermo, coming in from Boston on a relief mission to rebuild neighborhoods that had been devastated by a recent fire. As part of the terms of his probation, Orsini was assigned to the rebuilding program.

Although he was a tremendous physical asset, each day, one man would outwork him—the Bishop. Orsini was impressed with the Bishop's commitment and dedication to his mission and, over time, became refocused. The wages he received were enough to rent a small apartment. His needs were now different, now met. Orsini could live as a man.

With just six months to go on his probation, vandals broke into the church and robbed it of money stored in the office, plus religious items. They started a fire, but it self extinguished, causing repairable damage, sparing the church and community of a horrible loss.

When he learned the thieves' identities, his rage was too much to suppress. The church and Bishop Vincent had saved him from a certain fate and these robbers not only stole, but attempted to destroy the house that saved his life. He found them and beat them, killing one, and almost killing the other.

The investigation was slow to make progress, as the local police were also members of the burnt parish. Questions were asked, and there were those who suspected Orsini, but there was little need to press on, as justice had been served. The case would never be closed. Weeks later, Orsini confessed to the Bishop.

When the Bishop was called to Rome to serve as cardinal, Orsini was offered the position of assistant and driver. But it was the other skills Orsini had demonstrated that got him the position.

He remembered every detail about the meeting where he was introduced to Dr. Leonard. Although bizarre, the belief that there could be a second coming was so intense that Orsini could not question the man who saved his life. His service would be instrumental.

The cardinal provided the access to the facility where the Shroud of Turin was kept. Dr. Leonard instructed him on exactly what type and size of sample was needed. The Sudarium in Spain, on the other hand, took two years to obtain. The process involved recruiting someone and funding him to live in Spain, then securing him a job at the museum. Finally, when the room that stored the Sudarium was scheduled to have maintenance performed, access was provided. The attendant, however, "stumbled" on some exposed live wires left by the construction crew and was electrocuted. His death was classified as an unfortunate accident.

Once the samples were safe in the laboratory on the second floor of the stone house in Vatican City, Orsini morphed into the head of security for the covert operation.

The two mothers were young nuns hand picked by the cardinal. It was only when he was certain of their loyalty that he approached them with the opportunity to be the birth mothers to a new world order.

The birthing doctor Diorio would also be let in on the experiment, just prior to the births, but the midwives, the Lombardo sisters, had no need to know and were told they were illegitimate children of the nuns.

When it was done, Orsini's skills were called on again. The clean-up was necessary. The house was cleared of lab equipment. The doctors and midwives were dealt with. Only the mothers remained. While they believed their existence depended on their silence, the news of their death was deemed more of a risk to the operation. They would be watched closely, remaining on the cardinal's staff.

Glen Jennings and Father Henry were in place for over a year, unknowingly waiting for the babies to mature. The unknown source of funding seemed endless. Whatever was needed: funds to buy the brownstone and orphanage outright; the laboratory and scientist; real estate investments to legitimize Glen Jennings' presence in Beacon Hill; and, of course, Orsini's compensation.

After delivering Bryce to Boddington House, he arrived in Basel to an apartment he had never seen. Once inside, there was a briefcase containing the deed to the property and a bankbook, both in his name. The savings account showed a two million Swiss Franc balance. The payoff was not hush money, but a life long retainer, as the project, if successful, would not end in his lifetime.

Until now, only one call had come in the years that followed. Orsini responded loyally, backing the cardinal's story to the Inquisition of the failed experiments.

The last 10 years yielded a simple, solitary life in Basel, going to the cathedral each day to pray and light five candles, one for each life that he had taken.

His head bobbed forward, the movement shaking him out of his fog. The Chunnel train had come to a stop.

55

The rain had reduced to a drizzle as they parked the car three blocks down from Boddington House.

"I'll check it out," Brian said, as he pulled a maroon sweat-shirt out of his daypack.

Brian held up the sweatshirt with its large silver shield and initials BLC on the chest, and, before anyone could say something, flipped it inside out and pulled it over his head.

"Be right back."

He took off around the block so he would cruise past Boddington House on the return trip, while the rest waited at the car. David removed the bag of ice on his foot and got out, still limping and wondering if he could get the hiking shoe off without too much pain.

Brian returned, pulling down the hood.

"No sign of them," he said, answering the questioning looks that greeted him.

"Let's go see if anyone knows where Bryce is," David said.

One block before the house, they approached a group of young teenagers dressed mostly in black, all with body piercings and dyed hair. Most were smoking cigarettes as they hung out on the corner.

"Hey," one of them called out.

"Hi," responded Luc.

"American?" he asked back.

"Yeah."

"What brings 'ya here?"

The group had slowed to a stop to allow Luc's exchange to run its course, when Brian spotted the Jaguar.

"Problem!" he announced.

David and Heather's view was blocked by the small group as the Jaguar approached from the opposite direction and pulled into the driveway, disappearing between the orphanage and the neighboring house.

"It's in," Brian reported.

"Visiting a friend," Luc continued, the group oblivious to Brian's comments.

"At Boddington House?"

"Yeah."

"Do you know the man who runs the house, a Henry Jones?" Heather interrupted, no longer in a rush to keep moving.

"Yeah, sure."

Brian kept a fix on the house while they chatted. Another kid, maybe 15, hopped off the stone wall and removed the cigarette from his mouth.

"You know Father Henry?" he asked in a pure English accent.

He wore a black leather jacket over a black AC/DC tee shirt, dark, baggy jeans with dangling chains, and black leather boots. His head was mostly shaved and the remaining hair was gelled into a Mohawk, dyed green on the very tips.

"Well, no not exactly," Heather answered, as she counted four silver hoops mounted to his left ear. "How well do you know him?"

"Bit of a boozer. Usually passed out in front of the tele'," he said in a disgusted tone as he flung his cigarette into the storm drain.

"Do you live there?" asked David.

"Boddington House, yeah. But Father Henry lives in the house next door."

"Do you know Bryce Jones?"

The kid narrowed his eyes, shifted his weight to his right leg, and crossed his arms.

"Who's askin'?" He said in a defensive tone.

"My name is David," he said, speaking for the group, "and this is Heather, Brian, and Luc," he added, pointing to each individual. "We have some information regarding Bryce's family."

The kid raised an eyebrow.

"Yeah, I know him, but his family is dead. Plane crash when he was a baby."

"He has a brother—a half brother he doesn't know about," Heather said.

"Really? Well, Bryce comes and goes, as do most of us in the house. Not much supervision with the old man bein' that way."

"Is Bryce there now?" asked Luc.

"Haven't seen him in a while."

"Can you help us find him?" asked David.

"Sorry, ain't got time or interest in that."

David unzipped his vest pocket and pulled out a one hundred dollar bill.

"I'll pay you."

The kid's eyes opened wide.

"Well, that's a little different now."

David handed him the bill.

"And another hundred when we find him," David smiled.

"We are in a bit of a hurry," Heather added.

"Let's go then," he said, nodding the Mohawk to his friends and bidding them goodbye.

"Do you have a name?" asked David.

"Benny."

Benny started walking down the block toward a main street. Luc followed admiring the daring style of this kid. The earrings, the hair, and the Union Jack that spanned the upper back of his jacket caused Luc to think this kid wanted to be some kind of rock star. Luc caught up alongside.

"Like your hair. Pretty sick," Luc said.

"Thanks, mate."

They walked by a parked car with its window open. Benny spied a pack of cigarettes on the dash. He grabbed the pack, removed two cigarettes, and placed it back on the dash.

"No reason to be completely rude," Benny shrugged, as he lit one and slid the other into the inside vest pocket of his leather jacket.

They reached a small pub with a billiard table.

"Isn't Bryce a little young to be hanging out in bars?" David asked, limping a bit as they entered.

"The lads shoot pool. And, they have good food here," Benny retorted. "Lots of kids hang out here, just to have a place to get away. He's not here anyway," he said, completing his scan of the room.

They walked around the downtown area, stopping in at a couple more pubs and an arcade, but no Bryce.

"What about the amusement park?" Heather asked.

"Sometimes we go there to hang at night, but there's no action during the day."

They walked further down the main drag and found an empty park with a playground.

"Sometimes he hangs here, especially at night," Benny said, lowering his voice as if there were others nearby, "At night, this is where you can score just about anything you might want—or need."

Heather looked at David and raised her eyebrows. Benny sat on a swing and gave it a little push.

"So how do I know I'm not sendin' trouble my friend's way? You guys just show up outta nowhere and flash money around looking for Bryce Jones. Don't seem right. Americans too, at that. So just why are you here?" he asked as he gently swung.

"Have you noticed the men in dark coats at the orphanage?" asked David.

"Yeah, I see one or two from time to time. They check in with Father Henry. There's been a few of them hanging around lately, now that you mention it. Why do you ask?"

Luc hopped on the swing next to Benny and kicked himself going.

"*They* are the trouble. They don't want Bryce to know he has a brother," Luc responded.

"That's friggin' ridiculous. What in Christ's name do they care about Bryce Jones?"

"Hey, HEY! Careful," cautioned Brian.

"What do you mean?"

"Uh, nothing. Is Father Jones a priest?" Brian changed the subject.

"Sort of retired, as it were. I mean he's got no parish, but I think the church helps out with the finances in running the house. That is, if you define runnin' it as being drunk and not even carin' what goes on."

David continued: "Does Father Jones…"

"Now what about those men in black coats and Bryce's brother?" Benny interrupted.

"Let's find Bryce and we'll fill you in," Heather said, motioning to move on from the park.

"Where to now?" Brian asked Benny.

"'Bout all I can do right now; he's just not around."

"Will he come back to the house tonight?" asked Heather.

"No tellin'. I don't go snoopin' in his room to see when he comes and goes. I'll meet you on the corner tomorrow morning. I want that other hundred. If he comes home tonight, I'll bring him to you."

Benny walked out of the small park and rounded the corner in the direction of the orphanage.

"Back to the hotel?" Brian suggested.

"Guess so. I'm hungry," David replied.

As Luc moved to get off the swing, something in the grass next to him caught his eye. He reached into the grass, and came up with a cell phone. As the other three walked with their backs to him, Luc stuffed the cell phone into his jacket pocket, then ran a few steps to catch up.

56

Scordo poured two scotches, sliding one to Father Henry and sipping the other. Henry sat at the dining room table as Scordo paced back and forth. The room was all but dark, only a single oil candle in the center of the table and the last bit of daylight illuminating the room.

"We must watch Bryce very closely," said Scordo. "No running around town where they might run into him."

"He is very hard to contain; always been a discipline problem," defended Henry.

"If they get to him, then he'll be considered a risk to the operation, like them, and be treated as such."

"So you're just going to gun those kids down in cold blood after everything we have done?" Henry asked.

"If security becomes an issue, I don't need to tell you what we must do. So watch him closely. Every time he leaves I want my men to know about it."

The dining room lit up from headlights turning into the driveway. Out the window, they watched a silver BMW disappear between the house and the orphanage.

Henry froze when he entered. It had been nearly 14 years.

"Or-si-ni," he whispered, his hand trembling over his empty glass.

He got right to business.

"I am looking for Scordo."

Scordo glanced at Henry, then back.

"Vincent sent you?" Scordo asked.

"Yes, are you Scordo?"

"Yes."

Orsini sat down at the table. Another Dark Man entered the dining room and stood silent, knowing very well the name Henry had muttered.

"How is Bryce?" Orsini asked Henry, as he picked up the bottle of scotch and studied the label.

"Good, uh—fine!" Henry said, his voice cracking a little. "He's all grown up."

Orsini poured three fingers into Henry's empty glass.

"And I trust you are taking good care of Luc, Mr. Scordo?" he said, turning to Scordo, simultaneously sliding the drink over to Henry.

Scordo didn't like this one bit. He controlled his rage at the thought that he had to answer to this man after so many years had passed, so many years where Orsini was just a distant dark memory and he was now the "go to man." By Orsini's presence it was clear Vincent no longer trusted Scordo—but then again how could one blame him. The initial compromising of the crucial documents, the bumbled attempt to finish things at the amusement park, not to mention having to wire funds to Nova Scotia for bail, all added up to a failure warranting the call. Yet, the question Orsini asked indicated that Vincent had not shared all of the facts with him.

"He's a straight 'A' student," Scordo replied with his back to him, staring out the window.

"Good. Now, tell me about your problem."

Scordo's blood boiled. He turned and answered.

"Americans—four students: three male, one female. They broke into my office and saw the files. They know everything."

Orsini shook his head in disappointment.

"Where are they?"

"Not sure. They came for Bryce, but we intercepted them. Then they got away."

"Four American teenagers," Orsini said as he shook his head again. "Well, they should not be so difficult to find around here. And where is Bryce?"

No one answered.

"Henry?" Orsini redirected the question.

"I don't know. I saw him at dinner," Henry said without looking up.

Orsini turned to Scordo.

"Maybe someone should check the house!" Orsini's voice grew louder as he lost his patience.

Scordo looked at the silent Dark Man and jerked his head toward the orphanage. The Dark Man moved quickly out of the room. Orsini slid the bottle over to Henry, who half filled his glass and took a large swig. The three remained silent until the Dark Man returned.

"Not there. No one has seen him for over an hour," he reported.

"Probably out somewhere shooting pool or hanging out in the park," Henry offered as an excuse.

"Excellent!" Orsini said in sarcastic disgust. "So we have a breach in security and don't even know where the boy is? I suggest you get someone over to that park and find him!"

Scordo slammed his empty glass on the table and left the room, the Dark Man following. A few moments later, the two men left through the front door. Henry excused himself, retreating to the kitchen and gulping down the rest of his drink. He then went upstairs, not noticing the partially opened pantry door, or the gelled green tip of hair sticking out from behind it.

Henry took a flask from his bedside table drawer. He put his feet up on the bed and sat propped up by pillows; he took a swig. As he swallowed, he picked up an opened envelope with *Sarah* in the return address block. It had arrived the day before; it was too late. There was nothing he could do.

It was nearly 15 years ago that he arrived at Boddington House. The job looked perfect. He never had his own parish, but after working closely with Vincent in the church in Palermo for many years, he was asked to come to Rome, where he served on his staff for five years. When Vincent was certain of his loyalty, the offer came. Boddington House presented the perfect way to ride out his career with the church. The private funding made it all possible; there was no competition for the job and no cleric policy to navigate through. He was very grateful to Vincent, until it all happened.

The project tested his faith. He was not sure this was a path to be taken for the sake of hope or belief. Then there was Orsini. The killing spree devastated him. He could not comprehend the act nor believe he was a part of it. While in Rome, he had befriended the Lombardo sisters and often assisted them in their helping young mothers. His heart was ripped out, his loyalty shattered, but it was too late. To now refuse his commitment to the project was to die. Even after Bryce was delivered to the house, his depression increased. Alcohol was the only way he could sleep most days. And at certain times, like April and May, the anniversary of the births and deaths, he would remain drunk for days to cope with his guilt and depression.

Now they were back, to do more killing, four or five more—and maybe even him—all to hide what they had done.

He put the flask to his lips one more time.

57

The town around the three amusement parks was jammed with shops and small hotels, but now off-season, there was a smaller crowd, a crowd that would all but vanish in a week, when the parks closed for the season. Some hotels offered cheap rooms with no frills to support the teens who would come to the beach to party; the kind that took cash and did not ask for identification.

Theirs was a two-room suite on the second floor with a view of the ocean. The Vauxhall was tucked away behind a closed souvenir shop a few blocks away. The rooms were clean and simple. Brian knocked twice and announced himself.

"Hey!"

Luc jumped up from the couch and opened the door. He carried two large paper shopping bags by their handles which read, "Mr. Fu's."

"Oh, man, that smells good!" Heather exclaimed, as Brian started unloading white take out containers of Chinese food.

Heather quickly emptied the other bag of cans beer, soda, and bottled water. David sat at the table with his foot up on another chair, his shoe finally off, icing two broken toes and holding another ice pack on his ribs. Luc grabbed a container of teriyaki beef on sticks and a soda and moved to the couch so David could keep his foot elevated.

"Think he'll show?" Heather asked, as she sipped some won ton soup.

"A hundred bucks is a hundred bucks," David responded, opening a container of lo mein.

"Actually, over here, it's more like sixty," Brian said as he guzzled half a beer.

"Maybe we should we go to the amusement park and look around?" she continued. "But we don't even know what he looks like."

Luc was on the couch, semi reclined, eating his food.

"I do," he said.

"How-zat?" Brian asked as he started to feed.

"Leather jacket and a green Mohawk."

"Sure, kid. No way!" Brian mumbled through a mouthful.

"Not kidding. I bet it's him!"

"He's a derelict," Brian swallowed.

"He's a good guy," Luc insisted.

He was now fully reclined on the couch, playing a game on his cell phone with one hand and eating his beef teriyaki with the other, while David, Heather, and Brian sat at the small table. Brian was in high gear loading his plate with some of everything. Luc stuck the half-eaten stick back in the container and pulled out the phone he found in the park and flipped it open, holding the two side by side, the rest oblivious to him as they ate.

"OK, so why is he takin' Davy's money and leading us around town on a wild goose chase?" Brian said after washing down his food with some beer.

"He just doesn't trust us. Not yet, anyway." Luc argued. "Can you imagine if some people came up to you out of nowhere and told you that you had a secret brother?

"Uh, no," Brian answered as he cracked open another can of beer.

"Well, I can!"

"Ouch," Heather whispered to David, "Walked right into that one."

They both smiled and chuckled.

"I'm still not buyin' it!" Brian continued as he shoveled a forkful of lo mein into his mouth.

"He's my brother. I can tell," Luc asserted, pressing the power button of the left phone and simultaneously playing a game on the right one. The left screen lit up with the message: *"Hello Bryce!"*

"There are things you know, you just feel, like when your brother is standing next to you, there's this connection, this bond you can't explain, but you feel it. You just know it's him."

"I think you're delirious, that's what you're feeling." Brian said, then downing his beer, and squeezing the aluminum can. He let out a loud belch as he tossed it into the wastebasket.

"Wanna bet?" challenged Luc.

"Sure, how much?"

"How about a hundred bucks?"

"Make it two hundred."

"Deal," Luc said calmly as he closed the phone and retrieved his meat on a stick.

"Hey!?" David squawked, choking on his food.

Heather and Brian cleaned up the dinner mess, while David rested his foot.

"I'll run this to the dumpster," Brian said, picking up the bags of trash.

Heather reached into the last bag and produced a bottle of wine. She opened it with her Swiss Army knife and poured the wine in plastic cups she found in the bathroom. She handed one cup to David.

"Here's to?"

"Being here," David finished for her.

They drank and Heather refilled the glasses as Luc played on his cell phone. David watched. It was good to see Luc in a mindless video game, being just a kid, after all he had been though.

Brian knocked.

"Hey, we are like the only ones in this hotel," he said as Heather let him in.

"Makes us easy to find, don't you think?" David said.

"We have the car hidden, and as long as we don't make any noise we should be fine," Brian assured them.

"I'm tired," Heather said, picking up the bottle of wine and heading into the bedroom.

"I think I'm done," David said, removing the ice packs and grabbing his cup as he stood up gingerly and hobbled off. "Later," he bid the two good night.

He closed the door behind him, and a moment later Brian and Luc heard David grunt in pain, along with the sound of bedsprings squeaking and Heather giggling.

"I SAID, AS LONG AS WE DON'T MAKE ANY NOISE!" Brian yelled through the closed door of the bedroom.

Luc set himself up on the couch that looked out the window to the ocean and the pier abutting the amusement park. He was under a blanket and playing a game on his cell phone, while Brian found a cot in the closet and opened it up. Brian grabbed another beer, and flopped on the cot with the remote. He turned on the TV and within a minute, was asleep.

At the sound of Brian snoring, Luc got up and turned off the TV. He could now hear voices from the street below. He moved to the window and saw the green tipped Mohawk and a couple other kids heading for the pier. Luc looked over at Brian; he was out cold. The door to the bedroom was closed and, mercifully, there were no noises coming from the other side. He closed the door behind him without even a click.

58

When he reached the street, he could see them out on the pier and the glowing red dots of their cigarettes.

I wonder what they're smoking?

As he got closer, the group returned as Luc reached the entrance to the pier.

"Whatta you doin' out this late, mate?" Benny asked.

"Couldn't sleep," Luc said. "Too much noise outside," he smiled.

"Wanna hang with us for a bit?"

"OK, thanks," Luc said.

The moon was full over Wonderland Park.

"Are we goin' in?" asked Luc at the gate.

"Yeah, but not that way. That way will cost ya."

Luc followed them into the dark and under a tree. One at a time, Benny boosted the others up into the tree, where they climbed over the fence. Luc was last.

"Come on," Benny said. "Up ya go!"

Luc placed his foot in Benny's clasped hands and was boosted up into the tree. It was a short climb out onto a branch to get over the fence. He dropped into a small, private yard near the entrance, the very one they rendezvoused in after freeing David from the Dark Men. Moments later Benny jumped out of the tree, dropping to his knees and popping back up.

"Like your American commercial—*that was easy!*" Benny laughed.

As they followed the others into the park, Benny seized the opportunity to question Luc.

"So, your friends aren't gonna miss you?" he asked.

"They're all asleep," Luc replied.

"So, do you know why those men would be interested in my friend Bryce?"

"Yes."

A moment passed.

"Well, gonna tell me?"

"You, uh, see, Bryce and his brother are special people. They come from someone very high up in the church. Very high."

"And how does this make the men bad?"

"Their job is to make sure no one finds out about it," Luc explained without offering too much.

They walked in silence for a minute, Benny playing it down.

"Do you want to come with us for a little late night fun?" Benny said, lighting up a cigarette.

"I think I'm good for a couple of hours. Sure," Luc replied.

They caught up to the others and walked around until they heard an announcement over the loudspeaker that the park was closing in 30 minutes. Rather than leave, Benny and company walked around the rides and entered the service area. In the furthest corner of the park, they approached a metal warehouse. As they got closer, they could first feel, then hear the beat. A large man in a leather jacket stood at the door.

"Five."

As Benny reached into his pocket, Luc stepped up.

"Will twenty American do for both of us?"

"Sure," the big man said, taking the cash and nodding toward the door.

The warehouse was jammed full with young people, most a few years older than Luc and Benny. Some were dancing, others socializing. A makeshift bar in the corner held a keg.

"Come on, I'll buy ya a beer," Benny said.

The music was deafening. As they walked to the corner, there was a strange smell in the air—strange to Luc anyway. As they passed a small group, the smell grew stronger. Luc witnessed one of them toking on a small metal pipe, then passing it to a girl. She took a long draw on it, holding the smoke in, and, as she saw Benny, smiled and offered it to him.

"No, not now," he said, as he walked past her.

Luc followed as she shrugged, then finally exhaled, passing the pipe to someone else.

It was all surreal: the loud music, partying late at night, no one to tell you what to do—and what *not* to do.

"I guess this is growing up," Luc thought.

He looked at the gelled Mohawk with the green tips and wondered how two brothers could be so different. Benny spun around with two beers in his hands, giving one to Luc.

"Thanks," Luc said.

"Beats Boddington House," Benny declared over the loud music.

"How long have you lived there?" Luc asked.

"All my life. Well, as far as I can remember, anyway."

"So why don't you like Father Henry?" Luc asked, as they retreated to the corner furthest from the speakers.

Benny was taken aback by the question and sipped his beer. Luc took a sip too, stifling a grimace.

"It's kinda like, he let me, uh, let us down," he explained. "He could at least care enough to get involved, you know be a bit of a…"

"Parent?" asked Luc.

Benny looked at him squarely. Luc pulled the cell phone out of his jacket pocket and handed it to him.

"You dropped it in the park."

"So you knew?" Bryce asked.

"I had a feeling before I found the phone," Luc smiled.

The two stood in silence, taking in the scene of the rave. A passerby said hi to Bryce, but for the most part they just watched people dancing and partying. Luc took another sip of beer.

"Can we get out of here?" he asked.

"OK, sure."

They dumped their beers in a trash can and headed for the door. Outside, things were much quieter in the crisp evening air, the metal warehouse holding in most of the racket of the rave.

"Thanks," Luc said.

They walked along the boardwalk as the waves crashed on shore. Bryce picked the conversation back up without prompting, now that he could be heard.

"Henry put me in the orphanage to grow up with the other lads, and I can see his logic. But he did adopt me, ya know. For frigs sake, my name *is* Jones, and the others knew it, but Henry didn't treat me any different. The others wondered why too. I mean no one there had a real family or any chance at one. But there was the man who adopted *me.* So I thought maybe I had a chance—a chance to at least have a dad. I guess that's why I got in so much trouble, you know seeking out his attention an all that."

Luc looked at Bryce. Bryce smiled.

"I'll bet it would have cost ten thousand sterling to have a shrink bring that out!" he laughed.

They continued toward the end of the boardwalk, both stowing their hands in their pockets to keep warm.

"Storm's comin'," Bryce finally said.

"How do you know?" asked Luc.

"You can tell by the birds. They behave differently when the weather's about to change."

"Really, you know how to tell? That's so cool."

Bryce could not hold back his smile.

"Naw, I saw the report on the tele'," he confessed, laughing.

Luc smiled and gave Bryce a friendly shove with his elbow.

"Very funny," Luc smirked.

Both gazed at the ocean in the moonlight.

"So what do you know about my brother?" Bryce asked, as he looked up at the moon.

"A lot!" Luc replied enthusiastically. "First off, he's a really great guy."

Bryce looked at him with surprise.

"But he doesn't really like loud music or beer…"

Bryce's eyes opened wide.

"Get the frig outta here!" he exclaimed.

"Way true," Luc laughed. "Bryce Jones, meet your brother, Luc Jennings," he formally announced, holding out his hand.

Bryce grabbed his hand and shook it hard.

"Well bloody alright then!"

They both beamed from the excitement of their new bond. For Luc, it was the first moment in a long time that he was actually happy.

Bryce remembered Henry's pantry.

"Hey, there is some serious shit goin' down here, mate. And you and your friends are smack in the middle of it."

"What do you mean?" Luc asked, returning to the reality from which he had escaped for the last several hours.

"I snuck into Father Henry's house and did a bit of eaves-droppin' after dinner. Quite a bit, actually."

"What did you hear?" Luc asked

"If they find you guys, well..." he stopped, not knowing quite how to word it.

"They'll kill us?" offered Luc.

"So it's of no shock to you then?"

"They killed my father."

"Nooo!" Bryce cried. "Say it ain't so! That's awful."

"Shot at me too—I dove off a ferry to get away." Luc said matter of factly. The whole incident now seemed so far in the past.

"What!?"

Luc started down the list: "We got one of them in Maine—crashed him into a river—car exploded."

"Stop!" Bryce interrupted.

He looked at Luc for a moment.

"This is no bullshit. You *are* tellin' me the truth aren't you?" he asked straight faced.

Luc nodded and continued.

"David came looking for you yesterday. They caught him and we got him back, but it was close."

"I heard there was some trouble. They said there was an intruder. So that's why he's all busted up. So why the hell would you come here if you knew they would be here? You knew they'd be guarding me didn't you?"

"Yeah, we came to get you out. Before they..."

The two looked squarely at each other.

"Kill *me*," Bryce finished. "So that's what they meant about a security threat," he said, his voice low.

"No evidence of any kind—including us," Luc affirmed.

Bryce was now the rookie in a game he could not fathom. They reached the end of the boardwalk and leapt up on the sea wall.

"So why then?" Bryce asked, still confused. "Who are we that it's so important that no one knows, that they would kill people over it? Who in the hell are our parents?"

Luc remembered when he heard it all and how confused he had felt. Maybe Bryce was better equipped, but then who could be? They stopped and leaned on the railing, looking out at the sea as the waves crashed in white foam.

"Can I bum a cigarette?" Luc asked, hoping it would relax him a bit.

Bryce produced one from his leather jacket.

"We call 'em *fags* over here," Bryce said with a grin, handing Luc his lighter.

He chuckled a little, then lit the cigarette, gagging on the first puff, quickly taking another without inhaling.

"You, uh, *we* are the results of a secret DNA experiment."

"Watta you mean, DNA? Like cloning?"

"Exactly!"

"Your not bustin' on me here just cuz I messed with you on the birds and the weather, are you?" Bryce pleaded.

"It's for real. That's why they're killing people to keep it quiet."

"Henry? Is he in on it?" Bryce asked.

"Yep. The Dark Men, as we call them, are the enforcers. Henry is your caretaker and…"

Everything stopped.

He was good at telling the story until now. The reality of the cost to the 14-year-old slammed home. He threw the cigarette into the ocean and turned his head so Bryce wouldn't see the tears. He was barely able to keep the sobbing back, when he felt a hand on his shoulder.

"Luc, thanks for comin' all that way just for me. I mean that. Your pop raised a brave man."

Luc looked back and sniffed.

"Thanks."

After a minute, Luc looked at Bryce, cracking a thin smile as he wiped a couple of tears. Bryce raised his eyebrows.

"What?" he said, watching Luc's smile widen.

"Take a guess at who we are?"

"Huh?"

"The DNA that made us. Guess whose it is?" Luc said with a giggle.

"Uh…" Bryce smirked back "'Dunno. Wait, you said someone very high up in the church, right?"

Luc nodded with a large grin. Bryce thought for a bit.

"And they will kill—have killed—to keep it a secret."

Luc gave another nod. Bryce paused. He took a drag on his cigarette and stared at the dark horizon as he exhaled. He leaned back from the railing.

"The pope! That's it! We—you and I, are junior popes!" he exclaimed.

Luc laughed and shook his head.

Bryce cocked his head in surprise, thinking he had guessed right.

"But that's as high as it gets!" Bryce said.

Luc leaned over.

"Way low," he whispered.

"Huh? Whatta you mean, low?"

Luc leaned back and took a deep breath, contemplating what he was about to say.

"Jesus and his brother, James."

Bryce just stared.

"No bull," Luc assured.

"You mean Jesus as in…"

"Christ," Luc firmly stated.

"But how?"

"From artifacts. They got blood samples from artifacts."

"I don't friggin' believe it," Bryce said shaking his head.

"Don't blame you," said Luc. "David has all the evidence. It proves everything."

"How did they do it?"

"Some genetic doctor in a lab in the Vatican. A Cardinal Vincent is in charge of the whole thing. They killed the doctors after we were born, plus others who knew. The church threw the cardinal out when they found out, but he told them the experiments didn't work. Nobody knows about it except us and the crew on the ship we came over in."

"Jesus Chri—oh, I guess I shouldn't be sayin' that."

"Pretty screwed up, huh?" Luc offered. "Now they are trying to kill everyone and get their evidence back, before the world finds out what they did. But if we make it, we could be famous."

"Never thought of bein' famous that way," Bryce said. "Ya know, the lads at the house said some Italian nun has been trying to get a hold of me. Uh….Sister Sarah, yeah, that's it."

Luc lit up.

"Sister Sarah is my mother!" he exclaimed.

"I thought we was from some test tube?" Bryce argued.

"To start. Then we were carried until birth by two nuns. Sister Sarah carried me and Sister Rose carried you. We thought they were dead."

"I wonder why she was calling me?"

"Maybe to warn you. Wait! My dad got a lot of hang up calls, you know he'd pick up and no one would be there. Maybe it was her."

Bryce stood in wonder, how could all of this be possible. This kid comes out of nowhere and lays this wild tale on him. Yet it all seemed to tie together.

"Hold on now, who is James? I never heard of him. Jesus didn't have a brother."

"Me neither. They never taught us that in CCD. But according to the documents, there was a brother James."

"So Luc, if true, who's who?

"I don't know. We don't know. We don't have all the records," Luc explained.

"Are you sure it was Jesus' brother?"

"Oh yeah, the records talk about it. They tried the brother's DNA first, and when that worked, they cloned Jesus. But our birth certificates were forged later, with the same birthday, so we can't tell who is who."

"They stood against the rail and watched the growing waves pound the beach, then coasting all the way up and tagging the seawall before retreating back.

"I got it!" Bryce exclaimed. "I know how we can figure this out."

"How?"

"Jump off the wall and walk right out there," Bryce stated, pointing out to the ocean. "If you sink, you're the brother!"

Luc looked at him and rolled his eyes.

"I promise to save you, because it would then be my job, as it were," Bryce assured him.

Luc laughed.

"A brother James, huh?" Bryce said, as he kicked a pebble over the wall. "Hey, I got an idea. Seriously," he said, looking up at Luc.

A red dawn revealed the town behind them.

"See that church on the hill?" he asked, looking over his shoulder. "It's never locked. We can go in there and find out about this brother. There has to be something on him in the

"What kind of church is this?" whispered Luc.

"I don't know, but, it's not a real one." Bryce cracked a sly smile and finished, "I mean, not Catholic anyway."

Bryce opened the doors to the side room, finding it pitch black. He confidently walked into the darkness and a few seconds later, the room flashed with disturbingly bright lighting, revealing a library of sorts with book shelves lining all four walls and stacked full with books. In the middle of the room was a conference type table and chairs. Luc walked over to a steam radiator and placed a finger on it and smiled.

He slid down to the floor warming his back against it. Where do you want to start?" asked Bryce.

"Do you think they use Dewey Decimal in here?" Luc answered as he looked around the scope of the room.

Bryce started in on the books.

"Most of these are not even in English," he said, handing one to Luc. "Here, this one's got a James on it."

Luc found his eyes getting heavy as he opened *"A Study of the Letter of James to the Twelve Tribes."*

59

Luc awoke to the sound of a door closing. He didn't know how long he had slept and couldn't remember anything he'd read. Bryce jerked his head up from being face down on the study table.

"Looks like we're busted," he said, as the footsteps that awoke them grew louder.

Luc sat up as the pastor entered the room. He looked at the two of them, a bit surprised to see them with books opened.

"Occasionally, I find a homeless person here or someone who's had a little too much and needs to sleep it off. But, today we have a couple of young scholars—a pleasant surprise," he said, holding a steaming mug of coffee.

The aroma made Luc's stomach growl. Bryce closed the book and placed it back on the shelf.

"Sorry Padre, we was just lookin' for some historical information. Meant no harm," Bryce explained.

"No worries, lads. Maybe I can help you. Just what information were you looking for?"

"Ya see," Bryce responded. "We heard that Jesus had a brother named James. But, Luc here, I'm Bryce by the way," he said rising up and extending a hand to the pastor, "never heard 'bout any brother of the Lord Jesus and just wanted to see what was what."

Luc was on his feet, placing his book back on the shelf and shaking the pastor's hand.

"Luc Jennings."

"Reverend Jim Gallagher. Call me Brother Jim," he said smiling. "As a matter of fact, Jesus had many brothers and sisters."

"Huh?" they both said in unison.

"Let me guess, you're both Catholic?"

They nodded.

"You look hungry," Brother Jim said. "I was just about to make scrambled eggs. How about it?"

"Thank you, yes," Luc said.

"Starved, thanks," replied Bryce.

The reverend led them through the rectory, into the kitchen.

"What can I get you to drink? Orange juice?"

"That coffee smells really good," Luc replied.

"Same here," Bryce chimed.

He poured them coffee and slid a bowl of sugar toward them and retrieved a bottle of milk from the refrigerator along with a bowl of eggs. Bryce sugared his coffee then slid the bowl towards Luc, who declined. They sat sipping their coffees as the reverend prepared breakfast.

"There's bread behind you, Luc. Why don't you get some toast going? I just love the smell of toast in the morning. I'll bet the smell will get my wife out of bed."

"Wife?" Bryce asked, jerking back.

"This is a Protestant church. We don't take a vow of chastity here."

Luc got up and found the bread as Reverend Jim scrambled some eggs. Bryce noticed his gray shirt did not have the traditional white collar.

"You don't have to wear the collar on the off hours, I see," commented Bryce.

"Actually, I don't even have one. Some of the traditions of the Catholic Church are just theirs. We are *all* Christians, we just practice it a little differently."

At that moment, Reverend Jim's wife appeared. She was an attractive woman of about 50, dressed for the day, as she heard the voices from upstairs.

"Breakfast smells good," she said, placing a kiss on the reverend's cheek. "Now, who have we here?"

Luc jumped to his feet. Bryce followed suit.

"Luc Jennings," he said thrusting out his hand.

"Bryce Jones—pleasure."

"This is my wife of thirty years, June."

"Please, sit," she said, pouring herself a cup of hot coffee.

"Your timing is impeccable. Won't you join us?"

"Thank you," she replied. "So, what brings these fine young men to us?"

"They seek knowledge, my dear. I found them in the library doing research."

"Indeed?"

"We were looking for information regarding Jesus and his brother James," Bryce offered.

"Isn't that a breath of fresh air. It's not that often these days we see young men seeking out the Lord Jesus."

June quickly set the kitchen table as the food was served from bowls passed around. Luc placed his hands in his lap. Bryce glanced over at him while reaching for his fork—Luc gave a quick shake of his head. Bryce followed suit and placed his hand in his lap, both now waiting for the reverend's wife to lift her fork before starting; the smell of the eggs and toasted bread had Luc's stomach crying for a revolt to ceremony. June missed the quick exchange and was impressed by the manners of these two young men. Her hand passed over her fork and reached out to her husband.

"Shall we pray?" she asked.

"Of, course," both guests muttered and bowed their heads onto their interlocked fingers.

The reverend audibly cleared his throat.

They both looked up to see the reverend holding hands with his wife, with both of their free hands reaching toward them. They each grasped a hand, then looked at each other awkwardly for a second, and joined hands, as the reverend started.

"Dear father in heaven, we pray to you in thanks for our many blessings and the abundance of privileges that you provide us. We ask you for your forgiveness for our many sins and thank you for the nourishment we are about to receive. We ask you to bless and care for these fine young, studious men who have joined us for this meal and we also ask for you to extend your gracious care and guidance to our loved ones that can not be with us here today. In Jesus' name we pray. Amen."

They both felt their hands squeezed, then released. Bryce and Luc then made the sign of the cross about their chest. When they looked up, the husband and wife were just looking at them.

"We got that wrong, too?" Bryce asked.

"Nonsense. It's all right, if it's for the love of God."

June Gallagher lifted her fork, the green light for Luc and Bryce. She smiled as she placed it back down and buttered her toast.

"Okay, so your question was…did Jesus have a brother named, James?" the reverend asked, passing the butter across the table.

"Yes."

"Unfortunately, there isn't an easy answer to that question. Many different religions around the world have different views. And most Catholics do not believe that James was the brother of Jesus. However, some religions, such as ours—do believe that Jesus had a brother. Not only one brother, but several brothers—and sisters.

"To us, James was the younger brother of Jesus. He is known as *James the Just* to many because he believed you would be judged on your actions rather than your faith."

Reverend Jim ate a few bites of his toast, then got up and picked up a Bible off a small table.

"Can you pass the salt?" Mrs. Gallagher asked Luc. She was again impressed, as he presented both the salt and pepper to her.

"I promise not to bore you with Bible verses or attempt to convince you of things counter to your faith, but my belief that Jesus had a brother comes from several verses in the Bible. For example, here in the book of Matthew, Jesus has been preaching and telling parables to the crowds in Nazareth. The people in Nazareth were offended and questioned his qualifications to give such sermons. They said, "Hey, you're just a man like us. You have a father who was a carpenter, a mother, brothers and sisters. You are just a man, like us. What gives you the authority to preach to us?" So, they kicked him out of the city. It says right here in Chapter 13 verses 55 and 56.

> "Is this not the carpenter's son? Is not His mother called Mary? And His brothers James, Joses, Simon and Judas? And His sisters, are they not all with us? Where then did this Man get all these things?"

He pushed the Bible over to the two boys who read the passage word for word.

"There are several other verses I could show you, like Mark 6:3 and Galatians 1:19."

The boys looked closely at the Bible as the reverend continued.

"You might be thinking 'that sounds pretty clear' but, to some it really isn't."

They looked puzzled.

"The passage you are reading is from the King James version of the Bible and there are several different translations of the Bible. Some believe that in the original language, the words *brother* and *sister* are the same or very similar to that of *cousin*. Some also believe that his siblings were actually step-brothers and sisters, not full blood related siblings."

Bryce and Luc looked at each other and nodded.

"I agree with you, reverend. I have it from a good source that your version is right," Luc said with a smile. "Bryce wasn't sure, but I think we have convinced my brother here," he said with a wink.

"So why would you two come up here in the middle of the night just to settle a bet?" the reverend inquired.

"I guess we're just a little closer to God than most," Luc replied.

Bryce snuck a smirk to Luc on that one.

"And just how good is your source that my husband is right on his interpretation of the gospel?"

"Oh, I have a relative who knows a lot about this stuff, Mrs. Gallagher," Luc replied picking up the silver bowl holding the bread. "More toast?"

"Oh, no, you take the last one, go ahead."

Luc looked into the bowl, then at Mrs. Gallagher. He calmly presented the bowl to her. She looked in and saw four pieces of toast.

60

"Thank you for the wonderful breakfast," Luc said to Reverend Jim.

"Likewise," Bryce said. "And the lesson on James."

"It was very nice to meet you," Luc said shifting his handshake to Mrs. Gallagher.

"My pleasure," she said with the questioning look still on her face.

They finished their good-byes and headed down the sidewalk back into town. Once assured they were out of earshot, Bryce gave Luc a gentle shove with his elbow.

"You really had her goin' with dividin' the toast up! How'd you do that?"

"Do what?"

"Aw, come on you were messin' with her."

"Was I?"

Bryce looked squarely at Luc. Luc couldn't hold it in. He burst out laughing.

"I forgot a few pieces. I guess she was reading along with the reverend when I tossed them in. I don't know why, but when she said 'take the last one,' I couldn't help myself."

"You're gonna burn in hell for that one," Bryce laughed.

They walked a few paces in silence.

"Is that possible?" Luc asked.

The both giggled as they turned down the main street.

"Why don't you just go to the police?" asked Bryce as they reached the boardwalk.

"We will once we get you out."

"Well, I'm out," Bryce said.

"Oh, duh! Right!" Luc said. "Let's get back to the hotel."

"Can we swing by the house? I want to grab some stuff, as it sounds like I won't be goin' back there for a while, if at all."

"Sure, I'll be your lookout," Luc said, putting his hand in his jacket pocket and feeling around. "Crap, my phone!"

"Dropped yours now?" Bryce asked.

"Not sure," Luc replied.

"Luc?" Heather said, looking at the motionless blanket on the couch.

She rounded the couch to see the pillow lacking his head.

"Brian!"

He cracked one eye open.

"What?

"Where's Luc?" she said.

He let out a yawn and answered, "Huh?" He shot up. "Where the hell could he have gone?"

David appeared from the bedroom, showered and dressed.

"Maybe he went out to get breakfast," David guessed.

"Bed is cold," Heather said as she slid her hand under the blanket.

Without getting out of bed, Brian reached over to a chair and pulled a cell phone out of his jacket. He pressed "one" and Heather's down vest started beeping. He pressed "two" and Luc's pillow started to beep.

"Shit," Brian said. "He must-a left it by mistake, playin' video games on it."

"What do we do now?" Heather asked David.

"Brian, why don't you go look around while Heather showers up. I'm sure he'll show."

Brian threw on his sweatshirt. He popped on his sneakers, no socks, wearing the gray sweatpants he slept in.

"Back in twenty," Brian said as he went out the door.

Heather was dressed and David had everything packed when Brian returned, sweaty.

"Did he come back?" Brian asked as he closed the door.

They shook their heads.

"Weird. I looked everywhere. No sign of him."

"What now?" Heather said, her voice cracking.

"OK, let's stay calm here," David said, stalling.

"I'll hit the shower," Brian said. "If he doesn't show in the next ten minutes, then we can panic."

"Options?" Brian asked as David zipped his pack.

"We have an appointment with that Benny kid. He may have Bryce with him," David said.

"You two go," Heather offered, "I'll wait here for Luc."

"I hate splitting up," David muttered, recalling the mess at the orphanage, his side still throbbing from Scordo's greeting.

"I'll wait in the car, down the block. No one will be able to get near me without me seeing," Heather said.

David rubbed her back and kissed her cheek. "That sounds better than sitting here," he said with a little relief in his voice.

David waited at the corner as Brian appeared on the far side of the orphanage, heading his way, wearing his sweatshirt inside-out.

"Jag and now a Beemer," he reported in. "But no sign of Bryce or Luc—might be a good thing with those guys still around," he added.

"Where are they?" David wondered aloud.

The winds gusted cold, the darkening skies announcing the inbound storm. Brian stuffed his hands in his pockets. Bundled up, they monitored Boddington House from a safe distance, using the same stone wall where they met Benny as cover.

"Back there!" Brian said, grabbing David's sleeve and tugging. From behind them, the familiar green Mohawk poked out from behind a parked van. Bryce motioned back. They retreated a block and met him around the corner, out of sight of the orphanage.

"Sorry," Luc said preemptively. "We had a little catching up to do."

Bryce took the hundred out of his pocket and handed it to David.

"No, you earned it," David said, refusing to take the bill.

Bryce stuffed it into David's fleece pocket.

"My brother, Luc, filled me in on everything."

Brian exhaled loudly in disgust, looking at Luc, who was sporting a grin.

"We was just going to duck into Boddington, so I could grab some stuff."

"N-F-L," Brian said.

Bryce looked at him, confused.

"*Not Friggin' Likely*. Bad guys are home."

"Phone," David said to Brian.

He pressed "one" and put it to his ear.

"We have both of them. Come pick us up at the corner where we met Bryce—Benny is Bryce," David said. He listened for a moment, then turned his head for a little privacy and whispered, "Me too."

Brian stared him down as he closed the phone.

"Oh, please!"

They moved back to the corner, reinstating a line of sight to the orphanage.

"I wasn't sure 'bout you guys," Bryce started in, "ya know, comin' outta nowhere, just like I said. Then I hid in Jonesies' pantry and got an earful. They brought in a guy to help find you. I couldn't see him, but he didn't sound like a friendly chap. A guy called Orsini."

David, Luc, and Brian's eyes popped wide open and their jaws dropped, simultaneously mouthing "Shit."

"Know 'em?" asked Bryce.

"Know *of* him," David said.

"Oh, this is bad," Brian muttered.

"Really bad," Luc added. He looked at Bryce, "Murderer— big time," he finished.

"Oh, not good news at all, mate."

"PA-NO!, PA-NO!, PA-NO!"

The police siren grew louder from around the block. Then, another siren sounded and a police car whizzed passed them.

"Heather!" David exclaimed.

He ran to the corner and peered around. From a block away he could see Heather standing next to the rental car in the middle of the intersection with another car that had run into her passenger side door. People were standing around the scene and others were streaming out of their homes to gawk. The two police cars blocked traffic as officers walked about. David walked closer and then looked back; the rest had made it to the corner and waved him on, staying back and watching out.

It was a solid fender bender. The elderly woman who was driving the other car kept apologizing to Heather and asking if she was all right.

"I'm fine. It's only a car. Don't worry," Heather consoled her.

David watched a policeman scan the rental papers while talking to Heather. As she produced her license from her pack, he heard her explain that she had lost her passport. Then, after some unintelligible dialogue, the officer opened the door to the police car and Heather got in. Another officer got in the rental car and drove it away. The police car carrying Heather followed.

David rushed back to the group.

"They took her in!" he exclaimed. "The car is in Brian's name and she doesn't have a passport—I think that they think she stole the car," he added.

"Easy to explain," Brian calmly said. "I'll say she's my cousin."

David panicked, "We need to get her out of there fast, before they start pluggin' her name into the computer. She's got to be wanted or at least listed as missing back in the States.

They paused, the reality setting in that they had been on the run for some time—a run that started with the murder of Luc's father. Surely they would have been missed. Then there was the incident at the police station in Provincetown.

"Do you know the way to the police station?" David asked Bryce.

"All too well."

"Brian, we need to be quick. It won't take them long to find out about her and maybe you."

"I think I'm clean cuz. Sully will tell them I quit school and my parents will cover the rest, if they can find them."

David turned to Bryce.

"It's best you're not with us, just in case."

"Maybe Luc and I should hide out while you take care of biz."

"You two together is not a good idea," David said.

"Why's that? We did fine all night," Bryce defended.

"Wait! Wait! We have everything—you, Luc, the micro-fiche. We don't have to do this!" David said, almost in a cheer.

"What are you suggesting we do, then?" Bryce asked.

"Go to the police together and explain everything. They can contact Scotland Yard or whoever handles this kind of thing. We can stop running!"

The three looked at each other—it was over!

"Not in that station, mate. Not with me," Bryce stated. "Let's just say I'm not their favorite person and, like the last few times they dealt with me, they may just dump us on old Henry."

"And in the lap of Scordo and Orsini," Brian finished.

"All right then," David conceded. "This is your town. Where's a safe place?"

Bryce thought for a moment.

"Father Henry has an old farmhouse north of here. Was left to him, I guess. Never uses it. Me and some blokes hang out there from time to time when we want to disappear for a couple days. It's about five kilometers up the main road on the coast on the right. There's a broken iron gate with the words 'Nightingale Farm' on it."

"Sounds good. From there we go right to Scotland Yard, OK?" David said.

"Look," Bryce said. "Those guys are lookin' for you *and* me. What say I give them the runaround? They don't know I met you and they wouldn't think I would walk right into the house if I did. It will keep them from poking around at the police station while you get Heather out. I can ditch them and meet you later."

"I don't like it," said Brian.

"If I see trouble, I'll bolt—promise," assured Bryce. "It's just for an hour, so you can take care of business at that police station."

"They are probably out looking for all of us right now," David speculated. "Maybe running them back to the house will help."

As he turned and walked away, Bryce zipped up his leather jacket to protect him from a light rain, which had just begun to fall.

Standing in a doorway a block away, Orsini pulled out his cell phone.

"I found them. Bryce was with them, so you can stop looking for him."

"Bryce was with the Americans?" Scordo asked.

"Yes, but not any more. He is on his way back to the house. I will now do your job. I will call you when I am finished."

Scordo closed the phone; Henry was starting in on the scotch.

"Bryce has been compromised," Scordo announced.

"Nooo, you can't do this!" Henry cried, shaking his head. "He doesn't even know who he's killing!"

"I have my orders," Scordo replied.

A second Dark Man entered the dining room.

"Get the others!" he barked at him. "I don't trust him to finish this alone."

Moments later there were three Dark Men in front of Scordo, awaiting orders.

"You two, watch Bryce. He will be here in a minute. When I tell you, bring him to me."

Scordo turned to the third. "You, come with me."

61

Heather was sitting in a chair next to a desk, just past the lobby of the police station when Brian ran in.

"Heather! Are you all right?" asked Brian.

"Yes, I'm fine."

A police offer approached Brian.

"And you might be?" he asked.

"Her cousin! That's my car she was in. Well, my rental," Brian explained.

"Hold on, Robbie!" The policeman yelled to another who was handing a file to a clerk at a computer terminal.

The officer returned and handed the file to the other officer.

"Looks like her story checks out. That is, if you are who you say you are."

Brian produced his license and passport.

"Well, I guess your only problem is explaining that dent to the rental service. Are you sure you're all right, Miss Connor?" He asked, handing a copy of the accident report to Brian.

"Yes, thanks. I'm fine."

Brian and Heather walked out of the police station and got in the dented Vaxhaul. Brian turned on the wipers as he pulled out of the station; the drizzle was getting heavy.

"Did they plug your name into a computer?" he asked.

"I don't think so; I think that's what they were doing when you showed up," Heather speculated.

"We can't be sure. We will have to assume they did—or will—and you showed up from the shit that went down on the Cape. We're gonna need a new car."

"Where are David and Luc?" Heather asked.

"Just around the corner."

As they stopped at the intersection, the rear door flew open and Orsini jumped in behind Brian. In one motion, he pressed the barrel tip of his revolver against Heather's cheek, and cocked the hammer.

"Now drive slowly, straight ahead," he commanded Brian, closing the door with his other hand.

Heather sat motionless, feeling the cold steel push firmly on her face, while Brian eased the car straight through the intersection, out of sight from David and Luc, who sat waiting in a café.

Bryce entered the orphanage and was startled to see the two Dark Men with one of the teens in the next room. He did an immediate U-turn and exited the house, but not before one of the men had rounded the corner to see who had come home. The Dark Man leaned back into the room.

"Let's go. He's running!"

The two Dark Men exited the building, one pulling out his cell phone.

"He's on the run—we're following," the Dark Man reported.

"Where?" asked Scordo.

"To the train station."

"Call me back in two minutes!"

Scordo flipped the phone closed.

"Take a right!" he said to his driver.

Bryce headed into the station, glancing back to see if his followers were still in pursuit. He hopped onto a train busy with people loading and unloading. His followers watched him head for the last car. The Dark Men boarded the train one car up.

Scordo flipped open his buzzing phone.

"He's on the train, one car back from us. We're pulling out for Liverpool!"

"Move back to the car! Do it now!" Scordo directed.

The two went through the door as the train lurched forward, entered the car and looked around. Bryce was not there.

"He's gone!"

"At least he can see you and think he has gotten away!" scoffed Scordo as he sat in the Jaguar on the overpass, watching Bryce look back as he crossed the tracks.

"Now get off that train and call me when you are in your car!" he barked.

Scordo flipped the phone closed.

"Idiots!"

"He's heading for the highway," the driver reported.

"Keep your distance."

The Jag eased forward with its headlights off, hiding in the early evening brought on by the rain.

"They should have been here by now," David said to Luc as he finished his coffee.

"Don't worry, they will be here soon."

David tapped his fingers on the table and kept looking out the window, growing more impatient.

"It's almost over, David. Don't worry," Luc assured him.

"Is it?" David grunted.

"We have Bryce and we will be safe soon. Thanks to you, by the way."

"You would be in Italy with your family if it wasn't for me," David said, looking down into his coffee.

"No, David, that wasn't gonna happen."

"We read the e-mail from your father. I'm so sorry," David said, feeling the pain returning to his gut.

"I heard Scordo. He laughed at my father when he told him they wanted to move to Italy. Told him it was ridiculous. He had the plan for the ferry all along. No one would find our bodies that way," Luc said firmly, "You can never blame yourself for this—why else would he come to Provincetown? You were right—they're killers, and you saved me."

Luc's cell phone buzzed.

"It's them," he said flipping open the phone.

"Hey, where are you?" Luc answered.

David looked at Luc, not hearing the response.

"OK, can do," Luc answered, ending the call.

"What's goin on?" David asked.

"They ditched the car at the fish pier. Someone was following them. They lost them at the amusement park."

"So, what do we do?"

"She said to get the car—keys are in it—and pick them up by the east gate where we got you out," Luc explained.

"Let's roll."

The fish pier consisted of a complex maze of commercial warehouses and docks. When they arrived, trucks and vans were clustered by the docks as fisherman carted their catch from the boats and staged it for market. They walked across the wooden planks as the drizzle turned into a steady rain that pelted the buildings with each gust of wind. They walked, finally spotting it between two abandoned warehouses, a stack of crab pots and a delivery truck partially blocking their view.

They stopped and looked around for a minute to confirm no one was in the area, then started down the alley. They passed the crab pots and the delivery truck, finding the car with the right side driver's door open.

"They probably ducked through there," Luc speculated, pointing to the larger of the two warehouses.

David got in and closed the door. Heather heard the thud and looked up from the passenger side floor of the delivery truck. Orsini had one hand on the wheel, which also held the gun on her, and the other on a screwdriver jammed into a hole in the steering column where the ignition key housing should be. She heard the other door close as he twisted the screwdriver.

David started the car, but it didn't sound right. It was as if the muffler had fallen off. The truck eased up to them, slowly connecting with the rear bumper just as David put the car into reverse. He released the clutch, and the car nudged backward, then stalled. He looked in the mirror and saw the grill of the delivery truck.

"What the!?" he said, Luc looking over to him.

The car bounced forward with the surge of the truck, jerking their necks back in surprise. David stomped the brakes as hard as he could, the tires slid on the rain soaked pier. Heather rose from the passenger floor slowly, Orsini glancing over as he did his work. Heather looked over the dash to see the car with David and Luc inside being pushed to the edge of the pier. The front wheels were caught on a wooden beam serving as a curb between the wharf and the harbor. The truck eased, then accelerated, rocking the car forward.

"How can you do this!" she screamed, as the car popped up and over the wooden beam. The truck kept pushing, the car's undercarriage now sliding on the beam.

"You know exactly why!" Orsini barked at her. "They are the future! Nothing can get in the way of that!" he said, as the truck slammed the back of the car.

The front wheels reached the end of the wharf, then dropped off, the rear bumper popping up and crushing the truck's grill. David and Luc looked down at the large waves crashing on the pylons below them, the churning waters of the storm leading the way to shore.

"Jump!" he yelled to Luc, as they furiously unlatched their seat belts.

The truck revved its motor and Orsini put it back in gear.

"How could you kill them? WHY KILL LUC?!" she screamed as tears streamed down her cheeks.

Everything stopped.

The only sound that Heather heard was rain hitting the windshield. The rental car stood still, its hood pointed down toward the water. The delivery truck's engine was off. She looked to her right. Orsini was staring down through the steering wheel, Then, taking a deep breath, he slowly raised his head.

"Don't move!" he commanded.

He jumped out of the truck and moved toward the car, the rear of which was propped up on the wooden beam. David opened the door and carefully climbed out as Orsini moved forward.

"Down!" Orsini yelled. David instantly dropped to his knees and launched his hands into the air at the sight of the aimed pistol.

Orsini squeezed around the back of the car to the passenger side while maintaining his aim on David. He grabbed the door handle and opened it to find Luc in the passenger seat, trembling and glaring down at the splashing water.

"Luc Jennings?" Orsini said as the rain soaked his face.

Luc did not respond.

"Are you Luc Jennings?!" he yelled, his eyes darting back and forth as he continued his fix on David with the gun.

Luc looked up at Orsini and nodded. He lowered the gun and collapsed to a sitting position on the wooden beam, the gun hanging limp in his hand. He shook his head as Heather slowly emerged from the cab of the truck.

"This can't be," he moaned staring down between his legs.

Heather and David remained fixed on the gun. His hand was limp, the barrel dragging on the ground between his feet. Orsini could not believe what he had almost done. For 14 years he lived in a personal purgatory, silent and alone, each day praying for forgiveness for the lives he took—lives he had to take to bring these children into the world. Their impact on mankind would certainly be worth sacrificing the lives of a few, and the soul of the man who took them.

Why didn't they tell me he was with them?

"Brian?" asked David.

"In back!" Heather cried.

David and Heather ran around to the back of the truck and pushed the door up. They found Brian sitting with his back against the sidewall, his hands tied behind his back and a strip of duct tape across his mouth. They climbed in and freed him.

"You OK?" Brian said to Heather.

"Yeah, fine!"

406

"Orsini?" Brian asked.

"Luc!" David exclaimed.

They scrambled out of the truck to find the scene they had left unchanged. Orsini sat on the beam next to the open door of the car, with Luc still sitting inside. The gun remained hanging in his hand between his legs.

"What happened?" Brian whispered.

"Dunno. He just sort of gave up," Heather whispered back. "He didn't know it was Luc."

Orsini raised his head and looked at Luc one more time, then stood up. Everyone froze for a moment. Orsini slid the gun into his shoulder holster. They watched him stand there, looking at Luc, unable to tell if his face was wet with rain or tears.

"Where is Bryce?" Orsini said, turning to them.

No one answered. He stepped toward them.

"Was Scordo's plan to kill him too?" Orsini asked.

"Only if we get to him and tell him what's going on. Then he becomes a security risk...yes," David responded.

"Risk?" he muttered to himself, shaking his head. "Where is he?"

No one answered. He stepped closer.

"They must be stopped. They're mad!" Orsini shouted.

"He went back to the orphanage," Luc said, climbing out of the car.

"They will kill him."

"But they don't know," Heather said.

"They do."

Luc opened his cell phone and punched in a text message. He then looked Orsini straight in the eyes, but said nothing. Orsini looked back. They stared at each other for a long moment before Orsini spoke.

"You children are a miracle," he solemnly said, "and I was to make sure of it. I cannot let this end, not like this. I *will* not," he said, gritting his teeth.

"Take care of him!" Orsini ordered Heather as he started to walk away.

"Wait!" Luc said, holding out his cell phone. "He's not there!"

62

Bryce typed in "on way to meet u," responding to Luc's "where u?" text.

He was out on the highway, hitchhiking in the rain. A small truck passed him, then its taillights lit up bright. He jogged up and got in. They pulled out, heading north along the coast and rounded a bend. Simultaneously, the Jaguar's headlights lit up as it pulled out onto the road, accelerating to the turn where the truck had disappeared, then slowed, its target back in sight. All four were in the car.

"Stay back!" Scordo commanded the driver. "When they stop, we don't want him to see us."

They followed for a short time until the truck pulled over in the middle of nowhere. The Jag slowed, its occupants trying to confirm Bryce's exit through the swipes of the windshield wipers. The truck pulled back out onto the road and disappeared over a hill.

"That must be it," the driver said, though they could not see if he actually got out.

"A little faster and don't stop," Scordo ordered.

The Jaguar sped up and passed the gate to the farm house. Bryce was walking along the long dark driveway when he heard it approach. He turned, only able to make out a dark moving car in spraying rainwater as it flew by. It disappeared over the hill and Bryce resumed heading for the farmhouse. At the next farm, the jag turned in, and headed up the driveway. Finding a break in the stone wall that lined the properties, the headlights went out and they turned onto an overgrown cart path that led back to Nightingale Farm.

Brian drove the banged up rental car past the gate with "Nightingale Fa" hanging from the broken wrought iron frame. The silver BMW followed, parking behind the barn. When they reached the house, it was pitch black inside. David reached into his fleece and pulled out his flashlight but did not turn it on.

"Gotta get something out of my pack," Brian whispered, going to the back of the car and popping the trunk. It clicked, but would not open. Brian gave it a hard tug and the lid freed itself, opening a bit cockeyed, broken pieces of taillight falling off as it sprung loose.

"Remind me never to loan my car to any of you," Brian said.

David entered first and turned on the flashlight.

"Bad guy's car!" Bryce's voice called out to them.

David searched with the light but couldn't find him.

"It's OK!" Luc whispered back in the direction he thought it came from, "He wants to help us."

There was just enough light for Heather to see the silhouette of Bryce's Mohawk as he passed by a window.

"How are you?" Heather asked.

"OK," Bryce said, as David spun around with the flashlight and illuminated Bryce.

Bryce blocked the light with his hand.

"Sorry," David whispered, jerking his aim to the ground, making the room dark again.

"Any lights in here?" Brian asked.

"No, electricity is shut off. I'll find a candle," replied Bryce.

"What's that sound?" asked Luc.

They all heard the whirring; the sound of tires spinning. The spinning stopped and car doors opened and shut.

"They're coming!" Orsini warned, startling them by his sudden presence.

David shut off the flashlight. The spinning sound started again.

"Get out of here, NOW!" Orsini yelled into the dark room.

Scordo was behind the wheel of the Jaguar with two men pushing it out a deep, muddy rut. The fourth Dark Man made his way to the house, gun drawn.

They ran to the car. Heather jumped in the right front seat and looked down to find steering wheel in front of her.

"Shit," she muttered, and grabbed the door handle starting to get back out.

"Let's go!" said Brian dropping the keys over her shoulder as the other doors slammed shut.

They sped away from the house down the dirt driveway. After a moment, Heather spied two white dots in the rear view mirror coming onto the path, right where the spinning noise came from.

"Here they come!" Brian shouted.

"Keep it moving!" David yelled.

The rain came down in sheets on the rutted driveway, the car bouncing almost out of control and Heather barely able to see. She launched the car onto the empty two lane highway with a sudden swerve as the tires gripped solid pavement.

The BMW's headlights popped on. As he drove out from behind the barn, the car lit up the rear of the house, displaying the dead body of the Dark Man on the walkway.

"There!" David pointed to a dirt road. Heather yanked the wheel and the car swerved again, now losing traction as they entered it. The visibility was so poor that every twist in the road required quick reflexes to navigate. The lights in the mirror grew larger.

"Which way!?" Heather yelled, as the Jaguar's headlights glared inside the car.

"Don't know. You pick!"

The car blasted through a puddle, spraying mud as it reached a fork. At the last second, she yanked the wheel to the right, sliding the car through the turn. The Jaguar followed but spun out, abruptly stopping. A moment later, the headlights were back in the mirror. Brian spun his head around.

"Still coming!" he reported.

They entered an open field, as best they could see in the rain which blew horizontally as the wind gusted. Heather noticed the dirt road was now grass, more like a wagon path than a road. The car swerved on the slick grass as Heather attempted to stay in the tracks. Suddenly, she slammed on the brakes, jolting all of the passengers, the car sliding to a stop. The path had ended. Tall grass surrounded them as they sat for a long second, everything still, except for the high speed thumping of the windshield wipers. Heather was riveted out the windshield. The rest looked out and let their eyes focus beyond the grass lit up by the headlights. The edge of the cliff sat five feet away. The ocean, a hundred feet down, crashed on the rocks as the storm raged. The inside of the car flashed white.

"Get out! They'll push us over the edge!" yelled Heather.

They all jumped out of the car as the Jaguar skidded to a stop behind them. Scordo exited the car from the driver's seat and glanced around, assessing the situation. With a fed up look on his face, he drew his gun and fired once at Brian's back. The shot spun Brian around and knocked him back, falling over the cliff's edge. Hearing the shot, Heather dove into the wet grass and scrambled around the front of their car, missing Brian's silent spin directly behind her.

"Get the boys!" Scordo yelled to the other Dark Men, rounding the front of the Jag.

The rain soaked her as she hid in the grass and listened to her predators change their priority.

David! Luc! Run! She thought as her heart pounded. She lifted her head to see Brian lying 10 feet below on a ledge that spanned the cliff.

"Brian! Noooo!" she cried, jumping up, and half sliding, half falling down the embankment.

David followed Luc and Bryce, who slid down to the ledge and ran to the left. They heard the shot and glanced back, but saw nothing through the deluge. After a few moments, the ledge ended. There was nowhere to go. They turned around as lightning flashed, providing a white backdrop to the silhouettes of three overcoats and fedoras closing in. The field was 10 feet up; they couldn't climb it in time. The Dark Men slowed to a walk, seeing their prey cornered. With the situation under control, one of them turned around and headed back toward Heather and Brian. Scordo and the other came to a stop face to face with David, Luc, and Bryce. David had no move, no options.

The film! he thought. *Negotiate the microfiche for our lives— before they kill us and find it in my jacket.*

It was the only chance.

"If I tell you where the film is, will you let us go?" David yelled through the rain.

The Dark Men stopped. Scordo adjusted the brim of his fedora.

"The film is here," Scordo said sternly. "You are finished."

"Are you sure?" David asked hiding the lump in this throat. "We made copies."

"I have your copies."

"Not all of them," David replied with a forced tone of confidence.

His mind raced. What would Scordo say next? What would he reply? Could he keep this going?

Suddenly, from above, a long black coat slid down the embankment, kicking rocks and gravel out in front of it and landing between the two groups. Orsini stood with his back to the kids, his revolver aimed at Scordo.

"We serve with our lives. You can't stop us all!" Scordo protested.

"At what price?!" yelled Orsini, "They are the reason we live. You cannot kill them!"

"Where is your loyalty? You disappoint Vincent. Now, get out of the way and let us do what you are not capable of doing."

"I am quite capable," Orsini replied, twisting slightly to the right and firing once, dropping the other Dark Man to his knees.

Scordo raised his gun and fired. Orsini stood motionless, holding his ground. The wounded Dark Man got to his feet holding his side. Staggering, he drew aim at Orsini. Bryce was to the side of the raised gun and lunged at it. He simultaneously grabbed the gun and tackled the Dark Man.

"No you don't!" Bryce shouted as he dragged him down.

They rolled and, in an instant, vanished over the cliff's edge.

"Bryce!" Luc screamed.

The ocean roared back.

For a moment, everyone stared at the spot where they disappeared, not believing what they had just witnessed. David clicked back to real time and sprinted around the collapsing Orsini and jumped Scordo, the gun flying free as they rolled. First, Scordo was on top and landed a solid punch to David's jaw. David scrambled and got an arm around Scordo's leg, tossing him off and placing a solid kick to his ribs, sending Scordo rolling along the edge. David dove on him and landed several punches about his head. Scordo took the blows then rolled David to regain the advantage.

"Don't move!"

Scordo looked up to see Luc and the barrel tip of his Beretta.

"I should have seen that coming," Brian said, hiding the agony. "Not too bright."

He was on his back, soaked, and bleeding from the shoulder. Heather knelt at his side. The rain howled and pelted them as she ripped out a section of her tee shirt and stuffed it under Brian's denim jacket to pad the bleeding bullet hole.

"It went through," she said, examining the exit wound and tearing off another section of her shirt and wadding it up. "I need to lift your shoulder and get this on the other side."

Brian did his best to lift his bloody shoulder as Heather reached around inside his jacket. He winced in pain as she shoved her hand around and stuffed the wad of shirt on the bullet wound.

Behind her stood the Dark Man with his gun hanging down at his side; the rain had drowned out any sound of his approach. He watched her tend to Brian, the rain dripping from the brim of his black fedora. Brian mumbled something.

"What?" Heather mouthed while leaning closer to hear him.

"Get down!" Brian grunted in agony.

With her hand still wrapped around him, Heather dropped to her elbows, her face landing on Brian's stomach. Brian's eyes locked on the Dark Man's, who cracked half a smile and raised his Beretta.

Pop! Pop!

The Dark Man took a step back and winced in surprise. Brian remained fixed on him, his right arm extended, carefully aiming his father's chrome semi-automatic. The Dark Man stumbled two quick steps to his right and fell off the cliff to the rocks and waves below.

Heather lifted her head to see the gun in his hand.

"Close one," Brian grunted, and collapsed onto his back.

Scordo released his grip on David and stood up, staring at the gun in Luc's trembling hand. They all spun at the sound of the two shots, the lightning producing a strobe light show of the third Dark Man's death fall from 50 yards away. Before they could refocus, Scordo moved quickly and started up the slope to the field.

"Stop!" Luc yelled as he pointed the Beretta.

David got to his feet and watched Luc draw a bead on Scordo scrambling up the embankment. He placed the gun sight on Scordo's back and tightened his grip.

He lowered the gun. He could not do it. The man who killed his father was walking away.

"It's OK," David said, gently taking the gun from Luc's lowered hand.

As Scordo disappeared to the field above, David pocketed the gun and spit out a mouthful of blood.

Heather appeared through the rain.

"Brian?" David yelled.

"We need to get him to a doctor. His shoulder is bleeding pretty bad!"

"What?" David asked.

"He got shot!" Heather replied through howling spray. "Where's Bryce?"

David shook his head and ran to Brian. Heather stood in horror as Luc scrambled to the spot where Bryce had rolled off with the Dark Man. He peered over the edge. Water shot up at him as waves crashed on the rocks below, only the white foam differentiating the black sea from the cliff's black rocks. Heather knelt next to him.

"What happened?" she asked.

"Bryce jumped one of them; they rolled off."

"No!" she screamed.

The both stared down and watched the waves explode on the rocks below.

"There!" Heather pointed.

A black object floated in the foam.

"Get David!" she yelled, scrambling down the wet rocks, maintaining a fix on the moving object.

A wave crashed below showering Heather in ice water. Her fingers quickly grew numb as she held on to the frigid rocks. She slipped, dropping a few feet and landing on a jagged rock, grunting in agony as her shin was gashed on impact. She grabbed on just in time—the next wave broke, dousing her.

"Get out of here!" Luc heard from behind him. He spun around to Orsini who was reclined against the embankment, holding his side. Luc offered his hand to help him up.

"Forget me! Just get out of here before anyone else comes. Get as far away from here as you can. You are very special, Luc. Keep running!" Orsini cried.

Luc stared at Orsini. Before him was a man who did unthinkable things, all for the sake of two boys.

Am I that special that he would do all those terrible things... and now die?

"He was the one, wasn't he?" asked Luc.

Orsini looked at him.

"From Jesus? Bryce from Jesus, wasn't he?" Luc persisted.

"No," Orsini said with a grunt of pain.

"Then, it's me," Luc said softly.

Orsini shifted his position to sit as upright as possible.

"You don't know, do you?" Orsini asked, wincing. "Come closer."

Brian was sitting up against the embankment with his hood tight around his head, in a futile effort to protect him from the pouring rain.

"Can you walk?" David asked.

"I think so."

David got him to his feet and helped him climb.

Heather stood up and scrambled down to the water. The next wave came in and submerged her to her knees. The pain from her shin was now indistinguishable from the ache in both legs and feet from the freezing cold water. She could go no further. The person was face down, the union jack on the leather jacket floating even with the surface—it was Bryce. Moving with the waves, his body was lifeless. Just out of reach, she called to him. The next wave surged by, knocking her off balance and drenching her to her waist. As it subsided, the outgoing wave took Bryce with it, Heather catching a glimpse of the green Mohawk as it vanished in the foam.

"Nooo!" she howled.

He was gone.

She got out of the water and watched the next wave come in, then another. The ocean had kept him. She pulled herself up the rocks, her breath shortening and body shivering, looking back with each step to the spot where Bryce went under—the scene did not change. Luc reached down and helped her up, Heather hugging him hard on the cliff's edge.

"I can't believe this is happening," she said, face planted into his shoulder, her sobbing reached into and twisted her gut.

"Get going!" Orsini grunted. "More will come! They will stop at nothing to protect their secret!"

Heather slowly released Luc to see Orsini lying against the wall of the cliff. She tried to comprehend what was happening, and what to do next.

"You…"

"Go! I can take care of myself," he said.

She put an arm back around Luc. They silently turned and climbed to the field.

David was helping Brian into the back seat when they arrived. Luc got in on the other side and wedged a daypack next to Brian to help brace him. David and Heather jumped in the front.

"What about Orsini?" David asked, looking to Luc.

"He said to get out of here, he'll be OK," Heather answered as she backed up, slammed the gearshift forward, and sped away into the night, her soaked sleeve useless to wipe the tears. As they disappeared into the woods, only Orsini's car remained on the cliff, with a door open and two headlight beams illuminating the hard rain.

Brian's head bobbed as Heather drove down the uneven dirt road, the car going in and out of water filled ruts. Luc made up more padding from tee shirts, ready to repack the wounds.

"You're gonna be all right," David said from the front seat, dabbing his bleeding mouth with his fingers.

"How would you know? Like you've ever been shot," a cranky response came back.

"That's how."

"Where are we going?" Luc asked, sniffling.

David looked back at him.

"Home, Luc. Let's go home."

Heather cranked up the heat as she swerved back onto the pavement and pointed the car toward Liverpool. The rain and wind were easing as the red Vauxhall got up to highway speed. She clicked the wipers down to normal, slowing the thumping beat inside the otherwise silent car as the rain softly sprayed the windshield and roof.

Brian rested his head against the side pillar. Any grunt or moan would only acknowledge the obvious. They would take care of him, but it was supposed to be the other way around. He was supposed to help Luc and his cousin. The bullet hole burned.

At least I'm alive, screw it.

David assessed his injuries, his foot throbbed, ribs ached, and he wondered if his jaw was broken. The sum of his wounds was nothing compared to what had just happened. His mind spun, recalling the last few days.

How the hell did this all happen? Why did I drag them into this? Is it over? What now?

Heather trembled. She was cold. She gripped the wheel and focused on her driving, ignoring the tears that continued to stream down her face. It didn't matter; it was time to cry. Bryce was dead. Glen Jennings was dead. Brian might die. Luc is…?

How friggin' bizarre is this? He's a kid. We are kids!

She accelerated, attempting to put distance between them and the nightmare on the cliff.

Luc maintained pressure on the backpack to hold Brian still. He was spent. There were no more tears left in the 14-year-old's body. His father was dead. His father was Joseph? His brother was dead. His brother was James? His friends almost died helping him. They were his saviors.

"STOP!" Luc yelled.

Heather lifted and coasted to the side of the road.

"We can't go home!" he announced, as Heather and David turned their heads.

"I'm sorry, Luc. I'm really sorry, but there's nothing we can do," David consoled.

"You don't understand."

"Luc, I—" Heather started.

"The birth certificates were right!" Luc interrupted.

"What do you mean?" Heather asked.

Brian rolled his head to the right.

"The birthdays."

Heather and David looked at each other.

"Bryce and I were twins," Luc calmly stated.

"But, they were forged," David said with a complete lack of confidence.

"There is another. And *he* is the one."

Epilogue

The bells echoed about the narrow streets of Vatican City. From an old building of yellow painted stone, three figures emerged and walked as a group to the cathedral. There was no mistaking Scordo in the black coat as he walked a pace behind the other two.

As they reached the cathedral, there was a crowd out front, preparing to go inside. Families, each one with a young man clothed in a hooded, white frock, assembled on the stairs; the confirmation ceremony was about to begin.

As they entered, Scordo took a seat in the rear, while Vincent—in a dark suit—escorted a hooded young man forward. They stopped halfway down the aisle.

"Phillip, this is a very proud moment for me," the former cardinal said, placing his hand firmly on the boy's shoulder. "I know what greatness you are capable of, my son."

The 14-year-old smiled from under his hood, then proceeded down the center aisle of the cathedral, joining the other young men.

Vincent took his place with Scordo and kneeled, grinning.

About the Authors

Pens and Needles is the result of a collaborative effort of three people.

Weldon Boyd, created the plot in the back of his head while performing his daytime passion of coding script.

Several years after sharing the idea with his business partner's family, 16-year-old Hannah Green demanded once again, that he write it. This time Weldon agreed, but only if she helped.

Her dad, Walt, then started to document the plot line and characters, all of which quickly became subject to Hannah's review—and revision.

The group traded ideas, paragraphs, and scenes, then compiled them, reviewing them together, over and over. The story quickly jumped to life and became—and still remains—a part of daily conversation between the Greens and Boyds.